Stand at Callenspire

By

Joshua Reynolds

ZMOK BOOKS

Stand at Callenspire by Josh Reynolds
Map by Ciaran Morris
This edition published in 2025

Zmok Books is an imprint of

Winged Hussar Publishing, LLC, 1525 Hulse Road, Unit 1, Point Pleasant, NJ 08742
This edition was published in 2025
PB ISBN 978-1-958872-84-0
EB ISBN 978-1-958872-96-3

Bibliographical references and index
1. Fantasy 2. Media Tie-n 3. Action & Adventure

For more information on Winged Hussar Publishing, LLC, visit us at:
https://www.WHPSupplyroom.com
Instagram: WingedHussarPublishing
Facebook: Winged Hussar Publishing LLC

An Introduction to Pannithor

The world of Pannithor is a place of magic and adventure, but it is also beset by danger in this, the Age of Conflict. Legions of evil cast their shadow across the lands while the forces of good strive to hold back the darkness. Between both, the armies of nature fight to maintain the balance of the world, led by a demi-god from another time. Humanity is split into numerous provinces and kingdoms, each with their own allegiances and vendettas. Amongst the most powerful of all is the Hegemony of Basilea, with its devout army that marches to war with hymns in their hearts and the blessings of the Shining Ones, ready to smite those they deem as followers of the Wicked Ones.

Meanwhile, the Wicked Ones themselves toil endlessly in the depths of the Abyss to bring the lands of men to their knees. Demons, monsters, and other unspeakable creatures spill forth from its fiery pits to wreak havoc throughout Pannithor.

To the north of the Abyss, the Northern Alliance holds back the forces of evil in the icy depths of the Winterlands. Led by the mysterious Talannar, this alliance of races guards a great power to stop it from being grasped by the followers of the Wicked Ones. For if it ever did, Pannithor would fall under into darkness.

In the south, the secretive Ophidians remain neutral in the battles against the Abyss but work toward their own shadowy agenda. Their agents are always on-hand to make sure they whisper into the right ear or slit the right throat.

Amongst all this chaos, the other noble races – dwarfs, elves, salamanders and other ancient peoples – fight their own pitched battles against goblins, orcs, and chittering hordes of rat-men, while the terrifying Nightstalkers flit in and out of existence, preying on the nightmares of any foolish enough to face them.
The world shakes as the armies of Pannithor march to war...

Pannithor Timeline

-1100: First contact with the Celestians

Rise of the Celestians

-170: The God War

0: *Creation of the Abyss*

2676: Birth of modern Basilea, and what is known as the Common Era.

3001: Free Dwarfs declare their independence

3558: Golloch comes to power

3850: The expansion of the Abyss

Ascent of the Goblin King

Tales of Pannithor: Edge of the Abyss

3854: The flooding of the Abyss, the splintering of the Brotherhood, and Lord Darvled completing part of the wall on the Ardovikian Plains.

Drowned Secrets

Nature's Knight

Claws on the Plain

Free Dwarfs expelled from their lands.

3865: Free Dwarfs begin the campaign to free Halpi – the opening of Halpi's Rift.

3865: The Battle of Andro;

Steps to Deliverance

Pious **takes place six months before the events in** *Steps to Deliverance.*

Through Thick and Thin **takes place a few weeks after** *Pious.*

Hero Falling **and Faith Aligned take place several weeks after the events of** *Steps to Deliverance.*

Honor's Price **begins in early spring and ends in late August.**

Pride of a King **starts in the winter of 3865, but most of the events take place in 3866. The story continues in 3866 with** *The Argument of Stone.*

3866: Halflings leave the League of Rhordia.

Broken Alliance

3870: Start of the Xirkaali invasion.

Stand at Callenspire

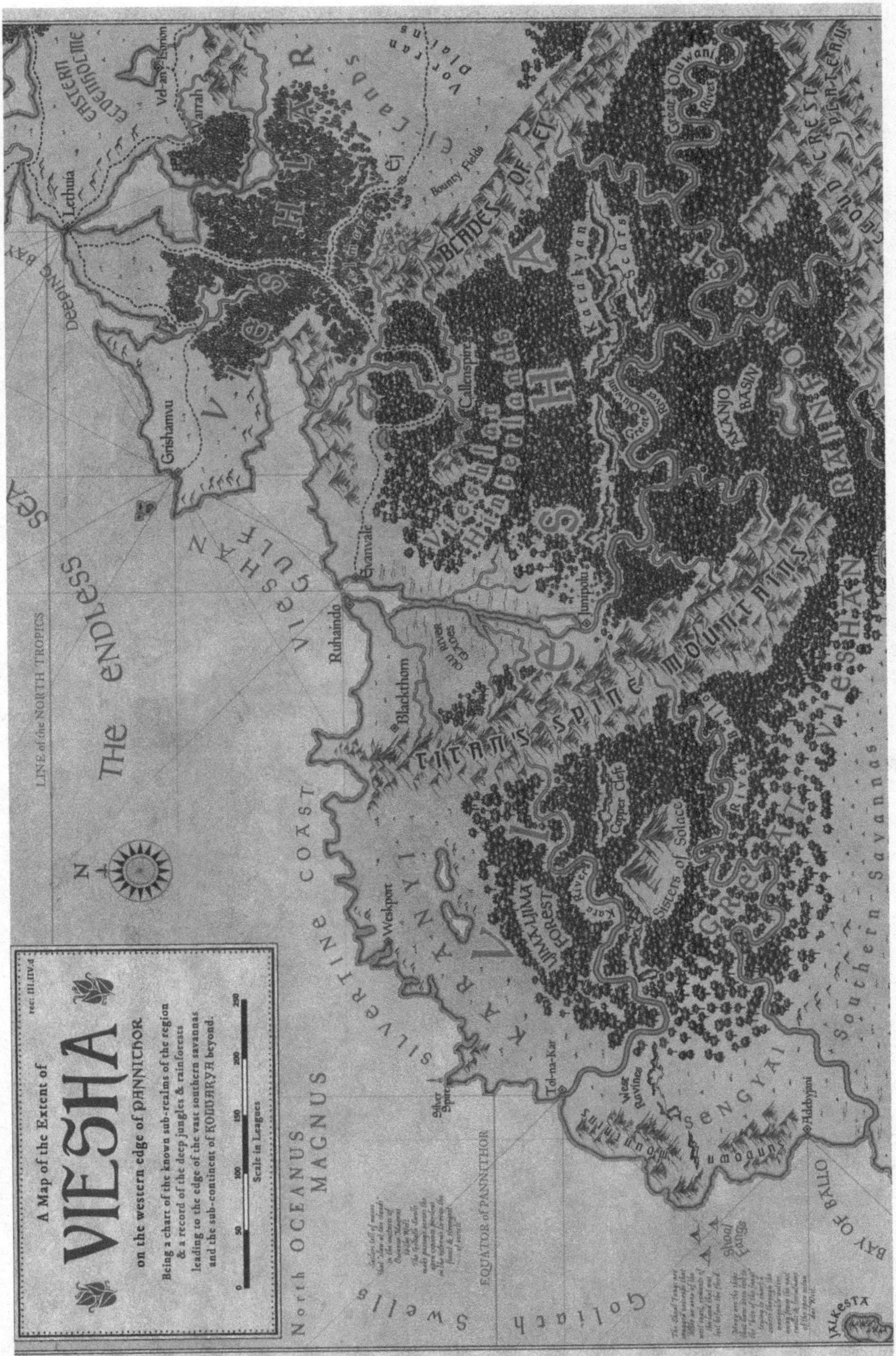
A Map of the Extent of
VIESHA
on the western edge of PANNITHOR
Scale in Leagues
THE ENDLESS SEA
VIESHAN GULF
LINE of the NORTH TROPICS
EQUATOR of PANNITHOR
North OCEANUS MAGNUS
SILVERTINE COAST
Swells
Goliath
BAY OF BALLO
DEEPING BAY
TITAN'S SPINE MOUNTAINS
GREAT VIESHAN RAINFOREST
BLADES OF EJ
Lethuia
Grishamu
Ruhaindo
Blackthorn
Weskport
Tol-na-Kar
Addobyani
Callenspire
Junipolu
Bounty Fields
Sisters of Solace
Copper Cliff
AKANJO BASIN
Great Oluwani River
Southern Savannas
SENGYAI

CHAPTER ONE

Hejun

Hejun Ironeyes, Matriarch-General of the Ironeyes pack and commander of the Tiger Claw horde, braced herself against the rail of the Xirkaali war-junk and studied the wide mouth of what the elves of Vieshlar called Breakwater Bay. The bay itself was a wild, roiling tumult of dark water that narrowed into an estuary, and an immense sprawl of insect-infested mangrove swamp that clung to the curve of the shoreline.

To either side of her vessel, the rest of the fleet was strung out in a rough battle-line, ready for whatever might emerge to meet them. She scrubbed her graying muzzle with a dark paw and growled softly in frustration. "The Neriticans cost us much time," she said to the other hemicyon who stood beside her.

Admiral-General Khulan grunted agreeably. "Not to mention material losses," she said, scratching her chin with a black claw. She glanced at her cousin and laughed throatily. "Still, we are here now, and you can finally stop complaining about my navigation skills."

Unlike Hejun, who wore the plain, unornamented steel scales of a spearwarden, Khulan preferred something finer. Her armor was lavishly decorated with the scales and fangs of dragons. But like Hejun, she had a heavy blade belted at her waist, and she could make the dance of steel as well as any hemicyon in Hejun's forces – though she preferred the halberd to the sword.

The two of them were of an age and had been whelped to the same pack. Khulan had found her calling in the sea, commanding a fleet of war-junks, and had earned the name Kaiju-killer at the Battle of Chunhai for an act of suicidal lunacy that had made her a hero of the Empire and a role model for pups with an excess of courage and little common sense.

Hejun had preferred a more traditional role: that of matriarch, and had gained the name Ironeyes for her unwavering determination in the Tangshan campaign, where she'd guided her forces through the dangers of the rainy season and the machinations of the enemy. Like her cousin, she had her own pack, now. Her own daughters to bully and guide, as the gods saw fit.

"If I saw that storm coming, you should have been able to," Hejun said, not taking her eyes off of the horizon. Control of the bay was split between two elven cities. Ruhaindo, on the western edge, and Evanvale, on the eastern. The pair, so she'd been told, had once been the hub of elven sea-trade in the southern region; now, they were little more than monuments to the faded glories of their builders.

"I saw it. That's why I sailed us into it. It shook the Neriticans off of us, didn't it?"

"For a few days," Hejun allowed, grudgingly. Khulan chuckled.

"Enough to get us here."

Hejun sighed. Here was not where they were supposed to be, but Khulan knew that. Tiger Claw was supposed to have made landfall on an isolated stretch of beach near a city called Grishamvu, but the constant, harassing attacks by the sea-going Neriticans had made that impossible. Breakwater Bay was the backup plan, though it was not particularly ideal from a military perspective. Two cities, that close, both with their own supply lines – difficult, even under ideal conditions.

These, needless to say, were not ideal conditions. The water was choppy, there were enemies before them and behind them, and the territory was unfamiliar. Hejun thought it boded ill but could not bring herself to say so. A matriarch had to project strength at all times, especially under difficult conditions.

Four Claws – a fifth of the empire's military strength – had been dispatched west to see to the pacification of Mantica and prevent the destruction of all that was. Khatun Temulun Warbringer had declared that their cause was a holy one, given to them by the Four-Who-Are-Two. The first three Claws had split Upper and Lower Mantica between them; Hejun's forces had been given responsibility for subduing the elves – a decadent, prideful race, steeped in forbidden magics.

Nearly eighty thousand hemicyon warriors had been placed under her command, and almost four times that number of human auxiliaries. The army was currently scattered across the war-junks of Khulan's fleet. The lesser matriarchs who served as Hejun's subordinates commanded a dozen similar landings to this one along the coast. Their orders were to establish beachheads, set up fortifications, and wait for further instructions. Most would; some would attempt to do more, because if there was one trait all hemicyons shared, it was a decided lack of patience. But that was no great sin. Not unless they got themselves killed.

Hejun had been proud to be entrusted with such a responsibility… at least, at first. To command so many was an honor few received. Now she was beginning to wonder whether it would be as easy as she'd imagined. She looked at her cousin. "If it comes to a fight on the water, we'll be caught between the Neriticans and the elves."

Khulan shrugged, seemingly little concerned by such facts. "The Neriticans haven't so much as poked their heads above water in the last week. I don't think they're much interested in what goes on, on land. So it's just the elves we have to worry about." She paused. "Well, you have to worry about. Since they don't seem to have much of a fleet to speak of."

The distant clangor of alarm bells sounded from the waters ahead. Hejun squinted, noting the delicate shapes of elven ships ghosting out of the twin harbors and arrowing toward the Xirkaali fleet. Too little, too late. The wind was with the Xirkaali, and the elves would have to tack into it to even attempt to intercept them. By then, they'd be close enough to Evanvale to begin disembarking troops. "We outnumber them," she said, in satisfaction.

"We outgun them as well," Khulan growled. "The larger ones have cannons or something like it, but they'll have to get in close to make use of them. Our rockets require no such proximity." She stepped back and turned to bark orders at the hwathca crew on the upper deck. A moment later, nine corkscrew contrails of red fire split the gloom of evening. The rockets sped across the water and struck the fastest of the elven vessels. Khulan gave a triumphant snarl. "Punched a hole in her hull. She'll be swamped before she sees our shadow."

More rockets were launched from the other junks in the battle-line. A roll of thunder passed over Hejun, and she clapped a hand to her ears as the horizon ahead was cracked open by fire. Thankfully the wind was blowing away from her, carrying the acrid stink of the Xiryan fire-powder with it. Not all of the rockets struck home; but enough did to render the waters ahead a tangled morass of burning vessels and black smoke. "It's as if they didn't even know we were coming," she murmured. Soon, more rockets would strike the crumbling harbor wall that protected Evanvale's docklands, opening the way for the fleet.

Khulan scratched her cheek and spat onto the deck. "Maybe they didn't. These elves are arrogant creatures, from what I've heard. Maybe they didn't believe that we'd dare attack them – let alone invade their lands."

"We told them we would," Hejun said, in disbelief. Could these elves truly be so haughty as to imagine that the Xirkaali would not carry out their threats? It seemed inconceivable to her, and yet, here they were. Perhaps the Khatun was right: the peoples of the west needed a strong hand to lift them up from the mire of their decadence.

Khulan shrugged. "Yes, but even so… who can predict the reasoning of such creatures? Their minds are stuck in the past, or fixed on the future. They are sick with magic. Frankly, they should be thanking us for this. Else what's coming would swallow them and their fancy towers whole." She clapped Hejun on the shoulder. "I must see to my crew. And you must see to yours, cousin. As soon as we get close enough, I want your warriors off of my ships. All twenty thousand of them."

"I have no doubt my warriors are eager to never set paw on one of these scows again," Hejun said, gripping her cousin's forearm tightly. "They stink of fire-powder and fish."

Khulan laughed. "May your steel stay sharp, cousin."

"And may the wind carry you to your prey," Hejun said. She stepped back and made her way swiftly belowdecks. As matriarch, the honor of being first ashore was hers. She needed her closest warriors ready to accompany her when they made landfall at Evanvale.

Of the two cities that girt Breakwater Bay, Evanvale was the smaller and nestled among the mangrove swamps like a fearful hound. It was why she'd chosen it as their staging point. Quicker to take, and quicker to repurpose. From there, they could lay siege to Ruhaindo, and then the rest of the coast. Once the coast was in their grasp, the hinterlands would be no challenge. That was what she told herself, at any rate. The truth was, a strategy lasted no longer than the first engagement.

She ducked her head as she descended the wide, plank steps. The war-junks of the Xirkaali were far larger than the Yan vessels that had inspired them, with capacious areas below for storage of fire-powder and other necessities. At the moment, much of the space in Khulan's vessel was given over to the troops she was transporting, including Hejun's bodyguard. The unit was composed of the finest hemicyon warriors in the pack. Sheathed in steel, and bearing two-handed halberds, they were the epitome of her people; the strength of the Kaali made manifest.

They waited belowdecks for her, where they, and their human auxiliaries, wouldn't be in the way of Khulan's crew. As she descended, the overpowering scent of weapon-oil and anticipation enveloped her. Turgo, the commander of her bodyguard, met her at the bottom of the steps. "Is it time, then, Matriarch?"

Hejun wrinkled her muzzle in acknowledgement. "Nearly. Are your curs ready, Turgo? Or have they grown fat from all the easy sailing?"

"Easy, she says," Turgo snorted. "I, for one, will be relieved to find solid ground beneath my paws. All this rolling to and fro does my digestion no favors." He clapped his paws to his sturdy midsection, causing the steel scales of his armor to clatter. He was big, for a male, with spotted fur and ragged ears.

"And yet you continue to eat like a starving pup," Hejun said, poking the warrior in the belly with her claw. Turgo grunted but accepted the chiding without protest.

"Eat heartily, for tomorrow you may starve," he said. "Old wisdom."

Hejun chuckled. "Get them up on deck, Turgo. If we are to lead the dance, we must be ready, eh?" She looked past him and saw the commander of her human auxiliaries lurking in the shadows. Han was an unassuming man; brusque, but swift to follow orders. As humans went, he was the sort she preferred. He was clad in armor composed of strips of lacquered wood, painted in a deep cerulean hue. There was a steel sword sheathed on his hip – a gift from Hejun. Ordinarily, human warriors carried only wood, but Han had done her pack a service once, many years ago, and she had rewarded him accordingly.

"That goes for you and your men as well, Han. Once we breach the walls around the harbor, we'll have to storm the docklands. By then, they'll be waiting on us."

"The sharks will get a feeding and no mistake, Matriarch," Han said. Turgo growled in pleasure and clapped the man on the shoulder, nearly knocking him sprawling.

"See? Even the humans are confident. That's a good omen. No doubt we'll be dining on elven delicacies before the day is out."

"More old wisdom?" Hejun asked, wryly.

"The oldest," Turgo said, licking his muzzle.

Up above, bells began to sound. Hejun heard the shouts of the crew and felt the throb of the hull as it cut through the water. They would be turning toward Evanvale now. If Khulan had done her job, the harbor walls would be broken and aflame. She gripped the hilt of her sword and gave a snarl of anticipation.

"The dance is beginning. *To your places*!"

CHAPTER TWO
Aeron

Aeron Cadwallader inhaled the cool mountain air and released it as a sigh. It was morning in the mountains, and he felt an all-too familiar sadness as he contemplated the troubles ahead. War was never a pleasant prospect; not to one who'd fought in his share. More than his share, even. He rubbed his hands, trying to ease the old familiar ache that accompanied early mornings.

He stood atop one of the many watchtowers that dotted this part of the Blades of Ej, each one a sturdy fortress in miniature, constructed by halfling engineers. An array of curved mirrors sat to his left; positioned properly, they could send a message to the next peak or even the townships in the lowlands. To his right, a heavy ballista, capable of knocking down a charging troll when fired by a trained gunner.

Far above, a gas-balloon swayed in the mountain breeze. A small crew of Ej-folk manned it, watching for any threats that the watchtower might not catch. The balloon-crews were rotated every three hours to prevent them from getting bored and possibly missing something.

Though the watchtowers hadn't been his idea, they were a necessary component to the strategies he'd been working on since Anas Macadrian had come to him and asked him to help the folk of Ej build their own army. Thankfully, that had been less difficult than he'd feared. Volunteers weren't in short supply in the valleys, and trained bands had been mustered from as far away as the Windblown Basin.

But for all their willingness, the Ej-folk had never had a proper scrap – not in the same way that the Shires had, of late. They'd always had the elves to protect them. Only now, the elves were calling in the favor, or so Anas had implied.

He sighed again and looked at his hands, with their litany of old scars. Sometimes, he wondered what his life might have been, had he never attended the College of Warcraft in Eowolf. Since that fateful day when he'd left, he'd endured more war than he'd ever imagined. The last one, against the Riftforged Orcs, had taken it out of him; he'd felt exhausted, not just physically but spiritually. It was as if something had shaken loose in him – something he had yet to repair.

He looked out again over the mountains and paused. Far to the west, a thin finger of what might have been smoke rose against the horizon. It shouldn't have been visible at this distance, not unless it was a big fire. He frowned and leaned out over the wooden rail of the watchtower, trying to ascertain where it was coming from. Was that the coast? He reached for the warning bell – paused – stopped.

Maybe it was just a wildfire, he thought. The Vieshan grasslands – the veldt, the Ej-folk called it – were prone to them, this time of year. But even as he dropped his hand, he knew better. The Xirkaali had come. He could feel it in his bones. He'd felt the same twinge the day the orcs had cut through the League of Rhordia like a knife through warm butter. But the coast was far from the mountains. Days of travel, if not weeks. If it was the Xirkaali, maybe the elves would hold them back. Maybe – maybe – *maybe.*

"You saw it, then?"

Aeron turned, startled. Anas Macadrian stumped up the final few steps of the watchtower, pausing at the top to catch his breath. He was older than Aeron by a good few years and looked it. His hair had been white when they met, but it was thinning now, and the round cheeks had deflated somewhat.

"This thing gets higher every time I come up those bloody steps," Anas complained as he popped his back. "Why do you like it up here, lad? Air not thin enough in the mountains for you?"

"Height lends perspective," Aeron said with a smile.

Anas snorted. "Wouldn't know it from the humans. Or the elves, come to that. But it is a pretty enough view, I'll give you that." He frowned. "I don't like the look of that smoke though. That fire must be big indeed if we can see it from here."

Aeron nodded. "That's somewhere on the coast, or I'm a potato-fly. Can you hazard a guess as to where it's coming from?"

Anas made his way to the rail and squinted at the horizon. "Vieshan Gulf, maybe. Near Breakwater Bay, I'd wager – if I were a gambling man, which I am not." He tapped his nose as he said it, and Aeron chuckled. Anas was well known for his love of dice, save when his wife was in earshot, at which point he foreswore such vices loudly and often.

"Port town?" Aeron asked.

"City," Anas corrected. "Big one. One of a matching pair; Ruhaindo and Evanvale. Twin sisters of Breakwater Bay." He scratched his chin, a thoughtful expression on his face. "You think it's these Xirkaali we've heard so much about, then?"

"I don't know, but we should probably find out. How long do you think it'd take you to ready the *Windwalker* for a reconnaissance mission?"

"No more than a day," Anas said. "We should probably send riders to Callenspire and Ej as well, to alert them. I expect the elves already know, but it's always best to show willing. Especially where the elves are concerned. They can be awful touchy about such things."

Aeron nodded. His experience with elvish hospitality had been both somewhat unpleasant and thankfully brief. The Ej-folk were on mostly good terms with them, from what he'd seen. Privately, he suspected that was more due to the good nature of the former than any real effort on the part of the latter. "If it is the Xirkaali, we're going to need to muster at least a third of the army, as it stands."

"And go where?"

"Wherever the elves need us." Aeron hesitated. Anas saw it and frowned.

"Do you think our people are ready for it, then?"

Aeron paused, considering how best to answer. The truth was, he doubted that the folk of Ej would ever really be ready. For every village that sent a muster for drill, there were two that flat out refused, seeing no purpose to it. Those willing to be trained had been drilled to the best of his abilities, but would it be enough when it came down to it?

He didn't doubt their enthusiasm or their willingness. But excitement waned, and once things started, so too would their willingness. Would they stick it out, or would they scarper for home after getting a taste of how bad a war truly could be? He had no answers, just as he had no answer for Anas. Instead, he said, "I need to see what's happening on the coast, Anas. I need to *see*." He thumped his fist into his palm. Anas nodded.

"You will, lad." He reached out and caught Aeron by the shoulder. "We will. We'll get the *Windwalker* ready to go and head toward the coast – though, I fear that by the time we get there, it'll be over."

Aeron shrugged. "We can't change what's going on right now. But we can change what comes after. If we're ready. If I haven't made any mistakes." He ran his hand through his hair, probabilities bouncing around like shrapnel inside his skull. A few months wasn't enough time to build a professional army. It was enough time to make a start. A good start, even. But the army needed testing; it needed to face the enemy in the field. Until then, they wouldn't know anything.

"Strictly a reconnaissance mission though, aye?" Anas asked. "No tricky schemes?"

Aeron smiled. "Strictly having a peek, nothing more." He paused. "Though we might want to bring a few grenadiers with us, just in case."

Anas frowned. "You're thinking about the rockets these Xirkaali are supposed to have, aren't you?"

Aeron tapped the side of his head. "I haven't stopped." The reports of the Xirkaali weapons had been spotty at best; it was as if the elves couldn't quite believe the things existed, or if they did, they didn't want to admit how dangerous they might be. Not for the first time, Aeron wondered if the elves were trapped by their immortality. They didn't change, or at least not swiftly. Some halflings had the same problem, though not to the same degree, thankfully. Both assumed the world was the same as it always had been.

But the world was changing, and swiftly. It seemed like new dangers were always on the horizon, and threats were ever-multiplying. It was one of the reasons he was determined to see that his people were able to defend themselves against whatever the future might hold.

Anas sucked on his teeth. "I might have just the regiment. My sister's cousin's girl is in command, Hannah. Ambitious. Keen. Good head on her shoulders but could do with some seasoning. This sort of trip might be just the thing."

Aeron nodded. "I'll trust your judgment. No sense risking anyone else, though. If the Xirkaali have come, we'll be flying right into them."

"You'll be doing what now, exactly?" a sharp voice cut in.

Aeron flinched and Anas winced. Aeron turned to see his wife, Nesta, climbing up through the hatch, a knowing scowl on her face. Anas made his apologies and departed hastily. Nesta ignored him, the brunt of her wrath reserved for her husband. "Explain yourself, Aeron Cadwallader."

"How long were you listening?" he asked, trying to judge just how angry Nesta was. Thankfully, there was nothing to throw up here. "Because I can explain all of it."

"So explain. What is it you're doing – and were you planning to tell me?"

"Obviously I was," Aeron began. Nesta held up a finger, and he fell silent.

"We came to the mountains so that you might have some time for yourself. To recover. And now here you are, running off to get yourself killed – *again.* Are you mad?" Despite her words, she didn't sound angry, just upset. She had good reason to be.

"No. Just tired," Aeron said. He pulled her close; she resisted, but only for a moment. "You know as well as I do that if these Xirkaali aren't stopped, they might well decide to take the Shires next. Better we fight them here than there."

"I wish we didn't have to fight them at all."

He hugged her more tightly. "You and I both."

They stood for a moment, and Aeron wished it could last forever. Then, there was a shout from the balloon above. Both Aeron and Nesta turned to see that the thin plume of smoke had widened and darkened, and now it was like a scar on the horizon. Nesta's grip tightened around him, and Aeron kissed her head.

"You'll be careful, I trust," she said.

"I will. *Windwalker* is a marvel. I doubt they'll even see us."

"I'm not just talking about that, and you know it." She took his face in her hands. "You be careful, Aeron Cadwallader. And when this is done, you come back to me in one piece, you hear me? Or I will be having words with you." They kissed, and when they parted, he almost laughed to see Anas's head peeking up through the hatch.

"Safe to come back up?" he inquired politely.

"Daft fool," Nesta said, kicking at him. Anas cowered back theatrically, but his smile slipped as he met Aeron's gaze.

"I checked the maps. You were right. That smoke is from the Breakwater Bay and no mistake. The Xirkaali are here, Aeron. And I don't think they're planning to leave."

CHAPTER THREE

Axel

Axel Tricklebrook awoke with a start as the warm waters of the river convulsed around him. Struggling free of the tatters of his dreams, the gillkin mage sent out a questioning pulse. The water, or rather the elemental within the water, responded immediately. *We are here,* Splish murmured inside Axel's mind. The elemental's voice was like the tinkling of rain on leaves, or the drip of water on stone; soft and comforting.

Axel blinked his eyes, clearing the last vestiges of sleep from them. Trusting in Splish to carry him safely to his destination, he had slept for what felt like days, regaining his strength, both physical and magical, after his long journey south.

He sighed and stretched his aching limbs within the comforting envelope of the elemental's embrace. The air was warm here, and pleasantly so; gillkin like himself were cold-blooded, and they felt fluctuations in temperature more keenly than some. That was why, in ages past, during the War with Winter, his folk had scattered from their familiar waters and sent themselves into hibernation. Axel himself had awoken only recently, into a world far different from the one he'd left, and yet somehow still familiar.

Though the War with Winter had ended long ago, a new conflict was in the offing; equally apocalyptic, it haunted his dreams. Warnings and omens, delivered to him in those dreams by the being known as the Green Lady, had driven him south, in search of… something. All he had was a name: *Oskan.* He knew that name of old. An enemy of all that lived. But what did it mean? Was Oskan returning? Or, maybe he had been sent in search of something to stop such an event from occurring. The Great Current did not always provide clear answers to its children. Nor did the Green Lady.

On his journey, he had communed with the rivers and estuaries of this vastly-changed land, and he learned of the great fleet approaching; of the Xirkaali and their invasion; of the fires that would soon consume Vieshlar and the elves of the southern kindred. He suspected that the Xirkaali were the reason he had been drawn to these lands. But what it had to do with Oskan, he could not say as yet. The Green Lady might reveal it in time, or not. As the Great Current willed.

His dreams showed him flashes of what was, or would be. His dreams showed him flashes of what was, or would be. By following them, he followed the will of the Great Current. It had told him he would find allies here, if he waited. Allies necessary to succeed in what came next.

Up, then, Axel thought, and Splish obeyed. They surfaced from the river in silence. It was late in the evening, and the waters were undisturbed by river-craft or fishermen. Only the hum of insects greeted him as Splish carried him gently to the waiting jetty. As he stepped from the elemental's grasp onto the sagging wood of the docks, he took in the sight before him. The city was called Callenspire, though he did not know why. The elves had their own ways of naming things, and it was a mystery to Axel why they chose the words they did to describe things. What he did know was that the city hummed with the magic that had been used in its construction. Like all the great cities of Vieshlar, it was at once a part of the surrounding jungle and yet isolated from it.

In many ways, it resembled the ancient ruins which lay scattered upon the seabed to the west – or had, in his day. Whether they were still there or not, he could not say.

The docklands were extensive here; a great quay of wood and stone, and many small vessels docked there. Some were fishing craft, others were heavy barges, built to transport cargo up and down the river. He spied soldiers in silver and brass armor, armed with spears and shields, patrolling, and he resolved to stay out of sight. A simple enchantment was enough to thicken the air around him, obscuring him from all but direct sight. He pulled up his hood and thumped his coral staff against the ground, conjuring a ball of soft, hazy light. The puff ball settled on his open palm, and he blew on it gently, setting it into motion.

The puff ball was a simple form of magic; it would seek out the one he'd come to find, and quickly. All he had to do was follow it, and so he did. It led him away from the river and into the heart of the city, a network of tangled streets and buildings that seemed to have sprouted from the jungle. The streets were lit by puff balls much like his own, save that these were contained within glass jars hung from doorways and the undersides of the highest walkways. Their radiance painted the city in contrasting bands of light and dark.

He walked for some time. The city was lively, even at night. It was as if the inhabitants either didn't know, or didn't care, that an enemy was at their very doorstep. Maybe it was both. It was hard to tell with air-breathers. From what he remembered, they had peculiar ideas about such things.

The puff ball halted, quivering. Axel looked up. The building before him blazed with lights of all hues and intensities – more magic, but a wasteful type, the sort many elves were proficient in. Music slithered from the shuttered windows, agitating the air. It sounded like a celebration, but there was a stiffness to it; a lack of spontaneity that spoke to grim regularity.

Warily, Axel entered, and was immediately struck by a wash of heat and the smell of spilt alcohol. A tavern? No, something else. Something altogether less acceptable in polite society. The front room was crowded with bodies – dancing, laughing, reclining, and otherwise entangled in a fashion which both perplexed and amused him. Musicians roamed the floor, competing against one another and the general cacophony. Drinks flowed freely, much of it ending up in tiny rivers that ran along the floor and out into the street.

There were elves here, yes; but also humans, dwarves, and others. All had the look of travelers or sailors. Traders and barge-crews, spending their hard-earned wages on the entertainments available. Axel threaded through the crowd, his hood pulled low. If anyone noticed him, they gave no sign, for which he was thankful. He doubted they would know what to make of him, given that his kind had not been seen in these lands for centuries.

He urged the bobbing light on and followed it into the back room and up a set of rickety stairs. The raucous noise died away, muffled by a profusion of satin curtains and the curiously angled walls. He found himself in a narrow corridor, lined with heavy wooden doors, each covered in delicately carved images of decidedly curious acts. He could sense that all of the rooms were occupied, but only one of those occupants mattered.

Axel blew once more on the bobbing light and sent it whirling down the corridor. It raced back and forth for a moment, and then settled to hang in the air before one door in particular. Axel went to the door and used his staff to knock politely.

A muffled voice complained from within. A denial, Axel thought. An exhortation to depart, with all haste, delivered impolitely. Axel sighed. "Splish," he said, softly.

Open, Splish agreed. The elemental surged from beneath Axel's cloak and spread across the door. A moment later, it yielded to the sudden pressure and thudded open with an echoing boom. The room beyond was largely empty save for a bed, and several of the beings upon it let out a communal yelp of surprise, and some fright. Axel studied them for a moment, trying to ascertain just how many of them there were in the bed. The mating rituals of air-breathers puzzled him greatly.

"Valan Cormys," he said, in his half-recalled elvish. Thankfully, from what he'd heard in his travels, the language hadn't changed much over the intervening centuries.

A lean elf sat up abruptly, pushing aside the two human women who occupied it with him. "Speaking. And who might you be? Or rather, what?" He was handsome, as elves judged such things, with sharp, aristocratic features and eyes that blazed with something that might have been curiosity, or perhaps anger. Or maybe both.

"I am he that is called Axel Tricklebrook. I must be speaking with you."

"Must you?"

"I must," Axel emphasized.

"Now?"

"Yes."

"Well, it's hardly convenient," Valan said, lightly. "But I suppose I can make an exception this once. Ladies, if we might reschedule…? No? Ah, well." The two women stormed out, filling the air with venomous curses as Valan rose to dress himself. Axel watched them go, puzzled by their behavior.

"Have I upset them?"

"I expect so. But they are very forgiving, for humans. At least this time they're not throwing things. Axel, you said?"

"Yes."

"Neritican?"

Axel bobbed his head. "Yes."

"I've met my share of Neriticans. You don't look like any I'm familiar with, if you don't mind my saying it. From Medu'Syth, are you?"

"Once. Not for many years." Axel gestured, and Splish closed the door with a thump. Valan raised an eyebrow but said nothing. "I must be speaking with you, Valan Cormys."

"So you said. About what?"

"The Xirkaali."

Valan stiffened. "And what do you know of them?"

"I know that they threaten your people, as well as mine."

Valan's eyes narrowed. "Do they now? How unfortunate. But what can I do about it?"

"You are being one who is speaking for your people."

Again, Valan paused. "I do, yes. In certain circumstances." He took a deep breath. "But again, I am not certain what I can do to help. I am decidedly out of favor at the moment. Indeed, there are many who think I am solely to blame for the current… situation." He didn't elaborate, nor did he need to. The Great Current had shown Axel all he needed to know about Valan Cormys.

Valan was not of the southern kindred; rather, he was a citizen of Elvenholme. More, he had been among those diplomats assigned to first meet with the Xirkaali. Three times their envoys had come, always with the same offer. Surrender, become a satrapy of the Xirkaali Empire, and survive. Resist, and be broken. The elves, Valan among them, had laughed. For what empire could challenge the might of the kindred?

It was only now that they were realizing their error. "They believe you are being responsible for the invasion," Axel supplied.

"The *threatened* invasion," Valan corrected, doubtfully. Axel shook his head slowly.

"The Xirkaali are being attacking now. The invasion has begun."

Valan sagged back onto the bed, a look of horror on his face. "What? When?"

Axel felt a flicker of sympathy. The elf was clearly at a loss. "It was being a few days ago, according to the waters. They are making landfall at Breakwater Bay, and other places. They will being advancing inland soon. We must be preparing."

"We? Again, what can I do?" Valan shook his head.

Axel thumped the end of his staff against the floor, lightly. "An alliance between our peoples is being necessary. You will be helping me in this."

"Will I, now?" Valan peered at him. "You must be aware that the southern kindred warred on the river-tribes for a number of years; bloody years, those, according to what I've read. Wars that ended indecisively, with a treaty that satisfied no one but allowed for the fighting to end. I doubt either side is eager to help the other."

Axel waved this aside. "That is being not important. We must be working together. If we are not joining you, you will be eventually joining them."

"What do you mean?"

"The Xirkaali wish to be making the elves a part of their empire. They will be succeeding, if we are not stopping them."

Valan paled. "And how do you know this?"

"Because I have been seeing it, and you. The Great Current is bringing your name to me, as it is bringing me shadows of the future. I am seeing it all, though some of it I am not understanding." Axel paused. "A lot of it, in fact."

Valan frowned and sat back. "Elves are no strangers to prophecy, but why me? I'm just a diplomat, and not a very good one, going by my recent failures." He looked around. "That's why I'm drowning my sorrows here, of all places."

Axel shrugged. "I am knowing only that the Great Current is carrying me to you, and that through you, our survival is being secured."

"That fills me with no end of confidence," Valan said, sourly.

Axel gave a burbling laugh.

"That is making one of us."

CHAPTER FOUR

Shulgin

Rockets roared overhead as Shulgin Ironeyes, daughter of Hejun, drove her blade through the elf warrior's sternum, nailing him to the mooring post. The warrior stared at her in incomprehension as the light faded from his eyes; he had been skilled, but not so skilled as to defeat her. She gave her weapon a brutal twist and wrenched it free, allowing his body to slump down. She stepped over him and howled for her pack.

Around her, Evanvale, and its surrounding mangrove swamp, burned. Behind her, rockets hurtled skyward from the decks of the war-junks that occupied the harbor. Hemicyon spearwardens and Yan soldiers fought across the docklands, forcing back the small band of elves that sought to stymie them. Shulgin wiped blood from her muzzle and blinked smoke from her eyes as she took in the battle going on around her.

It had taken only three days to gain control of the harbor once the outer walls fell. The elven fleet was a pitiful thing; decrepit and few in number. The docklands were another story. The elves had used those three days wisely and had set up an admirable killing field. Arrows had accosted the first warriors to step onto the docks, and sorcerous balls of fire had splashed across the hulls of the junks, sinking them even as their passengers disembarked. The rumors of the elves' dependence on magic had not been exaggerated. The witch-smellers were no doubt salivating in anticipation of the culling to come.

Two more days had passed since then; two days in a slaughterhouse. The elves were cunning, and for every band that stood and fought, two others played deadly games of ambush, using the terrain to their advantage. Swarms of conjured insects and elementals of mud and broken wood had assailed the packs of spearwardens at the forefront of the advance.

But now, finally, the elves were falling back, retreating through the great iron-banded portcullis gates that separated the docklands from the city proper. Arrows rained down on the invaders from the internal walls, but Shulgin had endured worse storms on the plains. The gates were a concern, however; any further delay in taking the city risked them being caught in a pincer by reinforcements from Ruhaindo – or worse, the Neriticans.

A shiver ran through her as she thought of the fish-people. She'd believed them nothing more than a myth, or at the very least their prowess exaggerated, before the fleet had run afoul of them. The Neriticans had savaged the Xirkaali for weeks, destroying ships and drowning soldiers with their monstrous beasts. The thought of fighting them again, even on dry land, made her decidedly uneasy.

Barks of greeting reached her ears, and she turned to see her pack converging on her, human soldiers following more slowly. She ignored the latter as she growled a welcome to her warriors. "Barga, Katak – with me; the rest of you, spread out. We need to take one of those gates before the elves manage to get them fully shut."

The spearwardens snarled in agreement, and Shulgin started to lope toward the nearest gate. Hwathca vomited fire from somewhere behind them, and rockets corkscrewed through the smoky air to impact along the walls. Tiangou raced alongside the hemicyons, uttering shrill howls as they scented prey.

Arrows skidded off of Shulgin's mail; one tore a divot from her ear, and she hissed in pain. Barag howled as an arrow found a weak point in his mail and buried itself in his upper arm. He tore it loose and flung it aside without slowing. A few moments later, Katak toppled forward, the shaft of an arrow jutting from his eye. Beside him, a tiangou fell in a heap, limbs spasming as an arrow pierced its brain.

Heedless, Shulgin leapt over an overturned wagon; Barag followed, panting curses. The Yan tried their best to keep pace and shield their hemicyon betters from the deadly rain without much success. Their wooden armor was tough, but the elven arrows sliced through it with ease. Shulgin paid their dying no more mind than she had Katak's. There was no time for such things when the dance of steel had begun. Afterward, maybe. But during – never. To let one's mind wander was to risk missing a step and losing one's life.

Ahead of her, elves were retreating beneath the open portcullis. A small shieldwall of warriors remained outside, covering the retreat with their long spears. Shulgin bared her teeth and gave a great howl as she leapt up onto a broken column and sprang off into the midst of the shieldwall, her sword extended behind her.

It was foolhardy; that much she could not deny. But how else was a warrior to truly earn the glory that was their due without some act of wild courage? In any event, she gave it no real thought, pressed as she was by enemies on all sides. The elves went after her with a fierceness that almost surprised her. A spearpoint skidded across her chest; a second caught her in the arm, nearly knocking her back. She wielded her sword with brutal efficiency, hacking at the elves with no thought save to drive them back and break their formation.

They fought well; with forever to practice the killing art, they had become quite adept. Even these – mere garrison troops! – were practiced fighters, equal to any number of Yan soldiers. But they were unequal to the task of felling a warrior of her caliber. Soon, their line collapsed and Barag was by her side, chopping through an upraised shield with a howl of triumph.

"They're on the run," he barked as he dragged his weapon free of the dying elf.

"Not all of them," Shulgin growled. An elf – an officer of some sort, to go by his fancy armor and robes – glided toward them across the blood-slick stones of the wharf. Barag gave a snarling laugh and lunged before Shulgin could stop him.

He was dead a moment later, his head betraying a surprised snarl as it bounced off of her thigh and out of sight. His body slumped, geysering blood. The elf had not a drop on him. He studied her with a cold eye. "Curs. Street curs," he said in a mellifluous voice. She realized he was speaking in a dialect of the east, but an archaic one.

"Hemicyon," Shulgin replied in the same tongue. She swung her sword absently.

"A dog by any other name," the elf countered. "What is your name, dog?"

"Shulgin. Daughter of Hejun, Matriarch of the Ironeyes pack."

The elf sneered and brought his sword up in something like a salute. "Well, whelp of Hejun, I am Herys Sunstrike, prince of the fourth house and master of the second gate. And you will not take one step farther into this, my city."

"A challenge," Shulgin said, pleased.

"Not for me," Herys said, and slid swiftly toward her. His blade made a silver arc as it cut through the air, too fast to follow. Shulgin barely had time to twist aside as it sliced a scale from her armor. She responded in kind, and the elf danced back out of reach, a smile on his face. He was laughing at her; arrogant creature. Incensed, she bulled after him.

His sword flicked out, scratching steel and flesh alike. Blood dripped between the scales, and she retreated, baffled by his sheer speed. Herys pursued her, and it was all she could do to parry his almost-lazy attacks. Belatedly she realized that he wasn't just laughing at her – he was playing with her. As if she were no more than a pup.

Anger, true anger, flared in her heart, and she gave a roar of fury. They came together with a crash, their swords meeting and springing away again and again. The elf was as good as she'd thought; a natural swordsman, as such things went. But Shulgin had been trained by the greatest warriors of the Kaali, human, hemicyon, and otherwise. She had been born for war. And her anger lent her a strength he could not equal.

As if realizing this, Herys began to fall back before her. He parried a blow and sprang away in the direction of the portcullis. The remainder of the surviving elves were already through, and the rain of arrows was holding her warriors back. Rockets hammered the wall, filling the air with grit. Herys vanished into the resulting smoke.

Shulgin launched herself in pursuit of her opponent and nearly lost her snout for her troubles. Spears jutted toward her from all directions; there were elves all around her. Herys, safely out of reach, sheathed his sword and turned away dismissively, as if his part in the affair was completed. The arrogance of it stunned her for several moments, and it was nearly her undoing. The elves pressed close, hemming her in on all sides, giving her little room to move or swing her sword.

She slashed out, chopping through spears. For every one she shattered, two more appeared. The elves were trying to herd her back through the portcullis. She cursed herself for her foolishness in attacking alone. It wasn't the first time her anger had betrayed her, and hopefully it wouldn't be the last.

Elves advanced on her. She could hear the howls of her pack and feel the slow drip of her blood through the gaps in her armor. She growled in satisfaction.

Still, if this was to be her death, it was a good one; adequate, for the daughter of a matriarch. Her mother might not curse her name, or look upon her memory without fondness. She crouched, bringing her sword up. "Come then – come and learn the dance of steel!"

Spears jabbed at her, and she ignored them. If they pierced her armor, so be it. She spied Herys, watching her with growing alarm. She lunged for him, and his sword appeared in his hand as if by magic.

"If I am to die, I will have your head to carry into the afterlife," she howled, joyously. This was everything she'd ever wanted, even as a pup.

Herys obliged, fighting desperately now, without his previous arrogance. She wondered if he understood now what he faced. Not a street-cur or a barbarian, but an engine of war, honed to lethal perfection. And what was a mere swordsman against that?

Nothing, and less than nothing.

When the moment came, she seized it fiercely. Herys made an error. An overextension, a slow correction. Her blade looped out, and the elf's sword-hand went flying in a gout of blood. To his credit, the elf did not scream. Instead, he went for a knife on his belt with his remaining hand – until Shulgin took that as well. Then, she took his head. Herys's body stood upright for a moment, as if in defiance of the obvious, before finally crumpling into a defeated heap.

Shulgin looked at the surviving elves and gestured. "Come then," she growled. "Who's next? My blade still thirsts, and I have fight enough for you all."

None of them took her up on the offer. Instead, they began to fall back. She didn't pursue them.

The howls of her pack were louder now; closer. The arrows from above were fewer. The elves were fleeing deeper into the city. Their defenses had been breached. It would be street-to-street now. A moment later, hemicyon warriors loped through the open gate, followed by human soldiers. She allowed herself to sink to her haunches as the tide poured past. She would rest a minute and then find what remained of her pack.

Shulgin licked blood from her muzzle and gave a growl of contentment as she contemplated the fighting to come. Then, she rose and followed the others.

The dance was not yet done, and she still had elves to kill.

CHAPTER FIVE
Valan

In the gardens of the residence of the Lady Merytan, ruler of Callenspire, Valan Cormys paced impatiently. He did not like waiting; he never had. Waiting gave the mind time to concoct the most dreadful fantasies. Only this time, it wasn't a fantasy, but an awful reality. The Xirkaali had come, and time had run out.

Valan bit back an obscenity. He'd known it was a possibility they'd attack while he was in Vieshlar, but he'd hoped to be away before this, safely back in Elvenholme. That they might have a few years yet before the empire made good on its threats.

Then, his luck had not been the best of late. His star, once on a steady ascent, had tumbled decidedly earthward after his disastrous handling of the initial Xirkaali negotiations in Elvenholme, unfair though it was. After all, who could have predicted a folk like the Xirkaali? Their way of thinking was utterly alien to any rational person.

In the months after they'd sent the empire's envoys packing, rumors of invasion had flown swift across the lands of the Kindred and beyond. Most sensible folk dismissed them; but some knew better, even then. And now there was no denying it. News came in from across Mantica. The Xirkaali seemed to be everywhere, all at once. As if they'd been preparing for this for some time.

He'd been sent originally to convince the petty lordlings of the southern kindred of the seriousness of the threat, though his mission had met with mixed success. They were a curious folk, these southern princes. Suspicious of outsiders, and protective of their crumbling enclaves. Even Callenspire, grand as it was, was but a shadow of what it had been, and slowly being swallowed by jungle around it.

In need of distraction, he went to the low wall that bordered the gardens and looked out over the city. At first glance, Callenspire appeared to be thriving. It surmounted the jungle and the rivers like a crown of white marble. Its proximity to Ej had ensured that it was in better state than the coastal cities. Unlike them, it had never been completely abandoned, and centuries of river trade saw to it that the city coffers were rarely empty.

The highest towers, like the one the gardens occupied, were built onto the trunks of immense trees whose roots were the foundations of the wharves that lined the banks of the river. An immense bridge, made from stone and the magically shaped trunks of several trees, connected the city to the Eastway. The height blessedly alleviated some of the humidity that was the curse of these lands.

Callenspire was, in many respects, the largest of Vieshlar's cities. It was through Callenspire that all trade flowed and all travelers went. It was from Callenspire that those first fraught expeditions to reclaim the region had set forth, into the interior and eventually the coast. The Merytan College of Cartography made its home in Callenspire, and the Breakwater Trading Concern, as well as the Eastway Company.

Thus, it was only natural to expect that the lordlings of Callenspire were not receptive to his warnings in the least. Like the rulers of Evanvale and Ruhaindo before them, they had ignored him. Had not, in fact, even deigned to see him. What did they care for the warnings of their northern cousins? He'd resolved to drown his sorrows and move on to Ej at the first opportunity. Only now, at the behest of a strange Neritican, he found himself once more attempting to talk sense into people who had no interest in it. He sighed.

"It's an old ploy, you know," he said aloud. "Making the diplomat wait. It's meant to frustrate us; to throw us off."

"It is seeming to be working," Axel said. The gillkin sat nearby, on a bench made from a single, still-living root. His pet water-elemental played about him, gamboling among the flowers like a child, its shapeless form ripping with every twitch. Valan studied them both. The mage resembled a large axolotl, albeit one dressed in perpetually damp clothing. He leaned on a staff made from a twist of coral, which occasionally glowed with an azure radiance. "You are being angry."

"Frustrated," Valan corrected. "It's rude."

Axel tilted his head. "Yes."

Valan hesitated. Was that amusement he heard in the gillkin's burbling tones? "Politeness is important to the Neriticans, I understand. They take great pains to ensure no insult is offered, on the rare occasions I have met with their envoys."

"Insults among our peoples often are leading to bloodshed." Axel gave a whispery sigh and looked away. "Or did. It is being a long time since I have been among them."

Valan sympathized. From what little Axel had shared, he knew that the gillkin had not seen his own people in at least a century. But before he could reply, the doors to the gardens swung open. A pair of guards, in glittering mail, stepped out.

"Lady Merytan will greet you now, Lord Valan," one said. "Come with us."

Valan and Axel followed the guards into the keep. Lady Merytan was waiting for them in what he took to be her study. Great shelves, the height of the room, lined the curved walls from door to window. Merytan reclined on a divan placed on the balcony. She was beautiful, in the way of many of her generation; perfect and cold, like something carved by a devoted sculptor. Her hair was flaxen and braided into a pattern so intricate it hurt his eyes to look upon it; and her eyes, lovely though they were, had seen vast epochs of time, and it showed. She was older than himself, certainly. Maybe even older than Axel.

Merytan was absently flicking through a book, a decanter and glass on the ground nearby. She looked up as the guards showed them in and gestured for the former to leave them. As the doors closed behind them, Valan made a sweeping, effusive bow. "My dear Lady Merytan, how delightful to see you once more."

"Have we met, then?" she asked, her eyes still on her book.

Valan didn't hesitate. "We have, though I expect it was a more significant affair for myself, humble diplomat that I am." He glanced at Axel, who stood patiently by his side. "But I have been remiss. Allow me to introduce my companion, Axel Tricklebrook. A Neritican mage of no small ability…"

Merytan snapped her book shut and examined Axel coolly. "A gillkin." She sat back, a speculative look on her face. "After all this time? How interesting." She set her book aside. "Your kind supposedly vanished during the Winter War. An amphibious people, much like the riverguard, with whom they were closely aligned. Magic ran in their veins, but as the world grew too cold, their magic faded and they vanished. I had thought them all dead."

"One is surviving, at least," Axel said. If he was insulted, he gave no sign.

"And why are you here?"

"To be offering aid," Axel replied.

Merytan rose smoothly to her feet. "What sort of aid?"

"Against the Xirkaali. They come for you – for your people – even now. I would help you cast them back, if possible."

She raised an eyebrow. "And do we need help, then? I am assured that our forces are more than equal to the challenge."

Valan swallowed and glanced at Axel. "He claims to see the future. A future wherein we are subsumed by them and taught to serve their empire, as the humans do."

Merytan gave a soft laugh. "How fitting. They would teach us, as we taught them."

Valan blinked. "We… what?"

Merytan poured herself a cup of something from the decanter. "We taught them. The hemicyons, I mean. In the Time of Light. We taught them to resent slavery. To take control of their own fate. But we did not teach them anything about what it meant to be free. An oversight, I'm sure you'll agree."

Valan nodded slowly in surprise. That someone knew something of the Xirkaali was not unexpected, but that it was Merytan was unexpected. Idly, he wondered if this was why Axel had wanted him here. And if so, what was he to do with the information? "Yes. But – you've known about them all this time? Why did you not tell us? Surely you heard about the arrival of their envoys to Elvenholme…"

Merytan smiled thinly. "Stories, Valan. All I have are stories. I did not know them to be true. Not with any certainty. And in any event, by the time I heard, you had already insulted them and, well… here we are."

Valan grimaced. "Yes, here we are. In my defense, if I had known –"

Merytan waved this aside. "Would it have mattered? I think not. There are only two options when it comes to the Xirkaali. Surrender – or be conquered. No elf would accept the former. You might have delayed things for a few months more, but what is a few months here or there, in the grand scheme of things?"

"An eternity," Valan murmured.

If Merytan heard, she gave no sign. Instead she turned her attention back to Axel. "You say that you saw this… event come to pass. But what is it to you? Our peoples are not enemies, but nor are we especially friends. Indeed, the river-tribes would like nothing more than to see us driven from the jungles that they claim as their own. Why help us?"

Axel thumped his staff against the floor, and a web of water vapor condensed on the air. Vague forms, like those of marching soldiers, took shape and dissipated before Valan could tell who they were supposed to be. "Despite the beliefs of some, the world is not being a thing of separate parts. Rather, it is being a web of connection. If you fall, Elvenholme is falling. If Elvenholme is falling, so too does Medu'Syth and the other Trident Kingdoms. It is being all one war, and if we fight alone, we will lose."

Merytan digested this in silence. Then, "Will an alliance be enough?"

Axel shrugged. "Maybe. Maybe not. The Great Current is being showed me the path – not the destination. Success or failure is being up to us." He looked at Valan. "If you are agreeing to an alliance, I can be taking word of it to Medu'Syth. It might be enough to be convincing them to go to war with the Xirkaali. From what the waters whisper, as yet the lords of the deep are content to see the Xirkaali as a problem for the air-breathers."

Valan snorted. "Of course they do. So long as it's not taking place in their precious waters, why should they care?" He frowned and looked at the gillkin. "But you think you can convince them otherwise?"

Axel nodded. "I do. I must. If you are agreeing, I will be leaving here today and making my way west, toward the coast, and Medu'Syth. I will be telling them that the elves have been asking for their aid. Their honor will be demanding that they are acting."

"You make it sound so simple," Valan murmured. But the best plans always were. Complexity was the enemy of success. Simplicity was the knife that cut all things.

"It is anything but," Axel said. "Along the way, I will see if the river-tribes can be roused to war. If they are already fighting the Xirkaali, Medu'Syth will have less reason to deny my petition."

Valan frowned in surprise. "And why would they do that?" The thought of the frog-folk doing anything to help the elves was all but impossible to believe.

"Because the Xirkaali are being a threat to their spawning pools."

Valan studied him. "And are they?"

Axel was silent for a moment. *Aha,* Valan thought. Wheels within wheels. This Axel was clever; he was playing his own game. But Valan didn't mind. He'd always excelled at games. He hid a smile and said, "Well, I suppose beggars can't be choosers." He looked at Merytan, who gave him an amused smile.

"Indeed," she said. She bowed elegantly to Axel. "On behalf of the people of Callenspire, I accept your offer of an alliance between our peoples. Rest assured, we shall uphold our end of it, come victory or defeat." She paused. "But hopefully victory."

Axel nodded. "Yes." He hesitated. "But there is being one final matter to be discussing." He straightened. "There is being another that I am seeing in my vision. A general, skilled enough to hold off the Xirkaali. He is to be coming here, or so the Great Current is telling me. When he arrives, you must be giving him command of the city. It is the only way Callenspire will be enduring what is to come. Without him, the city will fall."

Valan exchanged looks with Merytan. "And what is the name of this prodigy?"

"Cadwallader. He is being named Aeron Cadwallader."

CHAPTER SIX
Aeron

Aeron shielded his gaze against the sun and peered up at *Windwalker*. The airship, with its golden lifting globes and sky-oars, was a magnificent sight, familiar though it was by now. It existed in defiance of the world; a thing that size ought not to fly. Or so it seemed to Aeron, though he rarely shared that view aloud, especially in Ej.

Windwalker, once unique, was now one of a small fleet. A half dozen such vessels, though none of them anywhere near as impressive looking, now drifted across the skies above Ej and the surrounding region. Most of them were in almost constant use ferrying supplies and travelers between the Shires and the mountains.

A rain of clanks, whirrs, and hisses drifted down from the upper reaches of the docking tower, attesting to the airship's soon-to-be-readiness to set off on its reconnaissance mission. Folk climbed up and down the tower in a steady metronome of activity, carrying tools and supplies. Aeron made sure to stay well out of their way.

He turned his attention to the rooftops of Gerinhaf. Smoke rose from the chimneys and hearths, painting the pink morning air in hues of gray. The township was the largest of the mountain settlements, comfortably situated in a long, wide valley.

The docking tower stood at the highest point in the valley, overlooking the broad sprawl of the town, now somewhat larger than it had been in decades past. Indeed, it seemed to be growing faster than it had any right to. Access to several sources of water had allowed for a steady increase in manufacturing capability, as well as population growth.

Aeron could hear the distant clang of hammers on steel; the hiss of super-heated metal being cooled; of creaking wheels and pulleys. Voices as well; some raised in song, or argument, or simply conversation. He closed his eyes, and for a moment, he was back in the Shires. But only for a moment. The passing rumble of a wing of grenadiers overhead ruined the illusion. Aeron watched them go, out over the valley and heights. A patrol, perhaps.

Not long after his arrival, he'd suggested that more might sometimes be seen from the air than from the ground, and the folk of Ej had agreed. Before, such patrols had been rare – occurring only when some enterprising captain took the initiative. Now they were a regular occurrence; one more routine instituted against the coming war. Just one of the many changes he'd made. He felt a twinge of guilt as he thought of it; of all the ways that he was transforming a peaceful people into something harder.

The bad part was, he wasn't even certain that it would matter, in the long run. The mountains were as secure as he could make them, but they wouldn't be able to hold out against the Xirkaali. Not even with the extra reinforcements on their way from the Shires. The first batch had arrived a few days ago, aboard the airship, *Thunderwing*. There'd been a few familiar faces among the new arrivals; old friends that he hadn't seen in months. But most of them he didn't recognize. He didn't know whether that made it better, or worse.

"You've got that look again," Anas said as he stumped across the yard to join Aeron. Engineers and airship crewmembers called out to him, and he waved to them.

"What look is that?"

"You know the one. Impatience, mingled with regret."

"Oh, that one." Aeron rubbed his face. The rain had delayed their departure by a day. It had been nearly a week since they'd spotted the smoke on the horizon. A week of sending riders to every town in the mountains and the lowlands, making ready for what he knew they'd find. The Xirkaali were here, and they weren't leaving any time soon.

The delay had necessitated a change of plans. Rather than risking *Windwalker* over what was almost certainly enemy territory by now, Aeron had resolved to go straight to Callenspire. The elven city was considered by many to be the gateway to Ej. It sat at the confluence of two rivers and was the endpoint of the ancient road known as the Eastway. The only sure way to get to Ej, or the mountains, from Vieshlar, was to go through Callenspire.

The Xirkaali would be heading there, once they'd finished up with Ruhaindo. Aeron was as certain of it as he was his own name. Which meant he needed to get there first. "How long before we can go, do you think?" he asked, not for the first time.

Anas snorted. "Within the hour, if the wind holds. If she turns, maybe two. Have no fear, we'll be in the air before lunch, and to Callenspire before dinner."

"And won't that be a sight," a new voice interjected. Aeron turned to see a handsome young woman, dressed in the leather gear of a grenadier, approaching he and Anas. She stopped before Aeron and saluted smartly. "Captain Hannah Bimson, sir. Reporting for duty and ready to fly, at your command."

"My sister's cousin's girl," Anas added, in a loud whisper. Hannah shot him a friendly glare. Anas pretended not to notice. Aeron looked her up and down. She did cut an impressive figure in her flight-leathers. Like all grenadiers, she bore a profusion of the deadly little devices. Each grenade was a hard sphere that, once activated, would explode with enough force to shred armor and whoever was unfortunate enough to be wearing it.

"You know this is just a diplomatic mission," Aeron began.

Hannah nodded. "Yessir. But sometimes things don't go according to plan."

"In my experience, things never go according to plan," Aeron said. "If it comes to that, you and your wing might be responsible for covering our retreat, and you might take heavy casualties doing so."

Hannah's jaw tightened. "We're not afraid of a little dust-up sir. If it gets bloody, then by the missing gods, we'll make sure it's theirs." She patted one of the grenades hanging from her belt. "Besides, that's what we're here for." She hesitated. "Is it true what they say… are the Xirkaali already here?"

Aeron nodded. "They're here, alright." Reports had been coming in from the foothills; traders spoke of what could only be refugee columns heading for the Eastway or Blackthorn. From the sound of things, Evanvale had been taken; Ruhaindo still stood, but even the most optimistic view of the matter gave it only a matter of weeks. The Xirkaali were efficient in a way that the Riftforged Orcs hadn't been. They were interested in acquiring territory and went about it swiftly and effectively – and brutally.

"Are we really going to join the elves?" Hannah asked, eagerly.

"If they'll have us." Aeron paused, thinking. "Hopefully they'll be able to give us a more accurate picture of the enemy's movements, so that we can devise a more effective overall strategy for countering…"

He trailed off as he realized that Hannah was staring at him as if he'd grown a second head. Anas chuckled. "See? I told you she needed some seasoning."

Aeron ignored him. "You should probably let your wing know that we'll be leaving in an hour," he said to Hannah. She saluted again and trotted away, shouting for her fellow grenadiers. Aeron watched her go. "She's very young."

Anas nodded. "Aye, she is that. But so were you. And she's brave enough; I once saw her stuff a grenade down a troll's gullet and take off before it exploded." He peered at Aeron. "But bravery isn't enough. We need our own Aeron Cadwallader."

Aeron looked at him. "I'm doing what I can."

"So you are, lad. And frankly, I don't know how much else we can do. Every village green is a drill field these days, and mock combats are being held monthly," Anas said. He patted Aeron on the shoulder. "If we're not ready, it's not for lack of effort."

"If we're not ready, a lot of people are going to die."

Anas smiled. "Then let's be ready, lad."

Aeron chuckled. "Easy to say. Hard to do."

Anas shook his head. "You're a barrel of laughs today, you know that?" He was about to say more when they heard a loud crash from somewhere across the yard. It was followed by a lot of shouting, and not a little cursing. Anas flushed in annoyance and Aeron sighed. "It's that boy of yours again. I feel it in my water."

"Young Taran means well," Aeron began, half-heartedly. Taran Bligh had come over on the *Thunderwing* with the first batch of Shire-reinforcements, courtesy of Dilwyn Brinmoor. The boy was mechanically gifted; if ran on steam or cider or clockwork, he could make it run faster, or better, or both. But sometimes he took his tinkering too far. When that happened, things got very exciting, very quickly.

Most sensible folk thought he was a menace and nothing more. Aeron found himself torn between sensibility and sympathy. Taran was clearly gifted, but, in Aeron's opinion, those gifts had not been properly aimed.

Taran had quickly found a home among the engineers of Gerinhaf, but he'd caused quite a bit of disruption. Anas stumped in the direction that the crash had come from, just beyond a set of storehouses, a scowl on his face. "He's a menace. There are explosive compounds less destructive than that boy, Aeron. I'm surprised the Shires are still standing, given his propensity for collateral damage."

Aeron said nothing. Ahead of them, the ground had been churned up by something heavy, and a number of chickens raced back and forth in squawking panic. Broken pallets and ripped sacks were scattered across the ground. Halflings were gingerly climbing down from ladders and bales of fodder, looking somewhat dazed by whatever had just happened. On the roof of a nearby bunkhouse, a trio of grenadiers whooped and applauded. Anas glared them into silence and stomped across the courtyard, following the trail of devastation. Aeron trotted sheepishly in his wake.

The trail led to a storehouse near the armory. Aeron whispered a silent prayer of thanks that Taran'd had sense enough to guide his device away from the building full of explosives and into the one full of dry goods instead. He and Anas picked their way through the wreckage of the doorway and into a sea of spilled beans.

The thing called Iron Crusher lay athwart the back wall, hung up on a set of fallen shelves. It resembled a plow, in some respects, albeit one mounted atop a heavy wheel. A profusion of whistles, vents, and funnels dotted its armored surface, all expelling steam. Its single, heavy iron-rimmed wheel spun slowly. Taran lay nearby, sprawled gracelessly among sacks of flour. He looked around as Aeron and Anas entered.

"Oh – Commander! It's not what it looks like," he began, as he tried to extricate himself from the ruptured sacks.

"I am sick to the back-teeth of this, boyo," Anas growled as he hauled Taran up out of the debris with a surprising show of strength. "If you can't keep that contraption of yours under control, I'll have it – and you – bloody dismantled. You understand?"

Taran nodded jerkily. "I – I don't know what happened," he said, apologetically. "Iron Crusher has a mind of its own sometimes!" He looked past Anas to Aeron. "It's a good machine, sir – really! You've seen it on the battlefield."

Aeron nodded tiredly. "I have, and it is. Which is why it should stay on the battlefield, Taran. And you should refrain from provoking it, if at all possible."

Taran slumped, chastened. "Yes, sir."

Anas released the boy and looked at Aeron. He gave the latter a crooked smile. "I say we just point this thing at the Xirkaali and let nature take its course. What about you?"

"I say if it comes to that, we're in trouble. Taran, get this contraption out of here, please." Aeron gestured, and Taran hopped to obey. "He's going to get himself killed," Aeron murmured as they retreated back into the yard. Anas nodded.

"He's going to get someone killed, that I believe. Let's hope it's the enemy."

Aeron turned away. "Hope is a funny word to use. War doesn't care about hope." He looked across the yard, toward the docking tower. "War is a fire, devouring everything in its way. Hope, despair, anger… it all feeds the fire, one way or another."

"You worry too much," Anas said, finally. He cut off Aeron's protest with a gesture. "No, no. You do. You have good reason to worry, and sometimes it's of benefit… but we need you focused now, Aeron. Not worried, not second-guessing yourself. The Xirkaali are here, and its war. The time for second-guessing is done."

A bell atop the docking tower began to clang, signaling *Windwalker*'s readiness to depart. Aeron took a deep breath and looked at Anas. "You're right. Now let's go see what the elves have to say, eh?"

CHAPTER SEVEN

Hejun

Hejun growled softly and rubbed her muzzle with a calloused finger. "Must I?" she asked in a resigned tone. "Let one of the others do it. You do it."

"It is your responsibility, Matriarch," her advisor, Obair, said lightly. They stood atop one of the small, flat-roofed warehouses that lined the docklands of Evanvale. Despite the humidity, she could smell the salted fish stored below, as well as unfamiliar spices. All of it would be put to use by her warriors. Nothing would be wasted. A contingent of human soldiers loitered nearby, keeping watch on the streets below.

She looked at Obair. He was old, as humans judged such things, and proudly bore the sigil of her clan on his chest. No longer a warrior, he'd stayed safely aboard one of the war-junks until Evanvale had been taken. Or most of it, at least. In truth, much of the outer city was still in contention; the elves were fighting fiercely, but they were outnumbered. Another day, maybe two, and it would be done. Then they could turn their attention to other matters.

"Fine. And stop smiling. It irks me." Her paws itched for the hilt of a blade. But such pleasures were to be denied her for the time being. As Obair said, she had responsibilities.

Obair genuflected. "I shall do my best, Matriarch." As he straightened, she saw that he was still smiling. "Still, one mustn't complain. It could be much worse, you know."

Hejun gave the old man a baleful look. He ignored it, as ever. "Every third thing out of your mouth is a complaint, Obair," she said, pointedly. "You complain about the food, about the condition of our troops, about our orders, and even about my strategies."

Obair nodded agreeably. "I am your advisor. Advisors advise. Some pups might confuse this for complaints, but you are old enough to know better." He clasped his hands behind his back. "Now, why don't you address the prisoners, eh? They're getting antsy."

Hejun looked down at the courtyard below them. It was full of elves; captives, taken in the initial push, surrounded by Yan soldiers. The elves were tradesmen and artisans. Representatives of the city's social strata. Elven society was an odd thing; it seemed to have no bottom rung. There were nobles, servants, and yeomen. But no peasants, not like the Yan had once had. Perhaps that was a good thing; peasants were too much like slaves.

She could smell their fear. They were a ragged bunch; some had tried to escape the city and been caught, while others had surrendered as soon as they caught sight of her warriors. They feared her, they feared what her presence meant for their people; but more than that, they feared the loss of the lives they had known. Their comforts, their profits… their privileges. She bared her teeth. They were a soft folk, and soft folk were pliable.

Obair gestured, and the soldiers below struck the ground with the butts of their spears, signaling that she was about to speak. The elves looked up expectantly. She paused for a moment, letting them see her. Then, with a slight shake of her head, she began to speak.

She had given the same speech many times in the past; it was as practiced as her sword-stroke. In many ways, it was simply one more weapon in her arsenal. Words or steel, what did it matter, so long as the deed was done – and done well.

"You will work as you have always worked," she said, her voice carrying down and across the courtyard. "You will serve, as you have always served. You will live, as you have always lived. We have no interest in making you slaves. But we will have your compliance. You are free to serve – or free to die." She gestured to Obair. "In our service, you might rise high; higher, even, than you might have under your old masters, those feckless lordlings who abandoned you. Rest assured that we shall not be so quick to flee our responsibilities. Where the Xirkaali stand, we rule. Where the tigerskin banners rise, our laws hold sway now and forevermore. Of that, if nothing else, you can be certain."

At her words, the Yan, in unison, struck the ground with the butts of their spears. She studied the elves, searching the sea of faces for any obvious signs of recalcitrance. Mostly what she saw was shock and disbelief. But there was anger there as well; and on some faces… consideration. Calculation. That was good.

Conquest could not be accomplished through force of arms alone, no matter how many of her peers might wish it so. It was a thing of many strands, woven together with expert skill. It required finding those among the conquered who could – and would – ensure compliance. She glanced at Obair, who gave a terse nod. He had likely already made note of several potential candidates for such responsibilities.

She gave the order to dismiss the elves back to their homes and shops and turned to Obair. "Now, let us discuss more important matters. You have the maps?"

"I do." Obair motioned for one of the nearby soldiers to bring forward a trio of tightly rolled maps, drawn on kidskin. The elves were a degenerate people, but they made good maps. Hejun sank to her haunches as the soldier unrolled them on the roof before her. Obair had them bring him a stool.

Hejun studied the old man fondly. Obair had advised her own matriarch, when Hejun was but a pup, still learning the dance of steel. She had inherited him, along with her position, and could not imagine life without him. Humans were too unpredictable, too soft, to rule; that was as the gods willed. But some, like Obair, made her wonder what they might make of themselves, if given the opportunity.

"Are you comfortable, old man?" she asked. "Can we begin?"

Obair scowled at her. "It's the humidity. Makes my joints ache." He rubbed his wrists and looked down at the maps with a sigh. "Fine. To start with, thanks to the heroic efforts of Admiral Khulan, we've established a half dozen holdings along the coast to the north," he said, indicating the points on one of the maps.

"Iron Beach is the largest; Gorcha has burnt half the tidal swamp there to clear it. She's put her auxiliaries to work building palisades and the plainstalkers to laying paths through the swamp. Once it's done, she'll march for Evanvale with a third of her command to reinforce us here, and free us up to take Ruhaindo."

"So she says," Hejun murmured. Gorcha was a troublesome one; she had ambitions. Not a crime in and of itself, but it made things difficult sometimes. Especially when it was someone like Gorcha, who combined determination with equal parts arrogance and stupidity. But she was a good warrior. Sometimes that was enough.

But only sometimes.

"I know that look, my lady. I saw it often enough on your mother's face."

Hejun grunted and looked at the old man. "Meaning?"

Obair hastily looked back down at the map. "I estimate a week, maybe two, to make this place livable, once we've taken it completely. Three, to make it defensible. Less, if the locals see the light of reason."

"They will. They always do." She sat back on her haunches and studied the maps. Her eyes found the river and followed it up to the mountains. "Are any of the vessels we captured salvageable?" They had laid claim to a number of rivercraft in taking the docklands and the wharves situated along the estuary.

Obair tugged on his wispy beard. "A few. And of those, barely any fit for hemicyon use, I fear. Not quite big enough, you see."

Hejun grunted. "That is to be expected. Our auxiliaries can use them to move supplies upriver as we advance toward Callenspire and Ej. It will be hard, but still easier than trying to move them overland, through all that jungle, and quicker than taking the Eastway."

"So I anticipated."

A boom from across the bay drew her attention in the direction of Ruhaindo. The immense seaward wall of the port city stood defiant against her authority, and likely would for some weeks. A line of war-junks currently blockaded the harbor gates, and other, sturdier vessels ferried hemicyon warriors and their human auxiliaries to the mouth of the estuary. The familiar stink of fire-powder rode the salt-breeze, stinging her nose. She sneezed and shook herself. "Every time," she muttered. Obair stifled a chuckle.

"The rockets do come in handy, you must admit," he said.

"I do not deny it, old man. I simply do not care for the smell." She tapped her snout. "You humans are lucky that your noses are such pitiful organs."

Obair sniffed. "Hurtful."

"Accurate," she said. More rockets spluttered across the bay from the decks of the war-junks. Most impacted against the berm or the walls themselves. A few managed to clear the high parapets and strike something within the city. She could hear the distant clangor of alarm bells and see thin contrails of smoke rising up into the sky.

Sometimes, the rockets were enough to break the enemy. Not this time, though. The elves weren't as soft as she'd been told. Then, that was all to the good.

Her warriors needed a proper blooding. She stood, and Obair joined her, as the soldiers gathered up the maps.

"Thick walls," he mused. "We might crack them, but I doubt we'll bring them down. Even if we manage to get a few khon-bukhan mortars properly placed, which isn't likely at the moment."

"I don't want to bring them down," she said. "I want that city intact. We need it."

Obair nodded. "So we do. Still, can't predict everything."

Hejun grunted. "No. We can't." The thought made her itch. Thinking of the future made her uncomfortable. The city was in front of her, and therefore its fall was the most important thing. She could worry about the rest after. Or, better yet, leave it to Obair. Humans were gifted at planning for the future. Indeed, sometimes it seemed as if they did little else with their time.

"You still think this is a mistake, don't you?" he asked, after a moment. Hejun sighed noisily and turned away from him.

"It doesn't matter what I think. I have been given my orders, and I will see it done. The elves were offered amnesty three times, as is our way. And three times they refused us. The time for negotiations is over. Now is the time of war."

"Yes, but it won't be an easy one."

Hejun licked her muzzle. "When is it ever?"

Obair chuckled. "Your daughter will be pleased by that, at least."

Hejun glanced at him. "Which one?" She had whelped many daughters for her pack before taking up her current position. Most of them were serving throughout the empire as lesser matriarchs, overseeing their own packs.

"The only one here," Obair said. "Shulgin."

Hejun clicked her teeth in annoyance. Shulgin was her youngest pup, and the only one not to have made a name for herself yet. She saw much of herself in the young hemicyon; too much, at times. Shulgin was brash, even for a warrior of her age. Desperate to prove herself, perhaps. Hejun had been as well, in her youth. All a warrior had was her honor, and one needed opportunity to prove it.

Hejun grunted softly. "She will get more opportunities to prove herself, of that I have no doubt." Shulgin had been at the forefront of the attack on Evanvale, leading her warriors against the town's few defenders. Even now she was overseeing the push against the remaining pockets of resistance in the outer city.

"She did well at the portcullis. Or so I hear."

"She was nearly killed," Hejun countered.

"Is that concern I hear in your voice?" Obair teased, gently. Hejun glowered at him without anger. Obair had more than earned the right to speak so freely to her, though other matriarchs might disagree. And he had always doted on Shulgin, especially after his own children had become grown. Humans were strange that way.

"Concern only that her actions will bring shame to our pack." Hejun scratched her ear and squinted at the distant city. "They're evacuating the city."

"Reasonable. Pragmatic. It's what I would do."

"Yes." Her warriors had orders to ignore the people streaming out of Ruhaindo's landward gates and concentrate on digging in for the siege to come. Of course, some of her subordinates had taken it into their heads to capture as many of these evacuees as possible, in order to use them as a labor force. Obair saw her lip curl and sighed.

"It's not the same thing as slavery, Matriarch. They will be released when the battle is won. And none will be mistreated. Even the rowdiest of your warriors knows better than that. But it is a sad necessity of an undertaking such as this. Without enforcing your will on the empire's new vassals – without putting them to work – we will fail. The elves will be taught the ways of the new order. Even as my people were, so long ago."

Hejun grunted. "Let us hope. Else this will all be for nothing."

CHAPTER EIGHT
Valan

Valan poured himself a drink and offered his guest the same. The latter waved the wine aside. "If I wanted to drink watered down swill, I'd drink in one of the human taverns down by the docks," the gladestalker said, gruffly.

Gladestalkers were odd sorts; half hermit and half scout, with a decided tendency toward the slitting of throats. Enemy throats, mostly, though not always. They lived lives of self-imposed isolation, haunting the forest trails that bound the enclaves of the kindred together, and hunting the occasional bandit or monster.

Kortys Helmyr was no exception. He was rangy and weatherbeaten beneath his patchwork cloak, with a hard look in his eyes that Valan didn't care for. He was heavily armed, with a bow slung across his back, a sword on his hip, and far too many knives for Valan's liking. He played idly with an arrow as they spoke, balancing it on his forefinger.

They stood in the private garden that Lady Merytan had bestowed upon Valan so that he might have some place private to conduct his business. Unfamiliar bird calls drifted down from the thick canopy overhead, and the sweet smell of jungle flowers coated the air. Valan sipped his wine – not watered down in the slightest, *actually* – and studied the gladestalker.

Lady Merytan had recommended him, avowing that Kortys knew the jungle better than most and enjoyed a fight more than was to be expected of a civilized elf. Two qualities they were going to need in abundance, in the weeks to come.

"I expect you know why I've asked you here," Valan began.

Kortys smiled nastily. "You want me to kill Xirkaali."

"Ideally, yes."

Kortys chuckled. "Happy to be of service." He looked around the garden. "Always wondered what was up in these towers," he added, tossing the arrow up and catching it absently. "Can't say I'm impressed."

"I will inform Lady Merytan of your lack of awe at the first available opportunity," Valan said drily. "Specifically, we need someone who speaks the river-dialect. I'm told that's you. Is that correct?"

Kortys frowned. "What do you want with the *Ril'uwa*?" he asked, referring to the river-tribes by their proper name. Valan smiled. If that didn't prove Merytan correct in her assessment, he didn't know what did.

"The riverguard are our allies in this endeavor. We need someone who can ensure that there are no… miscommunications while our forces are working alongside one another. It would be unfortunate if old grudges interfered with new alliances, don't you think?"

Kortys's frown deepened. "I speak a bit of Mudbelly, and some Treeleaper."

Valan raised an eyebrow. "Those are different, then?"

Kortys snorted. "Every tribe has its own dialect, and there's around thirty tribes in this region alone. Every stretch of water in Vieshlar has at least one." He sighed and tossed the arrow again; and again, he caught it without so much as a glance in its direction. "I can do it, but it won't be easy."

"I do not expect miracles. But we must show willing, else they might decide we're not taking this whole alliance thing seriously." Valan took another sip of his wine and closed his eyes as a breeze passed over the garden.

How much time did they have? There was no way to tell. For the moment, the Xirkaali were still gnawing through the coastal enclaves of Evanvale and Ruhaindo. But he feared it wouldn't be long before they turned their attention to Callenspire.

During their brief meeting, Prince Herys of Evanvale had not impressed him as possessing any particular military genius. Like many southern princes, he confused being a passing duelist with a talent for strategy. Prince Sarkan, of Ruhaindo, was made of sterner stuff, but even he could only do so much. Ruhaindo had high walls, but not much else. It too would fall. And then what?

Valan opened his eyes. "The Xirkaali will be coming this way soon enough. We must be ready for them. I need you to take as many gladestalkers as this city has and delay the enemy by any means necessary."

Kortys scratched his chin with the tip of the arrow. "I can muster maybe a hundred, possibly a few less. That'll be more than enough to cause some confusion, at least. We can do a good deal more than that, if you're right about the riverguard. With the river-tribes on our side, we can conduct substantial hit-and-run attacks on any force moving inland. The Xirkaali won't know what hit them."

"Excellent."

"Yes. Isn't it just?" a smooth voice purred. Valan started and turned to see another elf leaning against the doorway to the gardens. The elf pushed away from the doorframe and studied Valan coolly. Valan recognized him immediately: Solibos, one of Merytan's many cousins and heir apparent to the throne of Callenspire. He felt his heart sink. He'd expected this, but it didn't make it any less welcome.

"Lord Solibos," he began, in his most ingratiating tones. Solibos sneered.

"Lord Valan. I see you've managed to worm your way into my cousin's good graces. This garden used to belong to her father." Solibos strode toward them, his hands clasped behind his back. He paused before Kortys and gave the gladestalker a dismissive look. "What he'd think of a – a reprobate like this being allowed in here, I shudder to think."

Kortys flushed but said nothing. He knew better. Solibos was the current commander of Callenspire's military forces, such as they were. A garrison of several thousand elven warriors answered to him, and him alone. Merytan was a queen in all but name, but her cousin was the power behind her throne.

Solibos looked away. "You may go, gladestalker. I wish to discuss important matters with this… diplomat." Kortys hesitated, but Valan waved him out. The gladestalker went, grudgingly. Valan hid a smile. If it came to it, he thought he knew which side Kortys was on. That was something, at least.

"I thought you were planning to depart," Solibos said without preamble.

Valan took a long swallow of wine before answering. "I was. Circumstances dictated otherwise." He offered Solibos the cup Kortys had turned down, but the other elf turned up his nose at it. Valan shrugged and added the contents of the cup to his own.

"And what circumstances might those be?"

Valan paused. He'd assumed that Merytan had told her cousin about Axel's proposal, but evidently not. That was curious – but perhaps a blessing in disguise. Solibos might have tried to arrest the mage as a spy, or some similar nonsense. "The Neriticans wish an alliance," he said, carefully. "Against the Xirkaali."

Solibos blinked. "That is… unexpected."

"But welcome."

"Yes, well, how can we be sure that this isn't some ruse?" Solibos pressed.

"Can we afford to be suspicious, given what is happening on the coast?"

"Rumors, nothing more," Solibos said, dismissively. "The tall tales of itinerant peddlers and gladestalkers. Hardly has the ring of truth, does it?"

Valan bit back his first response. Solibos, like many of his peers, assumed that the Xirkaali were no threat to the armies of the elves. But they had not seen what Valan had; even the smallest hemicyon warrior towered well over his elven counterpart. Skilled as they were, the largely inexperienced soldiers of Evanvale and Ruhaindo were no match for such creatures. The reclamation of Vieshlar had bled the southern kindred white for generations, and the spreading of the Ophidian deserts had made it difficult for them to rebuild their military strength in any meaningful fashion.

He took a breath and said, "Sadly, it is all true. The invaders took Evanvale earlier this week. They'll do the same to the rest of the coastal cities before the month is out, if even one of these reports is to be believed."

"Nonsense," Solibos protested. "I have dueled Herys myself; a more worthy warrior I cannot imagine. His skill with a blade is unparalleled."

"Perhaps. But what about his skill as a strategist?"

Solibos frowned. "Watch your tone, diplomat. You speak of your betters."

"Forgive me. You're correct, of course. To Evanvale," Valan said, raising his cup in toast. "May she last a hundred years more." He took a swig and added, "Sadly, however, Herys is dead. Slain by the Xirkaali."

Solibos inhaled sharply. "How do you know this?"

"One hears things, when one listens. Whether you choose to believe it or not, Evanvale has fallen. Ruhaindo might follow it within the week. Callenspire will be next. We might have a month, maybe two, but the enemy will be at our gates before we know it. We must make ready."

Solibos drew himself up haughtily. "You mean I must make ready. After all, I am in command of the city's military forces."

Valan smiled. "Then why didn't your cousin inform you about the alliance with the Neriticans? Curious, that. Maybe she knows something that you don't."

Solibos stiffened. “What are you implying?”

“Nothing at all. I merely state the obvious. If you were truly in command, Merytan would have informed you immediately. She did not. Thus, one must consider the implications. Perhaps she fears that your… lack of practical experience might endanger the city. Or maybe I make too much of a simple oversight.” Valan emptied his cup and sniffed. “It’s not my business, at any rate.”

“No,” Solibos muttered. “No it is not.” Without another word, he spun toward the doors and stalked out of the garden. Kortys returned a moment later. Where he’d been lurking, Valan couldn’t say, but he was pleased to see the gladestalker nonetheless.

“He’s gone,” Kortys said.

“Good. How much did you hear?”

Kortys gave him an aggrieved look. “All of it.”

“Yes, of course, how silly of me. And what do you think?”

“A discretely loosed arrow would solve several problems at once,” Kortys said. “He’s going to be trouble. He’s always been trouble, but he’s going to be worse now.”

“Yes, that’s my fear as well.” Valan rubbed the back of his neck. Callenspire was, like most elven cities, a viper-pit when it came to politics. The noble families that made up the local court feuded incessantly, making, and breaking, alliances on a whim. They vied viciously against one another for the most meager scraps of influence and power; worse, their factionalism ensured that Merytan’s control of the city was a house built on sand.

From what Valan had seen since arriving in Callenspire, Solibos was a deft navigator of these treacherous tides, more so than his cousin. Merytan had her strengths, but dealing with a pack of mutinous aristocrats wasn’t among them. She left that tedious responsibility to her cousin, and he had taken full advantage of it.

“You really think she intends to remove him?” Kortys asked.

Valan shrugged. “I have no idea. I just wanted him to leave so that I could come up with a solution.” Solibos wasn’t one to sit idle, especially if he thought his position was in danger. Valan hoped he hadn’t made a bad situation worse – not again. He was about to ask Kortys his opinion when he saw that the gladestalker’s eyes were locked on something in the sky above the city. Valan followed his gaze and saw a curious shape sailing through the clouds. “Is that a – a ship?” he asked, in confusion.

“Airship,” Kortys said, as if this were a common sight.

Valan peered more closely at the approaching vessel, briefly wondering if it belonged to the Xirkaali, but – no. No, this was something else. It looked like a sailing vessel, complete with oars, but had somehow been modified to fly. He had heard stories about similar contraptions, sighted by travelers over the Blades of Ej, but had dismissed them as products of fancy. “Indeed,” he said, as he suddenly recalled Axel’s parting words. He smiled.

“And, unless I am mistaken, it’s the answer to our problem.”

CHAPTER NINE
Hannah

Hannah Bimson sat belowdecks on the *Windwalker*, testing the straps on her flight pack. She knew they were fine, but it was a sorry excuse for a grenadier who didn't regularly check their equipment. It wouldn't do to have a strap break while she was in the air. She gave one a tug and then moved on to the seals on the cannister. It used magic but still had a form of fuel inside to act as propellant. If it leaked, she'd fall – or worse.

Absently, she touched the knife sheathed vertically on her chest. Accidents were few and far between, but they did happen. Magic was a chancy thing, even in the most skilled hands. She didn't trust it as much as some; it had its uses, but she believed in being prepared regardless. The knife would allow her to cut the straps, if needed.

A shudder ran through the hull, and she paused, listening to the sound of the wind sliding past. The *Windwalker* could travel nearly twenty leagues on a good day, if the wind was in her favor and the skies clear. It had been the beneficiary of several years of constant tinkering and improvements. Its main hull was long and narrow, like that of a seagoing vessel; pointed at the fore and blunt at the aft. It moved through the air, its sky-oars creaking mechanically as the magically empowered boiler provided fuel to the lifting globes below. A wonder, by any stretch of the imagination.

Unfortunately, the wind hadn't been good. They'd barely come ten leagues a day since leaving the mountains. Three days in, and the river was still a slash of muddy blue on the horizon. Hannah hadn't quite realized how much jungle there was between the mountains and Callenspire. It made her feel small to think of it, so she tried not to.

The turbulence cleared, and the tremors faded. Around her, the crew that were belowdecks went about their business with the ease of practiced sailors. Her grenadiers, however, looked a bit green around the gills. She'd brought five of her best, including her second-in-command, Cogman. It was an honor to be asked. At least, that was how Anas had framed it, when the order had come down.

The truth was, she and Anas didn't see eye-to-eye much. He was a stick-in-the-mud. He liked being careful, too much so at times. She understood a certain need for wariness, but Anas took it to extremes at times. Though, given recent events, she figured their days of hiding what they could do were over. If they really were mobilizing to help the elves, they'd have no choice but to reveal what they were capable of.

She set her gear aside and made her way to the other side of the cramped hold, where they were awaiting the order to fly – or not. They were a good bunch; experienced, insomuch as they could be, given the decided lack of action. The youngest, Pinter, had killed his first troll the year previous. "How are we feeling?" she asked.

Cogman was the one to answer. "Bit peaky. Must not have our sky-legs, yet." He was a stocky lad, around her age, with muttonchops badly in need of a trim and a propensity for chewing on cheroots, as he was now. A chuckle ran through the group. Grenadiers had strong stomachs; they had to, to endure the takeoffs. But walking around aboard a flying vessel wasn't the same as flying alone.

"Well, get them in a hurry. We might have to make a jump."

Cogman rose and joined her as she returned to her seat. "I thought this was just a friendly visit," he said, softly. Hannah glanced at him.

"That's what Ser Aeron says. But elves are funny about uninvited guests."

Cogman grinned. "Ser Aeron, is it?" he asked, coyly. "Impressed with him, are you?"

Hannah flushed. "And if I am?"

Cogman shrugged. "I'm just saying, he doesn't seem the sort to care for hero worship. More the humble sort, that fellow." He stuck his cheroot back in his mouth.

Hannah felt a vague need to defend Aeron. "I like him. He knows his stuff."

Cogman gave her a knowing look. "Very attentive, are we?"

Before she could reply, the clangor of a bell sounded through the hold. "That's us," she said. She looked past Cogman at the others. "Grab your gear and assemble on deck!"

Hannah was the first on deck, tightening the straps on her pack as she went. The wind whipped past as she reached the open air. The coast was visible to her left and the long muddy stretch of the river. "What's going on?" she asked, as she climbed onto the aft-deck.

"Isn't it obvious, lass?" Anas shouted. "We've arrived!" He stood at the controls, the wind whipping through his white hair. "There it is… Callenspire!"

Hannah turned, and her eyes widened in awe.

Callenspire rose up over a split in the river. At first glance, it seemed small, due more to the limits of geography than the intentions of its builders. But the closer *Windwalker* got, the more she noticed the great trees which permeated the island and the city both, rising up and up over the surrounding jungle. Skyways of woven vines connected far-flung branches, and more traditional bridges extended between and around rooftops. What the city lacked in width it made up for in height.

"It's huge," she breathed.

"Small, as elves judge such things," Aeron said, at her elbow. She flinched in embarrassment. He must think her such a yokel. But the smile on his face reassured her. Aeron pointed. "Look there. The docklands."

Hannah followed his gesture and saw that much of the lower city was given over to extensive docklands that made up the western district, and all manner of rivercraft jostled for the numerous but still limited berths among the wooden jetties and stone wharfs.

"Callenspire is truly what it claims to be," Aeron went on, loudly. "All trade in Vieshlar runs through it, or did. From what I've read, its toll locks once dominated the Vieshlar River, all the way to the estuary, in better times." He studied the city the way one might study an opponent. "The Xirkaali will be here in a week. Maybe two. If we're lucky."

"And if we're not?"

Aeron shrugged. "Then we'll do what we can."

Hannah swallowed, suddenly uncertain. "We've trained, Ser Aeron," she said, though whether to reassure him or herself, she wasn't sure. "Trained hard. We're ready for whatever they throw at us. On the field or behind walls, we'll beat them."

Aeron smiled thinly. "It's not our prowess I doubt, Hannah. It's what comes after that first battle – and the second – the third."

She frowned in puzzlement. "What do you mean?"

Aeron was silent for a moment. "Everything we know about the Xirkaali, and it's not much, tells me that they're here for the duration. This isn't a war that can be won before the next harvest. Even if we beat them – beat them bad – they'll just retreat to the coast and rebuild for another go. How much stomach for war do your folk have? Can we sustain the muster for months, let alone years? Can the elves?" He looked at her.

Hannah had no reply. She hadn't even considered that the war might last so long. It was a sobering thought. Aeron nodded.

"And here's a grim thought: what if the elves surrender? Where does that leave us? Or worse, when the Xirkaali come knocking, how many of our folk will decide to err on the side of discretion?" He looked at the city again. "We're on borrowed time, I fear. Which means we really only have one option open to us."

"Which is?" Hannah asked.

"Callenspire," Aeron said, firmly. He pointed at the city for emphasis. "It's the route to Ej and the mountains both. If they take the city, they'll have a clear path to the elven heartlands and our own. So if we're going to make a stand anywhere, this's the place."

"The elves might disagree," Hannah said dubiously. "It's the lords of Ej who asked for our aid, after all. The lords of Callenspire might feel different about it." She knew enough about elves to know they were persnickety about such things.

"Then we'll just have to be convincing," Aeron said. He clapped her on the shoulder, and she grinned. Before she could reply, however, *Windwalker* shuddered slightly and began its lazy descent toward one of the great trees that dominated the city skyline.

Despite Anas's best efforts, the elves of Vieshlar knew a good deal about her people's airships, and the folk of Callenspire had magically constructed accommodation for them in a rare show of thoughtfulness – a small sky-wharf, built into the green canopy that shaded the southern edge of the city. It resembled a circular row of immense petals, if said petals were made from timber and vine.

Largely hidden from the rest of the city, it provided a modicum of privacy on the rare occasions the Ej-folk paid a visit to their westernmost neighbors.

The sky-wharf also had a number of mooring points on its oddly shaped jetties, situated to accommodate several airships the size of *Windwalker*. If the elves knew about *Thunderchild* and the others, they'd never mentioned it, but Hannah suspected that the structure was as much a message as it was a docking area.

That was the elves all over; meanings within meanings. They never said just one thing. A conversation with an elf was like peeling an onion; no matter how many layers you peeled back, there was always one more. Unless you were talking about an elf like Kortys. Simple and straightforward as a poke in the eye, that one.

The gladestalker had accompanied the last delegation from Ej to visit Gerinhaf, some years back. The taciturn elf had made quite the impression on a younger Hannah. He'd taught her a few tricks with a knife that had stood her in good stead during her duties. Even as *Windwalker* began the tedious process of docking, she wondered whether Kortys was in the city. Or was he out there in the jungle somewhere, fighting the Xirkaali?

The airship shuddered. Unseen devices clunked and clicked. Air cycled through pumps. Ropes were hurled over the side to snag mooring posts. Then, finally, boarding ramps were extended and lowered. Hannah watched from the rail as Anas and Aeron made their way down. Elves were hurrying to meet them. One was clearly some sort of official, from the cut of her robes. The others were definitely soldiers. None of them looked happy.

Hannah ambled toward the boarding ramp. Cogman and the others crowded behind her, eager to see what was going on. The elven official was saying something, and though Aeron maintained his pleasant expression, Anas was turning purple. She also couldn't help but notice the way the soldiers were taking a definite interest in the airship and her crew.

"Is there some problem, Ser Aeron?" she called out as she took up a position at the top of the boarding ramp, one hand on her knife. Aeron turned and waved her back.

"No, Captain Bimson, thank you. We're just discussing docking arrangements with these fine folk." He turned back to the official. "As I was saying, the Xirkaali are coming this way. Or hadn't you heard? So I thought it best that we come, and quickly."

The official looked down her nose at Aeron. "And who are you, exactly?" Hannah winced, annoyed on Ser Aeron's behalf. Of course they wouldn't know who he was. Why would they? Rhordia was a continent away.

"He's Aeron Cadwallader, unless I am sorely mistaken," a new voice interjected. The soldiers stepped aside as a tall elf strode across the jetty toward them. He had an easy smile and his hands were clasped behind his back.

"Well, well, isn't this wonderful timing?" He stopped before Aeron and bowed. "Valan Cormys, at your service." He straightened and dismissed the official with a flick of his fingers. She hesitated, but only for a moment.

Valan watched her go and then turned back to Aeron. "Welcome to Callenspire, Ser Aeron. You have no idea how glad I am to see you."

CHAPTER TEN
Axel

Axel rested on the bottom of the river, in a natural bole of interwoven roots and mud. He had been traveling along the river for two days now, moving as quickly as possible, and all signs of elven civilization had long since faded into the green shadows of the jungle. Here was the land of wild things; of snakes as long as fallen trees and great spotted hunting cats; of frogs that killed with a touch and birds that sang in human voices.

Vieshlar was a cradle of the wilderness. It was the world as it had been, before the young races began to raise their cities and tame the land. There was magic in the soil and the water, and if Axel but closed his eyes, he could hear its song.

He wished others could hear it as he did. Then they might understand what was at stake in the war to come. The Xirkaali were driven to break and tame the wild – no. Not just the wild… the world itself. To control everything, even that which could not and should never be controlled. To prevent that would require a unified effort; not just from Neriticans, halflings, and elves, but from other peoples and powers. He'd done what he could to start things; if Callenspire stood, then so might the world.

They are coming, Splish murmured, startling him from his reverie. The elemental surrounded Axel like a living mantle, keeping him safely suspended beneath the bole and out of the strong grasp of the current.

"How many?" he asked. The newcomers had been trailing him for at least a day. He'd decided to let them catch up and give them a proper greeting.

Many, Splish replied. The elemental only had a vague understanding of numbers. *Closer now. Almost here.* The elemental was growing agitated.

"Well then, let us introduce ourselves," Axel said as he grasped his coral staff and felt the comfort of the magical currents stirring within his slight frame. The shadows beneath the riverbank were driven back by a cerulean glow, and the lapping waters became as clear as glass. With Splish coiled about him, Axel slid into the river and rose to the surface with nary a splash to mark his exit. Instead, a swirling cyclone of water lifted him high over the new arrivals, who had steadily been creeping toward his refuge.

The newcomers froze. Their bulbous eyes fixed on him. There were around a dozen of the rangy, frog-like creatures. They wore wooden armor and carried spears and javelins. Axel felt a pang of relief, mingled with poignancy.

"Riverguard," he said, softly. "Oh, my friends, it has been too long." He loosened his hold on the waters and dropped to the surface of the river, where he hung just above the water. By the marks on their armor, he judged them to be one of the tribes aligned to the kingdom of Medu'Syth; a small tribe, at least when he'd last been in this part of the world. Who knew how much they'd expanded in the centuries since then. "I don't suppose you recognize me," he began, hopefully.

A loud, rumbling croak split the air. At the same moment, Splish thrummed in warning. Axel turned to see a massive form bounding toward him from the bank of the river. "Pondwarden," he gasped, in shock. The creature resembled the riverguard, but was massive, easily outweighing even the largest of them; it too wore wooden armor and carried a large mace made from driftwood and bone. Axel raised his staff, drawing up the waters into an impromptu shield as the mace descended toward him with fatal intent.

The force of the blow rippled through the waters and caused the river to surge up and froth. The riverguard scattered, croaking in agitation. The pondwarden gave a warbling roar and attacked again. Again, the shield held – but only just. He was strong, Axel reflected. Then, they had been made for strength, even as his kind had been made to harness the power of the Great Current.

"Stop, please," he began. "I mean no harm – I just want to talk…"

The pondwarden struck again and again. Axel felt his concentration slip with each blow. It wasn't inconceivable that his attacker might simply bludgeon his way through. A new tactic was called for. At his mental request, Splish erupted into view and coiled about the pondwarden's mace, dragging it down. Simultaneously, Axel drove his staff into the river, causing the water to rise up and punch the looming pondwarden backward, into the mangrove trees that clustered thickly near the bank.

Axel gave his opponent no time to recover. He sprang onto the bank and spun his staff, whipping the brackish waters about him. Even as the pondwarden made to rise from the broken trees, Axel hit him with the full force of the river. The pondwarden went down – and stayed down. Axel crept toward him cautiously. "Do you live?"

For a moment, there was only silence. Then the pondwarden sat up, his ugly features wrinkled in frustration. "You cheated," he croaked. He sounded younger than Axel had assumed. Almost petulant. Like the riverguard, he likely belonged to a tribe allied with Medu'Syth. They were farther inland than he'd expected. Then, much had changed over the intervening centuries. The whole shape of the world was much altered.

"I wanted to win. Why did you attack me?" Axel asked.

"You're a stranger," the pondwarden replied. He reached surreptitiously for his mace, but Splish dragged the weapon away. The pondwarden grunted and looked at Axel. "What are you? You look like us – but not."

Axel hesitated, suddenly all too aware of the riverguard closing in on him from all sides. They didn't look actively hostile, but he'd rather not provoke them. They'd always been a prickly folk – quick-tempered, especially when it came to their waters. As he recalled, they had not looked kindly on the gillkin's departure during the War with Winter. "I am gillkin. My name is Axel. Axel Tricklebrook. You may know that name. In times past, I fought alongside the Sythians against our mutual enemies. I calmed the waters of your spawning pools and sang the sweetwater hymns to your tadpoles."

The pondwarden's eyes widened – then narrowed. "My father spoke of you; and his father. Tricklebrook the traitor. Tricklebrook the coward. You left us to Winter's mercy."

"That is not what happened," Axel began.

"Lies," the pondwarden croaked. He rolled toward his mace, swatting Splish aside with a contemptuous blow. He reclaimed the weapon and surged to his feet, raising it over his wide head as he did so. Axel did nothing. He could have easily formed another shield or hammered the pondwarden flat once more. But what point would that serve? He needed their trust. So, instead, he closed his eyes and waited.

The expected blow never fell. Axel cracked an eye and peered up at the pondwarden, who was staring down at him in confusion. "What are you doing?" the latter asked, bewildered.

"Waiting?"

"For what?"

"Common sense to assert itself," Axel said. "I'm no threat to you, warrior. I seek no trouble. Not with you or your folk." He looked at the nearby riverguard. "Tell me, how fare the Sythians in this new world? Well, I hope."

"The rivers of Vieshlar belong to us," the pondwarden said, slowly. Axel nodded.

"Really? In my day, you only controlled one small estuary." He looked at the pondwarden. "What is your name, friend?"

"I am not your friend, gillkin." The pondwarden hesitated, as the instinct toward hospitality – ingrained in the amphibious tribes – asserted itself. "Gorrup," he added, grudgingly. Axel nodded again.

"I knew another by that name. A long time ago. I counted him a friend."

Gorrup was silent for a moment. Then, "You speak of my ancestor, I think."

"I expect I do. He was very brave. His courage warmed him when the seas turned to ice and there was no warmth to be had." Axel hesitated. Memories of that time were still fragmented, broken under the weight of his long hibernation. But he remembered Gorrup – the first Gorrup. A fiery warrior, willing to meet any enemy head-on, regardless of the odds. A lover of poetry – specifically, the puddle-verses of the gillkin sage, Oloxo – and a boisterous, though unskilled singer.

Gorrup, slayer of monsters. Gorrup, who had called him a coward. Axel hung his head, momentarily overcome by the shame and sadness of it all. "We had to do it, you know," he said. "Had to find places to hide and hibernate, until warmth had returned to the world. Otherwise we might all have perished…"

"Many of us did," Gorrup rumbled. But he lowered his mace. "We have not seen your kind in many spawning seasons. Why are you here, coward?"

"To help," Axel said. Gorrup's words stung, but he deserved it. It had been cowardice. That it had been necessary, made it no less such.

"Who?"

"You, among others. There is an enemy coming. A great and terrible force for destruction. I hope to stop it – or at least aid those who might."

Gorrup hesitated. "The Xirkaali," he said.

Axel sagged in relief. If the Sythians already knew of the enemy, that would make things easier – at least theoretically. "Yes. I am here to stop them."

Gorrup chortled and swung his mace up onto his shoulder. "You're too late, coward. They're already here. The cities of the elves burn, and blood stains the water. That is why I and these others are on patrol, to ensure that what is happening on the coast stays there. It is no business of ours if the surface-dwellers choose to kill one another."

"Save for when it is," Axel said, desperately. "The Xirkaali mean to have true dominion over the world. The land and the seas alike."

Gorrup licked his own eye in annoyance. "If so, then they are doing badly so far. The seas resist them so fiercely, they have given up and sought the safety of dry land."

"For now," Axel said. "But when they have control of the land, they will turn their attention back to the sea, and our people. To Medu'Syth and the other kingdoms." He paused. "And whatever else you might believe, your spawning pools are in danger now. Unless you think you can hide forever."

Gorrup made a sound of discontent that was echoed by the riverguard around them. "We do not hide. These waterways belong to us."

"Then you will die." Axel took a deep breath. "The Xirkaali are indiscriminate in their choice of enemies. A day will come when one of their envoys will show up here and offer you the same choice they offered the elves." Or so his dreams told him. He wasn't sure if it was correct, but Gorrup didn't need to know that. "And if you give the wrong answer, they will fall upon you with all the might of their empire."

Gorrup grunted and looked out over the river. "If you are right..." he began.

"I am," Axel said, firmly.

"*If* you are right," Gorrup reiterated, "then what do you propose, mage?"

Axel sighed. The Great Current had shown him what must be. It was how he'd known Gorrup would be here. And it was how he knew where to go next, to convince the pondwarden that he spoke the truth.

"I have a feeling you're not going to like the answer."

CHAPTER ELEVEN

Aeron

Callenspire's central keep was a tall, rounded dome of a building, with elegantly carved exterior staircases that wound around and around its circumference, allowing for entrance on every level. Flat, stone balconies extended over each landing, allowing for fine views of the city below and the river. Each of these balconies was a garden in miniature, guarded by impossibly detailed statues of ancient heroes and scholars.

From what Valan had told Aeron on the walk up those interminable stairs, the keep was less a holdfast than an immense manor house, originally built to contain the library assembled by Lady Merytan's ancestors. As such, most of the space inside was given over to shelves upon shelves of innumerable books, some dating back to the earliest days of the old elven empire. The enormity of it boggled Aeron's mind.

But that was only the lower area. According to Valan, the top of the dome was reserved for a massive meeting chamber, capable of holding thirty or forty people easily. It was to this chamber that Valan was taking him.

Gulls swooped by, squalling raucously as they sailed away out over the river. From the landing, Aeron could make out the sky-wharf, where his people would hopefully be unloading the equipment that they'd brought.

"I still find it hard to believe that you've heard of me," Aeron said.

Valan laughed. "I make it my business to listen, especially when it's interesting."

Aeron frowned, puzzled as to whether that was strictly a compliment. "Thank you, I think. Still, it's not as if this Lady Merytan will have heard of me. Why should she give any credence to my expertise?"

"Because she trusts me," Valan said, airily. Behind them, Kortys snorted, startling Aeron. The gladestalker was so silent that Aeron had forgotten that he was there entirely. Aeron gave Valan a hard look.

"I'm not sure whether I do, just yet."

Valan smiled. "Nor do I expect it. I'm a diplomat, after all."

"I thought diplomacy was all about trust."

"Diplomacy, yes. Diplomats? No. A more conniving bunch you've never met. Diplomats trust each other because they – we – understand that we are fundamentally untrustworthy. That levels the field somewhat."

Aeron shook his head. "If you say so. It gives me a headache."

Valan patted him on the shoulder. "Stick to the battlefield. It's honest work, at least." He paused. "Now, before we go in, fair warning: we might have a bit of difficulty with Lord Solibos, the local garrison commander. He has a high opinion of himself and not much else. Right now, I expect he's trying to convince

Lady Merytan – his cousin, albeit thrice removed – to give him command of the city's defenses."

"Why not let him?"

"Well, for starters, he's an idiot." Kortys gave another snort of amusement. Valan glanced at him and chewed his lower lip a moment. "Solibos is a – a traditionalist, you might say. A believer in the unassailable superiority of the elven race in all matters, including war. That several of our cities are currently being occupied by the enemy has only reinforced this belief. Because, as I noted, he's an idiot."

Aeron blinked. "Ah. Well, I've dealt with a few of those in my time."

"You are not alone in that," Kortys offered.

"Well, as I said, Lady Merytan trusts me," Valan said. "And I think you are the answer to our present difficulties."

"I hope you're right," Aeron murmured under his breath. If Valan heard, he gave no sign. Instead, his attention was on the pair of elven warriors guarding the next landing up. They stiffened at the sight of Aeron and the others.

"Let me handle this," Valan whispered to Aeron. Then, more loudly, to the guards, "I wish to see Lady Merytan. Please step aside."

"Lord Solibos has asked that he and his cousin not be disturbed," one of the guards said. Valan fixed him with a look.

"And is Lord Solibos the ruler of this city? No? I didn't think so. How funny. Step aside, there's a good fellow."

The guard's hand fell to his sword. "They are in council."

"Just the two of them? I can't imagine I'll be interrupting anything important." Valan climbed the steps until he was within reach of the guards. "Move aside, please."

One of the guards reached for him. "You will wait."

Aeron heard the hiss of a bowstring behind him, and he turned to see that Kortys had drawn and nocked an arrow in between one heartbeat and the next. The gladestalker said nothing, but the flat look on his face spoke volumes.

Valan, momentarily taken aback by the sight of the arrow, recovered more quickly than the guards. "I am certain that Lord Solibos will welcome the news we bring to he and his cousin," he said smoothly. "Now, time is of the essence. So…" He gestured for them to step aside. After a moment, the guards did. Aeron released a breath he hadn't realized he'd been holding. Kortys gave him a thin smile as he slid his arrow back into its quiver but said nothing. Valan ushered them all inside.

The chamber was as grand as Valan had said. Great tapestries hung on the walls between high windows that allowed in the sunlight from all directions. In the center of the chamber was a large, round table made of some dark, smooth wood. An elf woman sat in a highbacked chair at the table, a glass sat before her and a decanter close to hand. Standing across from her was an elf man – Lord Solibos, Aeron thought.

Solibos spun as they entered, his pale features flushing with anger. "What is the meaning of this?" He noticed Aeron. "Who is this… halfling?"

"Ser Aeron Cadwallader," Valan said. "The leader of the reinforcements from Ej that the southern kindred requested." The elf woman stiffened at the mention of Aeron's name, and Aeron wondered what had startled her so.

Solibos snorted. "I don't recall asking for reinforcements."

"Probably because no one thought to ask your opinion on the matter, dear cousin," the elf woman said in an amused tone. She studied Aeron with a keen gaze – so sharp that he felt it go through him, to his very soul. "Have they only sent one?"

Valan laughed politely. "Oh no, my lady. There are more on the way via airship, according to Ser Aeron here. Fortuitous, no?"

"And what do halflings offer us, save more mouths to feed?" Solibos sneered. Aeron had to admit that the elf cut a dashing figure. When one imagined an elven hero, Solibos was what they pictured. Tall, handsome – as elves judged such things – and flamboyant. Also arrogant, prideful, and utterly lacking in politesse.

Aeron cleared his throat. "We offer gunpowder, airships, grenades, and our experience – that is to say, my experience." He ticked the points off on his fingers as he spoke, more to hide his sudden nervousness. It was intimidating to have so many elves watching him.

Solibos laughed. "Experience? I have centuries of experience!"

Valan coughed politely. "Experience as a garrison officer, yes." He put his hand on Aeron's shoulder. "Whereas his experience is that of a battlefield commander. Besides, he's never lost a battle. Can the same be said of you?"

Solibos glared at the other elf. "How dare you impugn my…" he began, but Lady Merytan silenced him with a gesture.

"Enough." She looked at Aeron. "You are not one of the Ej-folk. Too pale. From the northern Shires, then? Somewhere around Hoddingshire, by your accent."

Aeron nodded, impressed. He suspected that most elves couldn't tell the difference between halflings if their life depended on it. "Yes, my lady. Picksbury."

Lady Merytan smiled. "Ah, Picksbury. Fine jam preserves, as I recall." She studied him more closely. "Cadwallader, you said? Yes, you were involved in that nastiness with the League of Rhordia, weren't you?"

Aeron bowed his head. *Nastiness – is that what she calls it,* he thought. "In some small fashion, yes."

Lady Merytan sat in silence for a moment. Then, "What would you do, then, Ser Aeron? How would you defend this city from the Xirkaali?" Solibos made a spluttering sound, but she ignored him, her attention never wavering from Aeron. Aeron swallowed and tried to visualize the city in his head.

"There are two approaches to the city," he began. "The Eastway, and the river. I expect the Xirkaali will use both, to some extent. If they're smart, they'll use the river to move supplies and siege equipment, and leave the Eastway for the bulk of the army." He paused. "How many toll locks lie between here and the coast?"

Lady Merytan frowned. "A few dozen. Most are in disrepair. The ones closest to the city are in the best shape, obviously."

"Those are where I'd start," Aeron said, his mental map expanding to include what he knew of the surrounding region. "Minimal fortifications. Just enough to slow any approach. The tougher we make their supply situation, the easier it will be to endure a siege."

"A siege is certain, then?" Valan asked, quietly.

Aeron nodded. "I fear so. But Callenspire is well-placed to endure one. There is water on two sides. If we destroy the Eastway Bridge connecting the city to the road, they'll be left with no option but to either build their own or circle around. All of that buys us – and the other cities – time."

"Destroy the bridge? Are you mad?" Solibos demanded. "That bridge has stood for centuries! Longer than your foolish race has stood upright, even." He slammed his hands down on the table. "We'll do no such thing!"

Lady Merytan gave him a lazy glance. "And are you now lord here, cousin?"

Solibos hesitated. "I merely meant –"

Lady Merytan smiled coolly. "I know what you meant. But surely a bridge is a fair price to preserve a city? After all, it is easier to rebuild the former. Why, I might even put you in charge of it, if you feel so strongly about it. Destruction, and construction. A good use of your time and skill."

Solibos stared at her. "I – I…"

"I encourage you to say yes," Valan murmured. Solibos shot him a glare but nodded.

"I would be honored to do so, cousin," he said. He looked at Aeron, his gaze indignant. "But let us hear what else the halfling would have us destroy – perhaps we should uproot our ornamental gardens and plant turnips?"

"Couldn't hurt," Aeron said, bluntly. "Food will be concern, if we can't hold the river. Turnips make good soup and jam." He stroked his chin. "We should probably begin evacuation efforts as well. We can help with that, with our airships. Get people into the mountains, or to Ej, as quickly as we can."

"You would have my people abandon the city?" Lady Merytan asked.

Aeron met her gaze directly. "For their own good, yes. Lord Solibos was right about that much. The fewer mouths to feed, the better." He sighed. "The trouble is – and you'll forgive me for saying so, my lady – but these cities of yours, pretty as they are, aren't meant for this sort of thing. Your walls are high, but not sturdy. Those Xirkaali rockets will tear through them quickly enough."

"Walls can be reinforced," Valan pointed out. Aeron glanced at him.

"That requires time and labor. We don't have much of either at the moment. Rather, I think we should concentrate on harrying the enemy as much as possible. Our best chance lies in them being in bad shape when they get here. We can help with that."

Lady Merytan nodded. "I find your concerns to be practical ones. In fact, I think we could do worse than to turn the defenses over to you, Ser Aeron. If you are willing, that is."

Aeron stared at her. "You want me to defend the city?"

"You've made a good start so far," she said. "It seems a shame not to take advantage of your skill. Lord Valan speaks highly of you, among others, and what I know jibes with their assertions. You might well be our best hope for success."

Aeron took a deep breath. Could he do this? This wasn't like defending a township in the Shires. Yet, something told him that he had no choice. Someone had to do it, and better here than on ground of the enemy's choosing. He looked at Lady Merytan.

"Very well. I will defend Callenspire. I just hope none of us have cause to regret it."

CHAPTER TWELVE
Hejun

Hejun strode through the streets of Evanvale, Obair trotting at her side. The city was looking less haphazard than it had the last few days. More orderly. Behind them stretched a line of scribes, adjutants, and quartermasters. All human, like Obair; all trusted. Her hemicyon subordinates had other duties. Logistics was left to the humans.

Normally, on such walks, she would have been accompanied by at least a handful of bodyguards. Turgo had insisted in this case as well, but she'd overruled him. She had to show her warriors that she was both confident in their ability to hold the city, and that she herself had no fear. There were still pockets of resistance all over the city. Evanvale was lost, but the elves weren't planning to admit it any time soon. A recalcitrant people, even defeated. In most cases, the elves were soon shown the error of their ways. But toward the outer districts, where the trees were almost as thick as in the jungle, things were still uncertain.

But it wasn't this that worried her. It was Ruhaindo. The city across the bay occupied her every waking moment these days. It resisted her efforts with commendable endurance; whoever ruled there was almost like a hemicyon in their pragmatism. She looked forward to meeting them, when Ruhaindo finally fell. Perhaps an elf of such practicality could be convinced that their interest lay with the Xirkaali.

"The alchemists have finally set up their workshops in the docklands," Obair said, as he awkwardly looked through an armload of scrolls. "We'll soon have more variety in terms of munitions, which is no bad thing."

Hejun nodded absently. Rockets were useful things, but awkward to transport in great numbers. Especially the ones that did something other than just explode. She'd decided to forego the specialist munitions until they'd made landfall. Now that they had space, work could begin on increasing their armory. Fletchers would turn out arrows for the auxiliaries and plainstalkers, armorers would repair the steel scale of the hemicyons, and blacksmiths would hammer the elvish weapons into something more suitable for their new wielders. They would turn the city into something better, if given the time.

Invasions were always tricky things; momentum had to be balanced against ensuring that the rear was protected. Hemicyon history was filled with tales of matriarchs who had led successful assaults, only to later be bled to death because they didn't bother to shore up their supply lines. She would not be so foolish. It was one of the reasons she was determined to bring Ruhaindo down before moving on.

"Any word from Khulan?"

Obair shook his head. "I assume she's still ferrying supplies to Iron Beach and the other landing points down the coast. If she's on schedule, that is."

Hejun clucked her tongue. "Is that any way to talk about a hero of the Empire?"

"I saw you both whelped," Obair said. "I can talk about you how I like."

"Within reason," she said, as she took in her surroundings, noting the strange nature of the architecture, at once delicate and somehow sturdy, despite the thick roots and trees that inundated it. It was as if the elves had somehow incorporated the very stuff of the jungle into the fabric of this place. It had somehow resisted centuries of neglect, and might resist centuries more, if some care was taken by its new masters. Or, rather, their vassals. Like logistics, masonry was best left to humans.

In time, Evanvale would become an industrial center of this new frontier. The extent to which the elves had left their city to go fallow appalled her. The surrounding jungles served little purpose save as a hunting preserve. Soon, with the resources of the other coastal cities added to what they had now, their invasion of Elvenholme could commence in proper fashion. A thought occurred to her, and she glanced at Obair. "Any more sightings of that flying vessel our scouts spotted near the mountains?"

Obair shook his head. "It was last seen heading toward Callenspire. Our alchemists are at a loss as to how such a vessel might be created, save by magic."

"Maybe they're those halfkin we were told about. The little folk."

"Well, they certainly weren't Neriticans." Obair paused. "Speaking of which, I should also mention that our logging efforts in the surrounding swamps have encountered a few… oddities."

"Elves?" Hejun asked, though she knew better. But one could hope.

"No." Obair hesitated. "River-folk. Neriticans."

Hejun bit back a curse. "Tell me."

"Nothing much to tell. We sent out work-gangs to collect timber for the new palisades and to clear out the jungle around the city. Scouts have reported sighting strange, froglike creatures lurking in the trees, watching them." Obair looked at her. "I've heard that these lands were crawling with river-folk. Whole tribes of them. They seem to have a wary peace with the elves. If we've encroached on their territory…"

"Then it won't be long before the rest of them are slithering ashore, looking for a fight." Hejun thumped her fist against her thigh, causing her armor to rattle. "I want pickets on the shoreline, especially around the bay. The last thing we need is for hostility with the Neriticans to resume. And warn Khulan."

"What about the timber?"

Hejun considered this. The wise thing would be to leave it alone and cease all logging activity. But she needed it. Especially if the river-folk decided to attack. "Keep at it, but increase the guard. Once the new rockets are ready, we'll smoke the river-folk out of their pools and send them hopping back into the sea."

"We could send envoys to them. See if they are willing to see reason."

Hejun considered this, but only for a moment. "No. Too late for that. From what little we know of the water-breathers, they are strongly aligned to one another. If these river-folk attack, it is because the Neriticans as a whole deem it necessary. No, we must resign ourselves to eventually fighting a war on two fronts." She paused.

They had come to what might once have been a market square of sorts. A group of elven children sat quietly huddled in the street, their parents barred from them by a line of human soldiers. Hemicyons in light armor and robes prowled around the children, sniffing the air. Witch-smellers. Hejun watched them, doing her best to restrain her distaste.

Magic was prohibited in the empire. Those who displayed even the smallest affinity for the arcane were culled from the population by the witch-smellers and sent to special monasteries where they would learn to control their abilities so that they were no longer a threat to the innocent. In some cases, these retrained witches were even able to put their magics to use in service to the empire, as the occupants of the black cages.

One of the witch-hunters noticed them and approached, bowing slightly. "Matriarch, you honor us with your presence," he growled. He was an ugly creature, with cropped ears and a scar-decorated muzzle, exposing his teeth in a permanent sneer. And what teeth they were: his fangs were fashioned from xirang-infused iron, enabling him, it was said, to bite through even the strongest mystical wards.

Hejun inclined her head in greeting. "Ah, Baidar. How goes it, Witch-eater?"

"Tolerably, Matriarch," Baidar growled. He was among the most skilled of the witch-hunters that accompanied the Claw, and, to hear some tell it, in the empire. His sensitivity to the tang of sorcery was, some believed, the reason for his brusque personality. Hejun, however, believed that he simply enjoyed his work and disliked anything that took him away from the hunt. He had a reputation for killing his prey, rather than capturing them.

"There are many here with the stink of magic on them, however slight. These elves are steeped in it. We do them a favor, by taking them in hand."

"Is that what you call it?" Obair murmured, looking elsewhere. Baidar glanced at him but said nothing, thankfully. Hejun nodded.

"So we do, and so we must. For the good of us all." She looked past Baidar. "The children… they are infected with sorcery?"

Baidar glanced back at the children. Something that might have been pity flitted through his good eye. "Some. We are splitting them up. The ones most at risk will be sent back to Chinlun, so that they might be taught how to control the evil within them." He scratched one of his scars. "We have found few with any real power, however. I thought these elves were supposed to have great sorcery at their command."

"Many of the mages fled with what was left of the garrison," Obair said. "Of those who were left, most fought to the bitter end."

"And the rest?" Hejun asked.

As if in answer to her question, Baidar suddenly whipped around, his eyes wide. The other witch-hunters turned in the same direction. A moment later, the square was filled with fire. It danced across the witch-hunters, catching their robes and fur alight.

At the far end of the square stood an elf in soot-stained, bloody robes, fire dancing in his palms. He gestured, and the fires twisted around several of the witch-smellers like snakes, reducing them to howling pyres. As if their deaths were a signal, the elves scooped up their children and scattered. Hejun's followers did the same, scrambling for the dubious safety of the nearby buildings.

Baidar tore off his burning cloak and cast it aside. "Take him," he howled, as he drew his weapon – a xuedizi, better known as a 'flying guillotine' – from his robes. "Slay the witch!"

Yan soldiers and the remaining witch-hunters raced forward to intercept the mage. He turned, sweeping flames about him like a cloak.

Hejun went for her own sword as the mage set several of the human soldiers alight. The elf had to know this was a suicidal endeavor. Perhaps he didn't care. She wondered if he'd come for the children specifically – a strange notion, but elves were much like humans in that regard. They valued the life of a child over that of a warrior, for reasons that escaped her. It didn't matter, however. He was a threat and needed dealing with. She drew her blade and shoved Obair behind her. "Get to cover as soon as you can, old man."

Obair protested. "Matriarch, you can't..."

Hejun ignored him as she stepped into the open. She reflected that perhaps she ought to have listened to Turgo after all. But a few more warriors wouldn't make much difference against a mage. She had to hope Baidar had some trick up his sleeve.

The mage was shouting something, but she couldn't hear it for the roar of the flames and the screams of dying men and the howls of burning witch-hunters. She spied Baidar stalking toward the mage, his xuedizi spinning slowly in his grip. The weapon was an odd one, for a warrior; it resembled nothing so much as a hat with a bladed rim, attached to a long chain. As Baidar spun the chain, the fires parted before him, peeling away to either side. The mage didn't seem to notice – or didn't care. He was more intent on burning the remaining soldiers alive. Perhaps he didn't regard Baidar as a threat.

If so, it was the last mistake he would make.

Baidar howled and the elf jerked back, startled. He gestured, summoning a blade of fire into his hand. As if only just then realizing how close the witch-hunter was, he slashed desperately at Baidar, momentarily driving the witch-hunter back. But so preoccupied was he with one opponent that he left himself open to Hejun. Seizing the moment, she lunged into the fray, singeing her fur in the process. Her sword chopped down on the mage's wrist, severing it, and sending both hand and flaming blade spinning away in a gout of blood.

The mage turned toward her, eyes wide; and before he could speak, or summon one final spell, Baidar's xuedizi settled over his head. Baidar gave a yank of the chain, and the elf's head was severed at the neck. His body collapsed with a sigh, and the conjured flames went out – snuffed at the moment of death. Hejun flicked blood from her blade and looked at Baidar.

"A handy toy, that."

Baidar nodded. "It is made from the same iron as we make the witch-cages. I have found it most useful on occasions like these." He paused. "I had no need of your aid."

"If I hadn't helped, he would have killed us both."

Baidar shrugged. "Maybe. Maybe not."

Hejun shook her head at his arrogance. Obair came out of hiding, an unhappy look on his face. "How many more like him are hiding in the city, do you think?"

Hejun looked down at the dead mage. "I'm not worried about the ones in hiding. I'm more worried about the ones standing on the walls of Ruhaindo." She sheathed her sword.

Obair nodded. "Let us hope they are all so easily slain."

Hejun looked around the square, at the few surviving soldiers and the pitiful piles of ash that marked the dead. "Yes, let us hope."

CHAPTER THIRTEEN
Kortys

Kortys drifted through the market lanes of Callenspire, listening to the hum of the city. There was, as yet, none of the panic of the besieged, but that would come soon enough. Valan was right. The Xirkaali would be here; it was only a matter of time. He smiled grimly at the thought, glad that he'd be leaving the city in the morning.

He'd never been one for cities. He preferred the jungle. Cities were just traps waiting to snap shut. Better to be among the trees, where one never had to worry about walls. At least there, one had plenty of escape routes if things went bad.

Then, perhaps things had already gone bad. There were soldiers everywhere he looked. They crowded close in wary knots and added to the undercurrent of tension that ran through the city as the evacuations began. A good many of the citizens weren't leaving willingly; protests were common. It gave the soldiers something to do, at least.

He looked around as he walked, taking in the stalls that lined the crowded thoroughfare. Most of the artisans were elves, but there were a few dwarves, a handful of humans, and even a pair of Ej-folk offering up clockwork toys for sale to uninterested passersby. Kortys studied one of the toys, admiring the craftsmanship even as he wondered why they'd bothered to build such a useless thing in the first place.

Elves, as a people, tended to keep to their own. They considered the works of other folk to be inferior as a matter of tradition. What they couldn't accomplish through ingenuity, they achieved through magic. Even Kortys, well-travelled as he was, knew that he shared his people's blind-spots at times. It was a flaw; a human arrow could kill a warrior just as dead as one made by an elven fletcher. Ej grenades could fill the air with fire as easily as a spell.

He'd had a few run-ins with the Ej-folk over the years, when his duties had taken him into the mountains. They were brave, and size was no indicator of capability. They had a great respect for elves that the lords of Ej made certain to cultivate, but Kortys thought much of that was more due to politeness than true awe. The halflings were grateful to Ej, and the elves in general. That was why they'd come to help, at least to hear them tell it.

Not that everyone believed them; Solibos certainly didn't. No, knowing him, he thought it was some scheme meant to deprive him of – something. The city, maybe, given his plans for it. He definitely didn't care to be pushed aside as commander in favor of Cadwallader. Kortys wondered if Valan was trying to provoke Solibos into doing something foolish. If so, he couldn't have found a better method.

For himself, Kortys liked the Ej-folk. They were hospitable; generous. A far cry from his own people. He'd come to know several of the families there quite well during his visits. They were brief sparks, but bright nonetheless. He feared for them in the coming war. They weren't natural warriors in the way of elves or even humans.

The sharp whistle of a bird interrupted his thoughts, and he turned to see Alisor, one of his fellow gladestalkers, motioning to him from a nearby artisan's stall. Kortys slowly made his way over, keeping an eye out for the city guard as he did so. It was about time Alisor showed up. Kortys had been wandering around for what felt like hours. "Well?" he murmured, as he pretended to look over the artisan's wares.

"We're ready. Solibos is making it difficult to get resupplied, but we know our way around that. He really doesn't like someone else giving us orders."

"Technically, we're still part of the army," Kortys murmured. "Even if they ignore us half the time." The Callenspire garrison left most of its traditional duties to irregulars like Kortys and Alisor. The gladestalkers were responsible for guarding the Eastway and the river-trails, as well as the traders who traveled by them. The regular army kept itself safely behind the walls and rarely ventured into the jungle if they could help it.

"Oh, and your new friend Valan was right; Solibos is agitating among his peers." Alisor studied the street. "The city is a tinder box waiting for a spark." He picked up a delicate statuette from the stall and examined it. "Can't you feel it? There's fear in the air. No one wants to admit it, but everyone is scared." He looked at the artisan in charge of the stall, as if for confirmation, and the other elf looked away.

Kortys grunted. "No panic yet. That halfling is smart. Evacuation solves a lot of potential problems in one go." He scratched his chin as he watched a pair of soldiers wander past, their armor rattling gently. "I imagine Solibos doesn't like that."

"From what I've heard, he's incandescent with rage. Thinks it's a sign of weakness. As if they're admitting that they can't protect the city."

"I doubt the Xirkaali care."

"It's not them he's worried about, it's the other noble families," Alisor said.

Kortys frowned. That made sense; Solibos only had his position because Merytan wasn't interested in arguing against it. He had no influence of his own; not enough to let him rule the city the way he so clearly wanted to do. But if the other families should turn against Merytan, Solibos might well find himself out on his rear – or worse. Unless he ingratiated himself with the others somehow.

Alisor looked around, then lowered his voice once more. "I think the princeling is planning a coup. I have the distinct feeling that both your new friend and the halfling will wind up on the wrong end of an arrow before the week is out."

Kortys smiled mirthlessly. "You're just now working that out? Of course he's planning a coup. I expect everyone in this market knows that. It's what princelings like him do. But Valan is smart – and so is Cadwallader."

Alisor frowned. "What do you think of him, then? Cadwallader, I mean."

"The halfling? Smart. Pragmatic."

"Smart enough to hold the city?"

Kortys shrugged. "Who can say?" He rubbed the back of his neck. "They're a curious folk, halflings. Small pools, but deep. And let's be honest, it's not really our problem. We're going to be out in the jungle, putting arrows into any Xirkaali stupid enough to wander into sight. That'll keep us busy for months, if not years."

Alisor chuckled. "You sound as if you're looking forward to it."

"Aren't you?"

Alisor grinned and Kortys laughed. As he did so, he caught sight of a small group of the newly-arrived Ej-folk ambling through the market, taking in the sights with no small amount of awe. Unfortunately, he and Alisor weren't the only ones to take note of them; several soldiers were converging on the halflings like hawks on a covey of quail.

"Halflings," Alisor muttered. "No common sense."

"I expect they say the same of us," Kortys murmured. The halflings had been circulating through the city in the days since their arrival. Most were sticking close to the sky-wharf in the canopy above, but some, like these, were moving farther afield. *Scouts,* Kortys thought, with some small amusement. That was what they were. Getting a feel for the terrain, the way he and his gladestalkers did.

He watched them stop at the stall belonging to the halfling toymakers. They spoke animatedly to one another, and he wondered if there was a familial relationship. Probably. The few halflings he knew all seemed to be related. Solibos's soldiers had noticed it as well, and in moments, they were surrounding the stall.

"You will come with us," one of them said, in the tone of someone used to being obeyed. Kortys pegged him as the younger son of a good family; ambitious, probably. Arrogant, certainly.

"And why would we do that, then?" one of the halflings, a woman, replied, in a clear, high voice. She was dressed in the leathers of a grenadier and had hair the color of dying fire. "This is a free city, ain't it?" she continued, giving the elf a pugnacious look. Kortys felt an immediate swell of kinship – as well as a nagging sense of familiarity. Had he met her before?

"It is an elven city." The soldier caught the halfling woman by the arm. She grimaced and balled a fist, but luckily made no move to use it. Kortys had to give her points for that. "You'll come with us now, small one, or I'll –"

"You'll what?" Kortys called as he strolled toward the altercation. Alisor followed, but slowly. The soldier turned toward him, words of dismissal on his lips, but paused as he realized who Kortys was.

"This is none of your affair, gladestalker."

"I disagree," Kortys said and dropped his hand to the hilt of his sword. He could feel Alisor tensing up behind him and knew the other gladestalker would think he was making a mistake. But he doubted Valan would appreciate them letting Solibos's lackeys take the halflings somewhere without protest. "They are here to help us, after all. And if memory serves, their leader is in command – not yours."

The soldier's face darkened. "How dare you speak so…" he spluttered, clearly at a loss. Kortys figured it wasn't often that someone questioned the guard's authority. Well, he needed to get used to it. Callenspire was on the front line now. Garrison duty was about to get a lot less comfortable for everyone.

"I dare many things," Kortys said. He bared his teeth in an ugly smile and tightened his grip on the hilt of his sword. "Would you like to press the matter?"

The soldiers looked at one another, and then, as one, backed off. "Lord Solibos will hear of this," the one in charge said, in as menacing a tone as he could muster.

"Good," Kortys said. He watched them go and then turned to the halflings. "You should be careful around here, friends – a city is not safe just because it has walls."

The halfling woman stared up at him. "…Kortys?" she asked, hesitantly.

Kortys blinked. The nagging familiarity crystallized into sudden recognition. "Little Hawk? Is that you?" He laughed explosively and snatched her up in an embrace. "It *is* you! Look at you, all grown up, and a grenadier no less!"

"Put me down, you great lolloping brute," she laughed, thumping his shoulders with her fists. "I have my dignity to think of! What will the lads say?"

"They'll say nothing in my earshot," Kortys mock-growled, but he deposited her on the ground nonetheless. "How long has it been? You were a mere sprat when last I saw you."

"And you look much the same. A bit scruffier." Hannah looked up at him. "I was wondering if I'd see you here." She made a playful punch at his knee and he hopped back, chuckling. She looked in the direction the soldiers had gone. "What was that all about, then?"

"Trouble," Kortys said, his amusement fading. "The sort you and this Ser Aeron of yours need to know about, I think."

"That bad, is it?"

Kortys smiled. "It only gets worse, Little Hawk. I thought I taught you that."

"To be fair to me, I mostly only recall the lessons in knife-fighting," she said, beaming up at him in much the same way she had as a child. She sighed. "But if it's as bad as all that, maybe you need to speak to Ser Aeron. He's up at the wharf, overseeing the unloading. Come on, High Boots, I'll take you to the man himself."

CHAPTER FOURTEEN
Gorrup

Gorrup inhaled the steamy scent of the mangroves and clutched the haft of his mace tightly. Through a break in the tangle of trees, the pondwarden could see a line of distant Xirkaali ships riding the tide along the coast. Where they were going, he couldn't say. Grishamvu, possibly. Or maybe one of the smaller enclaves the elves had cut out of the tidal swamps of the coast. "Ships," he croaked. Beside him, the gillkin mage nodded.

"Yes. Many. As I said." Axel spoke softly, in a voice like the trickle of water across cool stone. There was a weight to his words that annoyed Gorrup, though he could not say why. It was as if the mage were haunted by something he did not dare name.

"The Medu'Syth do not sink them."

"No."

"Why?"

Axel looked away. "I do not know. Perhaps for the same reason that the elves did not intervene when the Xirkaali warred on the Neriticans. They believe it is not their – *our* – problem. Unfortunately, it very much is."

Gorrup snorted. "So you keep saying. But I see no proof of that. The dog-men seem more interested in killing elves than threatening our spawning pools." The tidal mangroves provided the perfect mix of isolation and brackish water for the needs of the *Ril'uwa* – the river-folk. Some tribes preferred to use the hollows of trees; others dug down into the black mud. The elves knew this and, sensibly, made little attempt to cull the swamps for resources these days, compared to the way they once had before the river-folk had taught them better.

The truth was, the relationship between their peoples was strained even at the best of times. The elves regarded the river-folk as little better than savages; for their part, the *Ril'uwa* found the elves to be injudicious neighbors. He could think of worse things than the elves departing for other lands and leaving the marshes and jungles to their original inhabitants.

"They are distracted by the elves, true, but only at the moment," Axel said. Gorrup studied him warily. It was hard to tell what the mage was thinking. Some of that was a lingering distrust. The river-folk had long memories for treachery. "If we aid the elves now, we might be able to stop the Xirkaali here."

"To what purpose? According to you, they are attacking everywhere." Axel had told Gorrup something of his supposed visions; he claimed that the Great Current had sent him to stymie the Xirkaali. Gorrup wasn't sure whether to believe him or not. It seemed folly to him to become involved in the wars of the air-breathers. Let them kill each other. What did it matter to his folk? So long as their ancestral waters remained inviolate, they had no reason to make war on the dog-men.

Axel hesitated to answer. Gorrup blinked in sudden realization.

"You think to draw them away from whatever they are after by making so much noise that they cannot help but come. You mean to use us." He gave a croak of disdain. "I should have smashed you when I had the chance. You would have me declare war against the foe of another – why? To fight and die so that others do not have to? What is so important that you would betray us to such a fate for a second time?"

"I do not intend to betray you," Axel protested. "Whatever happens here, I shall not leave your people. I swear by the Great Current that I will defend your spawning pools to the death. But death it will surely be if we do not secure an alliance between the elves and Medu'Syth – and soon. The time is fast approaching when it will not matter."

Gorrup snorted derisively. "That will not happen. That particular current has carried too much water in the years since you went for your little sleep." He stirred the water with his mace, setting a cloud of insects into flight. His great tongue unfurled and snapped out, snagging many of them. He swallowed them with pleasure. "The elves of this land dislike our kin, and our kin despise them in turn. It is ever thus, between those of the sea and the land."

"Be that as it may, I still must try. I…" Axel trailed off, and the water elemental curled about his shoulders twitched and rose like an angry serpent. Gorrup sniffed the air and tasted the acrid pong of smoke.

"Something is burning."

"There," Axel said, softly. He extended his staff in the direction of the city that the elves called Evanvale. Gorrup turned and saw smoke rising above the mangroves. "The Xirkaali will need lumber… drinking water… and room to expand. The elven cities will not be enough, for the Xirkaali do not have their talent for coexisting with the land. They will seek to tame the jungles as they have their own lands. They will uproot the trees and divert the rivers – your rivers – to serve their needs. They will find your spawning pools and drain them. Or worse." Axel leaned against his staff, as if weary.

Gorrup felt the fires of anger grow in his belly. "This is why you brought me here, isn't it?" he asked with a glance at the mage. "You knew this was happening, didn't you?"

"I feared it. And yes. I needed to convince you."

Gorrup gave a gurgling growl and turned away. He heaved himself from the water and let loose a thunderous croak that set the mangroves to shivering. Then, with a single bound, he was away and plunging through the waters toward the distant smoke. He heard Axel call out behind him, but he didn't stop. If the Xirkaali were burning the swamps, he would stop them. It was his duty, and no spawn of his line had ever failed in that responsibility. He would settle up with Axel afterward.

He had played among the tidal swamps as a tadpole and knew them better even than his smaller kin. He had no trouble navigating the root-gripped shallows and moving through the close-packed trees with barely a sound to mark his passing. Smoke slipped through the tangled branches, borne on the bitter sea wind.

He reached the point where the shallows gave way to jungle; thick trees rose above the water, their nodding branches draping everything below in shadow. A crude logging camp had been set up here – or rather, the edge of such a camp. Tents jostled for space with stacks of raw timber and transport skiffs. Humans chopped at trees with axes and saws, and burnt the undergrowth away with torches. They had dammed the water, creating a pool to float the timbers to the skiffs. Others – soldiers by their look – stood watch.

The waters here were familiar to him; not a spawning pool, but they led to one. Or had. How long had it been dammed? One day? Two? Was there any water left in it, or had it all seeped into the earth without a constant stream to keep it wet?

Gorrup stared at the workers for long moments. They had not yet noticed him, so silent had his approach been. He could turn and leave them none the wiser. Find Axel. The mage had given him proof, though he had not asked for it. His hand tightened on the haft of his mace. Did Medu'Syth know? Did they understand? He could not imagine that they did. If so, they would never have allowed the Xirkaali to reach the coast.

He could leave. He knew that he should. There was nothing to be gained by fighting here. Nothing. Gorrup lifted his mace and studied it for a moment. Then he swung it out and slammed it against a tree. The dull boom echoed through the clearing.

The humans turned in surprise. In one bound, Gorrup was among them. His mace slammed down, reducing the nearest of the soldiers to red pulp. The others fled, shouting out in alarm. Gorup splashed after them, gripped by a killing haze. They would pay for what they had done – what they intended to do. He would see to it personally.

He turned and spotted the flat-bottomed skiffs, loaded with new-cut timber, tied up nearby. He paused and then smashed the first of them. A bark of command alerted him to the arrival of a new foe: a towering, doglike creature in steel armor and a plumed helmet pushed through the fleeing humans. Gorrup croaked a challenge, and the Xirkaali sprang toward him, sword raised.

Gorrup dove beneath the shallow water, leaving the Xirkaali to splash about in frustration. He rose up behind the dog-man and caught the creature a blow between the shoulder-blades. The Xirkaali toppled into the water without a sound. But the barks and yelps around him told Gorrup that there were more on the way. He looked down at the Xirkaali, who was struggling to rise, and planted one massive, webbed foot on the latter's back, forcing the unlucky creature back beneath the water. Gorrup held the dog-man there until his struggles ceased. Only then did he turn his attention to the final skiff.

He smashed it as he had the first and made ready for the arrival of the rest of the Xirkaali, whose barks were growing louder. "Come on," he grumbled as he took a two-handed grip on his mace. "Quickly now. I am impatient."

"No," Axel said from behind him. Gorrup turned, and water surged up about him, enclosing him like a cage. He glared angrily at the gillkin.

"Do not interfere, mage. This must be done."

Axel met his glare without flinching. "And it will be. But not here. Not now. The Great Current has shown me what we must do if we are to have any hope of success in this. But I cannot do it without you, or the tribes of the *Ril'uwa.*"

"You would have us fight where Medu'Syth does not?"

"I would have you fight, so that they might see and join. But if you cannot make cause with the elves – you, who share their land – then what hope have I of convincing our brothers in the sea to do so?" Axel twitched his staff and the waters subsided, freeing Gorrup. "If you insist on fighting, I will stand beside you. But it is likely we will die here and accomplish nothing, save alerting our enemies to the presence of your people. Is that what you want, Pondwarden?"

Gorrup stared at him. Behind him, he heard the clink of armor and the splash of paws. He turned and faced the Xirkaali – three of them. They stopped at the sight of him, and Gorrup extended his mace toward them.

"Next time," he croaked. He glanced at Axel. "Get us out of here. I would speak with the chieftains of the river-tribes." At that, Axel drove his staff into the water. It surged up about them, and when it cleared – they were gone, leaving the confused Xirkaali to no doubt wonder what they had just witnessed.

CHAPTER FIFTEEN

Valan

Valan looked out over Callenspire and wondered if the knot of tension in his stomach would unravel enough for him to eat breakfast. He stood on the highest garden balcony of the central keep, a book of poetry from Lady Merytan's own library in his hand. Reading it was proving an impossibility. His mind was awhirl with possibilities, mostly unpleasant ones.

There was smoke on the horizon; far away, but visible nonetheless. The tidal swamps were burning. As far as anyone knew, Ruhaindo was still holding out, but it was only a matter of time. Xirkaali war-junks had been sighted up and down the coast, and landings had been reported by gladestalkers and refugees seeking safety behind Callenspire's walls. Worse, traders on the Eastway had reported a fleet heading for Grishamvu. Thankfully the lord there, a grim-faced noble named Zeramyr, had listened to his warnings and was ready – or at least as ready as they could be. One less sin on his conscience.

The few estates in the hinterlands would soon be under attack as well. Some had been abandoned; others fortified. They wouldn't hold out for long, Valan thought. Not when the Xirkaali came in force. Right now, the enemy were content to make probing raids, testing the limits of elvish resistance. Kortys and his gladestalkers had departed at first light; they would do what they could to make the jungle an uninviting prospect for the Xirkaali, but it wouldn't be enough. Even Kortys admitted that much.

Valan wondered where Axel was, if the gillkin mage had managed to reach the coast yet. If he'd spoken to the riverguard, as he'd promised. There'd been little sign of the river-folk of late. The gladestalkers coming in from the hinterlands had reported that many of their old haunts appeared abandoned, as if they'd retreated to some unknown redoubt to wait out the war. Valan hoped that wasn't so. Callenspire needed them.

Thankfully, reinforcements were on the way from the mountains; airships full of halflings, spoiling for a fight, or so Aeron maintained. Valan feared they'd get it, and then some. But even with the addition of the halflings, their forces were too few. And, of course, Solibos had all but publicly refused to work with Aeron on their defenses.

Instead, he'd focused a spiteful degree of energy on tearing down the Eastway bridge, albeit in the slowest, most frustrating manner possible. Added to this, the army was complaining; they'd had it easy for years, doing little but toll-taking duties. Now they were being expected to labor and, worse, labor beside halflings. That the enemy were even now likely marching their way seemed to make no difference.

Frankly, things weren't looking good.

Valan sighed. Had he done the right thing? Impossible to say, at the moment. Axel's visions aside, Cadwallader was the best of bad options; a proven military commander, but not an elf. Word had already gone out, and complaints were rising from the expected quarters. Lady Merytan had used up much political capital in naming Cadwallader as commander; her reign was a brittle thing, upheld as it was by consensus. If the noble families decided to remove her, there was little she could do. And while the folk of Ej were not necessarily looked down upon by the southern kindred, neither were they celebrated. No one knew what to expect from them.

At least Aeron seemed willing to rise to the occasion. And there was no denying the effectiveness of the halfling weapons. Airships, gunpowder, explosives – all things that would be needed, if they were to see off the Xirkaali. He heard a horn sound, somewhere to the east. The evacuation was beginning in full. Riders had been sent to the city of Ej, warning them of what was coming and asking for elven reinforcements.

Lady Merytan, as befitted a noble of her house, had refused to go. She would stand or fall with her city. Most of her court was already gone, scampering for safety like the pampered aesthetes they were. Some few had stayed, however, including Solibos, who was being loudly and publicly unhappy about everything. He was going to be trouble, Valan knew. But there was nothing for it but to endure it. They needed Solibos, and the warriors loyal to him, to help defend the city.

Birds fluttered overhead, startled from the brambles of the garden as the doors to the keep opened to admit a guard. "Lord Solibos wishes to speak with you," she said.

I bet he does, Valan thought. He set aside his book and gestured for the guard to show his guest in.

A moment later, Solibos entered in a swirl of silk and a flash of mail. He did cut the dashing figure; the epitome of elven martial glory. The problem was, he knew it. There was a time and a place for arrogance, but Solibos took it to extremes. He oozed haughtiness, breathed egotism. He was everything wrong with their people, all in one handy package.

Valan decided to strike first. "Hello, Solibos. Finished tearing down the bridge yet?"

Solibos made a careless gesture. "I've left the details in the hands of my subordinates for the moment. I have more important business to attend to."

"Oh? Fomenting dissent, perhaps? Stirring up the remnants of your cousin's court against her, stoking fears of halflings in the larder and turnips in the rose gardens?"

Solibos paused. "Heard about that, did you?"

"Hard not to. Then, you haven't been trying to hide it. I shouldn't have to tell you that it's not really a good time for such foolishness, but – well. Here we are."

"I disagree," Solibos said. "Now is the perfect time. You know how these games go, Valan. Best to strike while your opponent is distracted. And nothing is more distracting than an approaching army."

Valan snorted and shook his head. "That will be our epitaph, you know."

"You exaggerate." Solibos looked away. "Besides, your new pet will save us – isn't that what you said?"

"Ah, and there it is," Valan said. He applauded mockingly.

"Are you a fool, or just spiteful?" Solibos asked as he joined Valan at the edge of the balcony. "Putting this city in the hands of a – a halfling?"

Valan glanced at him. "Well, the alternative was your hands, so – not much choice there." He turned away from the city and leaned against the wall of the balcony, arms crossed, the very picture of insouciance. He knew from past experience it would infuriate Solibos, which was all to the good. "Besides, now you're free to chivvy favor as you see fit."

Solibos glared at him. "How could you think he'd be a better commander than me?"

"Well, offhand, as I said, he's fought his share of battles. What was the last one you were involved in, exactly?"

Solibos snorted. "You're lucky my cousin is fond of you, Shining Ones know why." His hand fell to the hilt of his sword. Valan suddenly recalled that Solibos was exceptional with a sword. A good thing to keep in mind.

"I can be very charming when I put my mind to it." Valan examined his cuticles, trying to appear unconcerned. "You know, I warned you about the Xirkaali when I first arrived. As I recall, you laughed."

Solibos grunted and looked away. A touch of embarrassment there? Valan hoped so. "An error, I admit," Solibos said. "Who could have imagined that they would launch an invasion just because you insulted them?"

Valan frowned. "Yes, well, I have some thoughts as to that."

"I'm sure you do. Anything to avoid blame, eh? There's the Valan Cormys I know." Solibos grinned sharply. "I wonder, how much do you know about them?"

"More than you, I expect."

Solibos smiled nastily. "But do you know why they invaded us?"

Valan shook his head. "They wish to conquer us. What more do you need?"

"Yes, but why now? Why not a century ago, or a century hence? Why at this moment? Have you asked yourself that, Valan? I suspect not. It requires a certain intelligence to ask such questions; intelligence that you lack." Solibos braced a foot against the edge of the wall and leaned over, one elbow on his raised knee. The very picture of a master strategist at work. "It is a curious thing, isn't it? What is the purpose of this invasion? Not just of our lands, but all of it – where are they going?"

Valan was silent for a moment, thinking. Solibos had a point, however insultingly he'd made it. The truth was, no one had any idea as to why the Xirkaali had invaded here and now. It could have just been bad luck, but Valan feared otherwise. The Xirkaali wanted something; not just conquest, but something else. "A good question. Have you an answer?"

Solibos's poise cracked. "No," he admitted. He stepped back, a look of uncertainty on his face. "No. But that is the key, Valan, mark my words. We find the why, and we will know how to stymie this invasion."

"Brilliant. Let me know when you figure it out. Until then, try not to undermine your allies. I know it'll be difficult for you, but I would like to survive to learn whether you were right or not."

Solibos laughed. "Don't worry, Valan. I have no intention of usurping my cousin. Not unless things take a turn for the worse. Neither will I be dismissed like a dog. I am content to let your halfling play general for now. But when the time comes, and I must take over the reins of leadership, I will expect your wholehearted support. Else I will have no choice but to employ force in doing what is necessary. Do we understand one another?"

Valan nodded. "Oh, I think I understand you fine. But do remember that you are not the only one with plans for the worst, Solibos. Keep that in mind, and we should both make it out of this intact."

Solibos laughed again and departed. Valan sagged back onto the bench, mind churning over all the new ways that things could go very wrong, very quickly. Solibos was definitely a danger; this little visit had made that clear enough. Elves like Solibos saw opportunity in chaos; a chance to rise above their current station. To achieve that, they might be willing to do anything.

Perhaps even join the enemy.

Valan cursed under his breath. The thought was a ludicrous one, but – still. He wondered whether he ought to bring the matter up with Merytan, but – no. No. She was content to let her cousin be embarrassed a bit, to teach him his place, but an accusation of treachery was a whole different matter. As the saying went, a bell, once rung, could not be unrung. He retrieved his book and tried to concentrate.

After a few moments, he tossed it aside once more. It was no good. Axel's warning of what was to come hung heavy in his mind. Callenspire had to stand, to resist. It couldn't do that with a worm like Solibos gnawing at its vitals. He rose and straightened his robes. He needed to speak with Merytan and Aeron, in private if possible.

Something had to be done about Solibos… even if he had to do it himself.

CHAPTER SIXTEEN
Hejun

Eyes closed, Hejun listened to the song of war. Long windows behind her allowed in the sea-breeze, as well as the thunder of rockets. Ruhaindo still stood, far across the bay, but every passing day brought it an hour closer to capitulation. Or so she told herself. The elves, sadly, did not seem to agree. Another volley tore across the waters, accompanied by the dull hammer-blow of a mortar. She sighed and opened her eyes.

She had commandeered the central keep of Evanvale for her own, though she preferred to be in the open, where she could better oversee things. Obair had convinced her of the efficacy of a strong fortress, however. The Neriticans were still out there, watching from the depths, and the elves might well stage a counterattack at some point.

The chamber around her was made from some delicate, white stone, albeit pinkish in places. The furniture, unfit for hemicyon use, had been consigned to be broken up and used in making repairs or constructing temporary fortifications. Heavy benches had been brought in from one of the taverns; the wood still smelled of smoke, but Hejun didn't mind.

The only thing left was the table. It had been painstakingly carved from some sort of coral, and the rough surface was shaped like the bay and its tributaries. Though not quite a map, it now served that purpose, and had recently been marked with representational bits of metal, wood, and bone to mark the presence of nearby cities and villages – and enemy activity. An improvement, as far as Hejun was concerned. What use was a map that showed only the barest outline of the thing?

They were surrounded by enemies; mighty as her horde was, it could still die a death by a thousand stings if they were not swift and sure. Hejun popped a chunk of fruit from a nearby bowl in her mouth and chewed thoughtfully. She preferred pumpkin, but Obair claimed the fruit was an elven delicacy. It didn't taste like much to her, however.

Before her, on the table, was a recently drawn map of the coastline around Grishamvu. Khulan's cartographers had drawn it, and the admiral had kindly made her cousin a copy. The city was now all but cut off from the rest of Vieshlar by forces moving northward from Iron Beach and the other landing points. It was not quite under siege, not yet. But it would be soon enough. But first – Ruhaindo.

Obair laid another map across the first. "And here you will see the current situation around Blackthorn," he said. "Matriarch Yorgat says the walls are not as thick as Ruhaindo's, but are bolstered by sorcery of some sort. Our rockets and mortars hit, but the wall itself suffers no damage. She's requesting Baidar's assistance." He nodded to the witch-hunter, who stood near the table, pretending not to pay attention to matters he deemed beneath his station. Hejun glanced at

Baidar.

"Well, Witch-eater? Will you aid them?"

"Of course." Baidar bared his iron teeth in a ghastly smile. "I shall take a cadre of my best witch-hunters with me. We shall have this witchery dealt with in a few days."

Hejun dismissed him with a gesture, hoping that he would stick to it and not decide to go racing off with a new scent in his nose. Baidar was effective; probably the greatest witch-hunter the Empire had ever produced. But he didn't know how to follow orders.

"I do not care for him," Obair said after the witch-hunter had departed.

"Nor do I. But he is useful." Hejun glanced at him. "Has Gorcha arrived yet?"

"Yesterday evening. She's currently roistering in the outskirts, doing her best to amass favor with the troops, as is her custom." Obair frowned. "We need to keep an eye on her. She's ambitious."

"All hemicyons are ambitious. Ambition is a virtue."

"Too much is a vice." He paused. "I have heard that she approached Shulgin."

Hejun stiffened. That was unwelcome news. "Why?"

"To take her mood, no doubt."

Hejun's muzzle wrinkled in annoyance. Gorcha was clearly hoping to gain Shulgin's support for whatever she was planning. While Shulgin had yet to prove herself, she was still Hejun's daughter, and popular with the packs who made up the bulk of the army. Her opinion carried much weight. "And?"

"Shulgin's mood was bad."

Hejun sighed. When was it not? "Tell me."

"They squabbled a bit. In front of a large number of Gorcha's warriors, and an equal number of Shulgin's. The two packs nearly came to blows. Shulgin nearly took Gorcha's head, though I'd wager Gorcha will claim otherwise."

Hejun growled softly. "Foolish pup. I should discipline her."

"I thought so as well. Which is why I took the liberty of sending for her."

Hejun blinked, and was about to reply to Obair when a guard stepped into the chamber and announced the arrival of her daughter. She glanced at Obair, and then motioned for the guard to show Shulgin in. She busied herself studying her maps and only looked up as Shulgin was shown in. "Daughter," she greeted in a neutral tone.

Shulgin gave a growl of acknowledgement and peered down at the maps without being invited. Hejun bristled slightly but said nothing. Shulgin had always taken liberties, even as a pup. She'd been a gnawer of teats and a howler in the night. Never easy; never gentle. A warrior born. "Obair says you spoke with Gorcha."

Shulgin licked her chops but didn't look up from the maps. "Obair says many things. He barks at shadows, that one."

Hejun bit back a chuckle at the look on Obair's face and said, sternly, "Do you have ambitions, daughter?"

Shulgin grunted. "Should I not?"

"Obair says you and Gorcha nearly came to blows."

"Obair talks too much," Shulgin said, shooting the old man a glare. "In any event, she insulted me. Treated me as if I were a puling pup and not a warrior equal to her. I showed her the error of her thinking. Should I have not? Should I have accepted such dishonor?"

Hejun was silent for a moment. Honor was a tricky thing; the young knew its cost, but not its worth. She sighed. "I do not say that. I suggest merely that you think before you howl your rage to the skies."

"I thought, and did not act." Shulgin looked at her mother. "I could have slain her."

"Or she you. The result would have been the same. One less commander, and the horde weakened by her loss." Hejun gazed steadily at Shulgin. "You have much to learn, daughter. Hopefully your ignorance will not be the death of you."

"Did you summon me just to chastise me?" Shulgin growled.

Hejun considered her answer. Obair gave her a sly smile, and she snorted. "What do you know of Callenspire, pup?" She tapped the map with a claw, indicating the city in question. Shulgin said nothing.

"It sits at the confluence of several tributaries," Obair said helpfully. "It's the gateway to the eastern enclave of the elves, and Elvenholme." There was a twinkle of amusement in his eyes as he spoke, and again Hejun bit back a chuckle.

Shulgin shot him a glare and gave a bark of sour laughter. "So why are we wasting time here? Why not muster and move inland now?"

Hejun fixed her pup with a steady gaze. "Because if we do so, we leave our flank unprotected. Ruhaindo must fall if we are to maintain a defensible line of supply through the bay. Would you have me wage a war on two fronts, daughter? Are you so confident in my ability to overcome the enemy?"

Shulgin hesitated. Hejun snorted. Her pup knew a trap when she saw one, at least. "Good. Maybe you are not hopeless, at that." She paused, choosing her next words with care. The beginnings of an idea were stirring in her mind, and she needed to tease them out. "Gorcha wants to lead the attack on Callenspire."

In fact, Gorcha had demanded the privilege, as her reward for taking Iron Beach. Hejun had been tempted to see it as a challenge, but Gorcha was too valuable to waste in that fashion. Any confrontation between them would only end one way, and not the one that Gorcha assumed.

But she needed commanders of Gorcha's caliber, at least until the campaign was fully underway. She needed that fighting spirit if she was to take the region as the Khatun wished.

"What do you think of her?" she asked Shulgin.

"She is an… acceptable matriarch," Shulgin said, grudgingly. She traced the Eastway to Callenspire with a claw-tip, her eyes flicking to the river as she did so. Hejun could almost hear what her child was thinking; there was a first-rate strategic mind, under all the aggression. If only she could learn to temper her wrath, she might make a fine successor.

"Yes, but ambitious. Presumptuous. And impatient. Her idea of a siege is climbing over the bodies of the dead in order to reach the top of a wall. She would bleed us white, trying to take a city by force that might fall in a week, with a bit of patience."

Shulgin looked at her, head cocked quizzically. "Then who? You?"

"You."

Shulgin blinked. "What?"

Hejun continued quickly, before Shulgin could protest. "We are in an unenviable position. We must take Ruhaindo, else all this is for nothing. But it will take time. If we delay too long, Callenspire will strengthen its defenses, further slowing our progress. I cannot trust Gorcha to make a meal of it. So, daughter, what would you do?"

Shulgin shifted uncomfortably. Then, she straightened and said, "We must not allow Callenspire that time." She looked at Obair. "How much of our force can we spare from efforts here?"

Obair glanced at Hejun, who nodded. He cleared his throat. "A third, maybe less. Still a more substantial force than anything the elves have thus displayed."

Shulgin growled softly. "A third will be enough to open a second front and sustain it. Especially if our supply lines can be maintained." She looked at Hejun. "I propose we march inland via the Eastway and lay siege to Callenspire immediately. We might not be able to take the city – we can't, in fact – but we can prevent them from mustering a counter-attack against us here, or strengthening their defenses unduly."

Hejun nodded in satisfaction. The Eastway was already largely under their control, at least as far as the coast. The road was easy to patrol, and most of the smaller towns along the route had capitulated without much of a struggle. Many had been abandoned; others had surrendered and ceded authority to her warriors. It could no longer truly be considered enemy territory, until it started through the jungle. Then it became more dangerous.

"Good," Hejun said. "Only one criticism. Marching inland will be slow – too slow. You will use the river as well. And the boats we have commandeered from Evanvale. A two-pronged assault."

"Boats?" Shulgin hesitated. "I am not a sailor."

"No, but we have sailors. You will transport warriors, supplies, and siege equipment east, upriver, to Callenspire. It will not be easy, the current will be against you, and such a flotilla will be an irresistible target; but it is imperative that we control those rivers." Hejun tapped the map again. "That means we must take control of the toll locks as well as anything of importance along the way. Can you do this?"

Shulgin answered quickly. "I will do it."

Hejun showed her teeth, pleased. "Yes, pup… I expect you will."

CHAPTER SEVENTEEN
Axel

Axel leaned against his staff, watching as the chieftains of the river-tribes argued with one another in high, piping voices. The debate had been going on for more than a day and had long since become wearisome. The root-lodge where the meeting was taking place echoed with croaks of challenge and disdain.

Nor was it solely riverguard in attendance; besides Gorrup, three other pondwardens, each as large and bulky as he, crouched behind the chieftains. All of them glowered at him, as if it were his fault. And it was. No use pretending otherwise. Uncomfortable with their glares, Axel looked around at the sprawling root-walls and ceiling. The lodge was constructed so as to be all but invisible to those who were not privy to its existence. Sunk deep into the bank of the river, with the only entrance beneath the water, and the rest in the wet earth.

There were innumerable such lodges scattered across the region, some larger, some smaller. Some were built high in the canopy, while others floated on the water like lily pads. Wherever the river-folk made their home, the lodges rose. They were both hideaway and fortress for the tribes; places to cache food and supplies, but also bolt-holes in case of invasion. Places of war, and places of healing. And places of council.

Axel sighed and turned his gaze to the gathered chieftains. There were at least thirty of them, and the clamor of their voices was like the crash of the surf against the shore. The *Ril'uwa* had changed much in the intervening centuries. The tribes had adapted to a changing world; some still resided in their ancestral tidal swamps, while others had followed the rivers inland to the bogs and marshes of the hinterlands. Still others had taken to the high canopy. Some were the hue of mud and reeds, others so brightly colored as to sting the eyes.

"Where is Medu'Syth?" a chieftain croaked, his feathered headdress clattering as he gesticulated. "If they do not call for war, why should we?"

"Easy to say when it is not your swamps being burnt," another shot back. The wrangling swelled, going round and round as it had for the last few hours. Axel sighed. He had known that it would be difficult. Many among the riverguard, like their Neritican allies, saw the Xirkaali as an elf problem. But some were uneasy; the invaders were burning the swamps and pillaging the jungle – a direct threat to the *Ril'uwa*. All of them seemed to agree on one point: Axel himself was unwelcome.

They refused to hear him. Refused to let him speak. It was left to Gorrup to act as intermediary. The young pondwarden had long since passed through annoyance into a mounting fury that was easily visible in his body language. His earlier ire toward Axel had been all but subsumed by this new frustration. A blessing, of sorts.

Gorrup stirred impatiently. "Idiots," he muttered. Axel laid a calming hand on him, but the pondwarden shook him off. Gorrup heaved himself upright, his broad head scraping the ceiling. "Idiots," he croaked, more loudly. "Fools. Biting gnats!"

Silence fell. One of the other pondwardens glared at him. He was older than Gorrup, and his warty flesh was so calloused it resembled the bark of a tree. "Be silent, tadpole."

Gorrup slapped his chest. "Come over here and say that, Ruggo. I will show you who the tadpole is." He looked around and puffed out his chest. "As for the rest of you… are you frightened, or merely stupid?"

Axel winced. If Gorrup noticed, he gave no sign.

"Well?" he demanded.

"You should not have brought him here," one of the chieftains said. His skin was splotched and wrinkly with age, and the color of his daube marked him as a Mudbelly, one of the largest tribes. They claimed the Vieshlar River all the way from the mountains to the estuary. The lodge they were currently occupying rested at the edge of their territory, and they claimed it as a holdfast. "His kind are not welcome in these waters."

"He is bad luck," Ruggo added, crossing his massive arms. Rumbles of assent from the other pondwardens followed this, and Axel fought the urge to make himself smaller.

Gorrup snorted, clearly unimpressed. "Did he bring the Xirkaali here then? Did he dam the spawning pools or burn the mangroves? No. Do not ascribe to this mage more power than he wields." He shook his wide head. "The question is simple enough: fight, or no? All this debate is so much empty croaking."

Ruggo swelled in fury. He pointed at Axel. "We should feed his body to the mud and forget he ever lived." The others gave croaks of agreement, and Axel felt a chill run through him. He had known that there would be some lingering resentment, but he had not expected this much. If his people had not fled, they would have died. Could they not see that?

"And that will solve the problem, will it?" Gorrup croaked angrily. "The Xirkaali will vanish like ripples on the water, and all will be well again? Pfaugh."

The other pondwarden ballooned his throat wrathfully. "Watch your tone, tadpole. I have known more seasons than you have fingers."

Gorrup swelled his own throat-sac in reply. "Yes, you are very old. Congratulations. But what have you done to earn my respect, save sit in your hole and peer out occasionally?" He looked around. "What have any of you done?"

"We have watched. We have listened," another of the chieftains said in a lilting chirp. She had brightly-hued skin and wide fingers, marking her as a Treehopper. She looked at the others. "We have only the gillkin's word that these Xirkaali mean us harm. What does Medu'Syth say about them?" She looked back at Gorrup. "Have they said anything at all?"

Gorrup glanced at Axel and shook his head slowly. "No." And they hadn't. It was puzzling. From what the Great Current had shown him, the Neriticans had harried the Xirkaali fleet remorselessly – but ceased all hostilities the moment they landed. Was it simply a lack of concern for the land? But why had they not contacted the riverguard, if so? Why choose silence? The questions nagged at him.

"And why do you think that is?" the Mudbelly chieftain demanded.

Gorrup shrugged, though he had often asked Axel the same question himself. "Who am I to guess such things? More, why should I care?" He thumped his chest again. "I defend our waters, not theirs. If they wish to hide in the sea, let them."

A grumble ran through the assembled chieftains. The alliance with Medu'Syth had been a long one, and profitable for their people. The Treehopper chieftain spoke up again. "He tells us that the elves will help us. But where are the elves?"

"Running scared," Ruggo said before Gorrup could reply. He heaved himself to his feet. "They flee to the interior as the Xirkaali advance inland."

Gorrup faced him, big hands flexing as if readying himself for a tussle. Axel huddled back, out of the way. If it came to it, he would do what he could to help Gorrup – though he doubted the pondwarden would appreciate his efforts. "What the Xirkaali do is cut us off from the sea," Gorrup said, heavily. "A ring of iron all but encircles us, and it grows tighter with every passing day. You all know it. You have seen the fortresses they erect. Will you argue until the trap has snapped shut?"

"You would have us die on his word," the Treehopper said.

"I would have you fight!" Gorrup closed his eyes. "I have seen the devastation they intend to wreak with my own eyes. I bring you word of it, but still you prevaricate. What else would you have of me?"

"Your duty. Kill the traitor. Avenge our ancestors. And then we will go into the mud, or the sea, until the Xirkaali have finished with the elves. When they depart, we will return." Ruggo looked around, and there were many nods and croaks of agreement.

Gorrup waited until the noise died down to reply. "And what if they do not depart?" Silence. Gorrup chortled sourly. "Aye, I thought as much. You have no wisdom, no answers. Only fear. You have smelled the smoke of burning trees and seen the dams in our rivers. The Xirkaali wish to tame this land; to break it to their will. That includes us." He rose to his feet. "I did not believe either, when Axel first showed me. But I do now."

Gorrup looked around. "I do not know why Medu'Syth chooses not to come. I do not know why they have abandoned us. But I promise you that I will find out."

"How?" Ruggo demanded.

"We will go to Medu'Syth," Axel said, breaking his silence. All eyes turned toward him, and he pushed himself to his feet. "I will go to the sea, and down to the coral palace of the Trident King, if I must. But I do not think it will come to that."

"It will not. Because they will kill you, traitor," Ruggo said. But his tone was doubtful. Axel felt a flicker of hope. He knew that they hadn't simply killed him out of hand because of that doubt. They weren't certain what Medu'Syth wanted, and as such, had chosen to simply not act. But the time for waiting had passed.

"Maybe," Axel allowed. "But I will go regardless." He looked around. "I will go alone, if I must. I will fight my way past the Xirkaali, if I must. But I will do this thing, even if I must die to see it done."

"You will not go alone," Gorrup rumbled. He glared at the others. "I too will go to Medu'Syth. Let us depart now. Leave these cowards to the mud." He made as if to turn away, and a grumble of protest rose from the assembled chieftains.

"He is right," a chieftain said, silencing the others. A Tidewalker, Axel thought, by the sharkskin armor he wore. He shook his staff of office at the others, and shark teeth rattled against the fossilized wood. "I too have seen the dams and the burning. Many of us have. But we allowed ourselves to be swayed by the hesitation of a few – those whose territories are not yet under threat." He looked at the Mudbelly chieftain as he said this, and the older warrior looked away, as if ashamed.

The Tidewalker went on. "It seems to me that Medu'Syth does not fight because we do not fight. It is our duty to watch the waterways, to alert them to danger. But we have not done this. Instead, we have waited. I, for one, will wait no more. Gillkin or no, the facts remain. The enemy is here and we must meet them."

Another chieftain, her body daubed in the pungent green of the Slugeater tribe, stood. "Hulum is right. My shamans have read the entrails of one of the great red serpents of the mangroves and seen great death to come." She too looked at the Mudbelly chieftain. "Do your shamans say differently, Glump?"

Glump shook his head. "No," he said, finally. Reluctantly. "No, Surrop. No, my sister, they do not." He looked at Axel. "I do not trust you, gillkin. My father, and his father, spoke of your sort. How you left us to face the long winter alone. Will you do it again, I wonder? If the Xirkaali should be too strong, will you flee again?"

Axel met his gaze squarely. "No," he said, softly. "I will not flee again. Come a new winter, or fire or steel, I will stand with you. But I must go to Medu'Syth. I must make them understand what is at stake."

Glump nodded. "Then we will do as you ask. We will help the elves. We will stain the waters red with Xirkaali blood. But if you have lied to us, I will put you in the mud myself."

Axel bowed. "That is all I ask." He straightened and looked at Gorrup. "Thank you, my friend."

The pondwarden chuckled thickly.

"Thank me when the Xirkaali are fleeing back across the sea, and not before." Gorrup drove his fist into his palm. "Now, I think it is time we paid the Sythians a visit."

CHAPTER EIGHTEEN
Aeron

Aeron looked around the council chamber in no little awe. Everything was so grand here, and old as well. Trees grew up through the walls, their branches forming living roof-beams, and their roots acting as joists. Birds flitted through the windows and circled the great table, before fluttering off into the recesses of the room.

Servants occupied themselves in the background, removing dustcloths and sweeping the stone floor. The chamber had been sealed off for some years; centuries, even, from the number of cobwebs in the corners. He and the others sat at an immense table, made from a living tree, and somehow pruned into a useful shape. *Magic,* he thought. Everything the elves did involved magic somehow.

Lady Merytan sat at the head of the table, with Valan to her left. Lord Solibos sat to her right. Aeron sat across from them with a map of the region unrolled before him. There were two other elves present: one, in flowing robes, was clearly a mage, while the other wore fine armor – if not quite so fine as that worn by Solibos. Aeron, in contrast, had brought only two of his people. One was an engineer by the name of Makki. She was a stout halfling woman of middle years, with the shoulders of a stevedore and a wicked smile. Unlike most of the mountain halflings, she dressed flamboyantly, in garish reds and bright blues.

The other was Lance-Captain Trosbert, commander of the Hetronburg Dogs, a mercenary regiment out of Rhordia. The Dogs were a mixed force of stalwarts, gunners, and lancers. Trosbert was an old friend of Jarad Bligh – Taran Bligh's uncle, and a fellow of no small means, at least as far the Shires judged such things. When Taran had insisted on joining the Ej expedition, Jarad had sent Trosbert along to keep him out of trouble. Whatever the reason, Aeron was grateful to have the mercenary along. The Dogs had more practical military experience than the rest of Aeron's forces combined – something that Aeron feared was going to be sorely needed in the days to come.

Merytan started things off with an apology. "We have not used this chamber in many years; not since Vieshlar was retaken after Winter's War. We had a proper council then, as Callenspire was the gateway into the southern lands. From here, we planned to retake what was once ours." She ran her fingers along the edge of the table, her expression regretful. "Few of those worthies remain. Myself… Lord Velizar of Blackthorn. The mage-prince, Opiryn, whose tower lies east of Grishamvu. The rest… gone, now."

Valan cleared his throat. "Would that they were here with us now. But we shall make do – we must." He looked at Aeron. "Well, Ser Aeron. I hope you have some ideas for us, because word from the coast is not good. We've had reports from Grishamvu and Blackthorn. Both are under siege. There were signs that the

Neriticans might be getting involved, but sadly those seem to have been solitary incidents. I fear Axel's mission may have failed."

"Which is why we need to find him," Aeron said. He dearly wanted to meet the gillkin, especially since Valan had confided that it was Axel who had told them to put him in command. "If what he told you is true, we need the sea-folk in this. Especially once the Xirkaali on the coast start moving inland." He indicated the coastline on the map. "It's really quite brilliant, when you have a bit of distance from it. From what we've been told by folk fleeing the fighting, they've established fortified enclaves all along the coast, and they're expanding them... It's like a line of iron hooks dug into the land. Their fleet is running supplies and troops up and down the coast, day after day without stopping. Unless we can disrupt that somehow, those enclaves will just keep expanding and digging in, until we're completely cut off from the coast."

"Axel swore that the riverguard would do what they could, but it doesn't seem as if they're interested," Valan said, doubtfully.

"Maybe they need help," Makki said. "Or maybe they just need someone to throw a punch in good faith, eh?"

Trosbert nodded and looked at Aeron. "We could send an airship out along the coast, drop some explosives – take out a few of those camps, if we're lucky."

Aeron studied the map. "*Windwalker* and *Thunderchild* should be arriving tomorrow; if Anas agrees, we might be able to use them to soften up the coast. Each airship can carry a few dozen grenadiers; they can do an awful lot of damage in a short time."

"Bimson's lot will be happy about that," Makki said. "She's been champing at the bit to blow something up ever since she got here."

Aeron smiled. "Well, she's getting her wish." He looked back at the map. "That brings us to the next matter. The Xirkaali are no doubt already en route, or if not, they will be soon. The Eastway is the obvious route, and not much we can do about it."

"We could muster a force of cavalry to meet them and scatter them," Solibos volunteered. "One good hit should do it. Perhaps even chase them all the way back to Evanvale."

"And do we have that much cavalry, Alesha?" Valan asked, glancing at the other armored elf. She reclined in her seat and selected a piece of apple from a tray the servants had left on the table.

"No," she replied as she took a bite. Solibos shot her a glare.

"Preposterous! Our Stormwind knights are the equal of a dozen lesser horsemen."

She met his glare with one of her own. "Maybe. But they outnumber us at least twenty to one, and they have their own heavy cavalry; it's not just humans on unarmored ponies. We'd get one charge before we were cut to pieces. I'll not risk *my* riders in a suicidal charge for no gain save glory."

Solibos drew himself up and looked ready to argue, but Aeron interrupted.

"Trying to defend the road will only cost us casualties. Better to collapse the bridge and let them sit on the other side. Once the aeronaut corps arrive, we can send them out along with one of our airships. A few explosives dropped from on high might slow things down long enough for us to finish with the bridge." He indicated the Vieshlar River on the map. "The river is my real concern. Evanvale and Ruhaindo are port cities. Lots of rivercraft. Lots of captains who know how to maneuver a loaded barge upriver. I propose abandoning all but the last of the toll locks –"

"Abandon the toll locks? Are you mad, halfling?" Solibos demanded. He loomed over Aeron like a wrathful deity. Aeron met his gaze squarely.

"They are simply not fit to defend, my lord. By your own admission, they've been neglected for centuries." He indicated Makki with a gesture. "My engineers have determined that the only one in condition to endure any sort of assault is the one closest to the city. Why waste lives defending a bit of stone? Better to close the portcullises and evacuate anyone manning them. Have the garrisons retreat to the final lock and aid in efforts to reinforce it. I'll send Makki and some of the others downriver to help. We could turn it into a defensible position within a few days."

"You act as if the enemy will be sailing upriver," Solibos protested.

"As a matter of fact, they are," Valan interjected. Aeron and the others looked at him. Valan shrugged. "I just got the reports myself this morning. Kortys sent one of his gladestalkers back with word. Ser Aeron is right; they're coming at us from both directions."

Solibos rounded on him. "Unconfirmed reports, Cormys. Nothing more!"

"You do not trust the words of your own gladestalkers?" Valan asked. Solibos waved this aside with a snort of dismissal.

"They are prone to exaggeration. They spend so much time in the jungle that they jump at every shadow." He turned his attention back to Aeron. "You cannot take them seriously. And abandoning the toll locks will infuriate the merchant guild, as well as the Breakwater Trading Concern. We will have every trader in the city screaming for your head if you do this."

"I was under the impression that most of them had evacuated," Aeron said. Solibos frowned and stepped back.

"Someone must anticipate their concerns. If not you, then myself."

"I welcome such initiative," Aeron said. "Myself, I intend to concentrate on defending the city." He rubbed his face, suddenly tired. "I understand your concerns, Lord Solibos – I do. But we simply lack the means of defending the toll locks. If we close the portcullises, it will serve to slow down the fleet of barges approaching from downriver. That gives us time to reinforce the final lock."

"If you can't hold the others, what makes you think you can hold that one?" Solibos asked. "Why worry about any of them, if you are so afraid of a fight?"

Aeron sighed. "I don't think we can hold it. But I think we can delay their arrival by a few days." He looked around. "Make no mistake, our biggest enemy here is time. We don't have time to do what is needed. Everything and anything we can do to delay them will be helpful." He looked at Valan. "I don't suppose that gladestalker is still around?"

"I believe so," Valan said.

"Good. I'd like Kortys keep an eye on the river. I don't expect him to help with the evacuations, but if he felt like sending a few arrows over the Xirkaali way, I'd be obliged."

"I will send word. Truth to tell, he was probably already planning on it." Valan sat back. "Well, that just leaves the city itself."

Aeron pushed aside the map. "Yes. How many bolt throwers does the garrison have?"

"In good condition?" Valan asked.

Aeron paused. "Ideally."

Merytan spoke up. "Maybe forty. Already mounted on the walls. I can mark them on the plans, if you like. Between them and our archers, it usually does the trick. The crews are well-drilled, or so I'm assured." She looked at Solibos, who nodded.

"They are. I see to their training personally."

"I don't know about the rest of you, but that fills me with confidence," Valan said, blithely. Solibos stared at him.

"Are you impugning my abilities, diplomat?"

Valan's expression was one of affronted innocence. "Shining Ones, no. I meant it as a compliment." Solibos wasn't buying it, and neither was Aeron. Valan was clearly needling the other elf, and for no good reason that he could see.

The elf in robes cleared his throat. "According to the reports I've read, and what I have heard from those mages who escaped Evanvale, the Xirkaali have no affinity for magic. Indeed, they seem to despise it. Unfortunately, there are only a handful of mages in the city, and few have any battlefield experience, besides myself." He looked almost apologetic as he spoke. "Of those, most would rather evacuate."

Merytan gestured and an orb of dazzling light coalesced over her palm. "In my hedonistic youth, I was quite the battle-mage. I can lead our efforts in that regard, if Ser Aeron and Archmage Doromir here agree. I might even convince a few of the diehards to put their books down in time to defend the city."

Aeron watched the light for a moment, then nodded. "I would be pleased if you would. Magic has never been my strong suit. The only kind I'm familiar with mostly revolves around food. Or drakons."

Merytan smiled and snuffed the light with another gesture. "Sadly, we have no drakons here, nor anyone experienced in their handling. The beasts could come in handy." She sat back in her chair. "We shall have to rely on more traditional skills, I fear."

"Nothing wrong with that," Aeron said. "Better to stand on firm ground than hope for rain, as the gaffers say."

Valan frowned. "And what exactly does that mean?"

Aeron shrugged. "I have no idea. But it's what they say in situations like these." He ran his hands through his hair. "I've made some other preliminary observations. The walls along the river are in the worst shape, but that might be to our advantage."

"Meaning?" Merytan asked.

"The stone there has crumbled rather than shattered. It's become a natural berm. I know from experience that that sort of barrier absorbs explosions better than a normal wall. A bit of luck, that, if their rockets are anything like what we use." Aeron tapped his fingers against the table. "We should still reinforce it, and the wharves as well. We have to hold them, especially if we want to keep supplies coming in. Once the evacuation is complete, we can chain together any remaining barges and turn them into bastions to keep the Xirkaali from attacking them directly. A few archers, or some gunners, would be enough to hold them."

"The eastern walls are the real problem," Merytan said.

"The bridge, you mean," Valan said. He looked at Solibos, who huffed.

"Work is underway to destroy it, I assure you. It is a tedious process, and slow." He bowed shallowly to Merytan. "And with your permission, I will get back to it." He left without waiting for a reply. Aeron frowned.

"He's going to be a problem, isn't he?"

"You have no idea," Valan said. And something in his tone sent a chill of unease through Aeron. He glanced toward the doors, wondering whether he should be more worried about the enemy without – or the one within.

CHAPTER NINETEEN
Hejun

Hejun reclined on her bench and listened to her followers squabble. Deftly, she peeled a piece of fruit with her claw and waited for a lull in the conversation. A gull hopped across the floor, eyeing the hemicyons balefully, until Hejun threw it the remainder of her fruit and sat up. The stone floor was cold beneath her paws. The elves had done something – witchcraft most likely – to keep the interiors of their buildings cool despite the humidity of the region. It was unnatural, but welcome all the same.

She glanced at Obair, who stood nearby. He smiled slyly, and she almost laughed. It wasn't the first time she'd allowed her followers to snap and snarl at one another. She knew that many matriarchs could not countenance such behavior from their subordinates. But she had found that a certain amount of acrimony served a necessary purpose. So long as no one drew blood, things were fine.

"What I do not understand is their continued defiance," Gorcha snarled. She stared at the updated map the cartographers had provided as if it had personally offended her. "We encircle them, we bombard them – they have no way out. And yet here we sit, still staring at those blasted walls!" She thumped the table with her fist, and the other subordinate commanders growled in agreement. Hejun sighed and tugged on her ear.

She considered her next words carefully. Of late, these councils had become tedious exercises in bone-gnawing. Her subordinates were unruly; ready to move on to the next phase of the invasion. Patience was not considered a virtue among the hemicyon. Her gaze found the scattered faces of the human advisors who stood by their respective matriarchs. Only a few, and none equal to Obair in sagacity.

"As I have said, our strategy requires the cities to remain intact," she began. "Without them, we leave ourselves open to a counter-assault. The elves are disorganized, but only for the moment. They will soon rally, dig in, and prepare for our coming. If we do not have walls, we will be caught in the open. Our numbers are not limitless. Our supplies are finite. We must have infrastructure to prosecute the invasion successfully."

"Logistics," Gorcha barked, as if the word were an obscenity.

Hejun bit back a snarl of her own. "Yes. Logistics. Supply lines. The business of war, Gorcha. Not the dance of steel, but what comes after."

Gorcha blew out a noisy breath. "Better you than me, Matriarch," she said, grudgingly. If she was still angry about being passed over for command of the Callenspire expedition, she was careful not to show it. Then, a certain amount of nepotism was considered healthy among their people. Of course one would elevate one's own pack over another; it was only practical. Still, Gorcha had held longer grudges for less.

"We all serve as befits our abilities," Hejun said, piously.

If Gorcha noticed the insult, she gave no sign. Instead, she scrubbed her muzzle fiercely for a moment, then turned her attention back to the map. After a moment, she said, "What about a seaward assault?"

Hejun grunted and leaned forward. "Explain your thinking." The problem with Ruhaindo was the seawall that separated it from the bay. The wall encircled their docklands and was high enough that there was no easy way across. Unless it was brought down, or the sea-gates opened, their fleet would remain stuck in the bay.

Gorcha tapped a claw against the sea-wall that separated Ruhaindo from the water. "We hold the water, but that wall protects their docklands. The sea-gates are sealed by magic, according to the witch-hunters. We could spend a year hurling rockets at them and never crack them. So what if we leave them, and focus on the wall instead?"

Hejun clicked her teeth. "I told you, I want the wall intact…"

Gorcha bared her fangs. "Which is why we go over it."

Hejun blinked and stepped back. She glanced at Obair, who looked thoughtful. He peered at the map. "A long climb, and the elves raining arrows on you the entire way," he said, speculatively. Gorcha nodded.

"Which is why we use the rockets and mortars to cover our assent. It would not take many, especially if some of the special ones are ready. A bare handful of hemicyons could make the climb and take the wall. With luck, we could have the sea-gates open soon after."

"The elves would put up a fierce resistance," Hejun said, considering the matter. "We would need to launch a simultaneous assault on the landward walls; something big enough that they couldn't ignore." She tugged on her ear again, thinking. "Risky, Gorcha."

Gorcha nodded, licking her chops. "But glorious, Matriarch. And it has the added benefit of allowing us to take the city without much damage."

"Unless one of you sets another fire," Obair said, absently. Gorcha growled at him.

"Watch your tone, human. The Matriarch might be kindly disposed to you, but I am not. Continue to bark at me, and I will remove your tongue."

Hejun snarled. Gorcha and the others froze. "Obair is my advisor. He speaks with my words. Growl at him, and you growl at me. Threaten him, and – well." She fixed Gorcha with a steady look. "So, it is you who should watch your tone, Gorcha. If you please."

Gorcha bowed her head after a moment's hesitation. "As you say, Matriarch."

Hejun waited a half-beat, and then said, "But you are correct about the wall. Your strategy might be our best bet for taking Ruhaindo. Thus, I leave it to you to lead the assault on the seawall, while I oversee the feint."

Gorcha gave a yelp of pleasure. "I will not fail you, Matriarch!"

"I know that you will not," Hejun said. "Choose those you wish to participate in the assault. The rest of you will join me in the feint." She made a fist. "Together, we will take the city, and will be one step closer to fulfilling the designs of the Khatun. Now go – see to your packs. I wish to be ready by first light."

They departed in an unruly mob, barking and jostling one another in their eagerness to be about the bloodshed. She went to the window that looked out over the bay and stared at the city across the water. Obair joined her. "Clever," he said.

"Gorcha has always been troublesome. This will fill her belly for the time being." Hejun glanced at him. "Then, you knew that when you made such a foolish comment, I expect. You are lucky she didn't simply remove your head."

Obair nodded. "A calculated risk. If she wasn't annoyed, she might have realized that you've given her the privilege of leading a suicide mission."

"Hemicyons do not fear death," Hejun said.

"Nor do they seek it," Obair countered. "You must keep an eye on her. She might well seek to challenge your authority in a more formal fashion next time. That would be disastrous, for all of us."

"Gorcha is a competent leader," Hejun said, unconsciously echoing her daughter's earlier statement. Obair noticed, and smiled.

"Gorcha is a fierce warrior, but vainglorious. She has no patience, no foresight." Obair paused. "Besides, I would miss you."

Hejun snorted. "And I you, old man." She turned her attention back to the city in the distance. The waters before the sea-wall were thick with wrecks, both elven and Xirkaali. There had been two engagements thus far, the latter involving fire-ships. They had lost two junks outright to those, and three more were badly damaged and no longer fit for purpose. "Have we heard from my cousin?"

Obair nodded. "Admiral Khulan is overseeing the siege of Grishamvu, as you requested. The city is holding, but not for much longer. And Baidar sent word that the gates of Blackthorn have been cleansed, whatever that means."

"It means that Blackthorn will fall within a handful of days, if Han is as competent as I believe. If not, well, we shall have to lift the siege until Ruhaindo is dealt with." Hejun scratched her chin and pondered the direction of the dance. "What about the river-tribes? Any sign of them?" According to their scouts, the river-folk had seemingly begun to retreat from the coast, following the rivers inland and away from Iron-Beach and the other landing points.

"Sporadically." Obair looked at her. "I suspect that they lack the numbers for a sustained conflict. They have no choice but to retreat – to hide."

"You think they are going into hiding?"

"I think they might," Obair said, cautiously. "I think they will stay away from us, unless we provoke them. Unless the Neriticans decide to get involved, in which case who knows what they'll do." He sighed and looked out at the water. "I wish we knew more about the water-breathers. Are they finished with us, or just waiting for something? I don't like not knowing."

Hejun gave a bark of amusement. "You are not alone in that, old man." She looked toward the mouth of the bay, where a line of war-junks waited in a defensive formation, just in case the Neriticans decided to join the fray once more. The junks probably wouldn't be enough to stop an assault from the sea, but they would hold the enemy up long enough to alert the rest of the army. "If Gorcha's plan fails, how long do you estimate a siege will take?"

"Six days," Obair said. "Maybe seven."

Hejun glanced at him. "As many as that?"

"Those are very thick walls," Obair said, somewhat defensively. He sighed and pushed himself to his feet. She heard his joints pop as he did so, and once again reflected on his age. He would not walk beside her much longer, however much he protested the idea. "You are worried," he said, as he looked down at her. It wasn't a question.

"I am." She saw no point in dissembling.

"About the siege?"

"About many things."

Obair grunted and looked out over the water. "She will be fine."

Hejun shot him a look. "I am not worried about her."

"I didn't say you were," Obair said.

"You implied it, old man. And I do not care for the implication."

"It is natural to worry about your pup."

Hejun licked her muzzle in exasperation. "Hemicyons do not worry about their pups. They live or die on their own strength. It is not up to us to coddle them." She paused. "Has there been any word from them?"

"Nothing worth worrying you over," Obair said. "She appears to be following orders, for a wonder. At least three villages along the river have been taken. Well, burned." He paused. "And I say villages – more like country estates, really. Small fiefdoms, ruled by minor aristocrats. They'll reach the first of the toll locks we were told about in a day, maybe two. That's where she'll meet real resistance, I expect."

Hejun grunted. "How much?" The elves' lack of readiness still puzzled her. Surely reinforcements were already on march. So where were they? Hiding? Or perhaps waiting. The thought disturbed her.

"Nothing major." Obair frowned. "I doubt it will delay her."

"Let us hope it doesn't." She leaned forward, staring at Ruhaindo with the intensity of a hunter eyeing their prey. "The city will fall. I feel it in my marrow. We must plan for the next siege, and the one after that. Callenspire. Ej. The way to Elvenholme must be opened and soon, or we will founder here, chasing our tails round and round."

Obair smiled and bowed. "I will begin preparations immediately, Matriarch."

Hejun barely noticed when he left. Her claws tightened on the sill of the window. "Fall, damn you. *Fall*. For I have no more time to waste on you."

CHAPTER TWENTY
Kortys

Somewhere in the jungle, a bird whistled sharply.

The Xirkaali scout sniffed the air and turned in a slow circle, studying the trees with narrowed eyes. Kortys, laying flat against the trunk of a tree, watched as the scout was joined by two more of his kind. Unlike the other hemicyons he'd encountered, they wore leather armor and carried bows. They moved cautiously through the clearing, and their gazes were never still. They sniffed the air and growled to one another.

Kortys kept a map of the region in his head. He knew where the river could be forded easily and where the waters were so deep that even the riverguard avoided them. He knew where the old logging roads were and the remains of the outposts that had once dotted them. He knew, therefore, that these scouts had come upriver, rather than overland from the direction of the Eastway. There was no easy route in that direction; not one known to the Xirkaali, at least. They were outriders, marking the trail for what followed.

Without turning, Kortys held up three fingers over his shoulder. In reply, three arrows flew from the jungle behind him, so close that he felt their passage. The hemicyons fell without a sound. Kortys waited. When no more Xirkaali showed their snouts, he crept into the open and checked the bodies. Around him, Alisor and the other gladestalkers split up and scattered through the trees. Alisor paused at the edge of the clearing and signaled that he was heading for the river. Kortys gestured, silently indicating that he would follow shortly.

The scouts carried nothing of interest, but it was the third such pack they'd encountered – and dispatched – since leaving Callenspire. Kortys rose to his feet. It boded ill. It was obvious that they were ranging out parallel to the enemy columns advancing along the Eastway and coming upriver. There was no telling how many of them were in the area.

Kortys motioned for two of his warriors to drag the bodies out of sight and leave them somewhere that they wouldn't be easily found. It wouldn't be hard; the jungle was in a constant state of flux, thanks to the magics used in the retaking of Vieshlar so many centuries ago. Trees grew to enormous sizes, and the very soil was changeable in places. No doubt the bodies would be swallowed up if something didn't come along and eat them first.

He started in the direction of the river, moving silently through the undergrowth as he followed the sound of rushing water. The Vieshlar River ran from the estuary to the mountains, with hundreds of tributaries that branched off in all directions. A labyrinth of water, not easily navigated, save by the river-tribes.

That was the reason they'd come this way, hoping to meet up with a band of riverguard and put Valan's claims of alliance to the test. But so far, they'd seen no sign of the amphibians. Alisor was under the impression that the tribes had retreated to their lodges to wait out the war; Kortys wasn't so certain. Perhaps they were simply waiting for the elves to do something – to prove that there was, indeed, an alliance. If that was the case, he couldn't blame them. In their position, he would have done the same.

The ground began to slope downward, becoming a tangle of roots and vines. Soon, the drop-off would become a sheer slide toward the river. This part of the jungle was thankfully sedate; the toll locks that marked the river were more than just gates – they were lodestones for those who chose to make their life in the forest, away from the snake-pit politics of Callenspire. Towns sprang up around them and spread outward.

Kortys slid down the overgrown incline, careful not to disturb the soil. Alisor waited for him below, wedged safely against a fallen tree. He signaled for quiet as Kortys reached him. Below, the snaky brown ribbon of the Vieshlar River wound through the jungle.

Some distance west, an ancient toll lock rose over the water. It was the first of a dozen such structures that dotted the length of the river from the mouth of the estuary all the way to Callenspire. Many were in ruins; their foundations long since crumbled into the water. But a few, like this one, remained standing despite the rampant overgrowth.

The toll lock resembled a castle parapet, or a wide archway of stone, straddling the river. Vines clung tenaciously to the stonework, and in places, a green shroud of moss obscured the faded friezes that had once covered its surface. A portcullis of iron spikes prevented any water-craft from bypassing it, and the outbuildings of an ad-hoc trading post sprawled across either bank.

An alarm bell was ringing somewhere in the depths of the trading post, and elven soldiers were racing to their positions. Each of the toll locks had a nominal garrison of around thirty, but some had fewer; others, more. Some had become the nucleus of townships, like this one; others were isolated. He watched as archers took up positions atop those buildings closest to the water. But why were they still here in the first place?

"What are the fools doing? They were given orders to retreat upriver," Kortys murmured. The halfling, Aeron, had ordered a general retreat; toll-garrisons were to pull back toward Callenspire, where the last few toll locks were being reinforced.

Alisor shrugged. "Maybe someone gave them different orders," he said, pointedly.

Kortys grunted. That was always a possibility. "Their bad luck, then," he said. Below, more archers filed across the lock, readying arrows as they moved. A bolt-thrower was angled into position and loaded. At a shouted command, the first volley arced skyward. Kortys followed the volley's flight and turned his attention to the vessels fast approaching the lock. Most were barges, sailing upriver single-file. Difficult to do, even with the wind at your back. The Xirkaali appeared to be using muscle-power; oars thudded against the water, denying the pull of the current.

"Look there," Alisor murmured. "See the chains on the aft hulls? The first boat pulls the rest. Clever."

Kortys nodded. "I've heard that Xiryan merchants do the same, in their country. So long as they don't stop, or get bound up, you can keep a whole fleet moving on the momentum of the first boat alone."

Alisor laughed softly. "Looks like they're about to be stopped, though. That barge is big, but not big enough to ram through the lock." The lead barge was indeed big; someone had reinforced the prow with timber struts and iron plates, making it into a battering ram. The hull had been armored, and the rails were protected by a raised palisade of wood, turning it into a floating fortress. All of it must have added substantially to the weight of the craft, but the Xirkaali at the oars didn't seem to mind.

The first volley hadn't done much; the rowers were protected by a leather tent that did much to absorb the rain of arrows. The second volley was more effective. The humans who'd appeared on deck to return fire with their bows suffered several casualties and caused none in return. The third volley was composed of fire-arrows. These did little; the Xirkaali had obviously thought of that, and wetted down everything that could burn.

Kortys tensed when the mortar team appeared on deck. Alisor, who'd never seen the weapons in action, watched in confusion as the weapon burped fire. The first shot went wide, exploding on the shore behind the lock. There were screams from the trading post, but the lock still stood. By the second shot, the mortar team had gotten the angle right. The explosion, when it came, was powerful enough to wrench part of the lock off of its foundations. Elves were hurled into the air or cast into the swirling waters of the river. Black smoke boiled across the surface of the water.

The remaining archers somehow maintained their discipline, and a ragged volley followed both from what was left of the lock and the nearby buildings, but the barge maintained its steady approach. "What are we going to do?" Alisor asked, whey-faced.

"Nothing," Kortys said, flatly. There was nothing that could be done. A few more arrows here and there wouldn't make any difference, not against that. From the look on his face, Alisor knew it as well. "Fall back. We need to move upriver and warn the next toll lock what they'll be facing, if they haven't already fled. And send word to Callenspire."

They moved quickly, retreating the way they'd come. But as they climbed, Kortys felt something cut across his arm and saw an arrow embed itself in a tree ahead of him. He shouted a warning and flung himself to the ground. Alisor stumbled and scrambled out of sight. Bird calls sounded throughout the jungle.

Branches rustled overhead, and a hairy form plummeted toward him with a snarl. Kortys rolled aside as the hemicyon crashed down, stabbing the spot where the gladestalker had been only moments before. He'd been wrong – there were more than three scouts this time. He was forced to dodge aside again as the hemicyon's blade swooped out, chopping through a branch in the process.

"Kortys!" Alisor called out.

"Keep going!" Kortys shouted. "I'll keep him occupied. Find the others and head for the rendezvous point. *Go*!" He ducked back as his attacker slashed at him again. *A trap,* he thought, as he went for his sword. Had they used their own as bait to draw the gladestalkers into the open? If so, they were more cunning than he'd given them credit for. But it wouldn't be enough. His opponent was stronger; tougher, maybe. But not faster.

Kortys sprang to his feet and lunged. His blade danced across the hemicyon's flank and midsection, easily cutting through the creature's light armor and drawing blood. The hemicyon snarled and redoubled its efforts to kill him. In doing so, it left itself open to further debilitating cuts; legs, arms, neck. The creature wheezed and staggered. Kortys stayed out of reach. When his opponent finally collapsed, Kortys felt no relief. Only annoyance that they'd been sniffed out.

He turned to find the others. They had to keep moving before Xirkaali reinforcements arrived. He could see them through the trees and made to call out. But before he could, he heard the scrape of steel on wood and turned back to see the hemicyon clambering to its feet. Blood stained its fur, and froth gathered at the corners of its jaws, but it wasn't as dead as he'd assumed.

"Tricky beast," Kortys muttered, as the hemicyon charged, blade raised.

But before it could reach him, a green form leapt down from somewhere above, impaling the hemicyon with a trident. The warrior gave a strangled howl and slumped. Kortys cursed in surprise. A bulbous-eyed riverguard crouched atop the body.

"You are… unhurt?" the newcomer asked, in badly-accented elvish.

"I had him," Kortys said.

The batrachian warrior nodded. "I… apologize. I am being Glump," he croaked, as he pulled his trident free of the dead dog-man. "Of the Mudbelly tribe. You fight the Xirkaali?"

Kortys nodded. "We do." He suspected the Xirkaali scouts hadn't been the only ones watching the gladestalkers. He pushed aside his irritation and kept his expression neutral.

Glump blinked. "They be filling the river with elf blood."

"They are."

Glump was silent for a moment. Then, "You come with me. We speak. Perhaps we make war together."

CHAPTER TWENTY-ONE
Axel

Axel crouched among the roots of the great mangrove and watched the Xirkaali landing party splash along the small estuary, heading inland. There were more than a hundred of them, both human and hemicyon, formed into a winding column to navigate the shallows of the estuary; one of the many such expeditions now occurring along the Vieshan Gulf. The air was thick with the smell of smoke; the Xirkaali were burning everything as part of their effort to clear the jungle so as to make room for their fortified camps. These camps were like iron claws dug into the flesh of Vieshlar.

Gorrup, hunched nearby, asked, "Now?"

Axel gestured for him to stay where he was. "Not yet. Let them get a bit farther inland." As he spoke, he made a slow, circular motion with his hand, calling up a concealing mist to roll across the estuary. The swamp was full of noise; insects and swirling water and, now, the rattle of steel armor and the harsh laughter of hemicyons.

All along the coast, similar ambushes were being launched by the river-tribes. Or so they had promised to do. Axel hoped that Medu'Syth was watching; that when they saw that the riverguard was at war, they would have no choice but to rejoin the battle. If not, he would have to try more direct means of getting their attention – something he was loathe to do, despite the circumstances.

Ostensibly, this ambush was designed to get him closer to the sea. He had promised to go to Medu'Syth, and that was his intent. But the truth of it was he had not spoken to another Neritican in centuries… and a part of him feared what their reaction to his presence might be. Would they see him as a coward and traitor, as the riverguard? Would they recognize him as one of them at all? How much had changed since he had entered his hibernation? He feared the answers to those questions.

Worse, his dreams were growing more disturbing. The name Oskan echoed painfully in the vaults of his mind. He had become certain that the old terror was returning, but how or why was still unclear. Perhaps not even the Green Lady knew. He could not risk saying anything, for to say the wrong thing might endanger all he had worked toward since arriving in Vieshlar. For now, the Xirkaali were the only threat that mattered.

Pushing such thoughts aside, Axel raised his staff and tapped it against the trunk of the tree whose roots he sheltered in. The insect noise grew more pervasive as his magics called to the biting, stinging Vieshan gnats and incited them to swarm toward the Xirkaali.

He was rewarded by a cacophony of shouts and complaints as the human soldiers slapped at their bare flesh in agitation. Nor did the hemicyons escape the insects' attention. They scratched at their ears or snouts, whining in frustration. Between the mist and the insects, their attention was safely diverted. He glanced at Gorrup. "*Now*."

Gorrup gave out a loud croak and heaved himself from the water. As the echo of that cry faded, it was answered by a deluge of similar croaks, albeit not so loud. Moments later, the riverguard attacked. They rose from the shallows to either side of the Xirkaali column, wielding tridents and spears. Javelins arced overhead and fell among the enemy.

Axel knew that the river-folk coated their weapons in various poisons. A single cut was often enough to fell an opponent. Given their size, it might take more than that to bring down a hemicyon, but it'd slow them down at the very least.

The riverguard hopped in a seemingly chaotic pattern, darting close only to leap away at the last moment. The hemicyon warriors howled curses as their exposed flesh was stung. But more often than not, the riverguard weapons scratched harmlessly off of steel scales. While the poison was doing something, it wasn't doing it quick enough to be of much use.

Axel slammed his coral staff down into the water, and the river surged up in a frenzy. It enveloped a nearby group of human soldiers, plucking them away from their riverguard opponents. The struggling warriors were dragged into the water, where they vanished. Some might survive the attention of the river, but most would not.

Axel found himself saddened by the thought, though he knew that the humans would not think twice about killing him, if they had the chance. It did not have to be this way. Their peoples could learn to live in peace, if not harmony. And yet war never seemed more than a moment away at any given time, even in his day. And now more so than ever.

"Is that all you are going to do?" Gorrup demanded.

"I was saving some for you," Axel said, mildly. Gorrup snorted and launched himself into battle, mace swinging. *As impetuous as his ancestor,* Axel thought, not without some affection. He turned to find the chieftain of the Tidewalker tribe, Hulum, watching him. The riverguard licked his eyeball thoughtfully.

"He took a chance, not killing you," Hulum croaked.

Axel looked away. "Hopefully, he will be proven right."

"Hopefully," Hulum said. He watched the battle for a time, seemingly in no hurry to join the fray. Some chieftains leapt in immediately. Others were more pragmatic. Hulum was of the latter variety. "He has always been hotheaded, that one," he continued, his gaze fixed on Gorrup. "Forever leaping into deep pools without first checking that nothing was waiting to gobble him up. But more often than not, he was right. Good instincts."

Axel nodded. Gorrup was the only reason the diverse tribes of the region had listened to Axel's pleas. Their people had grown in the centuries he'd hibernated, waiting for the world to grow warm. Where once there had been only one sort of river-folk, these days there were the estuary tribes, the marsh-walkers in the swamps, and the jungle-wardens, who lived among the poison flowers of the high hinterlands. A great and varied folk; he hoped he was not leading them to their destruction.

Swinging his staff out, he sent another swarm of insects into the confusion. A howl from nearby pulled him about, and he spied a hemicyon warrior bounding toward he and Hulum out of the melee. Blood stained the warrior's armor, and his muzzle was swollen with insect-bites. He was in a frenzy; driven mad by frustration, perhaps.

"Where are they all coming from?" Axel murmured. The dog-man was large; sturdily built and armored in steel plates. Axel gestured, and the roots that ran through the bank rose like writhing serpents, snagging the legs and arms of the charging hemicyon warrior. The captive howled in frustration, and perhaps fear, as he was dragged down into the mud, and, moments later, entombed alive.

The warrior's open-faced helm, topped with a plume made from horse-hair, lay nearby. Axel stooped and picked it up, marveling at the weight of it. They were strong, these hemicyons. Tough. But not builders. Not scholars. A warrior-caste, then, much like the placoderms who fought Medu'Syth's wars.

"How far did you travel to get here?" he murmured. "And why? What is the point of such needless slaughter?"

There was no answer to be had; not yet. He wondered if the Xirkaali themselves knew, or did they act at the whim of another? The Great Current had been unclear on that point, as on so many others. Still, Axel hoped to find answers. He turned and saw that the battle had spread to either bank. The jungle echoed with the clash of steel.

Hulum rose from his crouch. He whistled sharply, and a deep, bellicose croak sounded. A moment later, something large and shaped vaguely like a toad burst from the undergrowth. Hulum was on the dambuster's back in a moment, and with a thump of his trident, the immense toad was bounding away into the river. Bemused, Axel watched its rampage for a moment before turning his attention back to the battle.

Most of the hemicyons had retreated from the water, leaving their human servants to fend for themselves in the shallows. Or maybe they'd simply been carried by the flow of battle. He could hear Gorrup bellowing somewhere back among the trees. But the bulk of the Xirkaali column was still stuck in the estuary, hemmed in by the ambushers.

Ride, Splish burbled in his mind. The water elemental quivered with excitement as Axel gave his permission. Splish slid down Axel's legs and formed an undulating walkway of water. Axel took a running start and slid up the slope and into the trees, carried by Splish's surging form. He whipped along the estuary at high speed, avoiding the struggling knots of riverguard and humans, or hemicyons, with ease. As he neared the rear of the column, he spied the supply-skiffs that the Xirkaali landing parties always dragged in their wake. Food and supplies, mostly. But also weapons; rockets. These were the true danger. The riverguard had nothing to counter them. Nor did the elves. Not yet. That would change, thanks to the halflings. But every rocket destroyed was one less that could be hurled at Callenspire.

Axel urged Splish up, and the water elemental rose like a wave, carrying him over the skiffs. Axel pointed his staff at them, and the river bucked like a wild dambuster, smashing the skiffs and sinking many of them. The humans responsible for them scattered in all directions, harried by the riverguard.

The ambush had dissolved into a free-for-all, and Gorrup was in the middle of it, adding to the confusion. As Axel sped past, he caught sight of the pondwarden and saw his mace catch a hemicyon in the hip, launching the dog-man snout-first into a tree. The hemicyon collapsed in a heap and did not move again. But where one fell, two more were ready to fill the gap. Gorrup was soon ringed about by foes and seemed pleased by it.

Too many, Splish burbled.

"Yes," Axel agreed. Too many. Always too many. The river-folk had indeed grown in population over the years, but the tribes were still outnumbered by the invaders. Each tribe could only muster a few precious clutches of warriors; good for ambushes and night-time raids, but not for a stand-up fight. Unless Medu'Syth became involved, the river-folk would eventually be forced to abandon the fight and retreat to the deep places. Axel knew that if that happened, the elves would soon be overwhelmed.

Even as the thought crossed his mind, he caught sight of an oddity; a large skiff, far behind the others. It had somehow come through his deluge undamaged. Atop it was a tall cage, made from what appeared to be black iron. Within it sat a human woman, legs crossed and eyes closed, as if meditating. The waters around the skiff were calm; as if by magic. The humans who crewed the skiff were calm as well, seemingly unbothered by the fighting going on about them. Something about the cage pulled at his attention, and he urged Splish toward it so that he could get a closer look.

The elemental balked. *No, bad,* he quavered, and dispersed, retreating to Axel's shoulder and dropping him into the river.

Axel splashed to the surface, nonplussed. "Splish?" he asked. His bewilderment almost cost him his life.

Axel heard a growl behind him, turned – and instinctively raised his staff to catch a blow that might have killed him, even as Splish screamed a warning. His attacker was a scar-faced hemicyon clad in raggedy black robes, bearing an odd sickle-topped chain. The dog-man struck at him again, and Axel twisted aside, using his staff to parry the blow. Chips of coral struck him in the face.

The hemicyon pressed his attack, forcing Axel to backpedal through the shallows. His attacker slashed out again, and Axel ducked beneath the sickle. Splish leapt from his shoulder and crashed into the hemicyon's legs, unbalancing him. Axel rose and brought the end of his staff across his opponent's muzzle, knocking him sprawling in the muddy waters. He retreated into the root-systems of the riverbank as the hemicyon scrambled to his feet.

Splish was wailing in his head, terrified beyond reason. He quieted the elemental and crawled through the roots. Behind him, the sickle slashed out, hacking through his protection.

Axel was no stranger to battle. He'd fought in many during the war against Winter, but always from a safe distance, using his magic to bolster his allies and hamper his enemies. This sort of close-quarters fighting had never been one of his strengths.

He gestured frantically, calling on the waters that permeated the humid air. They resisted at first, surprising him; it was if they were afraid of something, as Splish was. But they came at last, if slowly. At the last moment, he sent the roiling mass toward his opponent. The spell was meant to drown its target, to fill their lungs and dash them to the ground.

Instead, the waters cascaded off of the hemicyon like morning dew, leaving him damp but unmoved. Axel stared silently in shock. He'd never had anyone simply ignore one of his spells before.

Bad, Splish moaned. *Very bad.*

Axel retreated, trying to call to mind another spell, but something about the hemicyon had rattled him. It was hard to think – hard to draw on the mystical energies that were his birthright. He tried to conjure a concealing mist and failed.

The hemicyon surged forward, and only Splish's quick thinking saved Axel from a split skull. The water elemental jerked Axel out of the path of the dog-man's hooked blade and deeper into the network of roots. The hemicyon hacked at them in frustration, trying to cut a path to Axel. Axel's mind, normally so quick, stuttered into sluggishness. He pressed himself back against the roots and – *ah.*

Instinctively, he tried to concentrate on the point where the water and the roots met. Water-magic was easy for a gillkin; almost second nature. Trees were harder, for all that they were part of the same cycle. They were more stubborn, for one thing. It was hard to convince them to do anything, let alone move.

He could hear the panting of his opponent, the chop of the sickle, the crackle of the fire. He closed his eyes and tried to block it all out. He let his staff rest against his shoulder and thrust his fingers as deep into the mud as they could go. Splish vibrated in warning, but he ignored it; ignored everything but the mud and the tree.

Roots twitched; cracked… squirmed. He fell back with a cry of relief as the root network writhed around him like a nest of snakes, but his respite was short lived. The sickle tore through the last of the roots and fell toward Axel's head.

Only Splish's intervention saved his life. The elemental rose up like a living shield, intercepting the blow. The hemicyon gave a shocked yelp as the elemental flung itself full in his face, knocking him backward. Around them, the remaining roots pulled themselves loose of the muddy water and began to rise.

Axel squirmed out and up onto the shuddering trunk of the tree, followed closely by Splish. The mangrove continued to uproot itself with a long, echoing groan. "Go," he cried. "Go!"

He lost sight of the hemicyon as the great tree took its first, lurching steps toward the sea. A heavy branch swung out, sending the cage and its skiff sliding away. Inside, the occupant was staring at the tree in shock, and Axel laughed out loud. Then, the mangrove was toppling toward the sea with a bellow of splintering wood.

Axel leapt, and the waters rushed up to welcome him.

CHAPTER TWENTY-TWO
Shulgin

Shulgin sighed and paced the length of the boat's foredeck, her paw resting on the hilt of her sword. Every so often she paused and looked back at the vessels trailing in the wake of her own, her claw-tips tapping impatiently against the pommel of her weapon. The sun was setting, painting the waters in hues of orange and gold.

It had been two days since they'd left the last toll lock a shattered ruin and its defenders for the crows. Two days since her steel had tasted blood. Callenspire was still at least five days away, if not more. She scratched at a scabbed-over wound on her neck idly. All things considered, the advance was going well – at least this part of it. She just wished it was going quicker. It was as if the jungle were somehow actively attempting to stymie their advance.

On the maps that they'd procured from the elves, the jungle and the rivers were depicted as separate things; easily navigable. The truth, as always, was more complex. There were many, many rivers that cut through the hinterlands of Vieshlar, winding across the jungle like scars on a warrior's body. Some led all the way to the coast. Others fed into deep, murky pools where frogs sang incessantly.

This one led all the way to Callenspire, at least in theory. But the river was treacherous; it narrowed unpredictably at points and grew shallow without warning. More than once, they'd been forced to drag the lead barge across a sandbar or stop to remove an obstruction; a fallen tree, a collapsed bridge – even a sunken boat, at one point. Every day brought with it new challenges, and new frustrations.

Worse, it was now apparent that the riverguard had been shadowing them since the last toll lock. Occasional showers of javelins and arrows fell from the trees to scythe the decks clean, but by the time her warriors reached the shore, they were gone. She'd thought the frog-folk beaten, but apparently Gorcha had been exaggerating.

The barge passed underneath a set of low-hanging branches. They rattled as they struck the extra armor she'd had attached to the forward rail, and a swarm of insects flurried from them to spiral up into the darkening sky.

"Too hot," one of her warriors, Ryuk, growled, from where he lounged nearby. He was panting; they all were. The heat and wet of the jungle bore down on them like a physical weight. "It wasn't this hot before, I'd swear it."

"We were still near the coast," Shulgin said, licking her chops. She reached up to yank aside a dangling vine as it passed by and found, to her surprise, that it was a snake. A large one. It was as startled as she was, and it reared back with a hiss. She was faster, however, and her jaws snapped shut just shy of its head. She gave it a vicious shake and flung the body onto the deck, where it lay thrashing.

Ryuk grunted in pleasure. "Good eating on one of those."

"Then have at it, by all means," Shulgin snarled, as she spat out a mouthful of blood. "Cook it up with my compliments."

She wiped her muzzle with the back of her hand and prowled toward the rear of the vessel, ignoring the hasty salutes of the human auxiliaries she passed. Most were engaged in minor repairs; the barge had sustained damage at the last toll lock. There had been a witch of some small ability, and she'd frozen parts of the river and the barge itself before a well-placed mortar round had ended her blasphemy. Thankfully, the elves seemed to lack anything in the way of artillery, save for the occasional arbalest.

When she reached the raised aft-deck, she paused again to look at the long tail of river-craft that followed her own. Most were flat-hulled cargo barges, though a few fishing vessels were visible here and there. Anything that could carry cargo had been commandeered for her use. Her own vessel was driven upriver by hemicyon muscle; twenty warriors bent over the oars, pushing the barge against the current. They hauled the rest of the caravan in their wake by virtue of heavy chains and ropes – an old Xiryan trick, or so she'd been told. Of course, the Xiryan had used oxen.

"Bored, are we, Hejun's daughter?" Ushar, the expedition's second in command, called out from where he stood at the wheel. He was a skinny creature, with too many rings in his tattered ears and several teeth made from steel. He had been recommended by Admiral Khulan herself for his experience with river-craft, and Shulgin was grateful to have him – even if he was more informal than she liked in her subordinates. "Aye, always the way with these things," he continued, though she hadn't replied. "Nothing of interest for days and then, all at once, things get too interesting."

Shulgin sighed. "I don't suppose you've noticed anything amiss?"

Ushar scratched his muzzle. "Nothing of interest. If anyone is watching us, they're staying out of sight and downwind. Maybe they're too frightened to attack."

"Or maybe they're biding their time." Shulgin heard the hope in her voice and quashed it immediately. It wasn't seemly to be seen to be too eager for bloodshed. "We won't go unchallenged for long. They'll have to try and stop us before we reach Callenspire."

"Unless they've fled already." Ushar gave the wheel a twitch and looked at the trees stretching along the bank. "From what I've seen, these elves would rather run than fight."

"We caught them by surprise," Shulgin said.

Ushar grunted. "Maybe. Or maybe they're simply cowards."

Shulgin shrugged. "Some of them, maybe. Not all, I think. Which is all to the good, really. A cowardly people are no boon to the Empire." She sighed. "How many more toll locks between here and Callenspire?"

"At least three. Even the elves in Evanvale weren't sure of the exact number," Ushar said.

Shulgin snorted. "If they can't fight, and can't keep records, what are they good for?"

Ushar shrugged. "They make pretty things." He sniffed the air. "Do you smell that?"

Shulgin paused. She did, though she hadn't noticed it until just now. A particular odor; wet and musky. Unpleasant. Then, the whole jungle smelled unpleasant. She turned, studying the shore as it slowly slid by. Long shadows stretched across the waters, and the frogs were out. Their croaks sounded like music.

Then – silence.

Shulgin bristled. She had her sword half-drawn when the first bone-rattling croak sounded somewhere in the dark. "That's not good," Ushar growled. A second croak followed the first; almost painful in its volume and intensity.

The arrows came a moment later, falling like rain. Shulgin barked a warning, and human soldiers raised shields protectively over the rowers. Even so, some got through. One of her warriors convulsed at his oar, black foam splattering his muzzle as he keeled over onto the deck, overcome by poison. He was swiftly pulled aside and replaced by another, even as cries of alarm rose from the other craft.

A javelin thudded into the deck just shy of her paws, and she hopped back with a curse.

"Keep those shields up, or I'll feed you to the river myself!" she howled as a human stumbled beneath the impact of an arrow against his shield. She snarled in frustration. This was not the sort of fighting she'd been hoping for. "Cowards," she muttered, glaring at the shadow-darkened shoreline as a third volley fell across the line of boats.

Three volleys, and then they would be gone. That had been the pattern for the last two days. Always at different times of day, but otherwise identical. Three volleys, no more, no less. Then they would melt back into the jungle, leaving her caravan battered and flinching at shadows.

"Not cowards," Ushar said, as he plucked an arrow from his arm. "Cunning. Why risk themselves when they don't have to?"

"Where is their honor?" Shulgin snapped. "Do they have none at all?"

Another booming croak sounded across the river and was followed by the unsettling sound of heavy bodies moving far too swiftly through the water. Shulgin's ears pricked up. This was something new. She went to the rail and looked back. Torches had been lit on the line of boats to hold back the dark. By their light, she spied several bulky, toadlike forms bounding through the river.

She tossed back her head and howled a warning. Her voice carried eerily across the river – but too late. As she watched, the things bounded from the water and crashed onto one of the boats in the middle of the caravan, causing it to bob low in the water. She heard the boom of hulls striking each other and cursed.

By the light of the torches, she could see that the three were toads, but enormous. Each of them as large as a lionsnarl, at least. Immense, ugly things, and atop each was a rider; one of the river-folk, armed for war.

An instant later, the giant toads leapt in all directions, two heading to the rear, the third galumphing her way. Wherever they landed, they left death and destruction behind; mangled warriors and shattered decks littered their path. She drew her sword and howled again, calling for Ryuk and the others. The deck pitched beneath her feet as the giant toad landed on the aft-deck, shattering the rail as it did so. Shulgin blinked splinters from her eyes as the toad-thing took a heavy step toward her, its wide mouth falling open to vent a wafting cloud of impossibly foul breath.

The riverguard on its back wore a feathered headdress and armor made from bone, as well as a crudely-stitched back-banner that depicted some insignia that she didn't recognize. He too had a sword and gave a croak of challenge as she raised her own. The toad-thing lunged, snapping deck-boards as it did so. She leapt aside, and her sword drew a weal of blood from its warty flesh. The rider slashed down at her, somehow holding his balance on his bucking mount. The blow caught her on the edge of her helmet, and she stumbled back. She heard Ushar cry out and saw that the toad was making a bee-line for him.

So that was the plan; kill the pilot, set the barge adrift. A good plan. But doomed. Shulgin thundered across the spasming deck and drove her sword into the toad's flank, eliciting a bellow of pain. The rider stabbed at her, and she caught the blade in her paw and yanked as hard as she could. Pain flared in her arm, but she managed to pull the riverguard from his steed and send him crashing to the deck. Pressing her injured hand to her chest, she tore her blade free of the toad and turned on the rider. He staggered upright and raised his sword as hers descended. Her steel shattered the bone of his blade and completed its arc in his skull, right between his bulging eyes.

The riverguard collapsed, and she stumbled to one knee, off balance. She heard an awful sound and turned to see the toad rising up over her. Then – a shriek of fire, and the great beast was tumbling away in a shower of entrails and tissue. The smell of fire-powder stung her nose, and through teary eyes she saw Ryuk approaching.

"My apologies for taking your kill, Matriarch," he said. "We saw an opening and took it." He gestured to the rocket-team behind him. Shulgin gave them a nod of thanks and rose to her feet.

Croaks sounded from the shore, and she knew that someone was calling for a retreat. But the damage was no doubt done. How many had she lost this time? She shook her head and looked at Ushar. At least things were still moving.

Ushar met her gaze and inclined his head. "I suppose I owe you some thanks, Hejun's daughter." Then, with a laugh, he added, "I told you so. Nothing of interest, and then too much – all at once!"

CHAPTER TWENTY-THREE
Hannah

The airship, *Thunderchild*, drifted out over the shore, its sky oars deftly turning the vessel in the direction of the Xirkaali camp below. One of three such vessels now coasting through the skies of Vieshlar, *Thunderchild* was more heavily armored than its predecessors, being the first designed solely for war, though it had not yet been tested on the battlefield. But that had changed over the last few days.

A signal-bell attached to the main mast sounded, and the crew scrambled to positions. Guns were rolled out, and explosive charges readied for deployment, as they had been the last three times this operation had been performed. The airship continued its slow pivot, approaching the camp from the direction of the sea.

On the upper deck, Hannah gripped the rail, studying the approaching camp with interest. Like the others they'd hit, it was a well-built thing; not so much sprawling as expansive. She'd expected something cruder; more barbaric. A heavy palisade had been erected around the periphery of the camp, and an orderly arrangement of tents occupied its center. Larger structures – towers and outbuildings, mostly – were being erected, and the palisade was being extended in several places, as if in preparation for new buildings.

"They're settling in for the long haul," Cogman murmured at her elbow. She nodded in agreement. As Ser Aeron had said, the camps were like an iron claw, hooked into the coast. This one even had a makeshift wharf where supply vessels could dock. A war-junk sat some distance from the shore, and she marked its position. If they had time, they'd take a run at it, but the camp was their primary objective. She estimated there to be around five or six hundred Xirkaali in the camp, humans and hemicyons both. Too many.

"Get everyone up on deck," she said. "We need to hit them quick, before they can respond. I don't know about you, but I don't fancy trying to dodge any more rockets. Last time was bad enough."

Cogman saluted and headed belowdecks to roust the rest of the grenadiers. Hannah made her way to the aft-deck, where Captain Roob stood at the wheel. Roob was an older halfling, of the same generation as Anas, but with a sunnier disposition. He was missing an eye and had a propensity for chewing on sugar-root. His white hair was a fluffy cloud around his dark features, and he gave her a grin as she joined him. "We're on schedule, eh? In and out, and away before they pull on their socks."

"Hopefully," Hannah said. "Keep her steady for us, we'll do the rest."

Roob gave her a lazy grin and saluted. "Don't worry lass. I know my business."

Hannah returned the salute. Roob was right; he knew his business. He'd captained a barge for thirty years before volunteering to take command of

Thunderchild, and there was little he hadn't seen or endured. A steady hand, as Anas called him.

The vessel jerked suddenly, and she heard the groan of the sky-oars as they tried to compensate. Then – a burst of fire split the sky off the starboard bow. She stumbled against the rail. Another burst, this one on the port side. The crew weren't quite in a panic, but they were getting there.

"What's going on?" she asked, looking at Roob.

"Isn't it obvious, lass?" he shouted. "We're under attack!" The hull groaned thunderously as a rocket streaked past and burst overhead. "They must have finally looked up and noticed us, the dozy bastards."

As she watched, a rocket erupted from somewhere and arced upward. It couldn't quite reach *Thunderchild,* but the ship shuddered from the explosion regardless. It was clear that the airship was high enough up to be just out of range, but all it would take was one lucky hit and it would be no more, and every halfling aboard along with her. Roob grinned at her as he spun the wheel. "If you were planning to do something, lass, now is a good time!"

She turned and saw that Cogman and the others had assembled on deck. She hurried toward them as the deck pitched and yawed beneath her boots. Cogman helped her strap on her pack. "Alright lads, it's that time again! Let's show these Xirkaali what Ej ingenuity is capable of!" She motioned sharply, and the grenadiers hurried toward the rail.

She led the way, swinging herself over onto the outer curve of the hull. Then, with a silent prayer to the Missing Gods on her lips, she pushed off and away. A moment later, the cannister on her back vomited fire, propelling her into the air. She yanked on the wing-toggle, and they snapped out to full extension, enabling her to catch the wind.

It was always a heady moment, that first leap into the void. The world spun around her as she corkscrewed away from the airship before righting herself with a practiced roll of her shoulders and hips. She noted with satisfaction that Cogman and the others were right behind her and already falling into formation. They were still over the water, but that was all to the good. Dropping directly over the camp would have put them at risk of arrows. This way, they'd already be at top speed by the time they got in range.

It took months of practice before a grenadier was allowed to find their wings. Even then, some of them flamed out. Not everyone could handle the pull of the wind, the constant scream in the ears, the popping sensation as they hit the heights.

Hannah loved it all. She felt more at home with the wind rushing past her ears than anywhere else. She would stay airborne for days at a time, if possible. The world was beautiful from high up; the higher you went, the prettier it got.

She and the other grenadier captains had discussed strategy before the other airships had arrived from Gerinhaf. Until now, they'd simply been making supply runs to Callenspire, but Ser Aeron's strategy called for hitting the Xirkaali where it hurt; namely, their own supply depots along the coast.

The plan was the same for all the airships. Each was to hit a scattering of targets and then return to Callenspire along the Eastway route, doing any damage they could along the way. The airships gave them some advantage, but Ser Aeron was loathe to risk them – or their crews – unnecessarily. They only had the four at the moment that were sky-worthy, including *Thunderchild*. And it wouldn't be long before the Xirkaali brought one down, even if only by accident.

She banked, letting the wind guide her in the direction of the camp below. As she did so, she watched another rocket rise and explode. They were awkward things; unwieldy. At least these were. They reminded her a bit of the fireworks that her folk used on festival days, but these were far more dangerous. For one thing, they packed enough punch to set her wings wobbling even at a safe distance.

Hannah filed the thought away as she neared the target. She didn't bother to check on Cogman or the others. This was a standard drill for them. The camp rose up beneath them. She reached for one of the grenades that hung from her harness and palmed it, her thumb on the activator. She let the grenade fall. The palisade below erupted in a spray of fiery splinters, and Xirkaali scrambled for cover. A second grenade took out a section of tents. Fire licked across the canvas and spread swiftly through the camp. She rolled through the air, avoiding a ragged volley of arrows from a group of human soldiers, and palmed a third grenade.

Its detonation was like music to her ears. Explosions ripped across the camp in a symphony of destruction as Cogman and the others followed her example. They worked inward, hitting the palisade first and circling back to strike the tents and outbuildings. There'd be a supply depot of Xiryan fire-powder somewhere in the camp. Hitting it would limit the Xirkaali options as far as tactics.

She sent another grenade spinning out over the camp. The resulting explosion set men flying, or at least pieces of them. Three more explosions followed, hot on the heels of the first.

She heard horses screaming in pain, and men as well. Feeling slightly sick, she steeled herself for another pass. An arrow skidded off of the frame of her wing, startling her. She rolled instinctively and snatched a grenade from her harness. She primed it and let it fall.

Down below, the Xirkaali were attempting to regroup. She heard the rumbling thud of a mortar and saw a streak of fire cut through the air toward *Thunderchild.* Roob responded in kind. The explosive charges mounted on the hull were simply larger versions of the grenades she carried; flip a switch, and they rolled off to plummet to the ground below. In this case, they tore apart the crude wharf that the Xirkaali had built, as well as part of the seaward palisade. Rockets were launched from the camp to corkscrew through the air just shy of the airship's hull. Roob was cutting it close.

An arrow plinked off of her wing, drawing her attention back to her own flight path. She spied a group of human archers crowding one of the watchtowers. They sent another volley toward the grenadiers. A halfling – she couldn't tell who – cried out and veered off-course, slamming into the ground at fatal speed. The halfling's broken body bounced, carried by the still firing rocket, and pinwheeled out and away over the water.

She felt her stomach lurch and she banked toward the tower, reaching for another grenade. A lucky hit. That was all they needed. A lucky hit, and one of hers was gone. Who was it? No way to tell until she made it back – if she made it back. She swooped past the tower, tossing the grenade as she went. The explosion made the air shiver. She felt no satisfaction; the nausea redoubled.

Was this what war was? She'd imagined something more like a scrum against bandits, but on a larger scale. But this wasn't that; as on the estuary, she thought this was nothing less than a slaughter, and revulsion rippled through her. Ser Aeron was right – they weren't ready for this. Even if her people survived, they would be irrevocably changed.

The camp was burning. Smoke boiled up into the sky, obscuring much of the area. She could hear horses screaming, and other animals howling and roaring. She ducked her head and swooped low, trying to get below the smoke, to take stock of the damage they'd done. Was it enough? It was hard to tell.

Another grenadier had the same idea but went too low, too fast. He skidded off the internal palisade, and his efforts to correct course slowed him long enough for a hemicyon to leap from the palisade and bear him to the ground. Hannah made to go to his aid, but too late. The hemicyon's sword pinned the unlucky grenadier to the ground, igniting the rocket cannister's contents in the process. The resulting conflagration hammered the air and nearly sent Hannah crashing into an outbuilding.

Too many close calls. It was time to go. She made a circular gesture with her fist and pulled up. She shot toward the sky, away from the camp. Cogman was waiting for her.

"Time to go, I think," he shouted, laughing. Soot stained his face and gear. He made as if to add something else, but his eyes suddenly widened and he pointed toward the sea.

Hannah turned her head to see rockets streak from the decks of the war-junk toward the airship. Her heart seized in her chest as *Thunderchild* shuddered; one of the rockets impacted against her hull. Detonations ripped through the lower decks, and Hannah watched in horror as the airship banked awkwardly away from the camp, smoke billowing from the wounds in its hull. The airship wavered and began to lose altitude. More rockets spiraled toward the wounded vessel, and fire filled the sky as it began to limp toward the jungle.

Pushing her horror aside, Hannah angled herself toward the war-junk. Cogman and the others followed. She spied the rocket crews, and grenades rolled from her hands as she passed over the deck. She ignored the outraged howls of the Xirkaali and the screams of the human crew. The subsequent blasts gutted the war-junk, and she quickly banked away from it and in pursuit of the dying *Thunderchild.* Roob might be able to keep *Thunderchild* airborne, but Hannah feared otherwise. If the ship went down, there'd be no saving it.

The airship was reeling now, like a drunkard in the town square. It slewed low over the jungle, its hull smashing against the canopy in a slow collapse.

Smaller explosions somewhere inside caused it to shudder. As she watched, one of the golden lift-globes snapped off and vanished into the jungle.

And then, after what felt like an eternity, *Thunderchild* went down with a groan, breaking trees in half as it struck the ground!

CHAPTER TWENTY-FOUR
Valan

"He did what?" Aeron asked in disbelief. Valan took a swig of wine, emptying his cup. They sat together in the council room. Maps were scattered across the table, and stacks of reports from gladestalkers and those fleeing down the Eastway, as well as the occasional straggler from the jungle. Aeron had been going through them when Valan had interrupted him with the latest news.

The diplomat smiled sadly and poured himself another drink from the jug on the table. He didn't offer Aeron one; the halfling wasn't much of a drinker. "As I said, it appears he countermanded your orders, regarding the toll locks. Their garrisons are to defend them to the death. According to the last report from Kortys, we've lost three already to the Xirkaali explosives. And the soldiers defending them."

Aeron groaned and covered his eyes. "He must realize…"

"He doesn't," Valan said, firmly. "Solibos sees retreat as weakness. Even when it makes strategic sense." He sat back. "Thankfully, he didn't also countermand your orders to reinforce the last one. Work is going well on it, I trust?" The last of the toll locks was a half-day's travel from the city, at the first bend in the river. It was in the best condition of the lot, owing to its proximity, but it was still in a state of some disrepair.

Aeron nodded slowly. "Makki is doing what she can. I was counting on them having extra manpower from the other garrisons to help. My people can only do so much."

Valan nodded sympathetically. The halflings were as industrious as he'd heard. In the days since their arrival, they'd organized the evacuation, food collection, and the like. And, of course, their grenadiers were doing their best to loosen the Xirkaali hold on the coast and spy out the movements of the enemy.

The problem was, as Aeron said, the halflings couldn't do everything. Valan's people had to do the rest, and many of them weren't happy about it. It wasn't that they didn't understand the necessity; it was that they resented it. Callenspire had remained inviolate for centuries. Even during the worst of the war against the riverguard, the city had never been truly threatened. Many simply couldn't conceive of an attack on it.

Valan pushed the thought aside. "In good news, Kortys also sent word that he has made common cause with a tribe of riverguard. The Mudbelly folk. From what I've been told, their territories are mostly around the Vieshlar River and the estuary. That'll come in handy, I think."

"Definitely," Aeron said, studying a map. "We won't be able to hold the toll lock though. Even with the help of the riverguard. At best we can slow the Xirkaali down." He paused. "I don't suppose you've heard from your Neritican friend?"

Valan shook his head. "No, sadly. Though if the riverguard have decided to deal themselves into this game, he must be doing something." He set his cup down. "I don't think we can count on their aid any time soon."

Aeron leaned back and closed his eyes. He looked tired. Valan didn't envy him the responsibility they'd thrust upon him. "Why me?" Aeron asked, after a moment.

"What do you mean?"

"Why did he pick me?"

Valan sighed. "For what it's worth, I don't believe that he did. I don't think any of this is Axel's doing; not really. He is as much a victim of fate as we are." He paused. "No, say, rather, servant. Not victim. We are not victims, you and I."

Aeron slumped. "No. The victims are the innocent folk caught in the middle." He rubbed his face and groaned. "I haven't slept well since we heard about the Xirkaali. First the war in Rhodia, then the orcs, and now this. I feel like a piece of iron that's been hammered too long." For a moment, Valan wondered if he'd made the right choice, suggesting Aeron take command. Then the halfling looked up, and Valan saw a steely glint in his eyes. The strategist took a deep breath and reasserted himself. "The reports from the Eastway are fragmentary. I'll need to see it for myself. And the river flotilla as well."

Valan sat up. "Are you certain that's wise?" Solibos would no doubt take advantage of Aeron's departure to throw yet more mud on the halfling's all-but nonexistent reputation.

"Trosbert can oversee the preparations in my absence. My real work won't begin until the enemy gets here. And if all goes well, we won't have to face them immediately. Speaking of which… how's that going?"

"You're referring to the bridge," Valan said. The bridge was a continuing spot of contention; work had begun to bring it down, but slowly. Half of the older families in the city were threatening to riot over it, and the other half wanted to bring it down faster. "Solibos is dragging his feet on his responsibilities, I fear."

"Intentionally?"

"You could say that."

"Meaning?"

"I mean he's planning a coup," Valan said.

Aeron stared at him in incomprehension. "You can't be serious."

Valan smiled. In many ways, Aeron was as naive as a child; all the halflings were. They had no understanding of how politics worked among other races. "I am, sadly. He made his intent very clear not long after you arrived. He wants to take control of the city, for his own ambitions."

Aeron blinked. "This is because of me?"

"Not as such. Don't take it the wrong way, but you're incidental." Valan poured himself another drink. He paused. How much had he had already? That he had to ask meant it was too much. He set the cup aside. "Most likely, he won't strike until you've completed reinforcing the defenses. Then he'll move to take Lady

Merytan into protective custody and arrest me. Only then will he try and force you from the city. Likely by ordering you to do something foolish – a reconnaissance in force or some-such. Then he'll sit back and take the glory. Such as it is."

"He thinks it'll be that easy?" Aeron asked, incredulously. Valan smiled thinly.

"Yes. He's an idiot. More, he is a privileged idiot. Only rarely has the world deigned to deny Solibos his desires. He cannot conceive of failure; of defeat." Valan paused. "In many ways, he is the epitome of our people. He is skillful and arrogant, and also blind to the realities of a world which has largely left him behind."

Aeron was silent for a moment. "I knew he was up to something, but this? He must be mad. There's a war on!"

Valan sighed. "The truth is, we elves have turned politics into a form of entertainment. Games for the bored and the ambitious. Solibos sees nothing wrong with undermining you – us – because that is what a southern prince does when he finds himself in an awkward position. He schemes himself a way out." He tapped the table unhappily. "And, truthfully, we of the northern kingdoms are no better. It is in our nature, I think. Frankly, it is almost certainly what has led us to the current sorry state of affairs."

He felt the red kernel of a headache throbbing at the base of his skull. War was not inevitable, and yet, somehow, otherwise rational beings inevitably found a way to start one. He rubbed his brow and decided to have another drink after all.

Aeron sat back. "We don't know much about them, do we? The Xirkaali, I mean. Not really. Just what we've seen and heard, but nothing solid. It's all guesswork and assumption."

"It's hard to come by. They are a large empire, I know that much. And powerful." Valan paused. "I'm told the Ophidians might know more, but we can't very well ask them, can we? And the vaunted libraries of Callenspire know more about the Xiryan than the empire that now rules their territories." He smiled sadly. "The Xirkaali have long been an insular people. Given how the world treated their ancestors, one cannot blame them."

"What I'd like to know is why they invaded," Aeron said.

Valan studied his cup. A question he'd asked himself more than once. "I have no answers for you. Some months ago, these Xirkaali sent a delegation to deliver their demand for our surrender. We were to be made a satrapy of their empire; we did not have a say in how or when this was to occur, only that it must and refusal would be viewed… poorly."

Aeron said nothing. Valan cleared his throat and continued.

"Three times they came," he said, softly. He felt suddenly very tired. "We – I – didn't understand. I assumed it was some cultural miscommunication, but no. Three times, no more, no less. And when negotiations broke down for the third time, they declared war."

Aeron paused as the full import of Valan's words sank in. "You didn't believe them."

Valan smiled thinly. "No. We didn't. We assumed it was a ploy – a tactic, to soften our stance. We have often used similar stratagems ourselves, when the situation called for them."

Aeron sat back. "Except they invaded."

"Yes, and here we are. Perhaps we should have surrendered, eh?" Valan laughed sourly. "But no. We elves have armored ourselves in pride, and to kneel before another is unthinkable. As I said, Solibos is the epitome of our people… for better or worse."

Aeron was silent for a moment, and Valan wondered what he was thinking. Then the halfling knocked on the table with his knuckles. "It doesn't matter, I suppose. What's done is done, and now we have to do what we can."

"Another saying of the old gaffers?" Valan asked, in amusement.

Aeron smiled. "Something like that." He cleared his throat. "The airships should be completing their runs and returning here in the next day or so. I'll catch a ride with Anas and see what there is to be seen. Given what you've just told me, I have no doubt that Solibos will be ecstatic. Do you think you can keep him under control while I figure out what to do about him?" He hesitated. "Unless you have a suggestion?"

"We could kill him."

Aeron laughed sourly. "No. I don't think so."

"Are you sure? I know a poison-dealer in the market."

Aeron shook his head. "No poison."

Valan chuckled. "Your folk have a lot to learn about civilized discourse. A bit of poison never hurt anyone – well, anyone besides the person who ingests it, I mean." He slumped lazily in his seat. "But yes, I will do my utmost to keep him contained. I intend to inform Lady Merytan of his ambitions as well, though I expect she's had her suspicions for some time. He isn't exactly subtle."

"No. I thought you elves were known for it."

"Well, we can't all be perfect," Valan said. "Just me, really." He toasted Aeron with his cup. "Here's to a safe journey. Hopefully we're all still here when you get back."

CHAPTER TWENTY-FIVE
Gorrup

Gorrup paused, listening to the sounds of the jungle. It was never quiet; there were always noises. The hum of insects, the scream of prey-animals, the crackle of branches. But something different had intruded upon the usual cacophony. He couldn't tell what it was, only that it was something different – and unwelcome. Nor was it the first time he'd had such a feeling since setting out on this foolish endeavour.

The water here was murky and sluggish, and barely up to his thigh. But the *Ril'uwa* thought of it as a road. To them, such streams were as a cleared path through the thick forest. If one had the knack, one could follow them all the way to the coast, or even to the mountains. Thus far, the Xirkaali didn't have that knack, thankfully. It was one of the few real advantages that the river-tribes had over the invaders.

Absently, he scratched at his wounds. Shallow things, caused by human arrows. A bit of mud and they would be as good as new. But no time for that now. The ambush had not gone as well as they'd hoped; reinforcements had arrived too swiftly. Axel was nowhere to be seen, and the riverguard had retreated piecemeal into the tidal swamp. Gorrup had been doing his best to avoid Xirkaali patrols ever since, only surfacing when he had to, as he tried to get past them and to the sea.

Unlike the Neriticans, the river-folk couldn't stay under water indefinitely. Otherwise, he'd simply have stayed out of sight for the duration. Worse, the Xirkaali were clearing the jungle, building dams; not just for their own use, he thought, but also to hamper the movement of the river-tribes. They were clever, these dogmen. As clever as Axel had claimed; perhaps more so.

Were the lords of Medu'Syth afraid of the Xirkaali? Was that why they refused to fight? The question sat like an unpleasant weight on Gorrup's mind. He had only rarely visited that great city of coral and current, and only as a companion of the chieftains of the river-tribes, on their rare visits to the territories of their allies.

Gorrup had always had the distinct impression that the water-breathers found them useful, but nonetheless kept them at arm's length – save when they needed something. It galled him that they must beg for help.

He made to slide back into the water but paused again, balanced among the tree-roots. What was it that had caught his attention? A sound? No – the opposite. An absence of sound. The jungle was never quiet… except now it was. He turned, scanning the bank behind him. Nothing moved. Nothing out of place.

An arrow streaked out of the shadows beneath the trees and skidded across the side of Gorrup's warty skull. He grunted and ducked aside as two more arrows flashed toward him. He cursed and pushed away from the roots, into the current's pull. Dark shapes poured out of the trees, howling like damned souls. The hounds were massive beasts, twisted by some form of dark magic into reptilian monsters. They moved swiftly across the uneven ground, bounding into the water with an unsettling eagerness.

Gorrup swatted one away and crushed a second with his shield. A third and fourth leapt on him, their fangs tearing into his armor. He shrugged them off and sent them flying into the water. Before he could capitalize on his freedom, he saw that the hounds weren't alone. Xirkaali, lightly armored in leather and animal hides, emerged from the undergrowth. They carried bows, and loosed arrows at him as he plunged under the surface and began to swim. Arrows pierced the water around him, but none came close to hitting him. Almost as if they weren't trying to do so. But why –

He got his answer a moment later as he found himself tangled in a fishermen's net. Or rather several, woven together with steel hooks. He twisted and turned, trying to tear free, but the only way to do so was to surface. He erupted from the river with a roar, wrenching the net from him, ignoring the bloody gouges the hooks carved into his flesh. Immediately, a volley of arrows clattered against his armor. One punched into his leg, and he snapped it off with a bellow of rage, ignoring the pain of the injury.

The Xirkaali were all around him, splashing into the shallows, arrows nocked and ready. He tightened his grip on his mace and swung it out, driving them back.

"Back," he croaked. "Get back or I'll crush your skulls!"

"One, perhaps. Two or three, possibly. But not all."

The voice was sharp; ugly. Like a knife on flesh. A hemicyon clad in black robes stepped out of the trees to his left, carrying an ugly looking sickle attached to a heavy chain. The hemicyon was missing an eye, but the remaining one gleamed with savage glee. "Is that surprise I see on your face, mud-dweller? That one of us knows your savage tongue?"

Gorrup glowered at the hemicyon. The *Ril'uwa* tongue was a thing of liquid beauty; all clicks, croaks, and chirps. Few land-dwellers could grasp its intricacies. The hemicyon crouched on the shore and began to idly swing his sickle.

"I learned from a captive. Captives, I should say. Elves who spoke your heathen dialect. Witch-hunters must have skill with languages you see, the better to hunt our prey. My name is Kungas. Where is the witch?"

"Which witch?" Gorrup asked.

Kungas showed his teeth. "Are you stupid, then? If so, you are no use to me. A shame, that. Kill him."

As the command left him, Gorrup tensed and sprang, his immensely strong legs carrying him out of the water and onto the bank in a single bound. His club slammed into a hemicyon warrior and crushed him to a twitching pulp.

He was among them in moments, each blow casting a broken body into the air. But there were more of them – too many. Arrows pricked his hide, jutting like quills from his back and arms. He barreled toward Kungas, but the hemicyon leapt away from him, retreating. Drawing him in. He could see it, but he couldn't resist the urge to pursue, to kill his enemy.

Kungas dodged aside from every blow, moving swiftly. He spun his sickle in a tight arc and sent it hurtling toward Gorrup's legs. Gorrup caught it with his mace and yanked the chain from Kungas's grip. The witch-hunter looked startled by Gorrup's strength and backpedaled swiftly, whistling sharply as he went.

As if in answer, howls erupted from the trees. A trio of hairy shapes bounded into view. Hemicyons, but larger than the others, nearly matching Gorrup in size. They wore no armor, merely savage totems and decorations, and carried no weapons save their claws and fangs. They pounced on him, and he was hard-pressed to keep them from his throat. Claws tore at his flesh as he caught one a blow that sent it tumbling back.

The other two tackled him into the water. Teeth sank into his arm. He drove his mace into his opponent's belly, doubling the creature over even as its companion bit at his neck. He was forced to drop his mace and grapple with the second hemicyon. It was harder than it ought to have been. He was injured, perhaps worse than he'd assumed. The arrows, the bites – the water was full of his blood.

He had been injured before; what warrior hadn't? But this was different. There was nowhere to retreat to, and no allies to aid him. He was alone, surrounded by the enemy. The thought enraged him, and he wrenched his attacker from his back and slammed him against the river's bottom. He held the struggling hemicyon there as the beast clawed at him with increasing desperation.

The creature went limp, but he had no opportunity to celebrate. The second had recovered, and the hemicyon's claws tore a hole in his side. Gorrup roared in pain and floundered to the side. The hemicyon lunged for him again, and again, snarling and biting. It was all Gorrup could do to hurl the beast back. The creature was in a state of frenzy, and Gorrup, already off-balance, fell to his knees in the river, unable to fend off his opponent's attacks. He looked up as the hemicyon charged toward him. "Failed," he muttered, angry at himself. But mostly angry at the Xirkaali.

It lent him strength. He made to retrieve his mace but froze as he heard the snarl of a hemicyon. Kungas had reclaimed his own weapon and stood on the bank above Gorrup, spinning it. More of his bow-armed warriors crept into view, arrows ready to be loosed. Bowstrings hummed as they were pulled taut. Gorrup prepared himself for one last leap, but his strength was flagging. He flexed his hands. He might be able to catch Kungas and crush him, at least. That much he could do.

"No."

The hemicyons paused. Kungas turned. A second hemicyon, this one in ornate armor, decorated with swirling serpentine carvings, splashed upriver toward them. She was bigger than the ones who followed her and carried a large halberd in one hand. "I have never seen one of these before. It is larger than the others. Stronger, too. I would see how strong." She spoke the Neritican common tongue better than her subordinate, as well, Gorrup noted.

"Admiral, I –" Kungas began.

"Quiet, Witch-Hunter. You have had your fun. Now I will have mine." She removed her cloak and let it fall into the water. She looked at Gorrup. "You do not know me, savage. I am Khulan, called Kaiju-killer by the Yan. I have killed creatures larger than you, and with only my two paws."

Gorrup retrieved his mace. "I will not die so easily as all that."

Khulan nodded. "No. I expect not."

With a croaking roar, he sprang toward her, mace held high. Khulan slid forward effortlessly through the water, the blade of her halberd shining as it cut the murky light. Gorrup crashed down some distance past her. His blow had knocked the helm from her head, but she remained standing. Her own blow, however, had cut him open. Blood spilled down from his side and into the water. The pain came a moment later; sharp and unyielding. He staggered with a groan.

"Arrows. Hooks. Fangs. Blades. And still you stand," Khulan said, flicking his blood from her blade. "A warrior like you could find much renown in the Empire, once you know your place."

Gorrup raised his mace. "My place is wading through your blood."

Khulan gave a growling laugh. "Good. Good. Come then, brute – come and learn the true might of the Xirkaali Empire. And if you survive, maybe I will have some use for you."

Gorrup charged again. He would not yield. Could not.

Another flash of steel. More pain. His mace fell from his grip. He sank down into the crimson water, unable to catch his breath. He fumbled for his mace but could not find it.

Failed.

He had failed to keep Axel safe. Failed to protect his people. Failed to get to Medu'Syth. He tried to rise – and failed in that too. He heard Khulan approach. She crouched before him, studying him with a look of mingled satisfaction and pity.

"No," she said, looking into his eyes. "No, you will not die here, brute. I will not allow it." She rose and gestured. "Get him up. Take him back to camp. I want him healthy when I gift him to my cousin. She will be most appreciative, I think." She looked down at him. "You belong to the Xirkaali now." She bared her teeth at him.

"In time, you might even thank me."

CHAPTER TWENTY-SIX
Hejun

Hejun studied the captives with a careful eye. They knelt before her atop the sea-wall, bound and weaponless, overseen by human guards as well as Hejun's subordinate commanders. Several of the elves were injured, and the stink of their blood hung heavy on the salt-tinged air.

"They fought well," Gorcha said, grudgingly. She had a red cut on her muzzle and a bandage around her leg. Hejun herself was uninjured, besides a slight scorching she'd received as she'd led her bodyguard through a gap in the landward wall.

"Too well," Hejun murmured.

The climb up the sea-wall had proved a costly strategy, both in terms of lives and materials. They'd wasted too many rockets and lost too many hemicyons for it to be considered a rousing success. Gorcha knew this and was looking appropriately subdued. Hejun had no intention of chastising her further. After all, she had agreed to let them make the attempt. Ultimately, the blame was hers.

Even after the sea-wall had fallen to her warriors, it had taken days to take full control of the city. The elves had fought for every shop and street with a ferocity that had surprised her, though perhaps it shouldn't have. Two of her better commanders had died during the attack; one slain by elven arrows, the other burnt to death.

Still, in the end, Ruhaindo had fallen. The city was hers, and already her forces were moving to occupy it. There was, as yet, no sign of reinforcements from Blackthorn, but it was only a matter of time. A smart commander would seek to pen her up in the city and keep her from advancing any further west. For the time being, that suited her just fine.

She'd come to the realization that this invasion could not be accomplished as quickly as she might otherwise have hoped. It would take many months, if not years, to stabilize the Vieshlar region enough to expand as the plan called for. She pushed the thought aside and turned her attention back to the captives.

Only a handful of the enemy's officers had survived the final push into Ruhaindo. Most had died fighting; some had been killed attempting to escape the city. A few had managed a fighting withdrawal through a heretofore unknown passage in the sea-wall.

One caught her eye. His armor was of better quality than the rest, and he had the face of a warrior unused to defeat. "You are… Sarkan, yes?" she said, in a poor approximation of the elvish tongue. "Prince of this city."

He peered up at her like something he'd scraped from his boot. "And you are the leader of these street-curs?" he asked, in turn. She licked her jaws in annoyance and crouched before him.

"I am Hejun Ironeyes."

"I do not care what you call yourself," Sarkan said. "A cur is a cur, regardless of the name it gives itself." He looked away, out over the city that he'd ruled. "What now, hmm? Will you burn it, or turn it into a kennel?"

Hejun felt the eyes of Gorcha and her other subordinates on her. Such an insult could not be safely ignored as she was otherwise inclined to do. Sarkan no doubt knew things of value; but he had cast his challenge into her teeth, and now there was nothing for it. She sighed and rose. "Cut him loose, and give him his sword."

"Let me do it, Matriarch," Gorcha growled, limping forward. "Give me the honor of teaching this pitiable creature what it means to insult a warrior of the Kaali."

Hejun shook her sword. "No, Gorcha. He insulted me, and so I shall be the one to answer it. Now, who has his sword?"

One of her other subordinates, Ayjuk, stepped forward, holding a sheathed blade in her paw. "Good steel," she said as Hejun took the weapon. "Light."

Hejun nodded. She drew the sword partially from its sheath and peered at the delicate symbols etched into the gleaming surface of the blade. "Perhaps they will teach us the secret of its forging, when they have learned their place."

Sarkan was on his feet and rubbing his wrists. She tossed the sword to him, and he caught it smoothly. He drew it and cast the sheath aside. Hejun drew her own blade and eyed the elf warily. "It is a shame. Your people will need leaders such as you in the coming years."

"Puppet-rulers, you mean? No. I think you'll find plenty of those without me." Sarkan sniffed and looked around. "A shame. This was a lovely city once."

"It will be again," Hejun said.

"I don't think so." Sarkan slid toward her, moving with a sinuous grace. He struck at her, his sword darting swiftly – but she was ready. Her own blade batted his aside time and again. Yet he did not retreat or surrender. Instead he pressed her, knowing that the end was inevitable. She hated to kill him; it was a waste of a good commander and a good warrior, both of which would sorely be needed in the years to come.

For a few moments, she allowed herself the luxury of being lost to the dance of steel. Each instant stretched into the next, an infinity of such, where the only sound was the scrape of one blade against the next, and the harsh panting of their breath. It was beautiful and perfect, and as with all such things, it ended far too soon.

Sarkan stumbled, left himself open. She ran him through, felt the shock of her blade entering his chest and erupting from his back. His sword fell with a clang, and he looked up – and she knew that it was not he who had committed the error. His hands caught her arms and he shoved her back, toward the precipice of the sea-wall. Gorcha and the others cried out in alarm, but Hejun felt a strange calmness descend on her. It was glorious, this. Would she have done any less? She liked to think not. But it was not meant to be.

She planted her paws and pivoted, swinging Sarkan out over the waters. His gaze was cold; fierce. He was dead, but refused to die. Not alone. She forced her sword up, lifting him away from her. His slackening grip loosed her, and then he was sliding off of her sword and away. The sea-wind took him, snatched him – and he was gone.

Hejun looked at the blood on her blade and then at the others. "A brave warrior," she growled. "May such bravery come to serve us, in time." She tore a strip from her cloak and used it to clean her sword. She looked at the surviving elves. "What of you? Will you serve us, or will you join your lord in death?"

The elves were silent, but she could read the answer in their eyes. She looked at Gorcha and gave a terse nod. Gorcha growled in satisfaction and drew her blade.

Hejun watched as the elves died. It was the least she could do.

When it was done, their bodies were cast into the sea. She rubbed her muzzle tiredly as the work was carried out. Afterward, she dismissed the others. Only Obair remained behind.

"A foolish stunt," he said, after a time. "He might have taken you with him."

"He insulted me. It needed answering."

"You could have simply taken his head. Gorcha and the rest –"

"Would have judged me weak, old man." She looked at him. "Even after all this time, you still seem puzzled by this. An insult must be met firmly, and swiftly. Our honor is all we truly have in this world. To allow another – an enemy – to besmirch it, is unconscionable."

"Like mother, like pup," Obair said.

Hejun growled and tugged on her ear. "Yes, well, some lessons sit better than others." She paused. "Has she sent back word?"

"Everything proceeds according to plan."

Hejun studied him. "And this… worries you?"

Obair nodded. "Somewhat. Remember the old adage: a strategy is only a strategy until one meets the enemy, and then it is no more than a memory."

"You fear she will not react swiftly enough."

"The opposite; I fear she will react without thinking. Shulgin is clever; adaptable. But she is headstrong. Foolish, at times. Certain of her own prowess."

"Yes. Which is why I made the decision to send her, and not one of the others." Hejun looked out over the bay. "She needs seasoning, that one. A test, which she will either pass or fail, as the gods will. But she must endure it nonetheless, if she is to take up the mantle of matriarch." She looked down, to the rocks far below. "Honor seeps away like blood from a wound. It must be replenished; purified. One must strive against all odds, at all times, else one becomes soft." She glanced at Obair. "Your ancestors were soft. That is why we defeated them. They allowed themselves to imagine that they had overcome all challenges, and thus, grew decadent in their boredom."

"But we know better now," Obair said. Hejun nodded.

"Yes. The elves, on the other hand, do not. They thought themselves masters of all they surveyed. Some will use that certainty to hone themselves, like a duelist's blade. Others will become soft." Hejun clenched a fist. "We must make them into something better. Something stronger. Raw iron, forged into steel." She pounded her fist into her palm. "Only steel can survive that which is to come. Steel, wielded by a Xirkaali hand."

They stood in silence for several moments. Then, Obair cleared his throat. "A messenger from Admiral Khulan arrived earlier. She has taken a captive."

"Oh?"

"A Neritican."

Hejun turned, interested now. "When?"

"A few days ago. A brute of a creature that the elves call a – a pondwarden. One of the river-folk, or closely allied with them. It's uncertain exactly which."

"And?"

"She seems pleased. The witch-hunter accompanying her is less so. Apparently he was on the hunt for a witch of some ability. Another Neritican, but not a type we've encountered before. It seems the water-breathers are still interested in us." Obair joined her at the edge of the wall and shaded his eyes as he studied the mouth of the bay. "I think we should consider an attack imminent."

"How imminent? Today? Tomorrow?" Obair was silent. Hejun chuckled. "But you are right, old man. They will come. Whether it is to aid the elves or simply to destroy us, the Trident Realm will mobilize to challenge us. So will the kingdoms of the north and the south. If they have not already." She paused. "Has there been word from the other Claws? Anything at all?" Messages came by ship, when they came at all. But word from the rest of the continent had been sparse. The other matriarchs were busy with their own sieges and their own invasions. She knew this, and yet it still irked her. She desired the whole picture, if only for her own satisfaction.

Obair shook his head. "None, of late. I cannot say whether things go well – or ill. Perhaps it is best to concentrate on things we can control, and not on things we cannot."

"That sounds like something a Xiryan philosopher might say."

Obair smiled. "There are one or two in my lineage, much to the chagrin of my ancestors. But the saying is a good one, nonetheless." He looked back at the city. "What now, my lady? Ruhaindo has fallen. The bay is yours. Blackthorn and Grishamvu will follow in a few weeks, if not days."

Hejun bared her teeth. "Callenspire. Let us hope Shulgin is up to it."

CHAPTER TWENTY-SEVEN
Hannah

Hannah and her grenadiers trooped wearily through the close-set trees. They were bathed in sweat and grime, their muscles aching. Even with folded wings, the jetpacks were awkward to maneuver on the ground. It was like trying to lug a sack of grain with one arm. The crash had torn a deep trench in the jungle, and bits of burning wood were still scattered in its wake, even three days later. It made the trail easy to follow, at least.

"Do you think there'll be survivors?" Cogman murmured at her elbow.

"I don't know," Hannah whispered back, more harshly than she'd intended. Cogman had asked the same question every day since the crash, and she had no better answer for him now than she had the first time. Were there survivors? Maybe. Maybe not.

There was still smoke on the air; the humidity weighed it down between the trees, trapping it. She spied a chunk of golden metal, impaling a bent tree; bits of hull, resting in impact craters deep enough to drink from. Here and there, other bits of wreckage; some of it bloody. She could hear jungle cats crying out hungrily in the canopy above. No telling what else was prowling about, following the same trail that they were.

Thunderchild had crashed three days ago. It had taken them the better part of a day to find a clear place to land; one free of Xirkaali patrols. It had taken the better part of the second day to find the trail. A third, to follow it here, to its end.

And what an ending it was. Awful and impossible, all at once. *Thunderchild* had impaled itself on several now-shattered trees and lay half in the air, its aft section crumpled against the ground and its prow jutting up like a tombstone.

"Missing gods preserve them," Cogman muttered as they hurried toward the site as quickly as the packs allowed. The crash had scraped away a good deal of undergrowth.

The next few moments were ones of confusion and horror. Dead halflings lay scattered across the newly-made clearing. The survivors had dragged themselves or others from the wreckage and set up hastily-built shelters with whatever they could find. Some graves had been dug, but not nearly enough. Animals prowled the outer edges of the wreck, gnawing on the unburied dead with abandon.

Hannah froze for a moment, overwhelmed by the sight of it all. She felt as if she were standing outside of herself, looking at it all from some impossible distance. This was what Ser Aeron had been afraid of when he'd begun to train them. She understood now, though she wished that she didn't. She swallowed and led the others into the clearing.

"Chase those beasts off," she said, in a ragged voice.

Cogman picked up a rock and sent it hurtling into the flank of something that resembled a dog, but with a ridge of spines on its back. It yowled and leapt away; the rest of its pack followed suit, fleeing before the grenadiers' approach.

Several of the survivors approached. All three sported bloody bandages; one walked with the aid of a makeshift crutch. Hannah recognized the first mate, Hasslefoot. He clutched his side, as if it pained him. From the pinkish stain on his bandages, Hannah suspected it did. "Thank the Missing Gods," he said. "We figured you'd been killed. Or worse."

"We thought the same of you," she said. Hasslefoot stumbled as he moved to greet her, and she caught him. He grinned weakly at her in thanks. "How many survivors?"

"Fifteen, maybe twenty. At least five are unaccounted for." His gaze grew vague. "Must have fallen over the side." He looked away.

"What about Roob?"

"Still in the ship. He – he got pinned, somehow. We can't get him out. Done what we could to make him comfortable." Hasslefoot grimaced. "It was only because of him that any of us survived," he went on. "But he paid the price for his courage, and then some. What wasn't burned was broken. He won't last more than another day or two. That he's lasted this long without the attention of a sauceror is a surprise…" He broke off into a coughing fit, his body convulsing. Hannah helped him to sit. There was blood on his hand when he pulled it away from his mouth.

"Supplies?" Hannah asked, softly.

"We scavenged what we could." He looked up at her. "It won't be enough to last us until rescue. I sent a couple of the lads into the jungle with a spare rifle a few hours ago, to see if they could scrounge us up something to eat." He hesitated. "They haven't come back. I thought you were them, at first."

Hannah nodded, her mind working through the possibilities. Maybe they'd gotten lost; maybe the jungle had claimed them. Or maybe… something else. She took a deep breath. "Right. We need to get moving. If the Xirkaali aren't on their way here already, they will be soon. We can't be here when they get here."

There was no time for shock; no time for the twinge in her stomach. Her people were counting on her. Ser Aeron was counting on her.

"Get everyone ready to go. If they can't walk, we'll carry them." Her stomach rumbled insistently. "And grab whatever supplies there are." They'd had little more than a pack of jerky between them in the three days since the crash, and whatever small game they could catch. She turned to Cogman. "You handle that. I'll handle the ship."

"What about the ship?" Cogman asked. Hannah tapped her bandolier with its remaining grenades. She palmed one.

"Remember what Anas said. We can't allow them to have it," she said. "I'll see to that myself." She hurried toward the wreckage, unbuckling her pack as she went. It would only get in the way of what she had to do.

Anas had drilled it into them the first day *Windwalker* had sailed out of the mountains. The tall-folk couldn't be allowed to get their hands on halfling technology. Better it be destroyed than that. It was the one advantage they had over their neighbors.

Hannah wasn't so sure about that, but she followed orders nonetheless. She crept carefully into the wreckage; every creak and shudder made her flinch. She climbed up and down, leaving a grenade here and there, tucked into nooks and crannies. She avoided looking at the bodies, or what remained of them. Avoided thinking about the smell, the way something unseen dripped into the gaps between broken decks.

She found Roob soon enough. He was pinned between two beams, his lower body hidden beneath a collapsed section of decking. Two other halflings sat beside him, keeping watch. One murmured her name to him, and he lifted his head.

"Took you long enough," he whispered. His eyes were bandaged, but his mouth was free.

"Still with us, old fool?" she asked.

He raised a bandaged hand, and she clasped it gently.

"Aye." He grinned. "You'll have to do better than this to get rid of me. I'll be back aboard a ship before you know it."

He grimaced suddenly, and his grip tightened. He convulsed, obviously in pain. Hannah looked at the others, but one, a crewman named Sagria, shook her head.

She was about to say something when, from outside, came a sharp whistle. She climbed to a gap in the hull and looked down. Cogman stood below her and gestured silently. Out of necessity, grenadiers developed a form of shorthand; trying to shout over the whine of rockets or the wind was a fool's game. But gestures were easy to do, and easy to remember. This particular gesture meant an unfriendly was approaching.

She bit back a curse and returned his gesture with one of her own; hers meant retreat. Cogman hesitated, and she gestured again, more sharply. If the Xirkaali were close, they had to run. Only the wounded couldn't. That meant they needed a distraction. She glanced at Sagria and the other crewman, a little fellow named Umer.

"Change of plans," she murmured. "I was going to tell you to go, but I need you to stay. Are you up for it?"

The two looked at one another, and then Sagria nodded.

"Weapons?" Hannah asked. Sagria hefted a rifle. Umer, a slightly panicked look on his face, lifted a sheathed sword. "Any good with that?" she asked, indicating the rifle.

"My da was a poacher," Sagria said.

Hannah nodded. "Don't shoot until I give you the signal." She crept back over to Roob, who was clearly listening. "We have trouble, old man. The Xirkaali will be here soon."

"I'm not leaving," Roob said. "A captain goes down with his ship."

Hannah wanted to argue, but the truth was, there was no way to get him out; and even if there was, there was no time. Instead, she took one of her remaining grenades and pressed it into his hands. "You know how to use one?"

He gave an undignified snort. "Teach your grandmother to suck eggs, why don't you?" He fumbled the grenade around for a bit but found the primer soon enough. He sighed. "I'll not let them have the ship, lass. But you be clear of it, eh? Lost enough crew to last me."

Hannah patted his shoulder. "Trust me, old man, by the time it comes to it, I intend to be far away and running for home."

She rejoined Sagria and Umer at the gap. It had a decent view of the clearing. Sagria balanced the barrel of her rifle on a splintered plank and settled down to wait. Umer was breathing heavily, on the edge of panic. Hannah patted him on the back, and he nearly dropped his sword. How old was he? Younger than her. Too young. No help for it now, though.

Down below, she could hear the underbrush rustling. She hoped Cogman had managed to get the others out of sight. A moment later, the first snout poked out of the brush. These Xirkaali weren't the armored warriors she'd seen before. Rather, these wore leather armor and carried swords and bows. There were three of them, and they crept into the clearing warily, nostrils flaring as they sought the scent of their prey. But halflings – Ej-folk, especially – knew how to hide better than most. They had experience, hiding.

That was the whole point of the grenades, the airships, all of it; to ensure that they never had to hide again. Or so some maintained. She wasn't so sure herself, especially at the moment. She hefted her grenade and watched the newcomers prowl about the clearing. They sniffed the dead and checked them for signs of life. One stiffened suddenly, ears pricked like an aralez that had just scented a rabbit.

He turned and growled something to the others. *The blood,* she thought. They could smell the blood of the injured. Unless she and the others acted quickly, they'd be after Cogman and the wounded. She glanced at the others. Sagria nodded. Umer swallowed nervously but nodded. He only had his sword, but that would have to be enough.

Hannah primed the grenade and tossed it.

The explosion was loud. Two of the hemicyons scrambled for cover. The third rolled on the ground, howling in agony. Sagria fired, and the injured scout fell silent. She began to reload. Howls rose from the brush. There were more than two of them out there. Hannah reached for another grenade – her last. She'd have to make it count. "When I toss it, we need to go. Run fast – don't look back."

"What about the captain?" Umer asked.

Hannah swallowed. "Roob knows what to do." She didn't look back at Roob, laying in the dark, waiting for – what? Death? Or one last moment of excitement? Regardless, the captain laughed hoarsely.

"Aye, I know what to do," he said. "You just be quick."

Hannah hurled the grenade toward where she'd seen one of the Xirkaali go. Then she shimmied out of the gap and landed hard on the ground. The explosion rocked the clearing, throwing up a cloud of dust and smoke. Umer followed her, losing his sword in the process. She dragged him to his feet as he scrambled to retrieve it, and shoved him toward the jungle. "Move!"

A Xirkaali came out of the smoke, blade in hand. Hannah went for her knife – but too slowly. Sagria's rifle barked and the Xirkaali staggered; dead or just injured, Hannah couldn't say. Sagria pelted through the smoke and past the hemicyon. Hannah joined her, howls following in their wake.

She knew – *hoped* – that the Xirkaali would ignore them in favor of taking the airship. That was what she'd do, in their place. So they ran, as fast and as far as they could. Even so, when the explosion finally came, it bowled them over. Trees snapped and fell. Heat scorched the air. Silence fell.

Hannah rolled over and climbed wearily to her feet. A few moments later, the birds began to call out once more. She waited, barely daring to breathe. But the only sound was the birds. At least for now. Belatedly, she realized that she'd left her pack. The thought saddened her in a way she couldn't explain. She looked at the others. "We need to go."

"Go where?" Umer asked, panting.

"Away from here, to start with." Hannah took a deep breath. They had to find the others and see about getting home. Even as the thought crossed her mind, somewhere in the jungle, something howled. She shook her head.

"We'll figure out the rest later."

CHAPTER TWENTY-EIGHT
Aeron

Windwalker shuddered slightly as a sharp wind rolled in from the west. Aeron gripped the rail hard enough to turn his knuckles white. He closed his eyes and tried to will his stomach to stop its sudden flip-flopping.

"I thought you were supposed to be observing," Anas said, from behind him. Aeron reluctantly opened his eyes and turned to the other halfling. Behind them, the airship crew went about their business with brisk efficiency. Anas held his crew to strict standards; they were the elite, as far as crews went. The first and best trained.

"I am."

"What exactly? The inside of your eyelids?" Anas chuckled and slapped Aeron on the arm. "Don't worry, lad. It'll pass."

"When?" Aeron muttered. Then, "That's the Eastway, then?"

He risked a look over the rail and studied the long stretch of road that ran through the northeastern edge of the jungle. The elves claimed to have built it long before Vieshlar had been lost and then reclaimed it from the jungle after the Winter War.

The road was impressive, in the way that everything the elves built was impressive. A defiant scar across the green face of the land from the coast to the wastes, constructed from magically raised and bent trees that intertwined into a solid, living stretch of road. Broken statues lined its length; some were merely empty pedestals, while others depicted some hero or scholar from elven history. Many of these were now subsumed in green shrouds of vine and moss, their identities forever obscured.

Where once trade caravans had traveled the road, it was now solely occupied by an army and the dust thrown up by its advance. *Windwalker* was staying out of rocket range, and high enough that the clouds might well conceal it from the Xirkaali below, but Aeron could nonetheless pick out the myriad troops that loped along the road and through the trees to either side. *Missing gods, there are so many of them,* he thought.

Human horsemen ranged far ahead, accompanied by hemicyons riding strange, leonine beasts. Behind them came a vanguard of armored hemicyons, marching in perfect formation. Human soldiers trotted in their wake, some carrying spears, others with bows and artillery. There were stranger things as well; towering apelike brutes, accompanied by human handlers and a half-dozen strange black cages that hurt his eyes to look upon for too long. The latter, at least, he knew something about thanks to reports from survivors of Evanvale. The cages somehow absorbed and redirected magic; something Merytan and the other mages had been interested to know, though they'd offered no plan to deal with it.

Anas whistled. "Nearly twenty-thousand of the buggers down there. But not a siege engine to be seen, unless they're in the supply wagons."

"They'll be coming by river," Aeron said, without looking up from the army. "They're marching light. Trying to get to us before we've got our defenses completed."

Anas grunted. "At the rate they're moving, they might just do it."

"That's what I'm afraid of." Aeron stepped back from the rail. Calculations ran through his head; not complicated – simple, like the edge of a blade. The Xirkaali outnumbered the defenders of Callenspire five to one; bad odds, any way you looked at it. Worse, that was a veteran army. Blooded in other conflicts, fresh off of victories against the elves. Numbers meant a lot; numbers and experience were an even worse combination.

The problem was, his own forces weren't simply inexperienced; they were raw. The aeronauts, the bulk of the grenadiers, the howitzers, all of them were new. Oh, they'd been tested, but not under battlefield conditions. What if they didn't work as promised? What then? It might be better for the elves if they weren't there at all.

Maybe Solibos was right. Maybe the Ej-folk were just a drain on resources. Maybe they should have stayed in the mountains. Maybe. Maybe. Maybe. The Riftforged Orcs had appeared so suddenly that there hadn't been time for uncertainties. It had been do or die, just like with Rhordia. But this was different. There was both too much time and not enough, all at once. He pinched the bridge of his nose, trying to push the uncertainties aside.

Not that the Xirkaali had it all their way. If the Eastway bridge could be taken down, it eliminated their easiest route to the city. They'd have to erect their own, under fire and vulnerable to a counter-attack.

If the bridge could be taken down. If, if, *if*. More uncertainties.

"Can those charges of yours be set off from a distance?" Aeron asked.

Anas frowned, but nodded. "Theoretically. You'd need to remove the activators and timers. They'd just be cannisters full of explosive powder. Why?"

Aeron rubbed his jaw thoughtfully. "Something I've been thinking about. By now, they know to watch the skies. But maybe they're not so observant of the ground. We string a few at certain points, set them off with fire arrows, or other explosives. That'd be enough to rout anyone. At least once."

Anas shrugged. "That's not a problem. The issue is, we don't have enough to do it more than once, at least not until supplies arrive."

Aeron nodded. In his mind, parts of a strategy were cohering into a semblance of order. "Set aside as many as you can spare. If we're going to set a trap, we need to do so quickly, before they're on us."

"So it's to be a trap, then?"

"Anything to buy time. Speaking of which…" Aeron indicated the army below. "Any ideas?"

Anas sucked on his teeth. "Aeronauts and grenadiers would be easiest."

Aeron nodded. There were both on board. All they needed was the order to make a run, but he hadn't given it yet. Part of him didn't want to. They'd have to get close; not too close, but close enough. A risk. A small one – but a risk. "I want to avoid any extended engagement with the enemy before time. Hit and run keeps our people alive."

"You're still worried we'll crumble at the first charge," Anas said, though not accusingly. He sounded more amused than anything else.

Aeron considered denying it. Instead, he sighed and knocked on the rail. "I'm worried that you don't understand. Not you, in particular, but… all of you." The Ej-folk knew how to fight. They'd fought trolls in the mountains, and bandits, and wild beasts. But this was not that. War was not bandits; war was a meat-grinder.

Anas nodded solemnly. "We never will, lad, unless we see it for ourselves. How can we prepare for war without experiencing it? Training is all well and good, but until you feel the fear, you can't know how you'll react to it."

Another shudder ran through the airship; a bit of turbulence, driven by storms out over the sea. Aeron swallowed thickly and pushed away from the rail. "Well, we'll get it. Especially if we can't take that bridge down."

"And how's that going, then?"

Aeron grimaced. "Badly. Valan says Solibos is planning a coup."

Anas's eyes widened. "That bad, is it?" he said, after a moment.

"That bad, and then some." Aeron went to the mast and leaned against it. The queasy feeling was subsiding, if slowly. Maybe it was just the way the wind was pushing against the ship. "Solibos is going to be trouble. He's been countermanding my orders, stalling… anything he can do to undermine me with his people."

"Why?"

Aeron shrugged. "Who can say? Who knows why the tall-folk do anything? Jealousy, maybe. Or maybe Valan's right, and he's just an idiot. It doesn't matter. The end result is the same regardless. He'll cripple us before the enemy arrives."

"Maybe he'll think better of it. Elves are pragmatic sorts."

"Too much pragmatism is the same as foolishness." Aeron grimaced as another slight tremor ran through the airship. They were turning now, swinging back toward Callenspire. The army would be passing below them. Three, maybe four days out, he judged. "I'll have to do something about him."

Anas was silent for a moment. "Like what?"

"I don't know."

Anas frowned and looked away. "There's always some bugger who thinks they know better than you, and tries it on. The tall-folk don't have a monopoly on that. Granted, I don't think Dunner Pashik would try and embarrass me during a siege, but who knows?"

Aeron blinked. "Dunner Pashik? The wool importer?"

"Aye. Nasty little reprobate. Called my airship a cheap fairground trick. But he's not laughing now. Especially after I gave him a thump." Anas paused. "I don't suppose that elf friend of yours had any ideas?"

"Poison," Aeron said, absently. Anas laughed.

"Aye, that sounds like an elf solution." He hooked his thumbs in his belt. "You could try and talk to the fellow, I suppose. Make him see sense."

"I don't think that will work. From his point of view, he is the sensible one. We're the crazy ones." Aeron shook his head. "And maybe he's not wrong to think that. Valan wanted me to be in command because a Neritican mage told him it had to be that way, else the whole of the elven lands would be lost. I don't know about you, Anas, but that is too much bloody weight for these shoulders." He realized he was shouting and forced himself to calm down. "What if that mage was wrong? Worse, what if he was right – and what if I fail?"

Anas stared at him as if he'd grown a second head. He laughed harshly. "If I thought you might fail, I'd have never brought you here, lad. I'd have never brought you to the mountains or put you in charge of training our folk to fight. And I'd certainly have never sent *Thunderchild* out along the coast to attack the Xirkaali camps."

Aeron flinched. *Thunderchild* was overdue for its return. Its tardiness might be due to a hundred factors; everything from mechanical failure to weather conditions. But part of him knew the truth. It had likely been knocked from the sky, and all hands lost. Including Hannah Bimson. He wondered if Anas blamed him for that. In Anas's place, Aeron probably would.

Instead, Anas said, "The first lesson you taught us was that war means casualties. Losses. Death is no stranger to us, not in those mountains. We've all lost someone. And aye, we'll lose more before this is done. But unless we fight, the Xirkaali will be on our doorstep before the winter comes. And when that happens, I don't plan on bending the knee." He took a deep breath. "Win, lose, or draw, we're in the game now. All we can do is play the hand we have and hope for a miracle."

"And am I that miracle?"

Anas laughed again. "Not the one I'd have picked, certainly. But you've done all right so far." He squeezed Aeron's shoulder. "You done your missus, and the Shires, proud, Aeron Cadwallader. You've done us proud, getting us this far. That's why I know that you'll do your damndest to preserve Callenspire – whatever some overprivileged elven idiot figures." He blew out a long sigh. "Now, what'll it be then? Should we let our aeronauts out for a run… or do we hold off a bit?"

Aeron hesitated. Part of him wanted to hold off until the last possible moment. Another part wanted to see what the aeronauts could do in the open. Would they stick to their training, or would the excitement be too much for them? It would be the first real test of the devices, for good or ill.

Aeron took a deep breath. "Give the order. If we're going to do this, we may as well start now." He clasped his hands behind his back and went to the rail to watch as a bell began to ring and a hatch opened in the lower hull. Three shapes dropped into the open air, balloons swelling to catch the wind. The aeronauts skidded out over the Eastway, rotors humming. A few minutes later, the first explosions rippled across the front ranks of the advancing army. Small ones, not big enough to do more than disturb the serenity of the horde.

But small drops of water could eat a hole in stone, given enough time.

"Time," Aeron murmured. They needed time.

And he would buy it for them, one way or another. Whatever the cost.

CHAPTER TWENTY-NINE

Valan

"Surely you must see the necessity, Master Hrinmeer," Valan said. Hrinmeer snorted and took a swig from his cup. He was broadly built for an elf; Valan dimly recalled some rumor regarding a drop of human blood in Hrinmeer's family line, best left unspoken of course. Some elves were sensitive about that. Hrinmeer was dressed in sumptuous robes and had a silver circlet on his head, after the fashion of Elvenholme.

"All I see is a troop of uncouth halfkin occupying my best hostelry." Hrinmeer held out his cup for a refill, and Valan obliged. "As yet, I have received no compensation from the city's coffers for the commandeering of the Red Star. So, do not talk to me of necessity."

"Do you think the Xirkaali will pay you better, then?"

Hrinmeer frowned and set his cup down. "That is unworthy of you, Cormys. It is not treachery to want reimbursement. I must have funds if I am to buy passage to Ej."

"You are one of the wealthiest kindred in the city," Valan pointed out. They sat in the chamber given over to Valan for his use, surrounded by ornate statuary of brilliant craftsmanship and no aesthetic value. It had belonged to Merytan's father, once upon a time, and the former lord of Callenspire's tastes had run to the mundane, at least in Valan's opinion. The doors to the garden were open, allowing in a warm breeze and the omnipresent hum of labor; the walls were being reinforced, and palisades set up in the market squares.

"Have you ever been to Ej, Cormys? They charge for the air you breathe."

Valan snorted. "An exaggeration, surely."

"Not by much. Besides, I'm not planning to stay there long. I intend to make my way north, to Elvenholme. As you should." Hrinmeer leaned forward. "They say the Xirkaali will be here in a few days. Solibos claims they'll never breach the walls, but – well."

"Yes. Not the brightest, our lord commander. And yet, you are happy to support his efforts to discommode our allies?"

"Solibos can get me to Ej. I don't see the halflings offering to do the same."

Valan sighed. The airships weren't built to carry passengers with significant assets. Evacuees had been encouraged to leave behind all but the necessities. Elves of Hrinmeer's station couldn't conceive of leaving any of their wealth behind. Few of them had taken the halflings up on their offer of a berth. Rather, they'd hired barges – when barges were available to be hired – or set off in a long caravan of horses and wagons that was even now still in sight of the city. Hrinmeer was one of the stubborn few who'd remained past the point of easy escape and now intended to make it everyone else's problem.

"Solibos is lying."

Hrinmeer raised an eyebrow. "Harsh words."

"But true ones. Solibos can no more ensure you a berth than he can himself. He does not possess the authority –"

Here, Hrinmeer chuckled. "He has more than you might think. Especially with your friend, Cadwallader, out of the city. And what about that? Has the little fellow run back to the mountains?"

"He's on a scouting expedition," Valan said.

"Is that what we're calling it?"

"What would you call flying out over the Eastway to gauge enemy numbers?" Valan asked, waspishly. "Unlike Solibos, Cadwallader is an experienced military commander."

"He's a halfling."

Valan sighed. "And Solibos is the scion of a proud dynasty, yet he has no practical military experience beyond hanging the occasional bandit. Is that the person you trust to defend the city? Really?"

"This is an elven city, Cormys," Hrinmeer said, softly. "There is a certain way of doing things, and this is all highly irregular. What of our proud military traditions?"

"Oh, you mean nepotism and bribery?"

Hrinmeer laughed. "Among others, yes. What profit victory, if it is earned by another?" He leaned forward. "I and the others understand why you backed him. But will the end result be worth it? Think of morale!"

Valan stared at him in bemusement. "Are you saying that you would rather the city fall to the Xirkaali, than be held by a halfling?"

"I am saying that there is little difference between them in the long run."

Valan shook his head. "Is this… feeling shared by many?" The thought wasn't a pleasant one. He'd known there was an undercurrent of unrest in the city; how could there be otherwise, with a hostile army on the approach? But if unrest had soured into unhappiness, things might become untenable.

Hrinmeer sat back. "I like you, Cormys. You know to keep the wine flowing, and your words truthful. But you've made some mistakes of late. This is only the most recent. If I were you, I would make peace with Lord Solibos very quickly. Else you might find yourself on the wrong side of the walls when the Xirkaali finally get here."

Valan was about to reply when there was a polite, but officious, knock at the door. When he called for them to come in, he recognized one of Merytan's personal guard.

"My Lady Merytan requests your presence in the south library at your earliest convenience, my lord," he said, stiffly.

That, Valan knew, meant *now.* The guard paid no attention to Hrinmeer, who looked back and forth between them in obvious curiosity, and not a little envy. Merytan did not often socialize with her court, not in the way Solibos did. Rather than isolating her from her supporters, however, it made her attentions all the more desirous to social climbers like Hrinmeer and his peers. To be invited anywhere by

Merytan was a social coup.

Valan dismissed the guard and rose from his seat. "The mistress of Callenspire calls," he said, in mock-apology, as he saw Hrinmeer out.

Hrinmeer, to his credit, didn't protest. Instead, he paused at the door and said, "It's good to have friends in high places, Cormys. You should remember that, and cultivate as many as possible." Then he was gone. Valan composed himself, and then made his way quickly to the south library.

There were three libraries in the keep; the south was the largest and oldest. It had been grown in the centuries prior to the Winter War and contained volumes nearly as old as Elvenholme. Merytan was justifiably proud of it and rarely allowed anyone other than herself and a few specially-chosen academics to peruse its contents. It was rumored to be one of the largest collections in the south.

This was the first time Valan had been invited to see it. Whatever the reason, it must be important. A pair of guards – both from Merytan's personal guard, rather than the army – stood on duty outside the doors.

The guards stepped aside before he'd even announced himself, allowing Valan into the library. They'd obviously been awaiting his arrival.

Merytan stood before a table piled high with books and scrolls, paging through a heavy-looking leatherbound volume. A high ladder extended from the floor to the top of the nearest shelf, and an elf in the robes of an academic clung to its uppermost point. As Valan entered, she drew a book from the shelf to examine, and nearly fell from her perch.

"Ah, Valan. So good of you to pull yourself away from your politicking," Merytan said as she snapped the book she'd been perusing shut. A cloud of dust billowed from the pages as she did so, and Valan waved a hand in front of his face.

"I am at your beck and call, my lady. What can I do for you?"

"It is more what I can do for you. Might I introduce Eran Hrthil?" She indicated the young elf clinging to the ladder. "She is an academic of some note; the prize student of Essilor Deryn himself."

Valan raised an eyebrow. "Is that so? I studied under the Sage of Ej myself for a time in my youth. Is his tongue still as sharp as I recall?"

Eran looked down at him, her eyes large and her hair so fine as to be iridescent. "Master Essilor has strong opinions," she said, diplomatically.

"Which he enjoys sharing at every available opportunity," Valan laughed. Essilor was one of the most eminent historians of the elven empire. The breadth of his knowledge was impossible to gauge; it was said that he knew things that only the Shining Ones were supposedly privy to. Whether this was the case or not, Essilor certainly acted as if he possessed all of the answers. He looked at Merytan. "Why did you ask me here?"

Merytan smiled thinly. "Were you busy?"

Valan grimaced. "Yes, now that you mention it." As Hrinmeer had implied, Solibos had begun to throw his weight around as soon as Aeron had departed. Elven soldiers had taken over fortifying the docks – or, rather, not fortifying the docks. Instead, trade was encouraged to continue as normal. That few merchants of any real standing remained in the city, and that trade along the river had all but halted, was of no import. Worse, there were rumors that Solibos intended to kick the halflings out of the buildings given over to them as temporary barracks. Hrinmeer's property was one such.

Valan had intended to head that off, if possible. But it was difficult. Solibos was merely stirring the embers already burning. Unless the Xirkaali showed up soon, the whole city might well be in revolt.

"Well, this is more important. Eran's specialty is in history. Specifically, that of the lands of the Xiryan – or, rather, the Xirkaali."

Valan blinked. "What?"

Eran carefully descended the ladder. "Her ladyship speaks the truth. I – I have some small knowledge of the Xirkaali dialect and their customs." She flushed. "I wrote a monograph on their reverence for pumpkins. Master Essilor thought very highly of it."

"Did he now?" Valan looked at Merytan. "I don't think pumpkins are going to win the war for us, my lady."

"Idiot," Merytan said, genially. "Eran knows more about the Xirkaali than anyone, save possibly the Ophidians. If we want to know why the war has started, we must first understand the enemy. Only then will we have any hope in stopping it."

"I was rather hoping we'd win and they'd go away," Valan admitted.

"They won't go away," Eran said. She shrank back as both Valan and Merytan looked at her. She swallowed and added, "They – they advance. Always. They don't retreat. Not for long. They can't."

Valan frowned. "Why?"

"I – I don't know. I have theories," Eran added, hastily. "There has to be an answer somewhere. A reason behind this invasion." She looked up at the shelves of books looming above her. "Once, we knew everything about them. They've changed in the centuries since, but the answer is in their history, somewhere. I know it."

Valan nodded slowly and looked again at Merytan. "That's all very well and good, but what does it have to do with me?"

"Because you have met one," Merytan said. "You've spoken to them. Moreover, you are a trained diplomat. You observe more than the average person. So, you will tell Eran what you observed, and she will read her books; and together, you might well find the answer we seek." She smiled. "As I said, this is important."

"What about Solibos?"

"I can handle Solibos. Or did you think this was the first time he tried to install himself on my throne?" She laughed lightly. "Please. He's been trying to usurp me since he was a boy. Callenspire is like a wild horse; you just have to know how to talk to it, and then it's as docile as a lamb."

Valan frowned but knew that Merytan was probably right. If anyone could quiet the fears of someone like Hrinmeer, it was her. He looked at Eran.

"Very well, then. Let's get started."

CHAPTER THIRTY

Axel

The outskirts of Yth'Medu sprawled across the ocean floor like an immense garden of shimmering coral. Much of its foundation had once been an elven city – or cities – according to those who knew such things. A city long dead, even in Axel's time. It was larger now than it had been. Even at this distance, he could make out the great towers and domes of its heart. Gorrup had told him that the great kingdom of Medu'Syth now spanned the equator, and looking at it, Axel could easily believe it.

Axel stood on a ridge far above the kingdom. The shoreline was more than a day's swim in the opposite direction. The ridge was a demarcation point; a sheer drop to the sea-bed far below. A series of fortified coral watchtowers lined the ridge for leagues in each direction, allowing the city's defenders to maintain vigil on the coasts of Vieshlar and the lands beyond.

It was to one of these watchtowers – the largest of them, built atop the remains of some great stone structure, now shot through with coral – that Axel had been escorted by the aforementioned defenders when they had intercepted him. The placoderms had not been violent; aggressive, yes – but not viciously so. A better greeting than he had expected, even if they had all but ignored his entreaties.

That said, he had been confined since his capture with no one save Splish to speak to. Indeed, for a time, he'd feared that he'd been forgotten. He had considered escaping more than once; a trick of no difficulty, with his magic. But he knew that the placoderms might well take offense at such an action. So, instead, he'd bided his time until they'd announced he was to see the garrison commander, though it had not been easy. He could not help but wonder what had happened to Gorrup and the others. He hoped that they had survived; that they had fled. That they still fought.

"You will come with us now, mage," a rough voice said from behind him. Axel took a deep breath and turned to face the trio of placoderm warriors who had come for him. "Tidewarden Nemon would speak with you."

Axel bowed his head. "Excellent."

He swam beside the warriors as they led him once more into the watchtower and up into its glimmering interior. As he swam, he noted the faded sigils which adorned the ancient stones; elvish, he thought. A remnant of some outpost, swallowed by the resurgent seas. What the elves had forgotten, the Neriticans had made use of. Nothing went to waste beneath the sea. Everything had its use.

Everything had a reason.

Axel wondered what the reason for the Neriticans abandonment of the war against the Xirkaali was. He pushed the thought aside as he was ushered into a circular chamber, crafted from striations of coral and what appeared to be the thick bones of deep-sea predators. At the far end of the chamber was a heavy seat, made from the skull of something with far too many teeth for Axel's liking. Occupying that seat was a large placoderm; battle-scarred and muscular, with scales like dark stones. A heavy trident rested against the side of the throne. This then was Tidewarden Nemon.

He was impressive. Like Gorrup, he radiated a physical might that far outmatched anything in Axel's experience. Here was a warrior that could win any fight, defeat any foe. Axel did his best to hide his sudden unease as he waited for the invitation to speak.

He didn't have long. The placoderm sat forward on his grisly throne. "You are… gillkin, yes?" He sounded intrigued, but not especially curious. Wary, perhaps.

Axel nodded. He would have to tread carefully here. The placoderms were fierce. They craved war in a way that was utterly alien to him. Or such had been his experience, centuries ago. "Yes, Tidewarden."

"Your kind vanished long ago. How do I know this is not a trick?"

Axel met the Neritican's black gaze. "If you believe it so, strike me down." He waited, even as he had with Gorrup so many days ago.

The placoderm paused, as if considering whether to do so. Then he gave a rumbling snort of something that might have been amusement. "You are brave. I will give you that much. Speak, then, cousin. What news do you bring us? Have your people finally come out of hiding? Do they wish our forgiveness for their abandonment?"

Axel forced himself not to slump. "It is just me, my lord, insofar as I know. I am the last. And I come to request your aid, not your forgiveness."

Nemon's scales rattled as he leaned back. "What sort of aid, mage? Speak, and perhaps I shall not tear the flesh from your bones." Despite his words, he sounded more amused than upset.

Axel swallowed. Despite Nemon's seeming good humor, he suspected that time had not softened the outlook of the placoderms. They were still as savage as ever. They made the river-folk look positively harmless in comparison. "Vieshlar is under attack. The Xirkaali –"

"We know about the Xirkaali," Nemon said. "We reddened the waters with their blood. And now they are no longer in our waters."

"They invade Vieshlar."

Nemon's gaze glittered as he studied Axel. "And so? What is that to us?"

Axel tightened his grip on his staff. "I have seen things – visions of what might yet come to pass. The Great Current spoke to me. The visions it sent awoke me from my hibernation." He let a scrap of magic slip into the water, and images of what he'd seen coalesced around him. Nemon growled in surprise, and his guards moved toward Axel, spears leveled.

"You show us nothing we are not aware of, mage. Do you think we lack for seers? They have all seen the same. And none of it matters. At the moment, they threaten neither our kingdoms, nor the balance of nature." Nemon sat back. "Why then should I hurl our people into war?"

Axel shook his head. He could hear the regret in Nemon's voice – and the frustration. He thought, if it were up to the placoderm, the Neriticans might still be at war. But Medu'Syth was not only the kingdom of the placoderms. There were other voices to be considered, and not all of them were as eager for war as Nemon and his folk. "Is the fate of the riverguard not enough of a reason? They are at war with the Xirkaali even now. Would you leave them to it?"

"A war you led them into, gillkin, if what you told my warriors is to be believed. A war on behalf of air-breathers… elves and half-men. Pfaugh. What use is there in dying on their behalf? Where is the profit to Medu'Syth?" Nemon studied him, and there was something almost pleading about his expression. Axel wracked his brain, trying to think of the right combination of words to give Nemon what he wanted – an excuse.

"I did not lead them into it," he said, finally. "I merely showed them what the Xirkaali were doing to the jungle and the rivers. They hew down the trees and dam the waters. They drain the spawning pools and crush the eggs. They are heedless, and worse, remorseless. They will not stop until they win, and they cannot win until all are under their yoke. They will break the river-tribes. The *Ril'uwa* are our allies. They have bled for Medu'Syth… will Medu'Syth bleed for them? Or are they too merely air-breathers?"

Nemon's muzzle wrinkled back from his fangs, and he hissed in obvious anger. His guards echoed him, and for a moment, Axel thought they might fall upon him and tear him to pieces. But Nemon held up a hand, and the other placoderms fell silent. "Your arguments echo my own, mage. And I have made them many times since the Xirkaali first set out for Mantica. But I have been denied. As I must deny you."

"Why?" Axel asked.

"Because the Trident King has said no, and his closest advisors agree. And that is the end of it. They do not threaten our waters, and so, we have no call to war on them. Even if our allies disagree. So we wait. Patiently."

Axel paused. "What if they were? Threatening our waters, I mean."

Nemon looked at him. "Explain."

"The bastions they have built on the shores – they erect wharves. Jetties. Impinging upon the sovereignty of the sea. Their ships occupy Breakwater Bay, and the estuary. Laying claim to that which is not theirs." It was a desperate gamble; but it might be enough, if what he read in Nemon's eyes was correct.

Nemon snorted. "As do the elves."

"The elves asked and were given permission to do so. I recall it well, for I was there when that privilege was granted to them. But the Xirkaali have not – they do not think that they require Medu'Syth's permission to sail Medu'Syth's waters. To dam Medu'Syth's rivers. If that is not justification… what is?"

Nemon stared at him. "Flimsy, gillkin. Very flimsy." Then he slammed his fist against his throne and rose to his feet. "Ha! But good enough, I think. At least for the moment." He growled an order to his guards, and they shot away from the throne room, swimming in all directions. Nemon looked down at Axel, a glitter of satisfaction in his dark eyes. "You will stay with me. I will lead the attack on the closest of their camps."

"You have been preparing," Axel said, in sudden realization.

Nemon chuckled. "Of course! What sort of fool do you take me for, gillkin?" He shook his wedge-shaped head in amusement. "The Xirkaali crouch above us, waiting. The balance is maintained so long as they do so, but I do not think it will hold for long, whatever the naiads claim. There have been…whispers, of late. I have heard thuul and naiads alike say that the Great Current is disturbed. That this is but the first ripple in a seaquake that may well consume us all." He reached down for the heavy trident propped against his throne.

"Our king is careful; wary of being drawn into a cataclysm not of our making or the machinations of those who might not have the best interests of the Trident Realm at heart. But sometimes wariness is simply fear under a different name. Fear of facing an enemy who shrugs off our magics and claims the seas as their own." Nemon lifted his trident and examined the steel prongs, as if searching for signs of blemish or weakness. "Or maybe he fears that we have already failed in the task that the Great Current has set for us. That perhaps we should have harried them onto the land and smashed them wherever they fled."

Somewhat taken aback, Axel peered at the placoderm. "What do you mean?"

Nemon looked down at Axel. "We could have stopped them before they made landfall. I pleaded to be unleashed, to let the fury of Medu'Syth wash over these arrogant Xirkaali. But I was denied then, and every time since. I was reminded that the way of the sea was waiting. In *patience*." He tapped the side of his head with a claw. "But I hear a voice that comes to me in the slow hiss of the night tide, and it whispers of what is to come. With it came a visitor from elsewhere. A strange naiad, her flesh covered in burn scars. A representative of the Green Lady."

Axel froze. "Her name?" he asked.

"She calls herself Shesh'ra, or so I am told. Even now she attempts to convince the Trident King that we should make war on the Xirkaali. Recommence war, I should say. Our initial assaults were at the Green Lady's urging, to repay a favor owed. But now the Trident King wonders if it was a mistake."

Axel sagged as relief flooded him. Shesh'ra. The name echoed in his mind, like some half-forgotten memory now rising to the surface; an ally, perhaps, against the return of Oskan. "Have you spoken to her?" he asked, softly.

Nemon nodded. "Yes. It was she who told me that I should expect a sign. I would say that your arrival here counts as such."

Axel considered this. All this time he had assumed he was the only one whom the Great Current was speaking to. But if there were others, it implied things were worse than he'd thought. The thought was an unpleasant one, and he pushed it aside for now. "What shall you do now?"

Nemon slammed the ferrule of his trident against the floor, and the sound shivered through the water like the peal of a bell.

"Now? Now Medu'Syth marches to *war*!"

CHAPTER THIRTY-ONE

Shulgin

Shulgin hacked through the thick vines with a curse. Trees crowded the rough trail, their roots coiling through the hard earth like sleeping serpents. Behind her came Ryuk and the others. Besides the scouts, she'd brought only a small group; five of her most trusted warriors, and nearly twice that of human auxiliaries. A dozen scaly-limbed war-hounds gamboled alongside their human handlers. A scouting party, nothing more.

They'd left the river, and the rest of the flotilla, behind some days ago in order to cut across the jungle and get a lay of the land. According to what she'd been told, there was only one toll lock left. She intended to see if that was the case for herself. It wasn't that she didn't trust the maps, or the elves – though she didn't – but that experience had taught her that no report, no matter how trustworthy, could replace one's own eyes.

Too much depended on the success of her mission. The flotilla had endured several days of constant, sniping attacks. Not just the river-folk, but elves as well. As if they'd made common cause; an unpleasant thought. And without the flotilla, the forces advancing along the Eastway would have no siege engines, and fewer supplies.

According to her scouts, the other column had been attacked as well. Flyers, with grenades. Airships. One, at least. Harassment, much like the attacks her flotilla had weathered. The thought of an airship did not worry her beyond a mild strategic anxiety; it was merely one more problem added to the pile.

It was obvious to her that these attacks were designed to slow her down; to buy time for the enemy to consolidate and reinforce. It was what she would do in their position. The problem was, there was little she could do, save endure it. They knew that and were counting on it. She'd lost four boats so far. Not many, in the greater scheme of things, but it irked her all the same. She wanted to avoid losing any more. Hence the scouting mission.

"We should be close to the bend in the river," Ryuk said.

"Until we see it, we're not close enough," Shulgin said. She paused and sniffed the air. Someone was coming. A moment later, she caught sight of one of her scouts making his way back along the trail. He moved at a slow amble, as if he had all the time in the world.

"Arrogant curs," Ryuk muttered. Shulgin shushed him with a gesture. Plainstalkers and spearwardens didn't get along; the divide between hunters and warriors was a large one, and some rivalry was to be expected.

"Report," Shulgin growled.

Like the other scouts, he was dressed in hard leathers and a heavy cloak, the color of dirt. He had a bow clasped in one paw and a quiver of arrows on his hip. When he reached her, he thumped his chest in salute and said, without preamble, "Ruins up ahead. Looks like an old waystation."

Shulgin signaled for Ryuk and the others to spread out. "Ambush?"

The plainstalker waggled his paw. "Maybe yes, maybe no. Hard to tell. Can't smell anything, but the elves are tricky. Might be hiding. Might be watching us right now." He looked about, as if expecting to see an elf leap out of hiding right there. Shulgin glared at him and he shrugged. "Probably not."

Shulgin looked at Ryuk. "Stay here. I will check it out."

Ryuk made to argue, but she was already moving before the words left his mouth. The scout fell into a lope beside her. She ignored him. Like Ryuk, she found the plainstalkers annoying. They had a part to play in the wars of the hemicyons, but it was one that grated against her sensibilities. Skulking about, loosing arrows – that wasn't fit sport for a warrior, whatever the elves seemed to think.

The waystation proved to be a single structure, surrounded by the collapsed remnants of outbuildings and long-abandoned stacks of lumber, left to molder in the humidity. The main structure wasn't large, at least as Shulgin judged such things; more like a hut than anything else.

"Loggers must have used it," the plainstalker opined absently. "Drag the lumber out of the forest, set it here, it gets collected for transport to the city."

"Not for some time, I think," Shulgin muttered. She wondered what had possessed the elves to abandon such a place. She had seen others like this while moving upriver. Forgotten signs of industry, abandoned for no reason that she could see. Left for the jungle to swallow up, the way it had parts of their cities. She wondered if they were mad, the elves. Or maybe they had simply given up, decided to use magic rather than steel and stone. Perhaps immortality had dulled their edge in some way.

She pushed the thought aside. The scout was already inside the building, an arrow nocked and ready. She followed him and saw a large hole in the roof, and a pile of broken tiles beneath. The scout slid his arrow back in his quiver, slung his bow, and leapt upward lightly, grabbing the edge of the roof and hauling himself up. He turned and extended a paw. "Coming?" he asked.

Shulgin took the proffered limb and clambered up onto the crumbling roof. She rose carefully to her full height. The trees hung close over the roof, but there was a gap where an old road had once run in the direction of Callenspire. She could make out chunks of what might once have been paving stones extending away into the jungle.

In the distance, she could just make out the tall tree-towers of what could only be Callenspire, rising above a fork in the river. The city was still some days' travel away, but she could also make out smoke rising up from the direction of the Eastway. That boded ill. "Fires?" she asked the scout.

"Maybe. Maybe rockets." The scout paused, eyes raking the undergrowth. She wondered if he'd heard something. He was a mangy creature; scarred and ugly from a life lived on the fringes of the pack. "The small ones… the fliers… they've been spotted over the Eastway. Maybe they blew up an ordnance wagon. They seem to enjoy that."

Shulgin grunted and turned her attention east, back toward the city. The small ones were obviously the halfkin Obair had warned her of. A people from the mountains. A satrapy of the elves. A clever people, with a talent for making things… like airships and grenades. Something hove into view, sliding across the nearby horizon. She stiffened, ears perked. "Is that what I think it is?"

The scout followed her gaze and sniffed.

"Airship."

"Close," she said. And it was, and getting closer with every moment. She judged it would be over this part of the jungle within an hour or two.

"Patrol," the scout said, noncommittally. "Keeping an eye on the river, maybe."

Shulgin snorted. "Looking for us, I'd guess." The elves knew they were coming. They'd want as much of a warning as they could get. But more than that, the airship was a clear threat. Rockets aside, her warriors didn't have much that could bring down such a vessel. And worse, such craft would make a siege difficult.

Closer to hand, past the trees, she could see the bend in the river, and the bulwark of the toll lock. Even at a distance, she could tell that it was larger than the others; a small fortress, rather than a palisade. She scrubbed her muzzle in annoyance. "Big," she said.

The plainstalker nodded. "Lots of movement. Very busy."

Shulgin sank into a crouch. "They're ready for us."

The plainstalker nodded again. "Most likely." He picked at something in his teeth.

She growled softly. "It is a trap."

The plainstalker grunted. Whether in agreement or acknowledgement, she could not say. "A trap," she said, again. "They let us have easy victories so that we would be overconfident." She looked around. It was a good position for mortars. A few here, to cover an advance through the jungle, might be advisable. She growled again, but in pleasure this time. The fighting up until now had been desultory; hardly nourishing.

This would be her first real meal in some time. She slapped the hilt of her sword and made ready to drop back down to the ground. "Stay here. Keep watch. Sound the alert if there's any movement."

The scout said nothing. Shulgin paused, her hackles bristling though she could not say why. She reached out with a paw and gave him a nudge. He toppled over and slid off of the roof to lay unmoving on the ground below. Shulgin bit back a snarl of alarm and looked around wildly. The jungle was silent.

She heard a hiss to her left and instinct took over. She flung herself flat on the roof as something cut through the air overhead. An insect? No. She saw it, embedded in a nearby tree. A dart of some kind. She cursed and clawed her way toward the hole in the roof. She needed to get out of sight, and fast. She heard another wasp-hum, and something struck her armor and bounced off.

A moment later, Shulgin fell into the interior of the waystation with a clatter of steel plates. She scrambled heavily to her feet, already reaching for her sword as the first of the riverguard burst through the door, trident aimed at her muzzle. She fell back, narrowly avoiding the prongs of the weapon, and snatched her sword from its sheath. Or tried to; the enclosed area made it difficult. She was too large, and the waystation too small.

The riverguard bounded toward her, webbed feet connecting with her chest. She pitched backward, into the wall. Ancient masonry crumbled around her as she struggled to right herself. The trident flashed toward her again, and she was forced to drop her sword in order to catch the prongs before they reached her. Her attacker was strong, but she was stronger. She wrestled the trident aside and kicked her opponent in the belly.

He gave a croaking wheeze and stumbled back, leaving the trident in her clutches. She spun it about and sent it hurtling toward its owner. It caught him in the midsection, and the force of her throw carried him outside. She retrieved her sword and followed.

More of them were waiting. They studied first the body of the one she'd killed, and then her, with unblinking eyes, tridents and javelins in hand. Shulgin showed her teeth.

"Well? What are you waiting for?" she growled.

She could hear the approach of Ryuk and the others; how many more of these creatures were waiting in the jungle to ambush them?

She threw back her head and howled a warning. The sound echoed through the jungle. When she looked back, the river-folk were gone; as if they had never been there at all. She waited for several moments and then sheathed her sword with a snort of disdain.

"Cowards," she muttered. But she knew better. It wasn't cowardice that had seen them depart, but wisdom. Their ambush had been ruined by her howl, and they saw no reason to stay, if nothing of use could be achieved. A cold, pragmatic folk, much like her own. She could almost admire them. She wondered if, unlike the elves, they could be made to see sense. If so, the empire might gain a strong ally.

But that was for later, and for wiser folk to gnaw over. She was merely a soldier, and a soldier had her duty. A duty she was looking forward to more and more with every passing moment. She gave a snarl of pleasure as Ryuk loped into view, followed by a number of other warriors.

"What happened?" he barked.

Wordlessly, she pointed at the dead amphibian. His eyes were open in death, wide and staring. She crouched and closed them. Ryuk joined her.

"They die easy enough," he said.

She grunted and rubbed her chest. "Not so easy as all that." Her gaze swept the jungle, but there was no sign of them. She glanced at the body of the scout. Foam decorated his muzzle, and his body was clenched like a fist. Her skin itched to see it. She rose, all thought of mortars and sweeping the flank vanished.

Another trap.

Clever. They were clever. But she could be clever as well. A new plan began to form in her mind. They wanted to draw her in? So be it.

"What now?" Ryuk growled.

"Back to the boats," she said. "And watch the trees."

CHAPTER THIRTY-TWO
Kortys

Kortys took a deep breath, eyes closed. Bird calls sounded throughout the jungle, as well as the roar of a spine-cat. And beyond them, the dull, wet thudding of oars striking the surface of the river. He opened his eyes. "They'll be here soon. Is everything ready?"

"It's as good as we can make it," Makki said, as she gave the parapet a fond pat. The halfling engineer grinned up at Kortys. "It'll stand up to most of what they've thrown at us so far, but probably not for long. A day, maybe two if we're lucky."

She looked down at the reinforced sections of the toll lock, and Kortys followed her gaze; heavy stones had been used to brace the ancient brickwork in places, and magic used to encourage the sudden, expansive growth of thick roots to further anchor the structure. Heavy wooden pavises had been erected along the wide stretch of the parapet, and behind them, halfling riflemen and elven archers crouched, waiting.

The lock was the last obstacle between the Xirkaali flotilla and the city. Once it fell, the enemy would have nothing between themselves and Callenspire except an empty stretch of river. For obvious reasons, it was here that Cadwallader had decided they needed to make a stand. While he couldn't fault the halfling's strategy, Kortys wished he wasn't the one who had to enact it. Something told him it wasn't going to be easy.

Parallel wharves of stone stretched beyond the portcullis; more pavises had been erected on them, among stacks of abandoned cargo and ornamental statuary, and more warriors waited there for when the Xirkaali inevitably breached the portcullis and tried to come ashore, as they had at the other locks. Not many warriors, though; not enough. If the other garrisons had retreated as they were supposed to, their numbers would have at least been adequate. As it was, they had barely the numbers needed to complete the defenses. Kortys leaned over and spat into the river.

Makki applauded. Kortys gave her a look. "What?"

"Never seen an elf so mad he could spit before," she said and laughed.

Kortys snorted. "I am not angry. Merely impatient."

"Eager to be about it then?" The halfling extracted a cheroot from her equipment harness and placed it between her teeth.

Kortys looked downriver. "Not in the way you mean. I am eager to be done with the whole business. The war – all of it."

"And then what?"

"I go back to walking the jungle trails. Alone."

Makki lit her cheroot with a taper. She shook the stick out and said, "Aye, I understand. I'd prefer to be in my workshop. But needs must, eh?"

Kortys grunted. "You don't have to stay, you know. Your job is done."

"Not hardly," Makki said. She retrieved her rifle from where it had been leaning against a pavise and checked it over. "My job is to hold the lock until it's time to retreat. Which is what I bloody well intend to do. Besides, I'm not leaving my howitzer here for you elves to filch." She indicated the volley gun now mounted at the rail of the barge that had carried their building supplies downriver. The barge had been turned sideways in the river and now acted as a secondary emplacement. Archers and gunners prowled the deck, taking up positions wherever they could find them.

Kortys chuckled. "We don't even know how to use the blasted thing."

"Yet another reason for me to remain, eh?" Makki blew a smoke ring into the air. "Besides, what would you do without me?"

"Well, I wouldn't have to smell your cheroots, for one thing. Do me a favor and go downwind, would you?" Kortys waved a hand in front of his face for emphasis. Makki laughed loudly and shouldered her rifle.

"I'll just go check my lads and lasses are in position, shall I?"

Kortys watched her go with amusement. He found the halflings refreshing, next to his own folk. Their lives were so short, yet they did so much with that small span of time. He admired them, though he'd never admit it out loud. He turned his attention back to the river, and his mood soured almost immediately.

He estimated that they'd managed to destroy a third of the flotilla over the last few days. At least four of the barges had been sunk outright, and two others damaged to the point that the Xirkaali had been forced to set them adrift.

But that left a dozen, at least. And each of them carried enough fire-powder to put a sizable hole in the walls of Callenspire, plus substantial provisions for the enemy forces moving along the Eastway. Once they got past the lock – and they would get past it – they'd likely go ashore and start assembling the siege equipment. Kortys assumed Cadwallader had a plan for that. At least he hoped he did.

That was all someone else's problem, however. Kortys's only concern was the flotilla heading their way. Days of hit and run had made the Xirkaali wary. There was a chance they might abandon the river entirely and try to go overland. If that happened, their preparations would be for nothing.

Alisor called out to him from below, and Kortys saw the other gladestalker climbing the stone staircase that connected the upper parapet to the wharves below. A familiar green figure lolloped in his wake. Kortys recognized Glump, the chieftain of the Mudbelly tribe.

Glump and his folk had done their bit and more to stymie the Xirkaali advance, but they had their limits. Once the fight was done here, for good or ill, they'd be retreating to their hidden warrens. Kortys didn't blame them. They'd lost too many warriors to the enemy to stay in the fight much longer. But at least for this moment, he was glad they were here.

"Our friend has news," Alisor said.

"They try to come through jungle," Glump said, without preamble. "We make sure they stay with the river." He looked out over the defenses and then away, as if they were of no real concern to him.

"They're close, then?" Kortys asked.

Glump nodded, bulbous eyes blinking with an odd rhythm. "Coming around the bend," he croaked. "We wait. You signal. We attack."

"Just like we planned," Kortys said. "Hit them hard, and then retreat." The riverguard nodded again and then slipped over the side of the parapet, vanishing into the river and leaving barely a ripple in his wake. Alisor made an unhappy sound.

"I don't like those creatures," he said, leaning on his bow. "How can you trust something that lives in the water half its life?"

"I expect they feel the same about us," Kortys said with a glance at his second-in-command. "Besides, we don't need to be bosom friends to work together against a common enemy."

Alisor frowned but said nothing. Kortys understood how the other elf felt. They'd had too many bloody exchanges with the riverguard over the years to ever feel comfortable fighting alongside them. The water-breathers viewed the elven claims as to control over the entirety of Vieshlar – including the rivers – as tantamount to a challenge.

But so long as they remembered that the Xirkaali were the greater threat, he was happy enough to fight alongside them. At least for the moment. Who could say what the future might hold for any of them?

Kortys brushed the thought aside. He'd been alive long enough to know the futility of trying to plan for the future. Things changed, whether you wanted them to or not. It was why he'd taken up the duties of a gladestalker in the first place. Better to be a disruptor of plans than one whose plans were disrupted. He looked at Alisor.

"As we planned, then. We hold the line until we can't. Then we retreat – back to Callenspire, this time."

"I still don't understand why we don't make a real stand," Alisor said. "Between us, the halflings, and the riverguard, we could sink every boat in that column."

Kortys shook his head, though privately, he agreed. "Maybe. But what about the ones coming overland? Or the column behind this one? Whoever is in charge of them is smart. They're dividing their forces, giving us too many targets. Trying to focus will let something slip through. At least this way we can gnaw their flanks and bloody them some. Now get in position. They'll be here soon enough. I can hear keels cutting the water."

As he settled himself behind the palisade of pavises, Kortys considered the matter. Cadwallader's strategy was a conservative one, meant to husband lives and resources for a later engagement. They were to hold out only as long as seemed sensible, and then they were to fall back toward Callenspire. It was probably smart, especially given what they'd seen of the Xirkaali capabilities, but Kortys couldn't help but wish it was otherwise.

To him, it felt as if the elves had been on the defensive for too long. Not just now, but across the long sweep of centuries. Every battle, a holding action; every war, a conflict of last resort. Or so it seemed. Would this one be the last?

Alisor stiffened, and Kortys peered through a gap in the palisade. The Xirkaali barge hove into view around the river's bend a moment later, its prow bristling with the familiar extra cladding in the form of wooden planks and elven shields. The hemicyons learned fast. They'd had to fight their way past the other fortified locks and were prepared to do so here as well. They'd employ rockets and mortars first, to soften up opposition, and then deploy troops to the shore to move up and take control of the lock.

Kortys gave the signal. Alisor loosed an arrow into the air. On the banks to either side of the approaching barges, gladestalkers rose from hiding and loosed fire-arrows at the lead barge. Normally, barges were too wet for such tactics to work more than half the time. But the Xirkaali were particular about keeping their fire-powder dry. Flaming arrows tended to panic the crew as well. A burning barge became an obstacle and a distraction. It slowed things down and bought Kortys and his warriors time to reposition, in order to best take advantage of the subsequent riverguard attack.

But in this case – nothing. No shouts of alarm, no movement. He frowned and signaled for a second volley. More arrows rose from the trees and fell, sinking into boards and deck alike. Where was the crew? The rowers?

"The barge – *it's still coming,*" Alisor said, panic rising in his voice.

"I have eyes," Kortys snarled. How were they – ? His eyes narrowed, running through possibilities. "They must be pushing it somehow. But why...?" He grimaced. There was no time to figure it out. "Signal the riverguard. Have them attack the other barges. *Now.*"

Alisor hesitated. "What about the third volley?"

"No time. Do it now!"

Alisor leaned over the palisade and loosed an arrow into the water. It was the same signal they'd used before. The moment the arrow vanished, the first of the riverguard leapt from the water and onto the side of the second barge, javelin in hand. More followed, attacking the other barges in a surge of green. But still the first barge came on.

The howls of Xirkaali filled the air, accompanied by the clangor of weapons. But the first barge did not slow; did not falter. Kortys loosed an arrow at the second barge and heard the peculiar snap-bark of halfling rifles as the second barge finally came in range.

The wind turned. He suddenly smelled the thick, bitter odor of fire-powder and realized what the Xirkaali had done. He spun toward Alisor and shouted, "Get everyone off of the lock – *now!*"

Too late.

The explosion, when it came, was like the hand of a god falling upon him. A moment of roaring red heat and pain and then –

Nothing.

CHAPTER THIRTY-THREE

Aeron

Aeron walked along the bridge with Solibos, taking in the demolition efforts. The elf was on his best behavior, but Aeron could feel disdain radiating from him nonetheless. Valan had warned him against meeting Solibos on his own. It was clear to everyone with half a brain that Solibos was aiming to be in charge. More, he wanted to be the hero of Callenspire. Aeron knew something about that.

There was a hunger in certain folk for glory; they saw war as an opportunity, rather than as what it truly was – a failure on everyone's part. At the end of the day, excuses aside, wars happened because some folk couldn't just talk around a table and hash things out.

But Solibos hadn't yet had his fill of such awfulness. He was like a starving dog, rooting around for any scrap of adulation from his lessers. It made him foolish; dangerous. He would send his own people into certain death, just so he could have the privilege of dying heroically. Or worse.

Aeron had known folk like Solibos before – humans, mostly. A few halflings. It took a good few hard knocks to shake the stupidity out of them. And when that happened, only the strongest recovered. Most… broke. Went the other way, and fast. He figured Solibos for one of those. Once his arrogance was punctured, he'd run and take half of the army with him. Or worse, attempt to surrender the city to the Xirkaali.

It was a problem that needed dealing with, quickly. He took a deep breath and looked up. River-birds circled the bridge, squalling. He'd been told there were nests in the root-infested pillars that supported the bridge. They were probably unhappy about what was being done to their home. He felt a moment of sadness, then pushed it aside. He cleared his throat. "Your efforts look as if they're coming along well," he said, politely.

"Destroying a thing is easier than building it," Solibos replied, haughtily. He glanced at Aeron. "Are you absolutely certain that this must be done? This bridge has stood for hundreds, in not thousands, of years. It is a testament to the skill of our people."

"It's also the only easy route to the city," Aeron said. *Which you know, of course,* he thought. *You just don't want to admit it.* "At the very least, we need to make sure there's a sizable gap between it and the land. They can cross a gap, but it'll be hard going while we pepper them with arrows and shot."

Solibos frowned. "I still say that we should hold the bridge and use it as a sally point. Hit them as they arrive and push them back in disarray. It will be a glorious display of our might and remind the Xirkaali with whom they are dealing."

"I don't think they've forgotten," Aeron said. *Better to say that they don't care,* he thought. From what he'd seen of the Xirkaali, they didn't look as if they minded a fight. Indeed, he reckoned that they were enjoying themselves. He paused, choosing his next words carefully. "How many times do you think you could do it? Push them back, I mean."

Solibos snorted. "As many times as needed."

"Give me a number, please."

Solibos looked at him. "Why? What are you thinking, halfling?"

Again, Aeron paused. He had the glimmerings of a strategy; a harsh, unpleasant one. But it was exactly the sort of thing that neither Solibos nor the Xirkaali would see coming. "A field of explosives, placed just before the bridge. Buried under a light spread of soil."

Solibos blinked. "Explosives? Why?"

"To blow up the first wave to reach the bridge. To put them into disarray, and make them easy prey for your warriors."

"My warriors?"

Aeron put on a thoughtful expression. "One of the first things I learned at the war-college is that strategy should be fluid. Every battle is an ocean, with its own currents. My job is to identify those currents and ride them to victory." He met Solibos's gaze squarely. "How many times do you think you could drive them back, if they attacked the bridge?"

A slow smile crept across Solibos's face. "Ah. I see. You want to bait them in. Make them commit forces to securing the bridge, and then chop them to pieces. First with your toys, and then with our steel. Clever. Well, if that is the case – three times should do nicely. But then what?"

"What do you think?"

Solibos pursed his lips. "We fortify the bank on the opposite side of the bridge. Push outward from there, sally by sally. We keep them from consolidating. It will require a certain ferocity of will – do you have such fire in you, Ser Aeron?"

Aeron was silent for a moment. "A better question is, do you?"

Solibos frowned. "Meaning?"

"What if I were to put you in charge of such a strategy?" Before Solibos could reply, Aeron went on. "My people would provide support, obviously. I think even you'll agree that the grenadiers, at least, would be useful in any sallies. We hold the city – you drive them from it. A glorious victory, and all yours."

Solibos studied him warily. "Why?"

Aeron shrugged. "I'm no babe in the woodshed, whatever you and Valan might think. We have our own disagreements in the Shires. Politics is a game everyone plays. You want to be the hero, because you want to rule here." Solibos's expression hardened, but Aeron went on. "Ambition is no crime, however some might see it."

"Yes," Solibos said, hesitantly. He smiled thinly, clearly pleased with the compliment. "Perhaps you are more clever than I thought, halfling."

I think you're an opportunistic snake, Aeron thought. What he said was, "We halflings know better than to show up you tall-folk. It never profits us." He sighed. "Your people asked ours for help, to pay back what we owed you. That is the only reason we're here. If you can show that we're not needed, I can take my folk back to our lands and out of yours. Trust me, we'll be more than happy to go. And you'll be pleased to be rid of us I have no doubt."

Solibos considered this. He went to the edge of the bridge and looked down into the swirling waters below. Aeron joined him. The river was deep here. Too deep to ford easily. The great stone pillars were as thick as towers and covered in carved reliefs of animals and gods and other things he couldn't identify. Green stains marked the rising and falling of the river with the seasons.

"It is not that I am ungrateful, you understand," Solibos said, with condescending gentleness. "It is simply that this fight is ours, and you are a distraction."

"I do understand," Aeron said. He clasped his hands behind his back. "We halflings aren't made for war. We don't have a tenth of the experience that you elves do. But we honor our debts. It is the least we can do."

Solibos nodded magnanimously. "It is good that you understand these things. I was afraid that you would be… difficult."

"Oh, no. Whatever spat is going on between you and Valan is your business. Tall-folk business, you might say. Just like this war. And once we've helped a bit, we'll leave it in your capable hands." Aeron forced a smile. "My wife will be happy to see me done with all of this."

Solibos chuckled. "I'm sure she will, my friend. Rest assured, your contributions will not be forgotten, after the fact. We elves have long memories." He made as if to pat Aeron on the shoulder but seemed to think better of it. "I shall call an immediate halt to this demolition."

"Why? As you said, it baits the trap. Don't stop, just… slow it down." Aeron turned away from the water. "In fact, let my people take over. Your people should concentrate on preparing themselves to meet the enemy."

Solibos glanced at him. "Perhaps you're right. Very well. I shall leave it in your charge, Ser Aeron." He rested his hand on the hilt of his sword and looked back toward the city. "It is a fine city, you know. Not a Xirkaali shall set foot in it while I live."

"I believe you mean that," Aeron said, honestly. "Let's say this; when it's time to sally out, we'll move our gunners and howitzers up to cover you."

"We have archers for that," Solibos protested.

Aeron nodded patiently. "Yes, but they'll be repositioning with you, in order to prevent the Xirkaali from folding up your flanks."

Solibos blinked. "Oh. Yes. Yes, of course. And then?"

Aeron smiled. "As you drive them back, we'll bring up palisades. Form a bulwark across the mouth of the bridge. From there, we can push forward, advancing the bulwark ahead of us and providing your warriors with respite, should they need it… though I don't expect you will."

"No. No, we will push them back, break their lines, and send them fleeing into the jungle." Solibos clasped his hands behind his back. "An excellent strategy. I am not surprised that you agree with me. We elves have perfected the art of war."

"So I've been told." Aeron took a deep breath. "Well, I'll leave you to it, Lord Solibos. I'll go inform Lance-Captain Trosbert and the others of our – your – new strategy." Solibos glanced at him, and for a moment, Aeron feared he'd pushed it too far. Then Solibos nodded and looked away, dismissing him with a curt gesture.

Aeron made his way back along the bridge. Now, he just had to find Taran Bligh. Taran was supposed to be hard at work, helping with the demolition. The lad was a good engineer, whatever else, and he'd put himself to the work with gusto. He spied Trosbert sitting on the edge of the bridge, peeling an apple with a knife.

"So, what did he have to say for himself?" Trosbert asked. He offered Aeron a slice of apple.

Aeron took it and chewed. "The usual. We're not fit to fight alongside the elves. The worst of it is, he's not wrong."

Trosbert looked at him. "Oh?"

"We have the tools, but not the know-how. I've sent for more reinforcements from the Shires, but they won't be here for days – if not weeks. The army is mostly green; there are a few veterans here and there, like yourself. But it's not enough. The Xirkaali already put at least two cities to the torch, and now they're coming for this one. If the elves couldn't stop them…" He trailed off and sighed. Trosbert swallowed a piece of apple.

"Then it's up to us. That's how it seems to me, at least. You'll forgive my simplicity of view, Ser Aeron, but it seems to me that this is an easy thing. Do or die. We hold the line or we don't. Anything else ain't worth worrying over." Trosbert sliced off another chunk of apple and ate it off of his knife. "You've done the work and trained our cousins to the best of your ability," he continued as he chewed. "From here on out, it's all down to luck and skill at arms."

"That's what worries me. That and this damn bridge." He looked at Trosbert. "Which is why I need young Master Bligh. Where is he?"

"Down below. He came up with some horrid pulley system that he says will revolutionize bridge repairs. He's trying it out now." Trosbert used his knife, a slice of apple impaled on the tip, to indicate the area below the bridge. "Some of the lads are taking bets on whether he falls in the water."

"They'll pull him out if he does, I hope."

Trosbert shrugged. "If they want to get paid."

"Could you bring him up here for me? I have a job for him."

Trosbert frowned. "What sort of job?"

Aeron turned away. An explosion sounded somewhere downriver. In the distance, a plume of smoke rose over the treetops. He felt a chill run through him, but he kept his expression mild as he replied.

"We're going to blow up a bridge."

CHAPTER THIRTY-FOUR
Kortys

Kortys coughed and rolled over. His body felt as if it were full of broken glass. He had a few cracked ribs, at least. Smoke filled his lungs and stung his eyes. He clawed blindly for his bow and found only its shattered remnants. Alisor lay nearby, staring at nothing. The echo of the explosion filled his ears, drowning out everything save its own concussive murmur. Coughing, he tried to pull himself to his feet. It took several tries, but he eventually managed it. He slumped against the parapet.

The lock had been burst asunder. The remnants of the barge lingered in the river, smoldering from the explosion. On the wharves to either side, elves and halflings fought and died as Xirkaali attacked. "Ambushed the ambushers," Kortys muttered, trying to clear his head. Clever. Sneaky. He could almost admire them.

The rest of the flotilla was under attack, but the riverguard were having their own difficulties. He watched as a hemicyon cut down one of the froglike warriors and booted the body over the side. Instinctively, he reached for an arrow but belatedly recalled the loss of his bow. His hand fell to the hilt of his sword. But what good would that do? There was nothing for it but to retreat and hope the defenses at Callenspire would hold.

He stumbled toward what was left of the stairs, one arm wrapped around his chest and his free hand on the hilt of his sword. He heard the mechanical whirr of the howitzer as it began to fire. Xirkaali toppled off of the wharf, their armor no protection against the halfling weapon. But there was only one howitzer and a lot more Xirkaali.

He stepped over the broken body of a halfling and tried not to notice the surprised expression on the dead gunner's face. It was mirrored in that of a nearby elf. Surprise – pain – shock. In life, different as could be; in death, identical. He stooped to retrieve a fallen archer's bow and saw the other survivors hurrying down the steps to join the fray, or maybe just escape. He hurried after them as quickly as he could.

The Xirkaali were waiting for them. Pain receded and training took over. "Down!" he shouted.

Halflings and elves sank down, and Kortys loosed a pair of arrows into a hemicyon climbing the stairs. The creature stumbled to a halt and blinked owlishly as he felt at the arrows that had suddenly sprouted from his throat, as if by magic. Then he toppled off of the steps with a disgruntled sigh. Kortys loosed three more arrows, as quickly as he could draw them from his quiver. The elves at the bottom of the steps rose and met the remaining Xirkaali blade-to-blade, allowing the halflings to slip past.

But the halflings didn't flee as Kortys expected. Rather, they turned on the Xirkaali, striking at their legs and fatally distracting them from their elven opponents. The melee spread into the smoke. There were no battle-lines, no structure. Just a disorganized mass of bodies heaving against one another in blind slaughter.

Kortys caught one of the elves by his shoulder. "Fall back. Form a shieldwall, cover the archers." He propelled the other elf toward a knot of his fellows. He lost sight of them as the wind turned, causing the smoke to thicken. He decided to keep moving, rather than attempt to bring order to the chaos.

It was all coming apart. No one was in charge except whatever god benefitted from confusion. The garrison troops were demoralized; one good push from running all the way back to Callenspire. The halflings weren't much better. The ones he saw looked as if they were in shock. Some were still firing their rifles, but mechanically – as if they'd forgotten all else but their training. The riverguard were still fighting with fervor, but they were on the edge of retreating as well. There was no sign of Glump. Perhaps he was already dead.

A dozen Yan soldiers burst through the smoke, heading in his direction. Kortys fell back, looking for somewhere to make a stand. He drew another arrow as he did so and sent it whistling into the chest of a charging human. The Yan fell with a guttural cry.

Kortys loosed a second and a third at the approaching humans, his eye selecting targets even as his mind calculated the odds and found them bad. A hemicyon burst through the ranks of humans and charged toward him, moving with surprising speed despite the armor that ought to have weighed him down.

The hemicyon slashed out at Kortys, clipping the edge of his cloak. Kortys leapt back and drew his own blade. The dog-man bared his teeth and lunged again, his sword whistling as it chopped the air. Kortys bent sideways, narrowly avoiding the blow, and let his own blade dance across his opponent's ribs. Elven steel proved stronger than what the hemicyon was wearing, and the scales parted. The dog-man howled in pain.

Kortys gave his enemy no chance to recover; his blade whipped out and opened the dog-man's exposed throat to the bone. Even as the dying warrior collapsed, Kortys had sheathed his sword and was sighting on another down the length of an arrow.

As he did so, something low and ugly bounded through the trees along the bank with a snarl. It was a dog, but unlike any dog Kortys had ever seen. Beneath its fur, there were scales, and its eyes blazed with an unnatural ferocity. It came right for him, moving far more quickly across the tangled roots than an animal of its size ought to have.

At the last moment, it sprang for him, jaws wide. He heard the bark of a rifle, and the beast convulsed in midair and collapsed at his feet. He turned to see Makki grinning at him as she lowered her smoking weapon. The engineer was crouched behind a line of barrels alongside a few other halfling gunners.

"I should have known you were too mean to die."

Kortys didn't reply. Instead, he sent an arrow winging toward Makki. She yelped and ducked, and the hound that had been creeping toward her collapsed onto the ground, whimpering. Kortys strode past the halflings and finished it off with a blow of his sword. More hounds appeared, tearing through the thickly-packed trees. Kortys reached for an arrow, but found his quiver empty.

Makki shouted, and Kortys heard the whirr-snarl of the howitzer. The hounds vanished into a pink mist. But more were on the way, and the howitzer had fallen silent. "Out of ammunition," she muttered.

"Too many of them," Kortys agreed. "Fall back," he added, as he retrieved a quiver of arrows from a nearby corpse. A black note of pain ran from his chest to his shoulder, and he bit back a groan, but managed to fill his quiver. "Get back to Callenspire with whoever you can. Let them know we weren't able to hold the lock. The enemy will be arriving sooner than they thought." He nocked an arrow and sent it whirring into the eye of a howling Xirkaali. The dog-man pitched sideways into the river.

Makki fired her rifle. "What about you?"

"We'll hold them back as long as possible. Give you time to retreat." Kortys loosed another arrow – a third – a fourth. There were plenty of enemies to choose from. He would run out of arrows again before he ran out of targets. "This is elf work now." A fifth arrow, a sixth. Gladestalkers converged, moving through the smoke like wraiths, killing as they went. It wasn't enough; but for the moment, the Xirkaali hesitated. Kortys paused and looked at Makki. "Go – *now!*"

The engineer hesitated, and then nodded. "We left barrels of powder on the wharf," she said, quickly. "Red X's. Don't miss." She clasped his arm tightly and then hurried away, shouting orders. Halflings fell back, and elven warriors as well. The gladestalkers remained, loosing arrows from wherever they perched, holding back the foe through sheer, relentless marksmanship. Each arrow bought a moment's respite. But only a moment.

The Xirkaali retreated slowly, drawing back. Readying themselves for another push, or waiting for reinforcements. Kortys thrust an arrow into a nearby fire, until the shaft caught. He loosed it at the farthest of the barrels Makki had indicated. The explosion was small, compared to that of the barge. But it was big enough to knock nearby Xirkaali sprawling. Some of them didn't rise.

Kortys whistled sharply. The signal to retreat. The gladestalkers who heard it melted into the smoke, breaking off from the enemy and falling back out of sight. Hopefully, they would be able to cover the retreat of Makki and the others.

He felt a strange sort of calm descend on him. He hadn't intended to die here, but here was as good as anywhere. He found himself standing beneath one of the old statues – some old hero whose name he couldn't recall. "Just you and me now," he said. Pain flared in his chest. The world blurred. When his vision cleared, he saw the Xirkaali advancing toward him. At a barked order, they stopped.

One stepped forward. "You fought well," the Xirkaali growled, looking about with what might have been admiration. "Better than I expected, given the circumstances."

Kortys tracked her with an arrow. "We do what we can." This was the leader, then. He wondered if he was supposed to feel honored by her attention. If so, she was in for disappointment. He'd never been much for honor.

"You are alone. Your allies have been slain, or fled. Surrender, and you will be treated with respect. Refuse – and die."

Kortys laughed and winced as the pain of his ribs flared through him. He'd been running on desperation until now, but it was wearing off. He felt like a waterskin that had been poked through with sticks. "That's no sort of bargain."

The Xirkaali nodded. "No. But it's the best I can offer you." She sniffed the air and studied the arrow aimed at her. "I am Shulgin Ironeyes, daughter of Hejun. My word is steel. If I say you will be spared, you will be spared."

Kortys hesitated, considering. He lowered his bow a fraction. "How about this? I've heard you Xirkaali like a good duel. So, we fight. If I win, you retreat downriver. If I lose – well. Doesn't really matter, does it?"

Shulgin gave a bark of laughter. "And why would I do that?"

Kortys shrugged. "Why wouldn't you? I'm hurt. Not much of a challenge. But I can still loose an arrow faster than you can blink, and I'll kill at least three more of your warriors before they cut me down. Do it for them, if not yourself." He slipped off his quiver and dropped it to the ground. He wondered how long he could last. A few minutes? Less? Not enough. A bigger distraction was called for. "Sword to sword. Your steel against mine. Unless you're scared, in which case, give the order and have me torn apart."

Shulgin bared her teeth. "You insult me."

Kortys smiled. "Yes."

Shulgin laughed again. "Very well. Steel to steel." She drew her sword and spread her arms. "Come then, and meet your fate, elf."

Kortys straightened and made to drop his bow. Red dots danced at the edges of his vision. It hurt to breathe. He sighed. "On second thought, I'd rather kill as many of you as possible." His bow rose and his arrow flew. It took her high in the shoulder, between the plates of her armor. She howled in pain and staggered back. The Xirkaali gave a great roar and rushed forward as one.

Kortys snatched a handful of arrows from the ground and loosed them as quickly as he could. True to his earlier assertion, three Xirkaali fell. Another two followed before the first warrior reached him. Kortys drew his sword and killed that one as well.

But not the one after that.

CHAPTER THIRTY-FIVE

Shulgin

"He shot me," Shulgin snarled, for the third time in as many moments. The arrow still jutted from her shoulder, and a red ache danced along her arm. She stared down at the elf's body in anger and not a little confusion. The blades of her warriors had done their work all too well, and there was little left that was recognizable, but somehow, she thought he was smiling. "Why? I would have spared him!"

"Maybe he didn't wish to be spared," Ryuk said, nudging the body with his foot. "Maybe it was simply as he said… he wished to kill as many of us as possible. If so, he gave good accounting." He looked at her. "I suggest we burn the body, just in case."

"Madness," she said. She reached up and wrenched the arrow loose, hurling it into the river without a second glance. "They're all mad, every one of them."

Ryuk nodded agreeably. "As you say, Matriarch."

Shulgin glanced at him, and then away. There had been amusement in his tone, but not quite the disrespectful sort. "Have Ushar bring up the rest of the flotilla. And get someone to drag the remains of the barge out of the way, as quickly as possible. We need to keep moving." She looked at the blood on her palm. "Madness," she repeated. The elves were mad. That was the only explanation.

She understood a token resistance; honor demanded nothing less. But this sort of hopeless courage was alien to her. Didn't they understand that defeat was inevitable? Why fight to the death when it served no purpose? Perhaps this was why the gods had sent the Xirkaali to conquer these lands. If this madness infected all of the kingdoms of this continent, then it was the duty of every Xirkaali to see it stamped out.

She pushed the thought aside and took stock of the situation. The explosion had damaged the toll lock, but not badly. It could be repaired and reinforced, in time. But she would leave that to whoever her mother dispatched to follow her. Her own priority was Callenspire. She sat on a cargo crate and summoned a human to bandage her wound. Around her, warriors began to clean away the bodies. The enemy would be burnt, according to imperial rites. If their families wished to complain, they could do so through proper channels once the war had ended.

She hissed in pain as the Yan surgeon knitted the wound in her shoulder shut. "Stop complaining, my lady," he murmured. "And stop tensing your muscles. It makes it harder to sew it shut." She grunted but did not chide him for his disrespect. Instead, she endured the momentary discomfort and called for the scouts. A plainstalker approached, a necklace of freshly cut elf ears hanging from his neck.

Shulgin wrinkled her snout in disgust at the sight of the grisly trophy. "Was such desecration necessary? These people will be a part of the empire soon enough."

The plainstalker shrugged. "I felt we were owed a little something, given how many of my pack they killed." He gave the ears a flick, and blood dappled the air. Shulgin looked away, out over the river.

"What do you have to report?"

"The remainder of the enemy garrison is retreating upriver, to Callenspire. Do you wish us to pursue?" From his tone, she could tell what answer he hoped for. There was nothing the plainstalkers enjoyed more than hunting a beaten foe. But she disappointed him with a slight shake of her head.

"Let them go. We have bloodied them enough for today, and there is no honor in savaging a beaten foe."

The plainstalker looked as if he wished to argue the point, but wisely refrained. Instead, he said, "As you wish, Matriarch. We should keep watch for the river-folk, though. They fled with the others, but I doubt that they went far."

Shulgin nodded, watching the effort to move the exploded barge out of the way. It required ropes, muscle, and teamwork; all things that the hemicyons possessed in abundance. But it was slow-going, even so. "Yes. Send out packs to patrol the jungle and the opposite bank. I don't want any surprises this close to our destination. Keep an eye out for patrols from the direction of the Eastway." As he turned away, she gestured for him to wait. "Oh, and find me a path to the city. I want to see it today, if possible."

The plainstalker bowed his head. "At your command, Matriarch."

Shulgin dismissed him with a wave of her hand. The Yan surgeon forcefully pushed her snout aside, leaned over, and bit through the thread he'd been using to sew her wound. He stepped back, cleaning his hands with a rag. "That should hold you, my lady. Just try not to pick at it, and it will heal clean."

"Will it scar?"

"Most likely."

Shulgin sniffed. "Good. Another for my collection." She turned as howls of greeting – and warning – erupted from the warriors on sentry-duty near the tree-line. She pushed herself to her feet and ambled over to greet the newcomers. She suspected that they'd come by the old paths she'd seen earlier, and they emerged blinking into the harsh sunlight that dappled the river. The group was small, composed of spearwardens, plainstalkers, and human soldiers. At their head was a familiar face, that of her opposite number, Parga.

"Parga," she called out, flexing her hand as she extended it. The ache from her shoulder had begun to fade, thanks to the surgeon's ministrations, but it wouldn't do for her sword-arm to stiffen up at an inopportune time. The other matriarch clasped her forearm and looked around with an impressed grunt.

"We missed quite the celebration, I take it."

"They welcomed us with open arms," Shulgin said, sourly. "I didn't expect you to come yourself. There are riverguard hiding in the jungle."

Parga chuckled. "Allow an old dog to stretch her haunches, eh?" She was older than Shulgin, and older even than Hejun; her muzzle was as white as snow, and her brown hide spotted with gray. One eye was filmy, and that side of her face was bisected by an old scar. But age had not weakened her sword stroke or tempered the fires within. Parga was in the final years of her service to the empire; come the final victory, she would retire to some comfortable posting where she could still be of use. She was a steady hand; reliable but lacking in ambition as well as initiative.

Shulgin had chosen her to lead the Eastway advance for those very reasons. If there was any glory to be gained from the battle to come, she wished it to be hers. Parga was no threat to that, but nor was she incompetent. "Any trouble on your end?" Shulgin asked, as she turned to look out over the river. Parga scrubbed her muzzle with a paw.

"Some. Nothing we couldn't endure."

"My scouts reported explosions along the Eastway. And airships."

"One airship. And some balloons."

Shulgin blinked. "Balloons? Like the Xiryan use on the plains?"

Parga picked at her teeth. "No. Not observation balloons, but something more… aggressive. They carried munitions. We knocked a few out of the air but recovered nothing. At least not intact."

"Elves?"

"Halfkin," Parga said. "Clever little vermin. I see they were here as well."

"Yes. They fought hard." Shulgin tugged her ear, thinking. "Elves, halfkin, and riverguard. That bodes ill for our campaign."

Parga made a sound of dismissal. "Thus far, things are going well. Why conjure shadows to jump at when there is no need?" She nudged a dead elf with her foot. "You'd think they'd fight better, given their supposed immortality."

"Garrison troops," Shulgin said. She crouched beside the body and rolled it over. The dead elf's expression was one of shock, as if he had not even considered the possibility of death. That was their great weakness; they lived so long that they could not conceive of life ending – or changing. She looked up at Parga. "You've seen the city, then?"

"From a distance," Parga said. "We made a camp about a day's march away – maybe two, if the weather turns. How long will it take you to get your boats moving?"

"We'll be past the toll lock by this afternoon. We should be in sight of the city by tomorrow, or the next morning." She paused. "Tell me what you saw."

Parga tipped up a barrel of halfkin fire-powder and sat on it. She began to massage one of her paws, as if it pained her. Maybe it did. She'd done a fair bit of walking, of late. "High walls of pale stone. Reinforced in places with what appeared to be sturdy wooden palisades – recently built, I'd wager. Half of the city is built into a tree, or so it appears from a distance."

Shulgin grunted in annoyance. "They do like their trees."

Parga laughed. "Indeed. The city sits on an island, roughly wedge-shaped, with two sides protected by water and the third connected to the Eastway by a massive bridge – which, according to my scouts, appears to be in the process of being demolished." She winced, plucked a bit of grit from between her paw-pads, and flicked it into the water. "They're ready for a fight, and no mistake."

Shulgin grunted. "Good. I don't know about you, but I was tired of easy victories."

Parga laughed hoarsely. "I never get tired of those. Best kind, in my opinion." She scratched her ear thoughtfully. "The rivers will make it hard work. We need that bridge. It's the only way to get our siege equipment anywhere close to their walls."

Shulgin nodded. "They'll make a fight of it." The thought wasn't an unpleasant one. As she'd told Parga, she was tired of easy victories. She wanted something better. "We'll need to be quick about it. Take it, and hold it. Else they'll just drive us back and finish what they started." She scratched her chin, thinking it over. "No rockets. We can't risk damaging the bridge further. We'll send the plainstalkers in first, and then follow up – take a pack, and as many auxiliaries as you think you might need. Drive them back and then hold position."

Parga shook her head slowly. "Won't work. They've already got defenses set up; if we attack with anything less than overwhelming force, they'll cut us to pieces."

Shulgin growled. That complicated matters. "I need to get closer. To see it for myself." There was only so much she could learn from second-hand reports. Nothing could substitute for firsthand experience. Her mother had taught her that much.

Parga shrugged. "No chance of that, unless – well."

"What?"

"Unless they agree to parley." Parga scratched her cheek. "You never know, they might decide to surrender after all."

"I doubt it. But a parley might be the thing nonetheless." Normally, the Xirkaali did not parley. Envoys asked for surrender, and if their request was denied, the horde would conquer. Talking to an enemy beyond that served little purpose. Yet, Shulgin was curious. Who would she be facing across the battlefield? Another mad elf? She touched her wound and winced. Part of her hoped not. Once was enough.

"At the very least I can size up my opponent."

CHAPTER THIRTY-SIX
Hannah

Hannah swung her knife out and wearily chopped through a low-hanging vine. Behind her, the tiny party of *Thunderchild* survivors plodded on, bent beneath their burdens. Some carried the injured, those not on improvised travois; others dragged litters of supplies, including the remaining flight packs of the grenadiers, and two wooden boxes of grenades.

Only eleven of them were left. *No,* she thought. Ten now. Hasslefoot, the first mate, had succumbed to his injuries the day before and been buried at the base of some towering tree covered in purple flowers that reminded her of bruises. Ten of a crew of over thirty, plus her small group of grenadiers, who'd taken their own losses over the last few days. Less than half, and likely to be smaller still in the next few days unless they found a source of fresh water. She licked dry lips and wiped the sweat from her stinging eyes.

"I can take point for a bit, Captain," Cogman said from behind her. Hannah paused to catch her breath and waved him forward. No sense wearing herself out just to prove a point. The last few days had taught her that lesson, at least.

"I'm really not enjoying this war anymore," she said. "What about you?"

Cogman snorted as he drew his knife and moved past her. He looked as rough as she felt, in his stained uniform and bandaged eye. A chunk of rock had nearly taken it out, but he wasn't complaining. No one was; none of them had the energy for it.

"It could be worse."

"How?" she called to his back.

He glanced over his shoulder. "It could be raining!"

Hannah allowed herself a brief laugh and leaned against a tree stump taller than she was, scorched hollow by a long-ago lightning strike. Something rustled within it, but she was too tired to care. The heat was unbearable and air here in the lowlands was somehow heavier than that of the mountains. Damp, too. It was like breathing soup in places.

She could still smell the smoke of *Thunderchild*'s destruction. A bandolier of grenades had been enough to rip what was left of the airship apart and prevent the Xirkaali from retrieving it. At least, that was the hope. But the Xirkaali had been hot on their heels ever since, pursuing them through the jungle. Driving them toward the hinterlands, and the Eastway, she thought. There would be more Xirkaali there waiting to capture them, as they'd captured the rest of the surviving crew. There were at least eight other survivors unaccounted for, and Hannah was fairly certain they were in Xirkaali hands. But what did the enemy want with them? She had no answers and pushed the thought aside wearily.

The others trudged past. Her grenadiers moved along the edges of the group and at the rear, carrying their grenades. The survivors of the crew were armed with a variety of implements; mostly tools. There were a handful of rifles, but not enough ammunition to go around. She wished they had a few more, maybe even an aralez. But wishing didn't make it so, as the gaffers said.

They were being followed; she knew that much. After the first go-round, the Xirkaali hadn't pursued in force. Instead, there were packs of scouts on their trail. They'd sneak close and come under cover of darkness, or in the rain that drenched the jungle periodically. She shivered slightly, thinking of yellow eyes gleaming in the dark.

They'd lost at least five of theirs that way. Two had been gutted and left in the mud, with no time to give them a proper burial. As to the fates of the other three, she couldn't say. Captured, probably. Taken to one of the camps along the shore, there to be interrogated or executed or whatever it was that the Xirkaali did to captives. And she had no way of getting them back, not if she wanted to keep the rest of her small group alive.

While that gnawed at her, it wasn't as painful as the thought of being out of the fight. She'd come all this way, only to spend the war lost in the jungle. It wasn't what she'd imagined when she'd first dreamt of being a soldier.

She made her way to the rear of the party where Umer and Sagria were keeping watch. They saluted as Hannah joined them, and she irritably waved it aside. "No need for that, either of you. It just annoys me."

"That's why we do it," Sagria said, lightly. She had her rifle cradled in her arms. Umer had his sword and a battered shield that he'd found somewhere.

"Maybe I should have left you to the Xirkaali," Hannah said, mock-sternly. Sagria grinned cheekily and patted her rifle.

"And then you'd have no one to cover your rear, eh?" She was about to continue, when a sudden, loud howl pierced the jungle gloom. It echoed eerily through the trees, and Hannah stiffened in fear. Sagria's face fell, and she raised her rifle.

"They've found our trail," Umer said, reaching for the hilt of his sword.

"I doubt they ever lost it," Hannah said. "Umer, tell Cogman to get everyone into cover. Sagria – you're with me."

Sagria swallowed nervously as Umer hurried after the others. "What's the plan?"

"The same as it was last time – we convince them that they've bitten off more than they can chew. Come on." Hannah sheathed her knife and plucked a grenade from her bandolier. Well, not hers; it had belonged to a grenadier named Winkle, who hadn't survived their last encounter with the Xirkaali scouts trailing them.

Sagria followed her into the trees. Hannah pointed to one. "Can you climb?"

"I did mention my da was a poacher, didn't I?" Sagria said as she shouldered her rifle and scrambled nimbly up the mossy trunk of the tree.

"Keep me covered," Hannah said as she advanced into the undergrowth, grenade at the ready. The howls were closer now. The Xirkaali were trying to scare them; had been since the crash. To harry them *somewhere*. To make them run – or surrender to whoever or whatever was waiting for them. But Bimsons didn't run.

"Captain," Sagria called down. Hannah paused and looked up. Sagria gestured for her to climb the tree the crewwoman sat in. "You need to see this."

Hannah climbed the tree quickly. As she reached Sagria's perch, she saw a clearing a short distance away. The group had skirted its edge but not gone in despite the need to make camp. At the time, she'd feared it was too open – too inviting. She'd been right. The Xirkaali had clearly been waiting – but not for them.

Something large now occupied the clearing, and the Xirkaali she thought were pursuing them surrounded it and loosed arrows at it, or jabbed at it with blades. It was a shaggy hulk, like a small, ambulatory hill covered in moss. Hannah flinched as arrows sank into the big beast's hide.

"What is it?" Sagria murmured.

"It's a troll," Hannah whispered. "Though I don't know what kind. Looks like a forest troll, but bigger. Maybe a swamp troll." Hill trolls were dangerous; ferocious and always hungry. Forest and swamp trolls were different; not as aggressive, for one thing, though they could be dangerous if angered. They mostly kept to themselves, in the forests of the foothills, or the swamps of the deep jungle. There were even a few in Gerinhaf, acting as laborers on farms or in workshops.

This one was having a bad time of it. Xirkaali hounds surrounded it, snapping and snarling. Several hemicyons approached warily, nets and ropes at the ready. They intended to capture the poor brute, but why? The troll groaned in consternation as a hound bit at his ankle, and he kicked the scaly beast away. The Xirkaali lassoed his arms and neck, and he bellowed in frustration.

Hannah looked at Sagria. "I don't know about you, but those odds don't seem fair to me. When I get close, shoot one of the Xirkaali."

"What are you planning?"

"To help. That's what we came here to do, after all." With that, Hannah dropped to the ground and moved quick, drawing her knife as she went. She couldn't match the Xirkaali in a stand-up fight, but she might be able to give the troll a fighting chance. She kept close to the trees, and when she heard the crack of Sagria's rifle, she primed a grenade and sent it rolling across the forest floor toward the Xirkaali archers.

The explosion rocked the clearing. Several Xirkaali were hurled to the ground, hair smoldering and bodies broken. Hannah was up and zig-zagging through the trees before the echo had faded. She sprang toward the nearest of the ropes that bound the troll and slashed through it before the Xirkaali had noticed her. She cut a second rope before a hemicyon came for her, sword in hand. Hannah tumbled away from the hemicyon's blow and was rewarded when the troll's hand shot out and closed on her attacker's head.

He rose, yanking several of his captors from their feet, and flung the hemicyon into a tree with bone-breaking force. Hannah palmed another grenade and sent it wobbling toward the edge of the clearing where the Xirkaali were regrouping. Before she could move again, a hound leapt and bore her to the ground with a gut-churning snarl. She managed to interpose her forearm between its jaws, and the thick leather vambrace she wore saved her from its teeth, if not the force of its bite.

Hannah jammed her knife between the hound's ribs again and again, trying to ignore the pain in her arm. It finally sagged atop her with a whine and released her. She tried to shove its dead weight off but couldn't quite manage it. She heard Sagria's rifle crack again, and a howl of pain. Then, a roar. She saw the limp body of a Xirkaali pass overhead and out of sight. The troll was loose.

For a moment, everything was loud and happening at once. Then, silence. The hound's body was dragged off of her and flung aside. She looked up into the primitive, slablike features of the troll. It – he – resembled a forest troll in coloration and size, but he was covered in a shaggy pelt that resembled moss.

He grunted something and nudged her with a warty knuckle. Hannah sat up slowly.

"Easy there, big fellow. Easy. I'm a friend."

The troll blinked and sank to his haunches. Then he threw back his head and howled. The sound reverberated through the clearing and drifted out through the jungle. Then, he reached over and hauled her to her feet as easily as he had tossed the hound aside, but more gently, thankfully.

"Friend," Hannah said again as he released her. She wondered if he understood. Trolls weren't the sharpest knives in the kitchen by any means, but he seemed to get that she was trying to help. That was something, at least.

"Captain," Sagria called out, nervously. Hannah looked up. The trees parted as another troll appeared. And then a third… a fourth… five, six… a dozen. They peered at Hannah with ponderous intensity, as if trying to decide whether she was food or not. The first troll gently lifted her up onto his shoulder and grunted something. He kicked one of the dead Xirkaali for emphasis.

The second troll looked at the others and gave a guttural snarl. The first replied with equal intensity. For a moment, the two brutes growled at one another. Then, a deep bellow sounded from somewhere back within the trees and another troll, larger than the rest, and wearing a headdress made from the skull of some large animal, pushed aside several of the others and ambled into view.

He pulled absently on his bottom lip as he studied Hannah. "You… fight?" he asked, haltingly. It was elvish, of sorts. But broken. Hannah nodded.

"We fight."

He sniffed. "Good." He looked down at the dead Xirkaali. "We fight too. They… take us. Take young ones. We… get back." He thumped his chest. He looked at her. "They… take yours?"

Hannah hesitated. She wasn't quite sure what he meant, but she thought it best to agree. "Yes," she said, quickly. Then, "Where?"

The big troll gestured vaguely in the direction of the sea. "Camp. Big camp."

"Is that where you were going?" she asked. If these trolls were anything like the ones she was familiar with, they were clearly on the war-path. But the trollish idea of strategy was largely just wandering in a random direction and hitting whatever they stumbled across. The big troll nodded.

"We… get back," he said, again.

Hannah took a breath. It was possible that her people had been taken to the same camp. She hesitated, but only for a moment. "We help," she said. The troll blinked.

"Help?"

"Help," Hannah repeated, firmly. Then, she tapped her chest. "Hannah."

The troll thumped his own chest. "Uk." He smiled, showing off a mouth of very large, very sharp teeth. "We get back."

"We get back," Hannah said. She turned to wave at Sagria. "Go get the others. Let them know we're heading back for our people." She turned back to Uk. "But we won't be going alone."

CHAPTER THIRTY-SEVEN
Gorrup

Gorrup cracked one eye and spat a gobbet of blood onto the coarse sand. "Is that all you've got, dog-man? I barely felt that one."

Kungas growled in annoyance and stepped back. "You are an obstinate creature." As always, he spoke in badly accented Neritican. Gorrup wondered if the Xirkaali was using this as an opportunity to practice his linguistic skills.

"I don't know what that means, but when I get loose, I'm going to eat you," Gorrup said. He flexed his aching muscles, but as ever, the chains held. He was bound to a post in the heart of the Xirkaali camp. His flesh was dry and cracked, and the sand at his feet was muddy with his blood. Kungas had been at him since Khulan's departure, trying to wring Axel's location from him. The hemicyon was obsessed with capturing the gillkin.

"You will not get loose," Kungas scoffed. "Those chains were forged to hold beasts far larger than you." He rubbed his paws, which were dappled with Gorrup's blood. "Why do you protect him? Would he do the same for you?"

"It does not matter what he would do. My honor is my own," Gorrup said.

"You know nothing of honor," Kungas snarled. "You are a savage. A worshipper of witches and an eater of mud. Were it up to me, I would kill you and place your head on a spike as warning to the rest of your primitive kind. But Admiral Khulan, in her infinite wisdom, has declared you to be useful to us."

Gorrup chortled, and Kungas hit him again. And again. He was strong, but Gorrup had been hit by stronger. Even so, it hurt. His wounds seeped through the bandages that the Xirkaali had used to treat them, and it felt as if every blow made them gape anew. Kungas stepped back again and studied him, as if considering a third blow. Then he turned and barked an order to two hemicyon warriors. "Take him back to the stockade. I will continue the interrogation later."

Having learned from painful experience, Gorrup didn't struggle as he was taken from the post and half-dragged toward the stockade by the hemicyons. He had been their prisoner for several days now and come to understand them somewhat. The Xirkaali could be brutal, when crossed, but otherwise were content to treat their captives as gently as possible. Most of them, at least. Kungas was a different matter; the witch-hunter seemed to revel in causing pain, at least where Gorrup was concerned.

As always, he studied the camp as he was escorted through its tidy confines. The Xirkaali had made themselves at home and had hammered crude pylons of mangrove wood into the sand in order to build atop a stable foundation. From there, they had begun to construct a shanty town of lean-tos and watchtowers. He could smell the smoke of industry creeping through the makeshift streets; of strange chemicals and spilled blood. Every day, the camp expanded – the palisade pushed ever outward, and more tents rose as supplies and warriors arrived from elsewhere.

Was this what they intended for his land? To uproot every tree and build over the mud and silt that his folk called home? Axel seemed to think so, and from what he'd seen, Gorrup could only conclude that he was correct. He wondered where the gillkin was now. Had he made it to his destination? Or had he been slain by some guardian beast of Medu'Syth? A depressing possibility, especially if the other Neriticans shared the *Ril'uwa's* animosity toward Axel's folk.

Gorrup hoped Axel was alive. Not simply for his sake, but for the sake of all the *Ril'uwa*, and all those who called the jungle their home. The Xirkaali had to be stopped, one way or another. Whatever the cost.

The stockade consisted of a heavy palisade made from mangrove posts, with a roof made from thick planks, bent to form an arch. Human soldiers stood on guard before the only entrance, and archers prowled the roof-planks, keeping watch on the prisoners below.

Once inside, Gorrup was chained by the leg to another post. The chain was long enough that he could circumnavigate the interior of the stockade, but couldn't quite reach the walls. The interior consisted of a single large space, with a huge iron pot of water at the center to be shared among the prisoners equally.

His fellow prisoners were a motley lot. Several riverguard; two elves; a trio of swamp trolls, all chained to posts similar to his own, equidistant from Gorrup and each other; and most recently, a small group of six halflings. Gorrup had never met one of the folk of Ej, but he had heard about them from those riverguard who had dealings with them.

The prisoners had little interaction, lost as they were in their own miseries. Even so, Gorrup had learned much, listening to them. Pondwardens were natural polyglots; they had to be, to deal with the various riverguard dialects. He knew some elvish, even. The halflings were a bit harder to understand, but there was enough similarity to elvish to help him.

The elves were soldiers from Grishamvu, taken by Khulan in some raid or other. The riverguard were from the Tidewalker tribe; some of Hulum's warriors, taken in the same clash that had seen Gorrup captured. The trolls were… trolls. Khulan had collected other monsters; swamp-cats and at least one of the great red serpents that slithered through the jungle canopy. The Xirkaali seemed to regard them as trophies of some sort.

The Ej-folk had supposedly been captured after their airship crashed. One was injured; she'd been barely conscious for several days. While Khulan had been assiduous in having human healers seeing to their needs, Kungas was of the opinion that such concern was a waste of time. In the time since Khulan's departure, the halfling's condition had taken a turn for the worse. At the moment, she was moaning softly while one of her companions tried to soothe her with a damp rag.

Gathering his chain, Gorrup painfully made his way over to the halfling. "Sick?" he croaked, in broken elvish. He knew a bit of the trade tongue; the elven boatmen used it to parley for passage through riverguard waters. The other halfling looked up at him, startled.

"She has a fever. I think her wound might be infected."

Gorrup crouched. "Let me see," he said. Reluctantly, the halfling did as he asked. Gorrup probed the injury as gently as he could manage. Nonetheless, his ministrations elicited a groan of pain from the small being, and the distinct odor of pus. "Get mud," he commanded.

"Mud?"

"Dirt with water on it," Gorrup said, still studying the wound. It wasn't deep, but it had become inflamed. He scraped a claw against his forearm, drawing a weal of blood. "Bring mud here, quickly."

The halfling did, and handed him a small sludge of mud, smeared on a tatter of cloth. Gorrup squeezed blood into it and worked it in with a finger. Then he placed the mass against the wound and used the cloth to bind it in place. The halfling made to protest, but Gorrup silenced him with a look.

"We heal quick. Our blood is clean."

"Some sages believe it has curative properties," one of the elves said, absently. "The mud as well. They say it is all due to the mud." He stood, flung back his sleeves, and came over. "I will tie the bandage. Your hands are too big."

Gorrup stepped back. "My people say sages pay bounty for our dead, so that they might be cutting them apart."

The elf paused. "Almost certainly," he admitted. He sat back on his haunches. "There. That should hold our large friend's poultice in place long enough to purge the infection."

"Thank you," the halfling said. He looked at Gorrup and the elf. "My name's Pinter. Oswal Pinter." He extended his hand to Gorrup, who clasped it gingerly.

"Gorrup," the pondwarden said.

"Talis," the elf said. He paused and then looked at Gorrup. "Would you like me to check your bandages, pondwarden?"

"If you wish." Gorrup continued to crouch as the elf checked him over.

Talis leaned close. "The halfling will die without proper medical attention," he whispered. "I have a plan, if you're willing to hear it."

Gorrup rolled an eye in Talis's direction. The archers were too high above to hear them, but even so, it was best to pitch their voices low. "Escape?"

"Yes."

Gorrup chuckled. "About time. What you need?"

Talis smiled. "A distraction would be most helpful."

Gorrup paused. "Can do that. But then?"

Talis hesitated, and then glanced at the riverguard. "Our *Ril'uwa* friends seem to think their people are close by. If we could reach the jungle…"

Gorrup frowned. "Big if."

"It would need to be a big distraction." Talis glanced at the trolls. "Those shaggy brutes might be of use to us. Set them loose, and the Xirkaali would certainly be preoccupied dealing with them…"

"They be killed."

"Better them than us."

Gorrup grunted and looked away. He hadn't expected any better from the elf, but even so, he was still somewhat surprised by the callousness of the suggestion. He studied the trolls carefully. Swamp trolls were voracious, and not picky when it came to what they shoveled into their maws. They viewed the spawning pools of the *Ril'uwa* as easy meals, and more than once in the course of his duties, Gorrup had been forced to fend off a hungry troll or two. But sending them to their deaths was a different matter.

He was about to reply when the trolls suddenly set up a clamor. They yanked on their chains and howled loudly. One began to slam his – her? – fists against the ground with a regular rhythm. Talis stepped back, a look of concern on his face. "What's gotten into them?" he demanded, in a concerned tone.

"Maybe they are having better hearing than you are thinking," Gorrup said as he heaved himself to his feet. There were shouts from the archers above, but whether they were directed at the captives or someone else, Gorrup wasn't sure.

Then, over the roaring of the trolls, he heard a thunderous explosion. Pinter shot to his feet. "Grenade," he said, breathlessly. "By the missing gods, that was a grenade!"

The other halflings were on their feet as well, save the wounded one. They were all excited. Before Gorrup could ask what a grenade was, another explosion – closer than the last – rocked the stockade. The trolls were wrenching at their posts now, trying to free themselves. It was obvious that they smelled something.

Gorrup hurried toward them, but his own chain brought him up short. He yanked at it with a croak of frustration, but the post was set too deep to uproot it. He took a deep breath and sprang back toward it, striking it with his full weight. The wood shuddered slightly but didn't splinter. He retreated a short distance and did it again. The archers above were too preoccupied to notice as he hurled his entire weight against the post a third and fourth time. Finally, it began to crack – or perhaps it was his bones. Either way, something was happening.

Another explosion. The stink of smoke permeated the stockade, and the howls of the Xirkaali filled the air. Gorrup roared in fury and crashed into the post once more, bludgeoning it to pieces with his sheer mass. He collapsed, panting, but not for long. He forced himself to his feet, snatched up his chains, and headed for the trolls. They looked askance at him, but soon realized what his intentions were when he looped his chains about the post of the closest troll and began to pull.

The troll gripped its chains and did the same, grunting with effort. Alone, neither of them had the strength. But together, the post began to wobble – then twist – and finally slide free of the ground. The troll hefted it in two hands and swung it at the one his nearest companion was chained to. The two posts shattered, freeing the second troll.

While they worked to free the third, Gorrup made his way to the iron pot. He dumped the water out and hefted the pot. "Get out of the way!" he bellowed.

Talis and the others scrambled aside as Gorrup hurled the pot with all the strength he had left at the doors to the stockade. The doors were barred shut, but the pot was very heavy and, even injured, he was very strong. The pot smashed through the doors and out into the yard. Smoke boiled in.

Gorrup reached down and scooped up the injured halfling over Pinter's protests. Cradling her against his chest, he rumbled, "Come!" He shouldered his way through the broken doors without waiting for a reply.

Outside – chaos. Confusion. Swamp trolls hurled Xirkaali aside like toys as explosions rocked the camp. Gorrup saw a small form dart through the smoke, armed with a sword and shield. Another halfling rode atop a towering troll, her rifle balanced on the great brute's skull. The attack had sent the camp reeling, but the Xirkaali were already regrouping. He could hear Kungas howling orders from somewhere nearby.

"We go," he said, turning toward the swamp. But the Xirkaali had anticipated this. Arrows rained down. Pinter cried out in pain, and one of the riverguard slumped with a gurgle. Talis snatched up a bow from a fallen human soldier and sent an arrow winging toward the roof of the stockade.

"You are going nowhere," Kungas growled as he prowled into view through the smoke, spinning his sickle in lazy circles. Armored hemicyons advanced on either side of him. The witch-hunter cocked his head, his good eye burning with kill-lust.

"And, I think it is safe to say that your usefulness has come to an end."

CHAPTER THIRTY-EIGHT
Hejun

Hejun sat on a bench atop the sea-wall of Ruhaindo, studying a pile of maps and field reports scattered across the table before her. She was slowly coming to believe that logistics was a curse placed upon warriors to keep them from getting too full of themselves. Taking Ruhaindo had only complicated her burden.

She sat back and stretched, trying to ease the cramp in her shoulders. Human guards patrolled the length of the wall, their attention split between the sea and the city. She wondered what they thought about. The human mind was a source of constant mystery to her. She knew that they felt the same about her people. Humans thought long; hemicyons thought short. It was hard for them to see past the present, to consider any future beyond the immediate. For humans, it seemed to come as naturally as breathing.

Sometimes, she envied them that. At other times, she found it infuriating. Nor was it the only thing she found to be so. As a pup, she'd imagined an invasion as a thing of fire and blood, pouring across the land. And it was, in a sense. But it was a slow fire. One could not invade and forget; gains were to be consolidated, fortresses manned, prisoners put to work. An invasion was a project of years, requiring a solid foundation for any future success to stand upon. It required an overseer who could think ahead, beyond the next day.

It made her head hurt.

The elven lands were bountiful; resource-rich. Even these lands, with the wastes encroaching steadily from the east, had treasures to be plundered. But such a task had to be undertaken with care. Hejun's responsibility was to see that things were done correctly, as much as it was to take the region for the Xirkaali Empire.

She paused for a moment and let her gaze roam across the bay, toward Evanvale. Smoke rose from the city; not the smoke of fires, but that of industry. Alchemists and forgemasters were working now, as the walls were reinforced and made ready. Things were proceeding as quickly as could be expected.

She picked up a scroll and noted Han's delicate script; the Yan reported that Blackthorn was mustering a sizable defense. He politely advised that they make a push to take the city before they became bogged down.

"With what forces, Han?" Hejun muttered. Fourth Claw was stretched thin as it was; her forces – those not already dispatched to Callenspire – were split between Evanvale and Ruhaindo, and were engaged in preparing defensive works. It was inevitable that the elves would counter-attack. Her warriors had to be ready for it.

She was confident the bay could be held against encroachment from the direction of Blackthorn or Grishamvu, both of which were still under siege. She was certain that Callenspire could be taken. But anything beyond that was murky.

She tossed Han's report to the side and selected another missive.

This one was from Gorcha, demanding to be given command of the Blackthorn expedition suggested by Han. She'd had a human write it for her, as in her opinion no proper hemicyon would waste time learning how to read and write.

Hejun considered it, wondering if there had been some collusion between Han and the other hemicyon. Gorcha had more than proved her abilities, taking the sea-wall. But she dismissed the idea. Gorcha needed a firm paw on her neck to keep her from rushing into foolishness. She would appoint one of the others and keep Gorcha close. If that provoked her into challenging Hejun's leadership, so much the better.

A polite cough caught her attention and she turned to see Obair standing behind her. "What now, old man?" she asked as she turned back to her maps. "What new problem have you brought me to gnaw on?"

"A report from Callenspire," he said. Hejun growled and looked at him.

"Tell me."

"There's been some resistance, but nothing they couldn't handle. Or so Shulgin claims. They managed to reach the city in one piece, at least."

Hejun tugged on her ear. "Small favors. And how does the city look?"

"They have made themselves as ready as such a place can. It will not be easy, but… she is confident." Obair hesitated. "I could go, if you wish."

Hejun looked at him. "And do what? Annoy her further?"

Obair smiled. "In a sense. Advise her, as I have advised you." He looked around. "She needs me more than you do, at the moment."

"Careful not to use those words with her. She will take it poorly." Hejun gestured. "But yes, go. Take a detachment. Tell her that they are reinforcements."

Obair bowed. "As you say, Matriarch." He paused again. "By the way, your cousin has returned. She wishes to speak with you."

Hejun perked up. Khulan had been gone for some time, leading the bulk of the fleet along the coast. "Does she? Send her out, then." Obair bowed again and left the wall. A moment later, a pair of human guards escorted Khulan out. Hejun waved them aside. "Greetings, cousin. Good hunting, I trust?"

Khulan collapsed onto the bench beside Hejun with a weary grunt. She stank of blood and fire-powder, and her armor was blackened in places. "I'm beginning to hate elves." She looked up at the sky overhead. "There's a fleet harbored at Grishamvu," she went on, still staring upward. "They were ready for us. We lost two junks."

Hejun grunted. "Did you accomplish anything else of note?"

Khulan chuckled. "Not as such. It's obvious to me that word of your victory over Ruhaindo has spread along the coast. The elves are digging in." She scratched absently at her jaw. "They'll be hard to shift, without more forces."

Hejun looked at her cousin. "Is that your subtle way of requesting aid?"

Khulan waved her words aside. "It can wait. I'm content to play corsair for the time being. There are many port towns along the coast. I can occupy my sea-dogs with burning those. We might get lucky and draw out that fleet."

"That would be ideal," Hejun said as she looked out over the bay. The water was littered with the remnants of war-junks and elven vessels, making it resemble a drowned forest. The wreckage would be salvaged, eventually. But not any time soon. She glanced at Khulan. "Any sign of the fish-folk?"

Khulan scratched her cheek. "Some. I captured a few of the frogkin, as well as some of the local wildlife. Trolls and the like."

"And?"

"I thought you might enjoy a hunt, when things are settled." Khulan stretched. "Or we can interrogate them and see what they know. At the moment, they're safely confined at Steel Mangrove Camp, under the watchful eye of one of Baidar's witch-hunters. A surly brute by the name of Kungas." She paused. "I also managed to capture a few of the halfkin, if you're interested."

Hejun looked at her. "What? How?"

"I shot down one of their airships. They've been prowling the coast, lobbing explosives into our camps. Nothing too damaging, save in terms of morale, but I thought it best to put a stop to it. So I waited for one to show and brought it down."

"You captured it?" Hejun asked, eagerly. The alchemists had been salivating over the thought of examining one of the strange vessels.

Khulan looked away. "Not as such. The little vermin blew it up, rather than let us have it." She sighed. "For such a small folk, they have courage in excess."

Hejun sat back. "They will make fine servants of the empire, when they have been tamed. You mentioned prisoners?"

"A handful. My warriors are hunting the rest. We'll have them soon enough, I expect. When they do, I shall have them brought here for you." She pushed herself to her feet and stretched again. "Now, care to spar, cousin? I feel like some exercise."

Hejun bobbed to her feet. "I was hoping you'd ask."

The dance of steel – the true dance, not simply the swirl of battle – was one of the oldest traditions of the Kaali. Part-meditation, part-ritual, it was one of their most sacred ceremonies. Hejun and her cousin came together with a crash and broke apart. They spun and lunged, came together again and broke apart. Again and again. Their blades whistled through the air, clashed, drew sparks. Hejun became aware of the humans watching, their expressions awed and not a little frightened.

Khulan laughed as their blades locked, steel scraping on steel. "You've gotten lazy, cousin. It's all this sitting around on walls, moping. You should get out more. Go pillage something. It'll do you good."

"And then who will see to all the planning, eh? You?"

Khulan stepped back. "Not likely."

Hejun laughed. "You see my predicament, then." She lowered her sword as a sudden, shrieking pillar of sea-birds rose from beyond the wall and hurtled skyward as if pursued by something only they could see. Khulan turned and watched the birds as well, her brow knit with consternation.

"Something has upset them," she growled, softly.

The first tremor hit a moment later. Faint; barely noticeable at all. But Hejun felt it, and her hackles bristled. What did the birds know that she didn't? Some instinct drew her to the edge of the sea-wall and she looked out over the bay. There was something odd below. The water moved in strange, uncertain directions as if caught by a storm. Only the sky was clear, and there was no sign of rain on the horizon.

The second tremor set the wall to trembling, ever so slightly. Khulan snarled. "Thunder in the deep, cousin," she said. "An ill omen if there ever was one."

Hejun didn't reply; couldn't. Her eyes were fixed on one of the junks prowling the bay, keeping watch for the enemy. It stalked among the wrecks that had yet to be cleared, like a hungry tiger wandering a battlefield. But it was not the only predator abroad in the bay. Shimmering forms – hundreds of them – darted along beneath the waves, moving quicker than thought. Hejun turned to shout an order – a warning – when Khulan suddenly gave a bark of alarm.

Hejun spun back to see immense, sucker-lined tendrils erupt from the sea and ensnare the war-junk. The tendrils convulsed, and the vessel shattered like a child's toy, spilling its crew into the bay.

"Kraken," Khulan said. She stepped back from the wall. "I must get to my vessel. It seems the Neriticans have decided to involve themselves after all."

Hejun blinked. "The camps," she hissed. Khulan nodded.

"I fear so. This invasion just got a good deal more complicated, cousin. I do not envy you what comes next." She paused and extended her hand. "May the gods be with you, Hejun." They clasped forearms.

"And you, cousin. Try not to get eaten."

Khulan laughed and started toward the stairs. "No fear of that. There's not a sea-beast alive that can swallow me and survive!"

Hejun turned back to the bay. Alarm bells were ringing now, in both cities. The water was full of sinuous movement. An invasion, or just a raid? Only time would tell. She watched as something that resembled a crab, but far, far larger, hauled itself up onto Evanvale's docks with a booming crash, followed by glimmering forms that moved with quicksilver swiftness. *Naiads*, she thought. She stepped back, already considering strategies.

She caught the attention of one of her guards. "Find Obair," she said. "Tell him he won't be reinforcing Callenspire after all." As the guard ran off, she sheathed her sword and looked back over the bay. The enemy had come. Shulgin would simply have to make do the best she could. Hopefully, her daughter was as competent as Obair insisted.

If not, things were going to go very badly for all of them.

CHAPTER THIRTY-NINE
Axel

Axel flattened himself against the shell of the immense crab-like gigas, as best he was able, as Xirkaali rockets corkscrewed through the air, too close for comfort. The gigas was one of six such creatures advancing on the enemy camp through the shallows. Behind them came Nemon and his placoderms, marching resolutely into the teeth of the enemy's firepower.

"Keep an eye out for our friend," Axel said to Splish. The water elemental held tight to him, wrapped about his shoulders and chest like a living cloak.

Friend, Splish agreed. While Axel hoped that Gorrup had escaped, the Sythians had observed a number of prisoners, mostly riverguard, being taken into the camp; it was why they'd chosen this one for their first strike. Nemon had taken a little convincing – he'd wanted to lead an assault on a larger target – but in the end, he'd acquiesced. The river-tribes needed to see the Sythians joining the fight; how better to do that than to rescue their people?

Unfortunately, it looked as if it wasn't going to be as easy as Nemon had promised. The Xirkaali had obviously been preparing for an attack from the sea. A trio of war-junks had been patrolling just past the shallows when they'd surfaced. Nemon had dispatched a contingent of placoderms to see to the ships and their crews, even as the majority of the Sythian forces struck the camp. Axel knew that the same fight was being played out up and down the coast, as Medu'Syth joined the battle against the Xirkaali.

Even the mysterious Shesh'ra had joined in, leading her naiads against the enemy all along the coast. Axel hoped she was successful. More, he hoped to meet her when this was done. He thought that they had much to discuss, especially about the dread possibility of Oskan's return, and what could be done to prevent it.

But for the moment, Axel had more important matters to attend to. Like staying alive. He leaned forward, using his staff as a conduit to the gigas's simple mind. The creature was powerful, but largely driven by hunger. With his magics, he could guide it where he willed, at least theoretically. Until it became too hungry – or too angry.

The gigas shuddered with rage as a mortar round exploded at its feet, throwing up a spray of water and sand. The gigas and its brethren plowed on until they reached the palisade at last. They didn't stop; instead, they slammed through the wooden posts at full speed, shattering the ones they didn't simply shove aside. Xirkaali leapt from the collapsing palisade and retreated into the camp. Mortars thumped the air, and Axel swept his staff out, protecting himself and his steed from a spray of debris.

As the gigas forced its way through the camp, Axel risked a look. The Xirkaali were falling back in good order, but they were on the defensive. The

Neriticans slammed against them, as remorseless as the tide. Placoderms and hemicyons strove against one another with brutal discipline. Axel wondered how long it had been since the dog-men had met an enemy as physically capable as they were.

Lithe, quick naiads slipped between the combatants, blades seeking any gap in Xirkaali armor. A gigas crashed into a watchtower and toppled it with a forceful heave. A placoderm roared in pain as a hemicyon blade removed his arm. A rocket struck a gigas and reduced it to smoking chunks of shell and meat.

Axel closed his eyes, wishing he were elsewhere. Anywhere but here, with the smell of death clogging his nose. *Swift,* Splish warbled, holding tight to Axel's form. The water elemental had been reluctant to accompany him; something in the camp frightened him – the strange cages, perhaps. But in the end, Splish's loyalty had been stronger than his fear.

Warning, Splish yelped, and Axel looked up to see a rocket heading their way. He conjured a lasso of water and snared the explosive in midair, redirecting it. It hurtled away, slamming into the palisade and sending chunks of burning wood into the air. Startled, the gigas reared up and gave a thunderous screech. Axel held on for dear life as the animal's jerky movements threatened to send him hurtling to the ground. He'd chosen to ride the beast because it seemed somehow safer than marching with the placoderms, but he was starting to regret his choice.

Friend, Splish murmured. Axel followed the elemental's mental urging and turned to spy Gorrup and several others – and facing them, a group of hemicyons, including one clad all in black. Surprise warred with pleasure; Gorrup was alive. A lucky chance, or perhaps the Great Current was carrying them all in the same direction.

He urged the gigas forward with a thump of his staff, and it sped toward the enemy with a hungry clatter of its mandibles. Around them, the battle spread through the camp. Nemon's warriors were relentless, striking on all fronts with a ferocity that seemed to stun the Xirkaali, if only momentarily. It wouldn't last; the Xirkaali would recover eventually. But for the moment, they were on the backfoot, and that was enough.

"Gorrup!" Axel called out. The pondwarden looked up, somehow hearing Axel over the din of battle. His eyes widened, and he shoved the elf standing beside him aside. Gorrup and the others scattered, but the hemicyons weren't so quick.

They tried to fight, but their steel was no match for the immense crustacean's shell, and their own armor crumpled beneath its crushing strength. The black-clad one survived the gigas's charge and sped around the great beast's back. Axel paid him little attention until he heard the chink of steel biting into shell. He twisted around and saw the black-clad hemicyon climbing steadily toward him. "Madness," Axel whispered.

Bad, bad, Splish quavered. Axel understood the elemental's fear. The warrior climbing toward him was the same hemicyon from earlier; as scarred and as ugly as Axel recalled. The one who'd shrugged off his magics like a light drizzle. "Yes, very bad," Axel agreed. He thumped his staff against the gigas's shell and sent a cascade of water sluicing toward the hemicyon.

The warrior swung his chain-sickle and hooked the edge of the gigas's shell, narrowly avoiding being washed off by Axel's riptide. As the deluge passed, the hemicyon howled and wrenched his sickle loose from the gigas's shell. He raced swiftly across the heaving surface toward Axel, whirling the sickle over his head. "You are mine, witch. At last, you are mine!"

"I do not even know who you are," Axel protested, as he conjured a gleaming shield of water over himself. The sickle pierced it as easily as if it had not existed at all, and the blade sliced through Axel's cloak.

"I am Kungas – I am your death!"

"Not likely," Axel said, as he drove his staff into Kungas's midsection, staggering the hemicyon – but only for a moment. The mage jerked back, only just avoiding the sickle's bite. His momentary bravado had bought him little, save a moment's respite. This Kungas was a deadly opponent and seemed to bear him some personal grudge for reasons unknown. He considered trying another spell, but decided against it. Why waste his energy against a foe whom it would do no good?

The gigas heaved itself up, crushing the struts of a watchtower in its fury. Kungas nearly fell but managed to hook a crack in the beast's shell with his sickle. Axel felt the shell shifting beneath his feet and leapt toward his opponent. Magic might not work on the hemicyon, but momentum was a different story entirely. Axel slammed into Kungas, and they both rolled from the gigas's back and to the ground below.

Splish cushioned Axel against the impact, but Kungas recovered first. He went for Axel's throat with a snarl. The mage only just managed to interpose his staff, and the hemicyon's jaws snapped shut on the coral. Axel fell back as Kungas worried at the coral like a dog with a bone.

"Get… off… *of me*!" he cried, kicking Kungas in the midsection and propelling him backward.

Kungas staggered back a few paces but recovered quickly. He made to lunge forward again, but a large shadow fell across him, causing him to look up. His good eye widened as the gigas's leg came down with crushing force. Kungas vanished in a spray of red. Axel stared in shock as the gigas continued its rampage, unawares of the life it had claimed by accident. He shakily wiped blood from his face as he rose to his feet.

"Axel!" Gorrup called out as he hurried over. "Are you hurt?"

Axel, dazed by his close call, looked at the blood on his hand. "I – I do not believe so." The gigas, freed from his control, stomped away, seeking something to sate its growing hunger. "Not for lack of his trying, though."

"The Great Current must have been watching over you, mage," Gorrup said, as he helped Axel to his feet. He glanced at the pulped remains of Kungas and gave a rumbling croak of satisfaction. "I would have preferred to have killed him myself, but I shall forgive you." He paused. "But enough of that. Your magics – can they heal, as well as harm?"

Axel nodded as Splish coiled about him, cleansing him of Kungas's blood. "Yes, why?"

Gorrup's answer was to crouch and lay something in his arms at Axel's feet. It was a halfling, and she was pale and shivering. Axel knelt beside her. He could feel her fever beating at the air like a hungry flame. Someone had made a crude attempt to help her, but it wasn't enough.

"Splish," he murmured. At his request, the water elemental surged off of him and around the halfling.

Cool, Splish burbled.

"Yes, cool her down," Axel muttered as he probed the halfling's injuries. He felt others gathering around them. The battle was still going on, but it seemed to have bypassed them for the moment. He heard the bellow of a swamp troll and the roar of a placoderm, and tried to block it out.

One of Gorrup's companions, an elf, said, "A – a gillkin? I haven't seen one of your kind in centuries." He crouched across from Axel and studied him with obvious curiosity. "This is an auspicious omen indeed."

"Can you help her?" a halfling, one of several now crowded around them, asked. Axel ignored them, and concentrated on his magics. As he'd told Gorrup, they could heal. Water could remove infections as easily as it stole breath, but it required guidance to do so. He placed his hands to either side of the wound, hidden beneath its mud poultice, and pressed gently. The injured halfling moaned as water and magic surged into the wound, cleansing it of infection, or so Axel hoped. It was always a tricky thing, healing.

He sat back. "She is being strong. She will be living a while longer." He hoped he sounded more confident than he felt. He did not wish to add another needless death to his conscience.

"Well, that's good to hear," a new voice exclaimed. Axel turned to see a soot-stained swamp troll ambling toward them, a halfling perched on his shoulder. She clambered down and hurried over, swiping a strand of red hair out of her round face. "Are you a mage, then?"

Axel stood wearily. He peered at the newcomer. Something about her face seemed familiar. Had he seen her in his dreams? "I am being called Axel Tricklebrook."

The halfling grinned. "Bimson. Hannah Bimson. And I think you and I need to talk."

CHAPTER FORTY
Aeron

The Xirkaali arrived at dawn.

From atop the gatehouse of the Eastway Wall, Aeron looked out at them and felt his heart clench painfully in his chest. It was the largest army he had ever seen, larger than he'd imagined an army could be. Even the League of Rhordia had never mustered so many soldiers. A glittering tide of steel, advancing slowly out of the shadows of the jungle. No siege weapons to be seen; not yet, at least.

"How many?" he asked, softly.

Valan, standing beside him, glanced at a haggard-looking gladestalker. "Around fifteen thousand, give or take, wasn't it?" The gladestalker nodded. Valan sighed and looked at Aeron. "Around five thousand more than I expected, I admit."

"That's more than three times our number," Aeron said.

"This is only the advance party," Valan said. "With Ruhaindo taken, I expect there'll be another ten thousand here within a few days."

"A cheerful thought," Aeron murmured. Valan laughed.

"I try to look on the bright side of things."

Aeron smiled sourly. "So I've noticed." He looked down toward the bridge. In the last few days, the temporary fortifications had been completed. Palisades extended outward from the towering gates, all the way to the end of the bridge. Heavy pavises, placed in an irregular fashion, lined the length of the bridge, creating a labyrinthine killing field. Two of their howitzers had been placed on wooden platforms on the bridge, overlooking the far end. Halflings armed with rifles scurried into position but stayed well back from the far end of the bridge where Solibos had overseen the defenses.

Aeron had to admit that the elf, arrogant as he was, hadn't done a bad job of it. Solibos had built up emplacements, set out stakes, and erected walls of mixed stone and wood, some of it reinforced with magic. If the hemicyons wanted the bridge – and they did, Aeron was certain of it – they would have to go through Solibos's garrison to get to it.

The strategy they'd worked out was simple; draw the hemicyons in and blow them up. Then retreat in stages, drawing them onto the bridge, where the Ej-folk could ply their trade as the elves fell back to the emplacements across the river. Of course, he didn't expect Solibos to do any of that, whether he'd agreed to it or not. But that was for later.

"They've stopped," Valan said.

"It'll be at least a day before they're ready to make a go of it," Aeron said. "Those hemicyons just marched overnight through a jungle. They're probably hoping for a sit down. And I don't see any human soldiers… they probably left them behind to set up a camp." He looked toward the western edge of the river.

There was smoke rising above the trees.

Makki had arrived the night before with a barge full of wounded halflings and elves, and a broken howitzer. The engineer had reported that the last toll lock had fallen, and explosively so. The Xirkaali, it seemed, had more than a few tricks up their sleeves. Kortys had died buying them time to escape. Aeron had only known the gladestalker briefly, but he'd liked him all the same. His death was a loss. Nor was it the only one they'd suffered.

When *Thunderchild* hadn't returned, they'd all feared the worst, Anas most of all. Surprisingly, however, Anas had shown no interest in casting blame. He'd simply redoubled his efforts to help strengthen the defenses, as had they all. The first disaster hadn't cracked them; neither had the second. Aeron tried not to think about how many they'd lost defending something undefendable. How many lives he'd spent to buy an extra few hours of peace.

He pushed the thought aside, to concentrate on the now. Makki had reported that the Xirkaali had found the old logging trails; Aeron had suspected they'd make use of them. It was nice to be proven right. It was the only way they could have gotten so many warriors so close without being immediately spotted.

The next step was clear-cutting the jungle. They'd need room for their camps, and the trees provided too many opportunities for mischief. Before long, there'd be the equivalent of a small town on their doorstep. Defensive works, tents, workshops, everything a besieging army needed to maintain itself. He reckoned it would take a few days, maybe less given how efficient they were proving to be. Aeron glanced at Valan. "Will they demand our surrender?"

Valan hesitated. "Possibly."

"Let's hope so. Anything that buys a few extra hours is all to the good."

"Unless we're simply delaying the inevitable."

Aeron nodded. "It's possible. But if your friend Axel can pull in the Neriticans, then the Xirkaali will be facing a war on two fronts. Strong as they are, that's not a good position to be in. If Axel succeeds, we just have to hold out long enough for whoever is in command over there to get orders to pull back and reinforce the coast. Then, we can harry them all the way back."

Valan frowned. "When you say it like that, it sounds so neat and simple."

Aeron looked away. "I assure you it's anything but. After all, we have no way of knowing whether he succeeded or not. Just like we have no way of knowing what happened to *Thunderchild,* or our people aboard her." He straightened abruptly. "I should probably get down there. Just in case they decide to parley."

"Wait," Valan said. He turned to the scribe who'd followed him up onto the parapet and murmured something. She'd been his constant companion for the last few days, though Aeron still didn't know her name. Valan turned back, with a slight smile. "I understand the Shires grow pumpkins. What about Ej?"

Aeron blinked. "What?"

"Pumpkins, Ser Aeron. Do they grow pumpkins in the mountains?"

Aeron shook his head slowly. "I – yes. Yes, they do. It's a staple crop. Shire seeds grow well in the mountains. Why?"

"According to Eran here, Xirkaali consider pumpkin a delicacy. And it is traditional in their culture to bring a gift to a negotiation. A sign of respect, if you like. You didn't happen to bring any, did you?"

Aeron nodded slowly. "Yes, we did. It makes good soup."

"I suggest taking a few gourds with you, eh? See if it earns us some consideration."

Aeron did as Valan suggested. He sent a runner to collect a few small pumpkins, and they were waiting for him in a sack down by the main gate. He hefted it onto his shoulder with a grunt and waited impatiently for the inner door of the gates to be opened. The small, reinforced door was set into a recessed alcove near the gates, and it opened out onto a narrow trail that wound down from the walls to the bridge.

Aeron followed it down, where yells of greeting met him. The Ej-folk on duty were excited; perhaps a bit fearful. For many of them, this would be their first taste of battle. For their sake, he hoped it wouldn't be their last.

Crossing the bridge was a nerve-wracking experience. It took longer than it should have, thanks to the burden he carried, and gave him plenty of time to wonder if he was making the right decision. Would the Xirkaali do anything so civilized as request their surrender? Or would they simply attack?

Solibos asked him the same when he arrived at the other end of the bridge.

"Are you mad, Cadwallader? These beasts have no intention of talking," he snapped, and looked as if he were on the verge of ordering his warriors to take Aeron into custody. Before he could give such an order, however, a horn blew from somewhere amid the Xirkaali lines.

The enemy battle-line split, disgorging a group of hemicyon warriors who trotted toward the bridge. Several carried tall staves, topped by steel disks from which hung tiger-pelts. *Banners,* Aeron thought. He hefted his sack and went to meet them. Solibos called out after him, but Aeron ignored him. He figured Solibos wouldn't try and stop him. After all, if he got killed doing something foolish, so much the better.

Even so, the walk to meet the Xirkaali was nerve-wracking. He imagined his wife's face, and those of his children, and could not banish them from his mind's eye until he finally stopped and set the sack down. The Xirkaali halted a short distance away. One stepped forward. "I will speak with your commander," the hemicyon said, in badly-accented elvish.

"That would be me," Aeron said.

"*You* are in command?" the hemicyon asked, clearly startled.

Aeron shrugged. "For my sins." He clasped his hands behind his back and tried not to show just how nervous he was. "Muster-Captain Aeron Cadwallader, at your service. And you are…?"

"Shulgin. Daughter of Hejun, Matriarch of the Ironeyes pack."

"Pleased to meet you." He hesitated. "I – ah – brought you a gift?" He indicated the sack of pumpkins with his foot. "Shire pumpkins. Best in the world. At least the parts of it we know about."

Shulgin paused, nostrils flaring. "A gift. For me?"

"I'm told it's a Xirkaali tradition."

Again, she paused before replying. "Yes. Thank you. They will be appreciated." She looked past him. "You should have collapsed the bridge."

Aeron laughed, despite himself. "You're not the first to think of it. But the bridge has great sentimental value for the elves." He glanced back at it, knowing she was watching. Hoping she took the bait that he was waving in front of her nose.

Shulgin cocked her head. "It will be your death. When we take it, we will be at your gates within the day." She rested her paw on the hilt of her sword. Aeron's smile faded. She was serious. He looked back at the bridge. Then, with a sigh, he shrugged.

"Possibly."

Shulgin made a quizzical sound. "You are not an elf. Why defend their city?"

Aeron looked up. It was a clear day. Good for battle. He wished it were raining. "They asked for our help. What could we do but give our aid? The folk of Ej remember their friends – even when their friends don't always remember them."

Shulgin grunted. "We would be better friends to your people than the elves." She looked down at him. "Those airships of yours are very clever. We will have much use for them, when you have learned your place."

"You make it sound as if we'd be slaves."

Shulgin snapped her teeth in irritation. "We do not take slaves. We do not *need* slaves. But you cannot rule yourselves – none of you. So we must do it for you. We will take on that burden and leave you free to live as part of the Xirkaali Empire. Surrender the city, and you will be spared."

"A tempting offer," Aeron said. "But I'm afraid our honor is at stake." It was a calculated ploy. Valan had told Aeron everything he knew about the hemicyons, about their culture and beliefs. Honor played a large part.

Shulgin was silent for a moment. Then she nodded. "Honor is a tricky beast. It demands feeding, even when you know better." She looked up at the walls, the bridge, all of it, and then finally back to Aeron. "I hope that you survive, Aeron Cadwallader. The Empire could use honorable soldiers." She paused. "Thank you for the gift. Next time we meet, I will have one for you." Then she turned away and made her way back to her bodyguards. Aeron waited a moment, and then went back to the bridge, sans pumpkins.

Solibos was waiting on him, an outraged look on his face. "What were you playing at, halfling? She might have killed you."

"No. She was offering terms of surrender."

"You didn't take them?" Solibos asked. "We might have bought some time."

Aeron paused. "It will take them at least a day to mount an advance. Besides, as I said to her, it's a matter of honor. I intend to hold this city while I am here. What you do with it afterward is up to you."

Solibos studied him. "You are an odd little fellow, Cadwallader," he said, finally. He patted Aeron on the shoulder. "Ah well, I'd have told her the same, I expect."

I bet you would've, Aeron thought. "My thoughts exactly, my lord," he said, forcing a smile. "My thoughts exactly."

CHAPTER FORTY-ONE

Shulgin

"So – he was quite tiny," Parga growled around a mouthful of pumpkin.

"Yes," Shulgin said, gnawing on a rind. Cadwallader was right; Shire pumpkins were quite tasty. "But clever."

She and the others sat under a newly-erected tent. The canvas had been wetted and bales of damp straw had been set in the corners to cool the interior. Besides Parga, Ushar and Ryuk were also present. A number of hounds lounged on the ground, panting in the heat.

"Oh?"

"Yes. He wants us to attack the bridge." Shulgin gestured with the rind in her hand. "Practically baiting us into it." It was the only reason the bridge was still standing, at least the only reason that made sense to her. An invitation to attack.

"Convenient, given that we also want to attack the bridge," Ryuk muttered, picking at the strings of pumpkin pulp in his teeth. Shulgin nodded. Ryuk saw it as well. That was something at least.

"Yes."

"You suspect a trap?" Parga asked. She was more dubious. She saw the scaffolds and the ropes, and thought only that they had arrived in time to interrupt the demolition efforts. But Shulgin thought otherwise. The defenders had had plenty of time to take the bridge down, if they'd truly wanted to.

Shulgin scratched her muzzle, thinking it over. Was it a trap? "Perhaps. Or maybe a counterattack. Maybe he's simply confident that they can hold it."

The bridge was wide and long, meant to hold caravans traveling eastward. But the elves – and the halflings – had turned it into a killing ground, full of staggered emplacements, ordnance, and the like. A cursory glance had been enough for her to understand what they were facing: a corridor studded with tiny fortresses that each needed to be taken.

Parga sniffed. "What about the docks? Why bother with the bridge when the docklands are the soft underbelly?"

Shulgin glanced at Ushar. He'd accompanied the plainstalkers on their scouting excursion. The old cur shook himself and said, "Not so soft as all that. From what I saw, they've turned the river into an extension of their walls. They've anchored heavy barges, linked by lengths of chain and long planks across the entrance to the harbor, and reinforced them with steel, to make them bastions. Half-folk gunners man them, and elven archers. The half-folk have even mounted one of their damned volley guns on one of the barges."

Ryuk spoke up. "Worse, their balloons and fliers can zip above the river as quickly as they can the jungle. Any boat that tries to get past the bastions will be blown out of the water."

Shulgin tossed her pumpkin rind to one of the hounds lounging at their feet. The draconic beast snapped the rind out of the air and fell to chewing it with gusto. "There are ways to break that line. Fire ships, rockets, mortars. Any of these will serve. The half-folk are clever, but cleverness isn't much use against a determined wedge of spearwardens." She rubbed her snout. Once broken, the bastions would serve her forces as well as they did the defenders. They had to know it. So what was she missing?

"Tainted meat," Ryuk grunted.

Shulgin glanced at him. "What?"

Ryuk plucked a seed from his mouth and flicked it into a nearby bucket. Wasting seeds was frowned on, and so buckets had been set out to capture them. "Tainted meat. Something I was told as a whelp. When it seems too good to be true, it's tainted meat. That there is tainted meat. Looks good, and we're hungry, but… something's off."

Shulgin nodded. "Yes. That describes both the bridge and the docks well."

Parga sniffed. "And so? As you said, we starve. But our stomach is strong enough to survive a bit of poison. What did your parley tell you, daughter of Hejun?"

Shulgin sat back. "It told me that you were right in your initial assessment. They are ready for us." She indicated the pumpkin. "This gift was proof of that, if nothing else."

Parga narrowed her eyes. "How so?"

"It says that they know more about us than we know about them. It was a warning, a challenge, and a sign of respect all in one." Shulgin reached down and stroked one of the dozing hounds. "My mother says that a respectful enemy is dangerous; an enemy that makes us a gift of one of our delicacies is a deadly opponent."

"That little thing? Dangerous? Ha!" Parga gave a bark of laughter.

Shulgin wanted to agree. She badly wished it were true. But she knew better. "It is true, nonetheless. He is clever, as I said. He is prepared."

"We have numbers and strength and determination," Parga said, in protest. "What does he have?"

"That is the question," Shulgin said. She was silent for a moment. "Trust me when I say that I want nothing more than to lead a charge across that bridge and rip that city from the hands of its masters. I came here for glory. For honor. Not to play games of what if. But what glory is there in defeat? What honor, in death? No. We must be wary, else we set a foot wrong and fail to accomplish anything."

Parga grunted. "I'd heard you were hot-headed, daughter of Hejun, but I see you are your mother's daughter after all. So then, tell us – what are we to do?"

Shulgin took a deep breath. She looked at Ryuk. "Ryuk, you will lead the assault on the bridge tomorrow morning. Take it, if you can. I will reinforce you, once you have gained a foothold." She turned to Ushar. "You, old beast, will take the docks at the same time. I want three of our remaining barges turned into fire-ships. Smash holes in the dock defenses, take what remains for our own use, but go no farther. From there, taking the docks should be easy. We will do it at our leisure."

"Tainted meat," Ryuk repeated.

"Maybe. But as you said, we're starving, and it looks good. So we go. We do the thing, and do it well." She hoped she projected confidence. What she actually felt was a sort of uneasiness. The halfling, Cadwallader, was clever, yes. Not cleverer than she, but – still. Clever. Unlike her mother, she preferred her opponents lacking in wit. Victory was no less glorious for being certain.

"And what is to be my role, daughter of Hejun?" Parga asked, dubiously.

Shulgin sat back on her haunches, pondering. Then, "Parga, take a third of your forces and circle around the city. Begin fortifying the banks of the river there. I want nothing getting in – or out – by water, and I want eyes on the road to Ej."

"You fear reinforcements?"

"I fear nothing. But we have had too many surprises of late; I would not have another. Commandeer any craft coming from the east; interrogate their crews. I want to know everything about anything, however seemingly unimportant." One of Obair's lessons, that. Information was the grist in the mills of war. The more one knew, the greater the chance of success one had.

"That is acceptable," Parga said. "Still, I expect you'll need me to do more than play sentry sooner or later. Just don't leave it too late, eh?"

Shulgin showed her teeth. "I will do my best."

Orders given, she dismissed the others. She was confident that they would carry out her orders to the best of their abilities. She filched a final piece of pumpkin and ambled out to the edge of the camp, accompanied by her bodyguards and several hounds. Trenches were being dug there, and stakes readied, for any possible counterattack.

The air echoed with the clang of forges and the calls of Yan laborers. It was never quiet in camp. There were always things to be built, to be repaired. A trio of plainstalkers trotted past, carrying wild game procured from the jungles, destined for the cooking fires. In a large tent, humans kneaded water into dough, making flatbread. Hemicyon warriors sharpened blades and made wagers on the feats they would perform the next day. Some of these greeted Shulgin and saluted, and she responded in kind before moving on.

Xirkaali field camps were always arranged along similar lines. A large, ever-expanding spiral of crude palisades and tents, providing fallback positions in case of enemy assault. Forges, workshops, and armories were confined to the center, while barrack-tents were on the outer. In many ways, they resembled cities in miniature. In the case of sieges, once each camp had reached an optimum size, a new camp would be begun somewhere close by, until the enemy was ringed about by Xirkaali fortifications.

Despite this involved process, the camps were not static constructs. They could be disassembled quickly, for rapid redeployment, should the need arise. Over the centuries, the Xirkaali had mastered the Yan martial philosophy known as *He'hijun Aoto* – Wave War – the strategy of always being in motion, like the ocean tide.

The Yan themselves had never quite managed to make it work, but the Kaali, a nomadic people, had taken to it quickly. Indeed, it had become the primary strategy of the empire; one taught to all would-be commanders. Constant motion, constant readiness to redeploy, to react. Shulgin chewed her pumpkin thoughtfully and eyed Callenspire. When morning came, it would become the eye of a roiling storm – or the spoke of a wheel. Her forces would turn and turn, moving around it, until the spoke splintered; until the eye shrank.

That was how it had been in the past, at least. But something about this city bothered her. Maybe it was Cadwallader. She knew how the elves fought. But Cadwallader was an enigma. He was clearly brave; clearly intelligent. He lacked the arrogance of the elves. She tried to recall what she knew of the halfkin. It wasn't much.

They were mountain-folk; at least these were. Not warriors. According to what she'd heard, they hadn't even had a proper army until recently. They should be easy prey. So why was it making her hackles bristle? Maybe Ryuk was right. Maybe it was tainted meat. Maybe the city as a whole was tainted meat.

The thought brought her up short. She swallowed a lump of pumpkin and looked at what was left. "Shire pumpkin," she murmured. Where were these Shires? Not in Vieshlar, she thought. Cadwallader even looked somewhat different from the Ej-halfkin. Paler. He was not one of them. So where was he from, and how did he come to be here?

Shulgin tugged on her ear. She knew that there were more Claws than the one Hejun was overseeing. That the invasion was larger than this one region. But she hadn't realized that the enemy might know it as well. Another ill-omen, or merely the promise of battles to come? Callenspire would not be the end, nor Ej. Not even Elvenholme. How many more battles awaited them? How many more sieges?

She pushed the thought aside. Such worries were for her mother. Her only concern was the city and its defenders. Tomorrow she would take their measure, and they would take hers. One or the other of them would be found wanting, and she was determined that it wouldn't be her. She popped the pumpkin into her mouth and chewed thoughtfully.

"Tomorrow, we will see just how clever you are, Aeron Cadwallader."

CHAPTER FORTY-TWO
Axel

As the sun rose, the Xirkaali retreated to the dubious safety of the jungle. Placoderms roared in triumph, and conch-shells sounded. Axel leaned tiredly against his staff and watched the enemy vanish into the trees. The air tasted of smoke and blood, and he closed his eyes, trying not to see the carnage that surrounded him.

The camp was in ruins; parts of the palisade had collapsed, and the watchtowers had all fallen. Tents had been smashed flat, and their contents scattered. The dead, both Xirkaali and Nerittican, lay in mangled heaps. The ruptured remains of a gigas slumped across the jungle-gate, its body still smoldering from the rocket strike that had killed it.

Despite Nemon's confidence, it had not been a one-sided slaughter. The Xirkaali had given as good as they'd gotten. The survivors were retreating, harried by naiad heartpiercers. They would no doubt seek to regroup at one of the other camps along the nearby coast. Then they would return, with reinforcements. Maybe not tomorrow, but soon.

"It is done," Gorrup said, from beside him. The pondwarden had a captured Xirkaali blade laying across his shoulder, its edge crusted with enemy blood. "They have fled."

Axel looked at him. Gorrup looked much the worse for wear but seemed in good spirits otherwise. Then, battle had a rejuvenating effect on the pondwarden.

"Yes," Axel said. "I am glad you are well, my friend." Splish, perched on his shoulder, burbled in agreement.

Gorrup snorted. "So you have said. I am just glad that you did as you promised."

Axel chuckled. Though Gorrup had not said it, he thought the pondwarden was happy to see him as well. "If I'm being honest, I did have my doubts. But it seems that the Great Current is carrying us all in the right direction." He turned and made his back through a gap in the palisade, and into the camp. Gorrup followed.

The placoderms weren't the only celebrants. Swamp trolls roared in triumph, pounding their chests or the ground. Some had already begun peeling dead Xirkaali from their armor in order to feast on them. The thought made Axel somewhat queasy, but Nemon seemed content to leave the trolls to their feast.

The trolls – and their halfling allies – had come as something of a surprise to Axel, though he supposed it was simply another example of the Great Current moving them as it willed. Less coincidence than fate; an assurance, perhaps, that he had changed what might have been into something better.

He spied Captain Bimson talking with one of the trolls – Uk. The big beast crouched low to the ground and nodded his shaggy head at intervals. Finally, he rose and lumbered off, calling out to his fellows. Bimson turned as Axel and Gorrup approached. She looked tired, but grimly pleased. "Uk and his chums aren't planning to stay, more is the pity. I think the Neriticans make them nervous. But Uk tells me they've acquired an – ah – taste for Xirkaali, so that's something at least."

Axel nodded. "Swamp trolls are not being the most reliable of creatures," he said, in the common trade tongue. "I am being surprised they did not eat you, Captain."

Bimson laughed. "Me too. And call me Hannah. But it's like Ser Aeron says, you can't always be picky when it comes to allies." As she spoke, she glanced at several nearby placoderms. The latter were busily dragging dead Xirkaali out of the camp, to bury them, or perhaps feed them to the remaining pair of gigas. "Never thought I'd see them in the flesh."

"I expect they are thinking much the same of you," Axel said.

She laughed again. But her face turned serious. "We need to be moving toward Callenspire. The Xirkaali are probably already there."

Axel hesitated. Gorrup spoke up. "Nemon is not being convinced." In point of fact, the placoderm commander saw no reason to take his troops that far inland. Not when the majority of the Xirkaali were concentrated on the coast.

Hannah sighed in disappointment. "Well, it'll be as the missing gods will it, I suppose." She pulled off her leather cap and shook out the sweaty tangles of her red hair. "Whatever he decides, we'll be going. The few of us who are left."

"Not make it," Gorrup said, bluntly. "Not without help."

Hannah gave him a challenging look. "Is that an offer?"

Gorrup looked away. Axel laid a hand on his arm. "Yes. We will be helping you. The question is, will anyone be as helping us?"

"What do you mean?" Hannah asked.

"Time is not being on our side," Gorrup said, as if reading Axel's thoughts. "The Xirkaali will be back, and the Sythians will be having to be retreating. The forces Nemon brought –"

"What about the forces I am having brought?" Nemon growled as he paced toward them, accompanied by several guards, as well as the elf, Talis. The latter had been one of Gorrup's fellow prisoners, but had quickly attached himself to Nemon in hopes of winning support for Nerittican reinforcement of his home city of Grishamvu.

Axel looked Nemon up and down. The placoderm commander had fresh wounds to add to his collection of scars but seemed otherwise in rude health.

"Is the army of Medu'Syth not being satisfactory, pondwarden?" Nemon continued, as he gestured with his trident. "Are my warriors not being good enough for you, child of the reeds?"

"They are being very skilled," Axel said, quickly. "We are being very grateful."

"Not enough warriors," Gorrup croaked.

Nemon thumped the ground with the ferrule of his trident. "These are being but my personal guard," he boasted. "Fear not, cousin, our army is to be advancing on all fronts. The Xirkaali shall be drowning in their own blood before another day is being out."

"And what about Callenspire?" Hannah asked.

Nemon looked down. "What about it, little one?"

"It is under siege."

"Many cities are under siege," Talis said, sharply. He looked down his nose at the halfling. "My own people are under siege in Grishamvu at the moment. Why should we not aid them instead?"

"Grishamvu is not being the key to Ej," Axel said. "Callenspire is."

"Grishamvu is closer," Talis said. "To reach Callenspire, Lord Nemon would have to march inland, through the jungle. But to aid Grishamvu, he would have to do nothing more than swim along the coast."

"Marching on Callenspire would free up the troops there to aid Grishamvu and Blackthorn, especially if the Neriticans can keep up the pressure on the coast," Hannah said. "With our airships, we can land troops just about everywhere… including Grishamvu and the other elven cities. That means artillery to counter the Xirkaali – though admittedly not in any great numbers. But it's something."

"A pipe dream. A fancy." Talis turned back to Nemon. "March to aid Callenspire, by all means – after you've helped Grishamvu. Together, we can catch the enemy in a pincer. It is the only practical solution."

Nemon peered at the elf in bemusement. "At the moment, I am having no intention of risking my warriors in either endeavor. Instead, we shall be making use of their camps as Shesh'ra is advising. We shall be using their walls to be mounting our ballistae and war-engines. I shall be leaving a hundred of my warriors here to be seeing to it. When they are coming to retake this place, we shall be making them pay."

Shesh'ra, Axel thought. Shesh'ra was a warrior of great cunning, at least to hear Nemon tell it. More and more, he wondered what the strange naiad might make of his dreams. He suspected that she shared them, or at least had answers to the questions that plagued him. He shook the thought aside.

Gorrup spoke up. "A hundred warriors is not being enough, if they are returning in force. Which they will." He glared at the placoderm. "So what is being your plan for that, eh?"

Nemon made to reply, but Axel quickly interjected with a question. "I am expecting that you came looking for us for reasons other than an argument, my lord. How am I being of service?"

The placoderm stared at Gorrup for a moment longer and then turned his attention to Axel. "We have been finding the cage you warned us of. If you are wishing to see it, now is being the time."

"Did you free the captive inside?" Axel asked. He dearly wished to speak to her, to learn more about the strange black iron cages and their purpose. It was vital to know if the Xirkaali had some method of disrupting magic. The elves, the Neriticans – others – all used magic as a matter of course. It was in the very air of Vieshlar.

"No."

"Why?" Axel demanded.

Nemon turned away. "Come and be seeing for yourself, gillkin."

Axel hurried after him, and Gorrup followed, muttering to himself. If Nemon noticed the pondwarden's grumbling, he gave no sign. Talis and Hannah joined them, still arguing with one another, albeit quietly. Axel listened for a moment, and then looked at Nemon.

"The Great Current showed me that Callenspire was essential," he began, quietly, in the Neritican tongue.

Nemon cut him off with a sharp gesture. "I know you have had your visions. Shesh'ra has as well, or so I have heard. I know you believe we must do this thing. But my only concern is what is best for Medu'Syth. Staying to the coast is a more practical strategy. Marching inland is a risky proposition."

"You would have the river-tribes to help you," Gorrup said.

Nemon shrugged. "We shall see. The representatives of the local tribe should be here soon. If they agree to help – perhaps."

Axel nodded. Several members of the Tidewalker tribe had been prisoners alongside Gorrup. They had departed before the battle ended, promising to bring aid to the Neriticans. Nemon stopped.

"There it is. Ugly thing. Stinks, too."

Axel peered past him and saw the cage sitting amid a field of debris. The broken carcass of a gigas lay nearby, still smoldering. A number of dead Xirkaali lay nearby. Nemon nudged one with his trident and looked at Axel. "They defended it to the death. They have courage at least, our enemies."

"Yes," Axel said, absently. His attention was wholly fixed on the cage and its lone occupant. She sat with her eyes closed, as if in deep meditation. Strange marks had been carved into her flesh, and tattoos girt the unscarred portions. Something about both set him on edge, as if they were harmful to even look at. Splish quivered and slid off of his shoulder, trembling like a frightened child.

"What is it?" Hannah asked, behind him.

"That is what I am hoping to be finding out," Axel said.

Nemon grunted. Then, in the Neritican tongue, he said, "Why you asked us to spare this one I cannot imagine. Even the Xirkaali must fear her, if she is in a cage."

"I wish to know why she is in there. The Xirkaali have no magic, and yet… I can feel it. But it is wrong somehow. Chained in some fashion I do not understand." He thought again of Kungas, and his accusatory words. *Witch,* he had called Axel. An ugly word. He took a deep breath and stepped toward the cage.

"Do you wish to be coming out?" he called, in common. The prisoner inside the cage opened her eyes and studied him with an unsettling serenity.

"Would you like to come in?" she replied.

"No."

"Why?"

"This cage – it is being for magic users, no?"

"Witches," she said.

"You are being a witch?"

"I was. But then came enlightenment. Now, I am a servant of the empire. As you should be. It is the will of the gods." She smiled thinly, and Axel shuddered. He turned away, and Gorrup looked down at him in confusion and not a little concern.

"What is it, mage?"

"I… am not certain." Axel looked back at the cage. The occupant met his gaze as serenely as before. It was as if she were an empty vessel, waiting to be filled – but by what? He was beginning to regret having asked Nemon to spare her life, though thus far she had offered no resistance. Something about her made him feel sick to his soul.

Her smile widened, as if she could read his thoughts. As he watched, the bars of the cage began to glisten – and then crackle, as if some strange energy ran through them. He raised his hand, but the magic would not come. He felt ill – no: *drained*. He staggered back, into Gorrup's steadying grip, as silent lightning limned the cage. *Ambient magic,* he thought. The magics that were the birthright of his folk, of the Neriticans. In the very air of this land. The cage and its occupant had somehow been drinking them in all this time, preparing to – what? "No," he muttered, as the realization hit. Then, more forcefully, "*No.* Nemon!"

At Axel's cry, Nemon hurled his trident through the bars of the cage, impaling the woman, killing her instantly. The lightning was snuffed instantaneously. Nemon wrenched the cage open and cautiously approached the body. He retrieved his trident and looked at Axel. "Satisfied, mage?"

"No," Axel said. Sickened, he looked away. "But it will do for the time being."

CHAPTER FORTY-THREE
Valan

As Aeron had predicted, it took the Xirkaali at least a day to make ready. By sunrise on the second day, they were moving into position. Valan climbed the walls to join Aeron at his command post, flinching slightly at every rattle of distant drums. Birds erupted from the nearby jungle and took to the skies. The halfling sat with the engineer, Makki, as well as his second-in-command, Trosbert, and both Captain Alesha and Archmage Doromir. Alesha greeted Valan cheerily as he stepped onto the parapet.

"A fine day for it, eh, Cormys?"

"Not so as you would notice," Valan replied, grumpily. His head ached; he'd over-imbibed the night before, trying to numb his fears about, well, everything. He collapsed onto a bench beside Doromir. The mage looked as unhappy as Valan felt. "Do they not sleep?" he asked, studying the distant Xirkaali. Lines of steel glittered in the rising light. From what he'd learned of them over the last few days, he knew the hemicyons would lead the advance, supported by their human subordinates. But it was more than just warriors out there; there were earthworks being raised, tents erected and heavy platforms – likely for their artillery – being constructed. "They must have worked through the night to build all of that."

"Some of them did," Aeron said. The halfling looked tired, and Valan wondered if he'd slept at all, or if he'd stayed awake to watch the enemy. "They have a lot of ground to cover before they reach the bridge. See those wooden pavises they've set up down there?"

Valan squinted. There were things down there that looked like high palisades, but appeared to be mounted on crude runners, as if someone intended to move them forward. "Is that what those are supposed to be?"

Aeron nodded. "They spent the night constructing them. I expect they'll advance behind those until they reach the bridge, to cut losses from the archers. They know by now that their armor isn't wholly proof against elven marksmanship."

"Clever," Alesha said. "Did you warn Solibos?"

"I did," Aeron said, and yawned. "He'd already taken the precaution of sending scouts out, thankfully. Thanks to him, we have a better idea of their strategy." He pinched the bridge of his nose. "They're moving into position between us and Ej, cutting us off from any reinforcements coming from the east. They've got troops massing on the river as well. If I were them, I'd launch simultaneous attacks on multiple points."

"And what do we do then?" Valan asked.

"We hold," Aeron said. "The docklands are as protected as we can make them. They might try fire-ships, like they did on the river, but that won't buy them much in terms of territory. I suspect they're looking at the barges we chained up like castle walls, rather than what they are."

"Which is?"

"A distraction," Makki said. She had bandages on her hands and scabbing cuts on her face. She'd been at the toll lock with Kortys, Valan recalled. She was the one who'd led the survivors back to Callenspire. He felt a dull stab of regret; he hadn't known Kortys well, but he'd liked the gladestalker. "The real defenses are on the docks themselves," she continued. "Once they take the barges, and they will, we'll blow them up from the air. They'll be forced to pull back, at least temporarily."

"And what happens when they come again?" Valan asked.

Makki fell silent. Aeron looked out over the bridge. "We fight, Valan. That's all we can do." He scratched his chin. "The problem is, we don't have many tricks to play. We'll catch them by surprise once or twice, but it's a finite resource, just like our gunpowder. For now, *Windwalker* can bring in supplies, but not enough. And even then, it'll soon become too dangerous to make those runs." Aeron looked at Valan. "Time is running out."

Valan felt a chill as he considered the halfling's words. "You're saying it's hopeless?"

"No. I'm saying the odds aren't great." Aeron looked at Doromir. "Solibos commandeered one of your people. Is she skilled?"

Doromir had a sour expression on his face. "Hestaria is quite skilled but lacking in experience. And she volunteered." He tugged on his chin. "I hope she survives." He cleared his throat. "I have warded the internal gates, as you requested. They will withstand most things, but they are not unbreakable. I have done the same with the dockland gates leading into the city. I myself shall remain here, to provide support. Two of my apprentices will be stationed at the docklands to lend aid to the forces there. Keryas in particular is skilled in water magics. I suggest you take advantage of his… creativity."

Makki nodded. "I'll do that." She pushed herself to her feet. "And on that note, I should best be getting down there. Hate for them to start without me."

Alesha rose as well. "I shall accompany you. With Ser Aeron's permission, of course," she added, speculatively. Aeron smiled and nodded.

"With my compliments, Captain Alesha," he said. She nodded but didn't salute. Valan knew that like Solibos, she wasn't entirely certain about the capabilities of the halflings. Unlike Solibos, she was better at not showing it publicly.

Valan looked back out over the city. It was strangely quiet; everyone who could be evacuated had been, and those who couldn't be were staying out of sight. There were soldiers at every intersection, raising defensive works around the internal gates that normally controlled the flow of traffic through the city. From what Aeron had said, it wouldn't be enough. Valan knew that Callenspire, like many elven cities, wasn't designed with sieges in mind. It was designed for commerce – for art – for magic.

Out past the bridge, drums thundered and a cataclysmic howl rose up. A cry of challenge – and of triumph. Aeron rose from his bench and looked out over the parapet. "Here they come," he said, softly. Valan joined him and felt his gut clench at the sight of the Xirkaali beginning their advance.

It was impressive, in the same way an avalanche or a flood was impressive. The sheer, raw inevitability of it. Hemicyons shoved the pavises forward, just ahead of their fellows. Armored Xirkaali, carrying heavy halberds or swords, marched at a swift trot in pursuit of the pavises. Behind these first ranks came human soldiers, carrying long spears or bows.

There was a significant expanse of ground between the Xirkaali and the gates that acted as an entrance to the bridge. The gates were as tall as the bridge and had been sealed shut with timbers, magically-wrought vines, and iron. The only way to reach the bridge were the wickets, set into the foot of each gate. Both of the small, narrow doors were open, providing access to the ramparts Solibos had erected along the far shore.

Solibos's ramparts were as tall as they were long; high scaffolds and walkways had been constructed across the front of the gates, allowing the archers a better view of the enemy. Valan had to admit that Solibos wasn't a complete fool. Even he knew that there was no way to hold back the Xirkaali with steel alone.

Aeron straightened. "Archmage, if you would."

Doromir spoke a single word, and there was a great flash in the air. Valan tasted heat and smelled burning. Ball lightning danced across the ground ahead of the advancing line of pavises, and the Xirkaali hesitated, just for an instant. But it was enough.

There was a sound like popping embers, and then from farther down the parapet, a group of halfling aeronauts launched themselves into the air. The odd balloon contraptions moved swiftly; each contained a single halfling, burdened with an inordinate amount of explosives. The aeronauts skidded out over the Xirkaali lines with a bobbing grace.

When he judged that they were close enough to the target, Aeron gestured. An archer sent a fiery arrow into the sky, signaling the aeronauts to drop their munitions. A moment later, the small craft were hurrying back toward the safety of Callenspire as explosions ran up and down the Xirkaali line, destroying pavises and scattering warriors. The detonations weren't particularly large; no bigger than a Xirkaali mortar strike. But they had the desired effect. The advancing Xirkaali wavered again, hesitating, as the resulting smoke covered the expanse of clearing before the foot of the bridge.

Aeron raised his hand, signaling the archers on the wall to hold their fire. "Now," he said, softly, almost to himself. "If it were me, I'd form up. Wait until the smoke clears to advance. But if I'm right – ha! *There!*"

The pavises stopped, and the Xirkaali charged through them, right into the smoke. Valan watched in bewilderment as the armored warriors punched through the smoke, weapons at the ready. "What are they doing? They must know we might have –"

"They do," Aeron said. "But they have to take the bridge. They have to, otherwise they'll have to build their own, under fire, and still have enough of an army left to take the walls. There's enough of them to do it, but I'm betting they don't want to risk it." He thumped his fist against the parapet. "Come on. *Come on!*"

The Xirkaali came, a roaring tide of steel and fury. They flowed toward the great gate that marked the foot of the bridge, moving at a speed that would put an aralez to shame. Valan could see the elves there, loosing arrows and magic in equal measure, but for every hemicyon who fell, two more filled the gap. "They won't be able to hold," he said.

"They will, if we placed those charges – *yes.*" Aeron gestured to the archers again, and again, a fire arrow was sent up. The aeronauts slowed their retreat and dropped their second load of ordnance, right onto the area where the halfling engineers had labored earlier to conceal a large scattering of explosives beneath a loose covering of earth.

The first explosion was barely noticeable. A muffled thump and some dirt spray. The next two, however, were highly visible. The ground ruptured, spewing smoke and fire. Hemicyons tumbled into newborn craters with yelps of confusion – and pain. Fire licked up, and the armored ranks reeled back, easy meat for the elves. Volley after volley of arrows sang into the smoke, and hemicyons fell.

For a moment, Valan thought they might rally. Then, horns blared and slowly, grudgingly, the disorganized mass of warriors began to fall back toward the pavises and safety. He noticed that Aeron was holding his breath, his expression oddly intent. Then came the clarion wail of an elvish horn. Aeron relaxed. "I knew it," he muttered. "I knew it."

"What? What are they doing?" Valan asked, watching in growing horror as the elves manning the wicket gates charged into the smoke in pursuit of the retreating hemicyons. Solibos was at their head, atop his steed, and a cadre of knights rode with him. "Is he mad? What is he doing?"

Aeron didn't reply. Instead, he spun to one of the elven messengers.

"Send word to the bridge. I want the gunners and the howitzers to pull back to the rear emplacements – *now!*"

"What's going on? Surely this isn't part of the plan?" Valan asked.

Aeron grinned mirthlessly. "No plan survives contact with the enemy. That's why he's called the enemy." He turned back to the elves and began relaying orders. More runners departed, carrying Aeron's commands across the walls and down below. "If Solibos is half the warrior I think he is, he'll carve through them right up until he can't. Then he'll come to his senses and fall back – and the Xirkaali will follow. They'll chase him right across the bridge, through the wicket gates… right into the howitzers."

"It won't be enough, surely," Valan said. But he was starting to see the shape of the thing now. "But that's why you pulled them back, isn't it?"

Aeron nodded. His grin had faded. "I didn't want my people caught in the blast."

Valan blinked. "Blast? What blast?"

"You'll see. Stay here and enjoy the show. I have to get downstairs."

Aeron gestured to Trosbert. "With me, Lance-Captain. It's time for your Dogs to earn their pay."

Valan watched the halflings go and then looked at Doromir. "What blast?" he asked again, feeling a cold sensation in the pit of his stomach. Doromir shook his head, seemingly as much at a loss as Valan. Valan cursed and turned his attention back to the battle.

"What are you planning, Aeron?" he murmured, even as he hoped that whatever the halfling's plan was, it worked.

Shining Ones, he thought, *please let it work.*

CHAPTER FORTY-FOUR
Aeron

Aeron took the steps down from the parapet two at a time; no easy feat for a halfling, but he managed without making a fool of himself. Trosbert followed. "This is it, then? We're riding out?" he asked.

Aeron didn't turn. "Not for the last time, I fear. But if this goes like I hope, we won't have to do much. Not this time, at least."

"I still can't believe you trusted Taran Bligh of all people to do what you asked," Trosbert said. "That's like arming a troll with a howitzer and expecting it to make sensible choices. I'm surprised he didn't blow himself – and us – up."

"Despite his exuberance, Taran is a good engineer. And he knows how to keep a secret, unlike many." Aeron paused. "Are you sure your lads are ready for this?"

"As ready as anyone can be," Trosbert said. He paused. "You didn't tell any of the elves what you were planning, did you?"

Aeron stopped and looked back at him. "No."

"Why?"

Aeron looked away. "Sometimes the fewer people who know about a plan, the more likely it is to work." He started down again, feeling the weight of Trosbert's gaze the entire rest of the way. It wasn't accusing; Trosbert was no brave, fresh out of training.

"The elves won't like it," the mercenary said, finally.

"No," Aeron agreed. A groom was waiting at the bottom of the parapet, holding the reins of Aeron's aralez, Wyn. In the forecourt of the gate-yard, a small force of halflings waited. Some rode aralez, while others were on foot. All of them were members of the Hetronburg Dogs. Trosbert's warriors were all experienced, and that was why Aeron intended to use them for the next part of his plan. He needed soldiers who knew how to follow orders and could be counted on not to get carried away.

Wyn panted happily as Aeron patted him on the head. He'd named the large, dog-like beast after his old pony, though their personalities were as different as night and day. "Are you worried about how they'll react?" Trosbert asked as Wyn slobbered on Aeron's pauldron.

"They'll get over it," Aeron said, though he didn't quite believe it himself. A runner, one of the halflings positioned on the outer bank, hurried toward them huffing and puffing. "Well?"

The younger halfling wheezed and said, "They're falling back. The elves are falling back!"

Aeron looked at Trosbert. "Told you," he said, with a sad smile. He heaved himself into the saddle and accepted a lance from the groom. Trosbert followed suit. "Let's go."

They rode out through the sally passages positioned to either side of the main gates. The area between the city gates and the bridge had been reinforced as thoroughly as possible along the shore line. Earthworks, bulwarks, and firing platforms for bolt-throwers and howitzers. Halfling-trained bands manned the defensive works here, at Solibos's request; he wanted the honor of defending the bridge to belong to the elves alone.

As the Dogs rode out of the city, engineering teams hauled howitzers up onto the firing platforms and positioned them to face the bridge. Gunners moved into position behind the earthworks, and trained bands moved up to support them. On the bridge, elven warriors moved toward the far end to reinforce the defenders there.

As Aeron watched, rockets struck the bridge-gates again and again, rocking them on their hinges. Dust sifted down, mingling with the smoke, making it hard to see anything. *Fog of war,* he thought, as he reined Wyn in at the end of the bridge. It was hard to make out, but he thought that Solibos's warriors were attempting to hold the wicket gates shut, though they weren't having much luck from the look of it.

He could see it in his mind's eye, as neat as clockwork. Solibos's glorious charge had likely bogged down amid the pavises. It would have been like attacking a fortified line. The elves didn't have the numbers. Stubborn as he was, Solibos would have seen the need to retreat almost immediately. The Xirkaali would have pursued and overrun the elven defenses – emptied of warriors as they had been in order to push forward.

A rocket corkscrewed along the side of the bridge and impacted against a dirt berm on the far bank. Aeron spied Xirkaali weapons teams setting up along the far shore, using the elven defenses to do so. The river was too wide for their mortars, but angled properly, the rockets could just about make it. *Rafts,* Aeron thought. They would use rafts to get closer. That was what he would do. Or perhaps barges.

An explosion caused the bridge to shudder and interrupted Aeron's reverie. Wyn whined, and he and the other aralez paced nervously, eager to be on the move. Aeron stroked his neck. "Easy," he murmured. "Easy. It's not time yet."

"Are you sure?" Trosbert asked. He licked his lips and fought to control his steed. "Because it looks to me like they're about to break through."

"They are – and I want them to." Aeron looked around. "Where's Taran?"

"Here, Ser Aeron!" Taran called out, waving excitedly from his perch atop his monstrous engine, positioned nearby. Iron Crusher grumbled thunderously, as if as excited as the aralez. Aeron grimaced at the sight of it but put on a stern expression.

"Are we ready?" he said.

Taran nodded. "Yes, Ser Aeron. I placed the fuse cord where you asked me to. You just light it and run." He grinned at Aeron. "The Xirkaali will never know what hit them, ser!"

"That's my hope," Aeron murmured, turning back to face the far end of the bridge. He took a deep breath. "Let's go." He thumped Wyn's flanks, and the aralez leapt forward with a wild bark. Trosbert and the others followed. Iron Crusher gave a screaming howl and rumbled into motion. It soon outpaced the aralez and crashed toward the far end of the bridge, with Taran clinging to it for dear life.

As Aeron raced along the bridge, the wicket gates collapsed inward, unable to withstand the pressures placed on them. Xirkaali warriors in soot-blackened steel flooded onto the bridge and steadily pushed the elves back. It was his first chance to see them up close and at work, and it wasn't pleasant in the least. The hemicyons had a weird, bestial grace despite the encumbrance of their armor. They could not match their elven opponents for speed, but were far stronger – and soon enough, it began to tell. In close quarters fighting, the elves simply couldn't match their opponents.

Hemicyons poured past the elves and raced to meet the wild lancers. As they'd planned, the aralez riders split into two groups, allowing Iron Crusher to lead the way. The Xirkaali paused, stunned by the sight of the thing. When it hit, bodies flew into the air or were ground under its iron-rimmed wheel. Taran yanked on the controls, and Iron Crusher veered to the left, scattering the hemicyons. The wild lancers hit them a moment later, swirling around their opponents, further isolating them from each other.

Aeron's lance struck a Xirkaali warrior full in the torso and sent the hemicyon rolling limply across the bridge. He hauled Wyn around, sighted a second target, and thumped the aralez into motion. The second Xirkaali was quicker than the first and managed to avoid the tip of the lance. He slashed at Wyn, and the aralez twisted aside, nearly throwing Aeron from the saddle. He repositioned his lance as Wyn loped past the Xirkaali and circled back.

Elves streamed past him, heading for safety. Others still fought at the gates; either unable to break away or unwilling. Solibos was among them somewhere, Aeron knew – unless he was already dead. Either way, there was no way to reach them, to order them to break away. But he'd known that when he'd come up with the plan.

Aeron shifted the weight of his lance, heart thudding. Memories of battles past fought to the surface of his mind, distracting him. There had been too many close calls, too much death – it filled him to the brim, and he found himself hunching forward as if in anticipation of a blow. Then the lance found its target, catching the Xirkaali in the neck. The force of the blow ripped the lance from Aeron's grip. He let it go and wheeled Wyn around.

The battle for the bridge had broken down into a confusing melee. It was the sort of fight that only benefitted the enemy. More and more Xirkaali were pushing through the wickets and onto the bridge, separating the elves from the halflings. Aeron spotted Trosbert nearby and caught his attention. "It's time," he shouted. "Fall back!"

"What about the fuse?" Trosbert called back. He had a sword in his hand, and his helmet was gone, but he looked none the worse for wear. Excited, even.

"I'll handle it. *Go!*"

Days earlier, Aeron had ordered Taran to set several barrels of gunpowder beneath the bridge. With the help of Trosbert and his Dogs, he'd done so, and all without the elves either noticing, or understanding, what was being done. There were enough explosives to split the bridge in half. At least that was the theory.

As Trosbert led his aralez riders back toward the city, the Xirkaali not otherwise engaged gave chase. Just as Aeron had hoped. He urged Wyn toward the ancient statue of someone Valan had called Halmwur of the Gold Flame, where Taran had hidden the fuse cord. According to Valan, Halmwur had been one of the first archmages and fond of conjuring fire. It had seemed appropriate to Aeron. He only hoped Halmwur, if he was able, smiled down on his efforts.

Wyn bounded over a palisade and past the elven archers defending it. Aeron shouted over his shoulder for them to retreat, but they ignored him. Solibos had ensured that his warriors had no interest in following Aeron's orders – even those designed to save their lives. Aeron tried not to think about it. They would buy him time. Their deaths would give the city a chance. That was all that mattered.

He saw the fuse, tied around the base of the statue. Now all he needed was a spark. He snatched his sword from its sheath and leaned sideways, so low he almost slipped from the saddle. The tip of his sword scraped along the bridge. Sparks danced – leapt – *caught.* The end of the fuse cord sputtered, dimmed, and then flared brightly. He jerked on Wyn's reins, aiming the aralez toward safety.

Behind him, the Xirkaali overran the archers. One of the hemicyons bounded toward him, halberd raised. Aeron bent low in the saddle, narrowly avoiding losing his head as the halberd whipped out and bit into Halmwur's ankle. The Xirkaali howled in frustration, but Aeron was already racing down the bridge. Wyn leapt over barricades and construction materials, racing so fast that Aeron lost track of where he was.

The explosion, when it came, was so powerful that it picked up the aralez and sent both dog and rider tumbling head over tail along the last stretch of the bridge. For a moment, a shroud of fire enveloped them, wrapping about them so tightly that Aeron felt the air crisping in his lungs. Then it released them, and left them laying on the bridge, charred but alive. Through bleary eyes, he looked back.

Taran's explosives had done their work well. The middle of the bridge had utterly collapsed, leaving an immense, impassable gap. Smoke boiled from the hole, and the broken bodies of the combatants littered either side. The gap wasn't as neat or surgical in form as he'd imagined. It reminded him of a length of shattered bone. The debris of the deconstruction efforts was scattered about by the explosion, and a mountain of collapsed crates blocked part of the remaining section of bridge.

Aeron clambered painfully to his feet, using Wyn for support. The aralez whined and favored one of his hindlegs, but seemed otherwise unhurt. Trosbert and the other riders gathered around him.

"Still in one piece, Ser Aeron?" Trosbert asked, as one of his people took Wyn's reins.

"For the moment," Aeron wheezed. He leaned forward, hands on his knees. His lungs thudded painfully in his chest, as if still shaken by the reverberations of the blast.

"You did it, Ser Aeron," Taran said, breathlessly. The young engineer stood nearby, hale and healthy, but pale. His wide eyes were fixed on the destruction he'd helped manufacture, and something in his horrified gaze tore at Aeron's heart. Taran swallowed. "We – we had to do it, right?"

Aeron nodded wordlessly. He stared bleakly at the smoking remnants of the bridge for long moments, and then turned away. It had been necessary. That was what he told himself.

It didn't make it any easier.

CHAPTER FORTY-FIVE
Hannah

Hannah wearily accepted a cheroot from Cogman as she watched the pumpkin soup bubble in the pot. They'd scavenged both the pot and the contents from the Xirkaali camp. It wasn't like the enemy needed either anymore. But she was getting tired of pumpkins.

She waved a fly out of her face and chewed absently on the cheroot. "How do you think it's going in there?" Cogman asked, indicating the large, central tent where discussions between the Neriticans and the riverguard – and Axel – were taking place. It had been two days since the riverguard had arrived. Half a dozen local tribes were represented, and they had been in deep conversation with Nemon and the others since their arrival.

"Hard to say. I don't expect either group is very interested in helping us." She leaned close to the fire and lit her cheroot. Puffing, she sat back. "Either way, we're leaving tomorrow. We'll scrounge supplies today, take whatever the Neriticans haven't claimed. It should be enough to see us back to Callenspire."

"And then what, Cap'n?"

"What do you mean? We get back in the fight."

"Yeah, except there'll be a whole bloody army standing between us and the city." Cogman stirred the soup. "We don't exactly have the numbers to break a siege ourselves."

"I'll think of something," Hannah said. She looked around their little camp within a camp at the others. Cogman was right. They didn't have the numbers. While some, like Sagria and Umer could be counted on in a fight, the rest were either wounded or in shock. And all of them were tired and not a little frightened. Including her.

War was proving to be nothing like she'd imagined. She'd seen herself making daring raids on the enemy, and instead she'd spent most of it in the jungle, either running from the Xirkaali or waiting around. Ser Aeron had tried to warn her; she realized that now. He'd tried to warn them all. None of them had listened.

Cogman clanked the ladle against the rim of the pot, startling her. She puffed on her cheroot and stared at the tent again, wishing she were in there. But neither she nor the elf, Talis, had been invited in. She could tell he was stewing about it. Talis didn't seem a bad fellow, really, for an elf. But he and his companion, Derech, were arrogant, as only elven warriors could be. Her gaze drifted to where the two elves sat nearby, in close conversation with each other. They too were watching the tent with rapt attention.

She sighed and picked up two bowls, also scavenged from the Xirkaali stores. "Dish me out two portions, Cogman. It's time I had a sit down with our friends over there."

"The elves? Why?"

"We're allies, aren't we? Time to put up a united front." Bowls filled, she headed over to the elves. "Hungry, neighbors?" she called out. Talis looked at her.

"What is it?" he asked, dubiously.

"Soup," she said. "The Xirkaali had a store of food. We helped ourselves. Thought you might appreciate some." She proffered the bowls, and, after a moment's hesitation, the elves took them. Derech even nodded in thanks, though Talis wrinkled his nose at the smell.

"You made soup from pumpkins?" he said.

"You can make soup from a lot of things. All it takes is a bit of water, some vegetables, and patience. Try it. You're probably starving." She puffed on her cheroot for a moment and then sat down beside the two. Derech made room for her, but Talis didn't so much as budge. Hannah didn't mind. "I understand, you know," she said, after a moment.

"Understand what?" Talis asked, not looking at her.

"Why you want them to go to Grishamvu. I understand."

Talis snorted. "And yet you argue against it."

"I did." Hannah took her cheroot out of her mouth and studied it. It was a gesture she had seen Anas do when he was trying to think. "And I think you know why." She watched a trio of placoderms stride toward the palisade, talking to one another in their harsh, snapping tongue. She could think of worse allies to have.

"Because your people are there, obviously."

"That's part of the reason." She looked at the tent. "Axel says Callenspire is important. That if it falls, everything in Vieshlar goes with it. I don't know about you, but that sounds bad."

"You trust the word of a gillkin?" Talis asked. He gave her a hard look. "Even the other Neriticans don't seem to like him." He indicated the placoderms guarding the tent.

Hannah shrugged. "The Neriticans don't seem to like anyone. But yes, I do trust him. And maybe you should as well." She looked at Talis. "Look, what I said earlier is true: if Callenspire is relieved, then we can help Grishamvu. We can take the fight to the Xirkaali, once Ser Aeron is freed to –"

"I don't even know who this Ser Aeron is," Talis said. He set his soup aside, untouched. "I don't know why you're even here, halfling. This isn't your war."

"It is now," Hannah said, flatly. Talis met her gaze, just for a moment, and then looked away. Hannah sighed. "We swung by Grishamvu, you know. Before *Thunderchild* was downed. It's under siege, but the army isn't large. And with the Neriticans putting pressure on the Xirkaali camps, they'll have to raise the siege. Because Grishamvu isn't that important."

Talis glared at her. "Watch your tongue, girl."

Hannah rose and matched him, glare for glare. "It's the truth, and you know it. I heard Ser Aeron say as much, though he was a good deal more polite than me, I admit. Grishamvu sits on the coast; well, guess what? The Xirkaali already control the coast. They can sit back and starve you out, or ignore you, because Grishamvu is just one city, far away from anything important. But Callenspire is a *gateway*. It leads to the east – to Ej. They take Ej, they can roll up the rest of Vieshlar at their leisure. You may not like it, but that's the way it is."

Talis flushed and rose to his feet. "I will never understand Ej's fascination with your kind. You're like goblins – vermin, taking up valuable resources."

Hannah punched him; since he was standing, it was below the belt. Talis wheezed and sank down, cradling himself. Derech finished his soup and set the bowl aside. He looked at Hannah.

"You're right, you know," he said, in a mellifluous voice. "But you have to understand, my lady, unimportant though Grishamvu is, it is still our home. And we are a proud people. Even we, humble soldiers that we are, are prideful of our city – our culture." He helped Talis to his feet. "But you are right. Talis knows it. It's why he's so angry."

"She struck me," Talis whimpered.

Derech patted him on the back. "I saw." He smiled at Hannah. "We'd already decided to lend our voices to yours, by the way. In support, I mean."

"Oh." Hannah stepped back, feeling suddenly ashamed. Talis had deserved it, but who wouldn't be angry in this situation? "I'm sorry."

"Don't be," Derech said, waving her apology aside. "Talis often confuses rudeness and pragmatism." He turned. "Looks like they've finally finished. Hopefully it's good news."

Hannah turned to see Axel and Gorrup stepping out of the tent, accompanied by Nemon and a riverguard chieftain. The quartet approached them slowly. Hannah stepped to meet them. "Well? I hope you've got good news for us."

Nemon grunted and looked at the others. "We have being discussed the matter and coming to the conclusion that when the enemy comes again, we will need every warrior."

"So why leave good soldiers penned up on the other side of the jungle?" Hannah asked. She looked from Axel to Nemon. "You need warriors. Well, we have them. In Callenspire. Help us, then we can help you."

Axel held up his hand, interrupting her. "We will," he said. He looked at Nemon. "Too much time has being wasted already."

Nemon snorted. "Yes, yes. And who's fault is that?"

"Yours," Gorrup said. "And I am still saying you will not hold this place."

Nemon growled at him. "Regardless, it is being our duty."

"But is he right?" Hannah asked, without thinking.

She flinched as the placoderm's blunt head swung toward her. But instead of growling, he nodded, with a sideways glance at Gorrup. "For a time, at least. Eventually, we shall be having to abandon it. But by then, preparations will be made ready along the coast, in case of reinforcements."

"Oh, there'll be reinforcements all right," Hannah said. "Ser Aeron said as much." She crouched and began to draw a rough map of the coast in the sand. "And from what we saw from the air, they've made landfall in a handful of places, like this one." She made several x's along the coast. "They're using them as supply depots. Then they spread along the coast in either direction, finding inlets and bays to go ashore." She made several more x's. "Each camp provides support for the others. And Ser Aeron thinks this is just the beginning, that there'll be reinforcements coming along and along, so that the forces in the camps can move inland. That's why they're building so much."

Axel leaned against his staff. "Yes. Nemon's scouts have been reporting such. We face the prospect of a war on multiple fronts. We are being like successive waves, consuming one another as the tide is going in and out."

"It is not being ideal," Nemon said. He crossed his arms and looked toward the jungle. "If we be marching inland as you are wishing, we might be able to be forcing them to be raising the siege of this Callenspire. But we will be leaving ourselves open to attack."

"But, breaking the siege will be freeing up the soldiers there to be aiding us here," Axel said. "And not just here," he added, looking meaningfully at the elves.

Derech nodded. "So we've discussed." He shot Talis a look before the other elf could so much as protest. "It is the only sensible alternative."

Nemon growled sourly. "This is all amounting to being nothing more than a feint. All we can be doing is delaying the inevitable." He looked at the elves. "From what Hulum has been told us, your people cannot be holding this land. Not even with our aid."

Derech hesitated but said nothing. Talis flushed. "We must. It is our home – it…" He trailed off and looked at Derech. "Where would we go?" Hannah felt a rush of sympathy for the elf. The idea of being forced to leave home was not one she liked to contemplate.

"North," Axel said, gently. "To Elvenholme. But unlike in my visions, you will not be doing so as servants of the Xirkaali, and that is what as being matters. Your people will be remaining free – at least for a little while longer."

Derech sighed. "That is better than nothing, I suppose." He looked at his companion. "Nonetheless, Talis and I will return to Grishamvu, if we are able. We will tell them of the Nerittican efforts, and those of your folk as well," he added, addressing Hannah. "At the very least, it will be good to know we do not face this alone."

"Hulum and his warriors will be accompanying you," Gorrup said after a brief consultation with the riverguard chieftain in their musical, burbling tongue. "They will be escorting you to the city by secret waterways as yet being unknown to the Xirkaali."

"And will they stand with us in battle as well?" Derech asked.

Axel nodded. "Wherever the water is flowing, Medu'Syth will be standing." He looked at Nemon. "We are making them fear the wet places, and the dark beneath the trees, and that too will be slowing them. They might be occupying this region, but they will not be taming it."

Nemon smacked a fist into his palm. "That is being well said, gillkin. Perhaps your people are not being the cowards we are thinking them. We shall rip and tear their flanks until every river in Viesha runs red." His eyes gleamed with battle-hunger as he spoke.

"But first, Callenspire," Hannah said, firmly. If Vieshlar was going to fall, Ser Aeron needed to know, though she wasn't sure what he could do about it. Maybe nothing – but maybe something. But they had to try.

Nemon lifted his trident over his head. At this signal, nearby placoderms cried out in eagerness. "Yes," Nemon roared. "*To Callenspire*!"

Yes, Hannah thought. *I just hope we're not too late.*

CHAPTER FORTY-SIX
Shulgin

Two days after the explosion, the last defender of the western side of the river fell. The elves had fought hard, ceding ground only grudgingly. But with nowhere to go, and no reinforcements coming, their efforts had been doomed from the start. Some had surrendered; others had fought to the death. In the final hour, a few dozen had attempted to break through the Xirkaali lines and head south. Led by a small group of armored riders, the ones the elves called Stormwind, they'd almost made it.

Almost.

Shulgin rubbed her shoulder. The Yan surgeon swatted her hand. Shulgin growled but didn't argue. The stitches had popped during the recent fighting, and blood matted her arm and chest.

"I warned you," the surgeon said as he cleansed the wound. "If you keep it up, it'll never heal – or worse, heal wrong. And then where will you be, my lady?"

"At least I wouldn't have to listen to your nattering," Shulgin grunted. The surgeon pretended not to notice. Shulgin grunted again and shifted her weight on the dead horse she sat atop. The animal's rider lay nearby, Shulgin's blade still in his chest. The elves had charged right into her lines, carving a red swathe through them before their lack of numbers had seen them driven back, encircled and chopped to pieces. It had been a brave effort, if futile. Wasteful as well. How many had they lost, attempting the impossible? Surrender would have served them better.

"Madness," she murmured. The surgeon began to sew up the wound again, clucking over the necessity. "They are mad, aren't they?" she asked him, not expecting an answer. Maybe a human might understand where she could not.

"They thought they could win, my lady. No madness in that; hubris, perhaps. But not madness. Unless you speak of their resistance to the empire as a whole, in which case, yes. They are quite mad. Victory is a certainty. Only the willfully blind cannot see that." The surgeon snipped the thread and stood. "There we are. Good as it was. Please try to be more careful, my lady."

"I will do my best," Shulgin growled as she pushed herself to her feet. She tightened the straps of her armor as she strode toward the remnants of what the elves had called the Eastway Bridge, pausing only to retrieve her sword along the way. The dead lay everywhere; not just elves, but her warriors as well. Carrion birds, native to the region, circled overhead, screaming out in almost human-like voices.

Smoke still hung heavy on the humid air, painting it in hues of ash. The bridge had been torn in two, as if by the hand of a god. Many warriors had perished on it, including Ryuk. Her subordinate was surely laughing at her from whatever afterlife awaited them. He'd been right. "Tainted meat," Shulgin muttered. Cadwallader had baited her in, using his own allies to do it. There was an almost Xirkaali-like pragmatism to it that surprised her.

Would her mother have been so surprised? Shulgin liked to think so. She scrubbed her nose in annoyance and brushed the thought aside. She turned her attention back to the bridge and the city beyond. The enemy had fortified the far bank, making any attempt to cross the river here hard-going. But with the bridge gone, she had little option.

Explosions sounded from the direction of the city docks. The fighting was still going on there, and her paws itched to join Ushar in his attack. She wanted to make the elves pay for Ryuk's death. More, she wanted to make them pay for costing her an easy victory.

But instead, Shulgin forced herself to walk out onto the burnt remnants of the bridge, in order to look at her enemy. As she did so, she gestured to one of the nearby warriors.

"Have Tarang bring me the prisoner," she said. Tarang was Ryuk's replacement; young, but a disciplined warrior with a list of honors to her name. Ryuk had been of her mother's generation, but Tarang was of hers. Shulgin found that oddly comforting.

The prisoner, on the other hand, was anything but a comfort. An elf – a noble. Highborn, as the kindred termed it. The leader of the defense of the bridge, according to her warriors. His armor was fancy enough for it. He had been caught on the wrong side of the wicket gates and swiftly captured. Thankfully, his skill with a blade had hardly been equal to that of the elf at the toll lock. Solibos, he called himself.

While she waited for his arrival, she conferred with the warriors stationed on the bridge. Human archers kept watch on the far side of the river, and hemicyon spearwardens kept watch on them. None of them had seen anything of interest, save the halfkin repositioning their volley-guns to aim across the river. *The better to tear apart any rafts I try and send over*, she thought, studying Cadwallader's preparations.

He was a cunning one. He had drawn her in and ensured that the shore closest to the city was properly defended. The halfkin had dug in; made ready. They would be hard to shift through traditional means. But she possessed more than just traditional means at her disposal. Before she had set out from Evanvale, she had requisitioned a small supply of special rockets – those in which the alchemical mix had been altered. These rockets did not simply explode but rather produced clouds of paralyzing gas, or showers of acidic rain, and fires that could not be extinguished.

The issue was, she had only a few of them. They had to be used sparingly. And once used, no certainty of acquiring more any time soon. Worse, there were witches in the city. The elves were steeped in magic. They might well have some method of containing or dispersing the ill-effects of the gas. And she had brought no witch-cages. There had been none to spare, and even if there had been, she would have had no way of getting them across the river.

The other issue with the special rockets was the comparative lack of range of the more lethal varieties. They needed to be fired from close range to avoid dispersing on the wind or exploding prematurely. Or even blowing back toward those who'd launched them. That meant taking chances with the rocketry teams.

Still. Perhaps…if the wind was right, and with the proper distraction…

Yes. Yes, it could work.

Tarang's arrival woke her from her reverie. She was accompanied by two warriors, and Solibos. The elf had been stripped of his fine armor and looked as if he'd been rolled in dirt and blood, but his expression was defiant.

"He is still complaining," Tarang said, shoving Solibos forward. He was not bound, but it wasn't as if he could go anywhere either.

"I expect he is. Is our hospitality not to your liking?" Shulgin asked.

Solibos spat at her feet. Shulgin caught him with a backhand and knocked him from his feet. So fragile, these elves. It was a wonder that they had their own empire. She gestured for Tarang to haul him back to his feet. "I have questions. You will answer them."

Solibos said nothing. She nodded.

"Very well. How many soldiers remain in the city?" she asked. Solibos looked away.

Shulgin caught a handful of his hair in a painful grip. She yanked his head back and bared her teeth.

"How many soldiers?" she asked, more firmly.

He met her glare with one of his own. "I'll tell you nothing," he hissed.

Shulgin paused, the urge to gut him warring with the knowledge that she needed him. Once, she might have killed him regardless. But now she tried to recall the lessons Obair had instilled in her. "And why should you?" she said. "After all, it is not your city, is it?"

Solibos frowned. "What do you mean?"

"Just what I said. If it was your city, they might have shown more loyalty to you. Instead, they abandoned you here, to my mercy. They would not have done that if you were important, or knew anything of value."

Solibos flushed. "I am a lord of the southern kindred!"

"And what is that to me? If you were lord of the city, you might be of some worth." She paused and looked him up and down. "What if you were?"

"What?"

"Lord of the city?"

Solibos frowned, perplexed. "What do you mean?"

Shulgin released him and turned away. "The city will fall, one way or another. Sooner or later. When it does, it will need someone to rule it, in our name of course. A trusted servant of the empire. I will have other duties, and in any event, I would prefer to leave it in the hands of someone familiar with it."

Solibos was silent for long moments. Weighing his options, she thought, not that he had many. Serve or die were his only choices. Those were the only ones the empire ever offered its foes. He swallowed and said, "If I agreed… what of my people?"

"They would be spared, should they be wise enough to surrender. But the time for negotiations is over. You will agree, answer my questions, and be taken somewhere safe to be educated in our ways, until the city has been pacified. When it is done, we will bring you back and install you as ruler."

"What of the halflings?"

"What of them?" Shulgin asked.

Solibos looked at her. "They are the ones who did this to me. They betrayed me. I want them dead. Promise me that, and I will serve you."

Shulgin paused, as if considering. He truly was a wretched creature. There was no honor in him. But she swallowed her disgust and said, "Done."

Solibos nodded. "There are fewer than six thousand troops in the city. A third of them are halflings." He said this dismissively, and Shulgin began to understand why the halflings had been so quick to abandon him. "They have a few toys; you've seen them already. They are running low on gunpowder, however. They have been relying on their airships to resupply them, but Cadwallader is too cautious – he does not wish to risk losing the ship to your rockets."

Shulgin nodded. That was sensible. "Witches?" There had been a witch on the bridge, but she had been slain early on. A lucky spear-thrust by one of the Yan soldiers.

"You mean mages? A handful, mostly apprentices. Doromir is the most skilled, but he is no battle-mage." Solibos hesitated. "My… cousin, Merytan, is also a mage. But she hasn't been on a battlefield in centuries."

Shulgin nodded again, taking in the information. If the witches were weak, so much the better. The rudiments of a strategy began to cohere in her mind; a risky one, perhaps. But where there was risk, there was glory.

She questioned Solibos for a few more minutes, dragging from him the particulars of the defensive works on the far shore and within the city itself. Then she had Tarang take him away. True to her word, he would be taken back to Evanvale at the first opportunity, there to be reeducated in the particulars of the imperial hierarchy.

She stayed on the bridge, watching the far shore from behind the safety of a repurposed elven palisade. She was still there when Parga arrived, atop a lionsnarl. The leonine reptile scrabbled to a halt, and the other matriarch dropped to the ground with an annoyed grunt. Shulgin turned to greet her, but Parga waved her words aside. "Neriticans," she said, without preamble.

Shulgin hesitated. "What?" Ever since the battle of the last toll lock, the riverguard had been all but unseen by her warriors. They'd retreated into the jungles and left the elves to fend for themselves. Or so she'd hoped.

Parga grunted. "My scouts have reported that the Neriticans are on the march. They're moving inland. Towards us," she added, pointedly. Shulgin growled softly. That changed things, and not for the better. Maybe the riverguard hadn't fled; maybe they were simply waiting for reinforcements.

"How close?"

"A few days, maybe less." Parga rested her paw on the hilt of her sword. "If we can't take the city by then…" She didn't finish the thought, but she didn't have to. Shulgin looked at the bridge again. Had the defenders – had Cadwallader – known? Had this been their plan from the beginning? If they were allied with the Neriticans… She pushed the thought aside. It didn't matter. Her duty remained the same, regardless.

"What about Ej? Any sign of reinforcements?"

Parga shook her head. "None thus far."

"Good. How soon can you mount an assault on the eastern gates?" Shulgin paused. "A full assault, not simply a feint."

Parga blinked. "A day, maybe two."

"Do it."

"It won't be easy. Victory is not certain."

Shulgin waved this aside. "I just need you to draw their eyes from me. Just for a moment." She felt the wind turn. Blowing east. She bared her teeth in a grin. "I will do the rest."

CHAPTER FORTY-SEVEN
Aeron

Aeron resisted the urge to flinch as a rocket barrage struck the walls somewhere to the west. Instead, he focused on the city plans before him. "How are we looking for ammunition for the bolt throwers on the east wall?" he asked the elf standing across the table from him.

"We've got maybe a hundred bolts left, and half of those are so old that they might turn to dust as soon as we launch them," the elf said. He looked as tired as Aeron felt. They were all tired. It had been three days since the bridge had been destroyed. Three days and nights of nearly continuous bombardment, from every side.

The enemy had surrounded the city and now rained fire from every angle. Sometimes, worse than fire. Some of the rockets carried strange alchemical compounds that burnt the skin and lungs of anyone unlucky enough to be caught in the area, or a type of fire that was impossible to extinguish, save with magic. The smell of smoke and other, more acrid things, tainted the air, and Doromir and his mages barely had time to rest.

The relentlessness of it was the hardest part. The constant rain of fire. The Xirkaali did not seem to sleep, or slow. They made constant attempts to ford the river, or attack the docklands. Or both. Fire-ships. Artillery. There was no lull, no peace. It reminded Aeron of a blacksmith, hammering a length of iron into shape.

The Red Star hostelry was empty of horses, but full of halflings and elves, all trying to accomplish a hundred different tasks at once. Aeron had commandeered the building as a headquarters, given its proximity to the Eastway Gates. It was situated along the main thoroughfare, meaning messengers had a straight shot to the Ej Gates and the docklands; both vital to his strategy. He turned to one of his people; a heavyset sauceror named Maggie Greenwell. "How are we on supplies?"

"We're provisioned well enough, thanks to Anas and the evacuations," Maggie said, rubbing her nose. "It's not food I'm worried about. It's water. The elves use magic to purify the waters from the wellspring. With their mages otherwise occupied, it's all we can do to keep our people from coming down with the flux." She glanced at Archmage Doromir, who sat stiffly nearby.

He mopped at his brow with his sleeve. "I can detail one of my apprentices to help with that, but it means one less person putting out those cursed alchemical fires."

Aeron nodded. "Do it. We can endure fires. Dysentery will kill us quicker." He scanned the room and found Trosbert sitting on a windowsill, beside the engineer, Makki, who slumped in a chair that was too big for her. The mercenary stank of smoke; he had been on the docks, leading his Dogs against the Xirkaali. "Captain Trosbert?"

"The docks are holding for now," Trosbert said, wiping the grime from his face with a filthy handkerchief. "They sent fire-ships in, as you expected. Now they're trapped on those barges, getting chewed to pieces by our howitzers. But when we run out of ammunition…"

"They'll be all over us," Makki said, tiredly. She scratched at her bandages.

Aeron looked at her. "How long?"

"A day. Maybe two, if I stretch it. Then it'll be bows or close quarters. Neither of which appeals to me, personally."

Aeron nodded. The thought didn't appeal to him either. He rubbed his brow, trying to think – to plan. He was about to speak when the room fell silent. He looked up to see Lady Merytan standing before him. His heart fell into his stomach; the moment he'd been dreading was here. He gestured for everyone to leave, which they did with alacrity. "Lady Merytan," he said, softly.

"Ser Aeron," she replied. She looked down at him, and then at the plans. "What are your thoughts?"

"We can hold the city for at least three more days," he said. "If nothing changes, if they don't have some trick I haven't anticipated."

"And what of you? Do you have any more tricks?" Aeron looked up at her but said nothing. He knew why she'd come down here. Until now, Merytan had been content to leave military matters to him. "Was there no other way?" she asked, softly.

Aeron sighed. "I wish there had been," he said, simply. Merytan nodded curtly.

"He was a troublesome child. Privileged. Spoiled."

Aeron said nothing. Merytan took a deep breath and looked away.

"He was my cousin, nonetheless. Highborn. Valan has had his hands full over the last few days, keeping Solibos's supporters from coming for you."

"He still has supporters?" Aeron asked in surprise.

Merytan laughed sourly. "Of course he does. More now than he did before, thanks to you. To them, he is a hero – the hero who held the bridge and was so cruelly betrayed by a jealous inferior. I expect his statue will join the others on the bridge, if we survive."

Aeron looked down. "That's a problem for tomorrow, I fear." He glanced at her. "I will step down, if you wish. Alesha could take overall command easily enough."

Merytan shook her head and made to reply when a messenger suddenly stumbled into the room. The halfling hesitated, staring at Merytan in bewilderment, but started speaking when Aeron cleared his throat. "It's an attack, Ser Aeron – on the Ej Gates."

Even as the messenger spoke, alarm bells began to sound throughout the city. Aeron rose to his feet. "A feint?" he asked.

The messenger shook his head. "It looks like they're sending everything they have."

Aeron frowned and looked at Merytan. "My lady," he began. Merytan cut him off.

"I shall see to the defenses at the east gate. You will stay here." She turned to go and paused. "We shall finish our conversation later, Ser Aeron." Then she was gone. Aeron retrieved his spyglass and sword, and was out of the hostelry a few moments after Merytan. If the enemy was attacking the east gate, it was most likely a feint.

Quickly, he climbed up to the parapet overlooking the bridge; no easy task with short legs. He was puffing in an undignified manner by the time he reached the top and had to pause to catch his breath. When he had, he hurried toward the edge of the parapet, pausing only to duck as a barrage of rockets impacted against the uppermost portion.

At the same time, a volley of mortar shells fell onto the fortified side of the river, hammering parts of the palisade there flat. He risked a glance below and saw injured braves being pulled from the wreckage by their fellows. He could hear someone was calling for a medic. Howitzers burped fire, casting death across the river.

On the remnants of the bridge, Xirkaali archers lobbed arrows at the elves across the gap, who responded in kind. Aeron watched the exchange through his spyglass for a moment, and then slid down. Captain Alesha sat nearby, sharpening her sword.

"There's been no change," she said, unhelpfully.

Alesha was somewhat more tolerable than Solibos, but she had a similar arrogance. Nevertheless, Aeron trusted her more than he had Solibos. "That's good," he said, risking another look in the direction of the enemy.

The Xirkaali closest to the river were largely keeping their heads down, thanks to the efforts of the poachers he'd stationed along the shore and in the scaffolding erected on the defender's side of the bridge. Every so often, the elven archers and gladestalkers stationed along the shore would loose a volley over the river.

The Xirkaali would inevitably respond in kind, sending a few rockets skidding across the water in desultory fashion. The rockets couldn't quite reach the gates. Occasionally, when aimed high enough, they struck the walls, where they did little damage. Mostly they hit the defensive works on the shore of the river, which had been reinforced to absorb those impacts as best they could. They wouldn't last forever, but for now it was enough.

That left things a stalemate. Or so it seemed. But Aeron knew they were up to something. He could feel it, in every reverberation of a rocket exploding. The Xirkaali were close-quarters fighters. They wanted swordplay. Needed it, in the same way Fatty Bumpo back home needed hard cider. Was that the reason for the attack on the Ej Gate? Was it signaling something? A change in the situation?

"Reinforcements," he murmured. That would make sense. If reinforcements were on the way from Evanvale or Ruhaindo, the Xirkaali might be emboldened to commit themselves to an all-out attack. He lowered the spyglass and looked down the length of the parapet. Elves patrolled the walls, watching for any attack. It was the same on all sides. Some distance away, a wooden launching platform waited for use.

In a few minutes, one of their few squads of grenadiers would head out on a bombing run over the Xirkaali camp. Similar platforms had been set up overlooking the docks and the eastern gates. Grenadiers and aeronauts made irregular runs against the forces there, using up a bit more of their rapidly dwindling supply of munitions. The Xirkaali didn't seem to have that problem, however.

"You'd think they would run out of munitions eventually," Alesha said, echoing his thoughts. She studied her sword's edge, clucked her tongue, and went back to sharpening it. Aeron wondered if it soothed her nerves. He hoped so, for it was doing nothing for his.

"They've probably brought what they need to make more. If you use arrows, you bring fletchers. If you use rockets, you bring alchemists." Aeron mopped at his face with a handkerchief. He was hot in his armor but dared not remove it. Not with rockets exploding every few moments. It was as if destroying the bridge had freed the Xirkaali to put their deadliest weapons into use. Maybe it had. "They're attacking the Ej Gate."

"They're attacking everywhere," she said. "No doubt they will pull back when they grow bored, as they have the other half dozen times."

"Maybe," he said. "Hopefully we have some time yet before they figure out how to come over these walls." Despite his words, something felt wrong with the situation. Why attack the gate now? The question nagged at him. If it was reinforcements, would they be able to hold the walls for a day, much less three? It would be street-fighting, then. He glanced at Alesha. "How are your warriors doing?"

"Morale-wise?"

"Yes."

"Not as well as might be hoped. Perhaps it had something to do with you blowing up a bridge many of them were standing on." She gave him a pointed look. "Solibos was popular with the rank and file. They liked him."

"I take it they don't like me."

"No," she said, flatly. She paused. "Then, they never really liked you to begin with."

Aeron paused. Then, "And what do you think?"

Alesha studied her sword for a moment. "I think you did what needed doing, Ser Aeron. Solibos was always going to be a problem, and you used his capriciousness against him. Indeed, you *planned* for it. A strategy worthy of the courtiers of Elvenholme. Valan could not have done it better." She pointed the sword at him. "But you are not an elf. That you, a halfling, did that is seen by some as an insult."

"Will they follow orders?"

Alesha looked away. "My orders, yes."

"And will you follow mine?" Aeron tensed as he asked the question. What would he do if she said no? Did he have it in him to do anything at all? Another rocket hit, and he flinched as slivers of pale stone rattled from his breastplate. Could he count on her, if it came to fighting the Xirkaali in the streets?

"Yes," she said, after long moments. "Valan is right. You are our best chance for survival, Ser Aeron. Neither Solibos nor I have any experience with sieges, or enemies like this. I would not have thought to destroy the bridge, or reinforce the docks. Callenspire would have fallen as surely as Evanvale." She looked at him. "But once this is done, you might consider leaving Callenspire – you and your people. We are grateful, of course, but…"

"Gratitude has its limits," Aeron said. Alesha nodded.

"Even so." She paused and stopped sharpening her sword. "Do you hear that?"

He did. The sound of wood striking water. He looked over the parapet and saw a small fleet of rafts riding the river toward the city's defenses. As they did so, rocketry teams moved into position at the end of the bridge to cover them. A familiar maneuver.

The Xirkaali had tried the raft trick before, but something was different this time. For one thing, instead of there being warriors on the rafts, there were more rocket teams. He frowned and focused on them with his spyglass. The howitzers on shore spoke, and a raft ceased to exist. Then a second; reduced to floating splinters. A risky gambit. So why –?

The answer came a moment later. There was a whoosh and a whining hiss as a volley spun away from the remaining rafts and struck the shore. As before, it impacted against the carefully arranged defenses. But there was no explosion, this time. Nor was there a whoosh of fire, or the hiss of acid.

Instead, from the points of impact rose an ugly colored cloud of mist. It spread swiftly, borne on the eastern wind. It enveloped one of the howitzer teams. Aeron watched in horror as the halflings stiffened and fell, as if dead. Worse, the mist continued to spread across the shore, circumventing all his carefully prepared defenses. "Oh no," he said.

"What? What sorcery is this?" Alesha demanded.

Aeron ignored the question. "Find Doromir. *Quickly!* We're going to need him." His hand fell to his sword. "I was wrong before. We're out of time."

CHAPTER FORTY-EIGHT
Axel

Axel bobbed to the surface of the river and peered at the nearby Xirkaali camp. Or at least its edge. In the time since the riverguard had first spotted it, the camp had expanded somewhat. Then, that was the Xirkaali way. They were rapacious; industrious. A camp became a fortress, became a town – a city. And then, when it was no longer needed, they discarded it as efficiently as they had constructed it.

The thought was repulsive to him, as he knew it would be to most Neriticans. The idea of imposing a false order on the world, even for only a short period of time, was inconceivable to one in tune with the Great Current. But then, that was the heart of the problem – whatever drove the Xirkaali, it was not any god or power that Axel was familiar with. Whatever their goals, they had yet to share them.

Axel drifted into the thick foliage that blanketed the shallows, with just his head above the water's scummy surface. He was tired, but also anxious. Over the last few days, the Neriticans had moved swiftly through the hidden waterways known only to the riverguard, crossing vast distances in half the time it would have taken another force of similar size, all in an effort to catch up to the Xirkaali forces marching on Callenspire.

They had arrived too late nonetheless. The Xirkaali were at the walls, and might soon be inside the city, if Splish and the riverguard scouts were correct. But all was not lost. On their march, they had been joined by warriors from the different riverguard tribes, who had spread out on the flanks of the placoderm advance, moving ahead of them to ensure that the army went unnoticed. Not a large force, but large enough to give the Xirkaali pause – or so Axel hoped. But even so, it wouldn't be enough. Not unless the elves and halflings joined them. Only then was there a chance of victory, however slight.

A slight noise from above shook him from his thoughts. A moment later, he spied the sentry, situated in the crook of a tree overlooking the river. The Xirkaali had not yet noticed him. Nor had he noticed the Treeleaper scout crawling down toward him, thankfully.

Not until it was too late.

The riverguard struck first. A blade, made from a sharpened bone of a Dambuster, slid into the base of the Xirkaali's skull without a sound. The hemicyon stiffened on his perch and half-turned, a silent snarl on his muzzle. Then he toppled from the branch and into the shallows of the river, where Axel's magic easily muffled the sound. The riverguard looked down and gestured. Axel nodded and waded to shore. Behind him came a bubble of shimmering water – Splish. And within the elemental's protective embrace, Hannah, and her grenadiers. Splish extruded the halflings as he reached the shallows, allowing them to spill out into the open air. Hannah looked around and said, "Well, that was… interesting."

Axel chuckled softly. "A polite way of putting it."

She turned and eyed the river speculatively. "You know, Anas has a theory we could make underwater boats the same way we have ones that fly." She turned back to Axel. "I might tell him not to bother. I don't think it'll catch on."

"I'm sure Medu'Syth will be thanking you," Axel said. He led them into the trees where the riverguard scout was waiting for them.

"The dog-men are being attacking the city," the Treeleaper croaked, in broken elvish for the benefit of the halflings. "We are getting as close as we can, but any closer and they will be scenting us."

Axel nodded. "Then be waiting for our signal. When you are hearing it, it will not be mattering whether they are smelling you or not." The Treeleaper bowed and was gone, his colorful form vanishing into the vibrant canopy overhead. Axel turned back to Hannah and the others.

The halflings were a motley lot. There were six of them in all, counting Hannah. The rest of the survivors had stayed in the jungle, a safe distance from the fighting. The ones named Pinter and Dopwell were all that remained of Hannah's original squad, besides Cogman. Sagria and Umer were not actually grenadiers, despite the equipment they carried, but Hannah seemed to trust them nonetheless. Cogman, her second-in-command, weighed a grenade in his hand and peered carefully around the tree at the enemy camp.

"That's a lot bigger than the one on the beach," Cogman said, doubtfully. "And us without our wings."

"No fuel, no wings," Hannah said. "But we still have these." She tapped the bandolier of grenades she wore as she studied the camp. "Not that there's many of them left either. Once we run out, we're down to bad language and fisticuffs."

"It will not be coming to that," Axel said. "Once the first one is going off, Nemon will be attacking. Perhaps even before then. They are being as eager for battle as the Xirkaali."

"I noticed," Hannah said, somewhat nervously. Axel chuckled.

"They are being fierce, but that is what is being needed now."

"No denying that," Hannah said. She looked back at Cogman and the others. "You all remember the plan, I hope?" It was a simple enough gambit, though Nemon had taken some convincing. Axel and the halflings would approach the camp from downwind, infiltrate and set off a few of the halflings' grenades where they would do the most damage. That would be the signal for the Neriticans to attack.

Sagria patted the tree the Xirkaali sentry had recently vacated. "This will do me. I can cover you lot from here easily enough." With that, she slung her rifle onto her back and shimmied up the tree almost as swiftly as the Treeleaper had. Hannah looked at Cogman, who bounced a grenade on his palm.

"What are we waiting for?" he asked.

Axel looked at Splish. *Protect,* the elemental burbled. "Yes," Axel said. "Protect."

The elemental rose over the small group and stretched out like a blanket, becoming a shimmering, reflective shroud. Within this damp shell, they would be all but invisible to the naked eye, and their scents muted by the pong of the river. Or at least that was Axel's hope. But when it came to the Xirkaali, nothing was certain.

They moved slowly – warily – across the clearcut expanse of jungle that marked the outer boundary of the camp. Stacks of felled trees, awaiting whatever use the Xirkaali might put them to, made a crude labyrinth of sorts, and Axel couldn't help but wonder if it was intentional. They could hear the whine of rockets, and the howled war-cries of the Xirkaali, if only dimly. No sentries cried out, no arrows hummed toward them, and Axel felt a flicker of satisfaction. When they reached the base of the palisade, he crouched and drew up the waters from within the soil to dig down and wash them a hole through to the other side.

It was a tight squeeze, crawling beneath the palisade, but with Splish's help, they managed it. On the other side, the camp was in a state of controlled chaos. Humans moved in all directions, carrying weapons, rockets, and supplies. Axel could hear the sounds of a smithy and smell the acrid tang of an alchemist's workshop. He looked at Hannah, who nodded grimly and pulled a grenade from her bandolier.

Once the first grenade went off, they would have no time to escape. Instead, they would have to find somewhere to make a stand – preferably within range of Sagria's rifle. Axel tried to relax; there didn't seem to be any of the strange iron cages here. But even his magic, at its most potent, wasn't enough to fight an army.

They moved cautiously around the edge of the camp, keeping to the shadows where they could. Splish's reflective camouflage was much less effective here. All it would take was one observant –

A shout. A shot.

Axel spun to see a human soldier collapse onto his face. The moment stretched. Other humans paused – turned. Some looked curious. Others concerned. Then, a Xirkaali hound stepped out of a tent, sniffed the air, and growled. The animal began to bark, and it was soon echoed by others. The beasts padded out of tents and from behind stacks of lumber, their eyes fixed on Axel and the others.

"That's torn it," Hannah said, grimly. She tossed a grenade toward a pack of hounds, and the resulting explosion tore apart tents and flung bodies into the air. Cogman, Umer, and the others followed suit, hurling their explosives in all directions. In moments, the air was filled with smoke and fire. But the alarm had been raised, and the camp alerted to the danger in its midst.

A hound, fur singed, scales blackened, leapt through the smoke, jaws wide. Axel conjured a gout of water and smashed the animal backward and out of sight. He could hear shouts; soldiers were gathering. Another grenade wobbled through the air, bouncing down among the tents nearby. The explosion nearly knocked him from his feet.

Warning, Splish cried. Axel spun as a human soldier, wielding a wooden spear, charged through the smoke. He twisted aside, and the spear point tore through his cloak rather than his flesh. Axel's hand snapped down onto the haft of the spear, and the wood swelled and ruptured with new life; vines swarmed up its wielder's arms and down his throat. As the soldier fell, two more appeared, racing through the smoke.

Umer crashed into the knees of one, bringing him down. The second raised a spear over Hannah, who had noticed too late. Axel stretched out a hand, summoning the water – but fell back as a hound latched onto his forearm, nearly cracking the bone. He fell and the beast was on top of him, snarling. His staff rolled out of reach and it was all he could do to hammer his fist against its snout, in hopes of breaking its hold.

As it thrashed atop him, he saw the spear descend – Hannah turning, too slow – then, Cogman was there, tackling his captain out of the way. The spear cut through the halfling's leathers and pierced his side. Hannah, trapped beneath Cogman, drew a knife, and flung it full into the spearman's throat. He fell back, releasing his weapon. Axel lost sight of Hannah as his attacker dragged him about, shaking him as if he were vermin.

The pain in his arm increased, wiping away his ability to concentrate. He threw out a mental cry for help, and Splish sprang onto the hound, enveloping the beast in a watery caul. The hound released Axel and whipsawed frantically as the elemental flooded its nose and mouth with water. Axel rolled toward his staff.

Then Hannah had him under the arms and was dragging him into the lee of a stack of lumber.

"Cogman…?" he gasped.

Hannah shook her head but said nothing. Her gaze was flat; calm. She had gone beyond fear, Axel thought.

Pinter and Umer were there as well. No sign of Dopwell. Axel didn't ask. He didn't have to. *Hurt,* Splish said, slithering up onto his Axel's shoulder. He felt the elemental's concern, and said, "Just a flesh wound."

"Grenades?" Hannah asked. Pinter held up one finger, and Umer shook his head. Both halflings looked as if they'd been in a fight and come out the worst. Hannah hefted her two remaining grenades and looked at Axel. "Not good odds."

Past the edge of the lumber pile, Axel could see men massing. Ten, maybe twenty. Hounds as well, and Xirkaali scouts, with bows. The Yan soldiers approached warily, shouting to one another in their own tongue. "No," Axel agreed. "Not good at all."

Hannah smiled sadly. Then she rose and rolled a primed grenade toward the soldiers. They scattered, and the explosion was loud enough to deafen Axel. A hum filled his head, drowning out all other sound. He saw, rather than heard, the next two explosions. Saw the dirt spray up, and felt the heat. But more than that he felt the ground tremble. A trembling that did not fade, but instead grew more powerful with each passing moment.

Help, Splish cried and Axel felt the elemental's joy.

The Neriticans had come.

CHAPTER FORTY-NINE
Aeron

A rocket struck the bolt thrower and exploded into splatters of clinging flame. An elf fell back from the weapon, screaming in pain. Aeron raced toward the elf with his cloak, hoping to put it out. But the alchemical fire proved as stubborn as ever and clung tenaciously to the elf's clothing and armor.

"One side, Ser Aeron," Archmage Doromir called out. Aeron hurriedly stepped aside as a jet of magically-conjured water enveloped the writhing elf, snuffing the flames. From his moans of pain, Aeron wasn't certain that they'd done the elf a favor. One of Maggie Greenwell's apprentice-saucerors hurried forward, stirring his pot of healing broth furiously.

Up and down the parapet, the story was the same. Rockets and mortars pounded the city from all directions, forcing the elves and halflings on the parapet to hunker down as best they could. The launch-platform for the grenadiers had been destroyed by a lucky strike; a few grenadiers swooped out over the river, doing what they could, but there weren't enough of them to make much of a difference.

Thanks to their alchemical rockets, the Xirkaali had taken the ground just before the Eastway Gates, and now they were hurling everything they had at the walls. They had crossed the river and used the deadly, alchemical gas of their rockets to drive back the defenders, and now they were at the gates.

Aeron looked up as a rocket arced over the parapet and landed somewhere in the city behind him. The explosion was muffled, but from the way Doromir winced, it had hit something important.

"Shrine district," the archmage said, as if in answer to the unspoken question. "One of the temples. I can't say which one."

Aeron looked out across the city. There were fires everywhere, dancing across the rooftops or crawling along the great boughs that stretched far above. Sorcerous rainstorms snuffed some, but there were always more. Too many.

"I thought they wanted to take the city – not destroy it," Doromir went on.

"They'll do one, if it means the other," Aeron said. He was slowly coming to grips with how the Xirkaali thought – *too late,* a traitorous part of him whispered – and found that there were some commonalities between their peoples. Industriousness, for one. Pragmatism for another. The difference was, the Xirkaali used those qualities for war and the folk of Ej… didn't. He imagined those steel-clad warriors marching through the streets of Gerinhaf, or worse, Picksbury, and shuddered.

Down below them, Captain Alesha was organizing a fighting withdrawal through the sally ports. She'd attempted to reinforce the warriors in the outer defenses but to no avail. The Xirkaali had been waiting. In fact, Aeron thought they'd been counting on it. After all, why knock down the gates when you can just bait the enemy into opening them up? He hadn't bothered to try and stop Alesha. She wouldn't have listened, anyway. The elves weren't in the mood for pragmatism.

"If they launch one of those gas-rockets into the city…" Doromir began, nervously.

Aeron looked at him. "Can you stop it? Conjure a wind to blow it back at them?"

"Perhaps." Doromir made as if to continue when there was a thunderous crash below, followed by screams and shouts. He and Aeron traded looks, and then the archmage was hurrying down the parapet steps to the forecourt below. Aeron hesitated before following. Was this it, then? Could they hold the Xirkaali from the redoubts scattered within the city? He'd thought so, at first, but his confidence was beginning to fray.

Was it worth it, trying to hold on? Wouldn't it be better to evacuate his people? He and Anas had discussed it before coming to Callenspire. There would be a moment where there was nothing more they could do, and when that moment came, it was Aeron's duty to get as many of the Ej forces home as possible – whatever it cost.

He looked down the length of the parapet, at elvish archers and halfling gunners, fighting shoulder-to-waist, and felt a flush of shame at the thought. Now wasn't that moment. The Ej-folk were fighting better than he'd imagined – and he wouldn't be the one to take that from them. Not yet. Not while there was still hope.

He started after Doromir, peering down into the forecourt as he descended. The forecourt was a large flat area before the gates, with an internal gate at its far end, leading to the city's main thoroughfare. The roots of the great trees that anchored the walls cut through the foundations of the wall and across the ground like tiny rivers of rough bark. A canopy of vines and leaves hung like bunting, and several wagons had been turned over to act as improvised bulwarks. Alesha was shouting orders, and elven warriors were forming up before the gates. Not enough, though.

Aeron was halfway down the stairs when the first rockets struck the sally gates and obliterated the heavy doors. The wall shuddered, and he was nearly flung the rest of the way down the steps. He stopped as the wind shifted, and he caught a whiff of something acrid.

Gas seeped through the apertures and stung the air of the forecourt. The elves nearest the doors began to gag and convulse. Doromir and Alesha pushed toward them, followed by several of the archmage's apprentices.

"Poison," Alesha called out, bewildered. "Magic?"

"No," Doromir shouted. "More alchemy." He flung back his sleeves and raised his hands, incanting swiftly. A strong wind sprang up and rushed forward to cast back the gas, but even as it did so, an arrow whistled through the gap and took the archmage in the throat. Doromir stepped back, eyes bulging in shock. He slumped into Alesha's arms, and she called for the other mages to help. More arrows sped through the gap, striking the staggering elves. The walls shuddered again. *Mortars,* Aeron thought. Explosions echoed from the other side of the city, and the alarm bells were ringing. *The fire is spreading,* he thought. He drew his sword as he made his way the rest of the way down. Trained bands hurried into the forecourt but slid to a stop as they saw the gas creeping toward them.

Doromir's apprentices spat incantations and wove determined gestures as their master gasped out his life in Alesha's arms. The wind turned once more, and the air caught fire, burning away the gas that wasn't rolled back. Yet as it faded, the first Xirkaali was through the gap and moving swiftly, blade in hand.

Aeron recognized Shulgin even as she chopped down one stumbling elf and beheaded another. She'd led the attack herself; of course she had. That was how the Xirkaali thought. She threw back her head and howled – and her cry was answered. More Xirkaali erupted from the gap, moving to engage the remaining elves and halflings.

There was no more time.

Aeron felt a strange sense of calm descend upon him as the battle unfolded. The Xirkaali were in the city now, and even if they drove them back, they'd lost the walls. They would have to pull back into the inner city. Plans unspooled in his mind's eye, and he pushed them aside. None of it mattered, if they didn't survive the next few minutes. He hurried across the forecourt, dodging elven warriors hurrying toward the enemy. When he reached Alesha's side, he said, "Start falling back. We've lost the walls."

Alesha looked at him as if he'd sprouted a second head. "Are you mad? We can stop them – we can…" She trailed off as she looked down at Doromir. The archmage was dead, his features slack. She gently laid him down. "We've – we've lost, haven't we?"

"No." Aeron shook his head firmly. "Just the walls. Pull your warriors back. This is a rearguard action now. We have to save as many as we can." A shadow fell across them – he noticed it first. He shouted a warning and shoved Alesha aside as a sword parted the air where they'd been standing.

Shulgin.

She glared down at Aeron. "You," she growled. Aeron scrambled to his feet, sword extended. His blade looked pitifully small next to the one she was carrying. A child's toy. He risked a glance at Alesha.

"Go!" he cried out. Then he lunged; a quick slash at Shulgin's legs. She leapt back with enviable grace. Her sword looped downward, nearly splitting him in half. He had no time to see whether Alesha had followed his orders. It was all he could do to stay out of Shulgin's way. She was faster than he'd anticipated. He retreated, trying to draw her back toward the wall. Shulgin obliged him and pursued.

"You are clever, halfling, but I am clever as well," she said. "I ask again: surrender. Yield to me, and your people will be spared."

Aeron didn't reply. Around him, his people were fighting; dying. He saw elves and halflings locked in combat with the Xirkaali. A hemicyon sheared through an upraised shield and slew the halfling warrior holding it. An elf sent an arrow humming into the open jaws of a Xirkaali clutching at a hamstrung leg as a halfling danced back with a bloodied blade. Bodies fell, carpeting the forecourt, and were trodden under by the living.

The world snapped back into focus as Shulgin lunged, and he rolled aside, striking at her in return. His arms and legs ached in a way they hadn't in years; he was getting old. Slowing down. His sword rasped off of her armor, and he ducked beneath her fist. The forecourt shook as more mortars rained down on the wall. Chunks of masonry and burning trees fell like rain onto the combatants.

A hunk of rock caught Shulgin a glancing blow on the side of the head and tore her helmet away. She staggered, momentarily dazed. Aeron threw himself forward, praying to the missing gods that his sword would find its mark. But the gods weren't listening. Shulgin's own blade intercepted his, and with a quavering scream, his blade shattered. Aeron was flung back onto the ground, face bleeding from splinters of metal. Before he could rise, Shulgin planted a paw on his chest, pinning him to the ground. She raised her sword.

"Three times, halfling – we offer terms of surrender three times. No more, no less. I ask again… will you surrender? Or do you die here, defending a home that is not yours?"

Aeron stared up at her and tried to muster words of defiance. Of courage and honor. But all he could think of was his wife's name… his children's faces… of all that he would miss. All for a war he did not wish to fight.

Everything slowed. Sounds became muted; distorted. Out of the corner of his eye, he saw one of his warriors fall, cloven from shoulder to belt by a Xirkaali blow. The halfling's empty gaze met Aeron's own, and he read confusion there – recrimination. He'd warned them; he had. But they hadn't listened. They never listened.

And now they would all pay the price.

Aeron looked back up at Shulgin and began to reply when the sound of distant explosions pierced the din. He knew the sound of halfling grenades when he heard them, though what it meant, he couldn't say. Shulgin stiffened and looked in the direction of the Xirkaali camp. She stepped back, and Aeron dragged himself to his feet. Shulgin looked down at him.

"Another trick?" she snarled.

Aeron slowly shook his head. "Not mine, but I can guess whose," he said, shakily. Hope kindled in his breast. Was it true? It had to be. *It had to be.* "If I'm right, we're not the ones out of time after all. You are."

Shulgin's muzzle wrinkled. "We can still take the city."

"And then get trapped here, fighting us inside and them outside. Not good odds." Aeron spoke quickly, hoping she was smart enough to see, and not stubborn enough to try it anyway. More distant explosions sounded from the direction of the camp. "But if you retreat now, you might just be able to save your army."

Shulgin eyed him fiercely, and for a moment, he thought she might strike him down regardless. Then she threw back her head and gave out a dolorous howl. All across the forecourt, Xirkaali stopped fighting and began to retreat back the way they'd come, some with more reluctance than others. Shulgin was the last to go. She paused in the gap and studied Aeron for a moment. Then she too was gone.

Silence fell, save for the groans of the wounded. Aeron sagged back and sank down, his head between his knees and his heart in his throat.

It was over.

CHAPTER FIFTY
Shulgin

Shulgin looked around the ruins of her camp and resisted the urge to throw back her head and howl. "Tainted meat," she snarled. Ryuk had been wrong. It wasn't the bridge that was tainted meat – it was the whole city. Callenspire was a trap. She could see it all so clearly now. They had been lured in, and now the trap had been sprung. A camp destroyed; a third of her forces slain over the course of a day of hard fighting.

It had taken much of the day to get back across the river and organize her forces to fight off the Neriticans. Too long. By the time the Neriticans had finally retreated back into the jungle, the elves and the halfkin had managed to reinforce the positions she'd thought as good as taken. Parga and Ushar had been forced to break off their own attacks to aid her. In a single day, they'd lost all the gains they'd made.

She'd been so eager to take the city, to earn the glory she thought due her, that she'd ignored the warnings, ignored the reality of the Neritican threat until it was right on top of her. "Tainted meat," she said again, more quietly.

"What was that?" Parga growled, picking her way across the bloody ground. There were bodies everywhere, both Xirkaali and otherwise. The Neriticans had come over the palisades like a wave and swamped the defenders quickly. When her forces had reached the camp, they'd found placoderms and riverguard waiting on them.

"Nothing," Shulgin said. "The Neriticans?"

She looked down at a dead placoderm as she spoke and wondered at finding such a creature so far from the sea. Why had they come here? Why was Callenspire so important that they would march inland to save it? She flicked the questions aside, irritated by her lack of immediate answers.

"They've pulled back. At least for the moment." Parga looked around the camp. "How many dead?" she asked. But what she was really asking was whether or not they could continue. Shulgin twitched her ear in annoyance.

"Too many," she answered. She gripped the hilt of her sword. "I had him."

"Who?"

"Cadwallader," Shulgin replied. She'd had him. She'd read it in his eyes. He might have surrendered, given a few more moments. The city would have been theirs, then. And maybe more, besides.

Parga snorted. "My condolences. What now? Shall we press the attack?" She didn't sound particularly eager to do so, Shulgin thought. Then, Parga had no ambition. She wasn't interested in glory, or honor. "We have the troops, still. Even now, we could take the city. Hold off the Neriticans until reinforcements…"

"What reinforcements?" Shulgin asked, bitterly. "If the water-breathers are attacking, they will be everywhere. There will be no reinforcements. Not until they are driven back beneath the waves. By then, the elves of Ej will have sent their forces west." She shook her head. "We can take the city, but we cannot hold it."

A clamor from across the camp caught her attention, and she waved Parga to silence. A Yan soldier trotted up. "A messenger, my lady," he said. "From the elves."

"Alone?" she asked, grudgingly impressed. She hadn't expected any overtures from them; not this soon, at least.

"Yes. He came under a flag of truce. There are mounted warriors awaiting his return – and a squadron of those flying halfkin."

Shulgin grunted. The flying halfkin were concerning. If they decided to attack, there was little her forces could do at the moment, save endure their barrage. *The besiegers besieged,* she thought, with bleak amusement. "Escort him in. No harm is to come to him."

The Yan nodded and trotted back the way he'd come. Parga sniffed. "Maybe they wish to surrender, eh?"

Shulgin ignored her. It was not a surrender; Cadwallader would see the situation as clearly as she did. He would seek terms – maybe a truce, maybe something else – that favored his position. It was what she would do, in his place.

The messenger was an elf, but not a warrior; not wearing robes like that. He came into the camp escorted by several of Shulgin's spearwardens, a nervous look on his face. He was brought before her and bowed low, almost obsequiously so. She gestured impatiently for him to rise. He cleared his throat and said, "I am Valan Cormys, a diplomat of the –"

"What does Cadwallader have to say?" she demanded, interrupting him.

The elf looked momentarily taken aback, but only momentarily. He recovered quickly and said, "Ser Aeron wishes to extend to you the offer of withdrawal."

"He is withdrawing from the city?" Parga asked, incredulously.

"No, he means our withdrawal," Shulgin said. The elf inclined his head.

"Even so. Ser Aeron realizes that you are in an – ah – spot of difficulty, shall we say? Rock and a hard place, as the humans say." Valan smiled thinly. "Funny expression, that. At any rate, it describes yours well enough, I think. The Neriticans on one side, and us on the other. And your holdings along the coast hard-pressed, to hear our Neritican allies tell it."

Shulgin grunted. "They would say that."

Valan nodded. "They would. Never known them to lie, however." He looked around, for all the world like some haughty noble examining a peasant's dwelling. Shulgin wanted to behead him on principle. She refrained, however. "As Ser Aeron sees it, you have only one strategically viable option."

"Withdrawal," Shulgin growled. Valan blanched slightly, but his nerve held. He was made of sterner stuff than she'd first assumed. Then, that went for the elves as a whole.

"Withdrawal," he echoed.

Shulgin was silent for a moment, thinking. Then, "We have a prisoner." Parga glanced askance at her, wondering what she was up to. Shulgin ignored her. The truth was, Solibos had no value if Callenspire could not be taken. She had no wish to drag his dead weight back to Evanvale, if there was no need.

Valan raised an eyebrow. "I wasn't aware you took prisoners."

Shulgin glowered at him. "We are not butchers." She rubbed her snout. "Do you wish him returned, in exchange for a peaceful withdrawal?"

"Who is he, if I might ask?"

"A noble of your kind. Solibos."

Valan's eyes widened, and he hesitated. Then, "No. Thank you, but no." He smiled coldly. "Keep him, with our compliments."

Shulgin bit back a laugh. It seemed Solibos had fewer friends among his people than he'd claimed. "Very well. Then what does Ser Aeron wish, in exchange?"

Valan spread his hands. "Nothing at all. It is mutually beneficial, after all." He paused. "Provided you begin your withdrawal tonight, we can promise no attempt to attack on our part. Tarry overlong, however, and we shall be inclined to provide… encouragement."

Now Shulgin did laugh. "Very well. We accept the terms." Parga goggled at her, but Shulgin went on before she could interject. "But know this – we will return. The city will be ours, one way or another. This is only a temporary cessation of hostilities."

Valan bowed. "Of course."

Shulgin gestured. "You may go, Valan Cormys. Tell Ser Aeron that I will see him again." Valan bowed again, and then turned away to be escorted out of the camp. Shulgin watched him go for a moment, and then turned back to Parga, who looked as if she were about to explode.

"What were you thinking?" she snarled.

Shulgin shrugged. "I was thinking that my mother has more need of this army than we do Callenspire. Do you disagree?"

Parga grunted and looked away. "No. I suppose not. I'm just not looking forward to the walk back. My paws are very sore, you know."

"So you remind me, at every opportunity." Shulgin tapped her claws against the ring pommel of her blade. "They didn't say anything about the Neriticans, of course."

"What?"

"The Neriticans. The elf was careful not to imply that the Neriticans had agreed to anything. Our truce is only with the elves and halfkin." Shulgin studied the jungle and wondered if the riverguard were watching them even now. They would have to fight every step of the way back to the coast. The thought did not displease her. She had grown tired of thinking; a few days of battle would be refreshing at this point.

Her thoughts were interrupted by the arrival of Ushar. He strode through the camp with his usual good cheer. "If you were wondering, Hejun's daughter," he said, "the river is full of frogs."

"I see nothing," Parga said, looking toward the river.

"That doesn't mean that they're not there," Shulgin said. Ushar nodded.

"Exactly so. But they're being quiet for the moment." He began to pick his teeth with a claw. "It won't last. Once the Neriticans have regrouped…"

"We're withdrawing," Parga said, flatly.

Ushar's nostrils flared. "Good. No way we can hold the camp, and I'd rather not die trying to do so." He surveyed the wreckage. "They caught us with our paws in the trap, and no two ways there."

"You say that as if you saw it coming," Parga scoffed. Ushar flicked his ears in amusement but said nothing.

Shulgin hesitated. "We'll need transport for the wounded."

"We have a few barges remaining," Ushar said. "Enough to carry most of the injured downriver. The rest can walk." He scratched his chin. "We'll have to leave nonessential supplies."

"Burn it," Shulgin said. "Burn everything that can't be carried. Parga and I will lead the withdrawal. We will use the remaining mortars to flatten the jungle and clear ourselves a path to the Eastway. Then we head for the coast without pause." She looked at Ushar. "Can you get the barges safely downriver?"

"I can get them downriver; safely is something else. They'll be all over us the moment we pass the bend." Ushar leaned over and spat. "Still, I expect they'll be more interested in you two." He sniffed and looked back toward the river. "We have a few of the alchemists' toys left. I say we make use of them. Gas the jungle, set it ablaze. The more we use, the less we have to carry all the way back."

Shulgin nodded. "Yes." She tugged on her ear, thinking. "Good. The quicker we move, the better."

"You think our gains in Evanvale and Ruhaindo are in danger," Parga said.

Shulgin nodded again, more slowly this time. She didn't know that. Not really. But the Neriticans could have only gotten this far inland if the forces stationed along the coast were otherwise occupied. She was not worried for her mother, or so she told herself. She was not a human, or an elf, to fear the death of a loved one.

"The Neriticans are a greater threat than the elves could ever hope to be," she said, simply. "We must reinforce the coast against them. There is no other choice."

"They will harry us," Parga said. "We shall have to fight the entire way back. If we make it back at all."

"We will," Shulgin said. "And then, we will return." She turned to look at the city. *Tainted meat,* she thought. But next time, she would be ready for it.

Next time, Callenspire would fall.

CHAPTER FIFTY-ONE

Valan

"You're certain, then?" Aeron asked, and not for the first time.

Valan nodded as patiently as he had every other time. "Yes. From the condition of their camp, our Nerititcan allies chewed them up and spat them out. They're caught between us, and that commander of theirs is smart enough to know it. This withdrawal of theirs is the real thing. Trust me."

He and Aeron stood atop the main gate, looking out over the remnants of the bridge and the Xirkaali camp beyond. Said camp was a hive of activity, though at this distance it was hard to tell what sort. Smoke still rose from it; the Neriticans had set a good portion of it aflame in their initial rampage.

The prospect of the Xirkaali rebuilding was there, certainly. They might even press the assault… drive off the Neriticans… lay siege once more. All of that was within the realm of possibility, to be sure. But Valan knew enough about them now to say it was not likely. They were not fools, whatever else. There was no glory in defeat. They would retreat; it would be bloody, if the Neriticans decided to oppose them, but they would retreat nonetheless. But how to convince Aeron?

Valan glanced at the halfling. Aeron looked haggard; beaten down. Soot smudged his round features and stained his clothing. He'd been right in the middle of it all, Valan knew. Yet he'd come out intact. He'd even saved Alesha. That alone had earned him the respect of the common soldiery. It had been the name Cadwallader they'd shouted when the Xirkaali had fallen back from the gates. When the histories were written, Aeron would be the acknowledged victor, even by elven scholars. Valan would make certain of it.

Nonetheless, Valan could practically feel Aeron's worry. The anxiety of battle still held him tight. It was possible the halfling wouldn't be able to relax until the Xirkaali were gone. Maybe not even then. "We've beaten them," he said, gripping Aeron's shoulder. "You've beaten them. They know it, we know it, and they've got no choice now. It is even as you said, if they want to save this army, they have to retreat – and swiftly."

"If the Neriticans let them," Aeron mused. "If they decide to attack again, it would be a disaster and no mistake. If the Neriticans make things difficult, the Xirkaali might see no option save to hunker down and hold their position. And what then?" He shook his head. "We need to shore up the defenses. Just in case…"

Valan cleared his throat. "Perhaps we should speak with the Neriticans, eh?"

"Perhaps you should," Aeron said, with a slight smile. A tired smile, but a smile nonetheless. Valan snorted.

"Yes, I suppose it is my job, isn't it? Very well. I'll leave you to your worries, then." He gripped Aeron's shoulder once more. "But from what I've learned, the Xirkaali don't lie. If they say that they're going to do something, they do it. Especially if it's something they don't want to do."

With those words, he left Aeron and descended down into the forecourt, where repairs to the defenses were underway. The dead had already been removed, but the marks of their dying remained. A reddish stain here, an impact crater there. It made him slightly nauseated to even think of it. A high price had been paid to buy Callenspire a few more days, one they couldn't afford to pay again.

Many of the defenders had been badly injured in that assault. The halflings especially had borne the brunt of it. Dozens had died outside the gates, choking on the fumes of the Xirkaali's alchemical weapons. Elves had done the dying inside, after the gates had been breached. Valan wondered if Aeron was the sort to keep a tally of such things; if he made it a point to know the names and faces of the dead. Few elven commanders would bother, but there were some who indulged in such sentimentalism.

Then, perhaps that was why Aeron was as good a commander as he was. He valued his soldiers, yet did not hesitate to cast them into the fire if that was what was required to win the day. It was something to consider, at least.

Alesha met him at the foot of the stairs. "How is he?" Like Aeron, she looked the worse for wear. Tired, as well. Then, she probably hadn't slept in some time. But her concern seemed mainly to be for Aeron.

"Pensive," Valan said.

"I would be too," Alesha said as she fell into step with him. They crossed the forecourt, toward the gates into the city proper. "We have no way of telling whether the Xirkaali will honor our agreement." She eyed him. "That was brave of you, by the way."

"Feh," Valan said, with a dismissive gesture. "It is what I do."

"And you are certain that they intend to depart?"

"Now you sound like him," Valan said. "Yes! Yes, a thousand times yes. Everything we know about the Xirkaali tells us as much. Our thoughts are crooked things, but theirs? Straight as an arrow. One of their few virtues is an abhorrence of falsehood. That's not to say they wouldn't trick us if they thought they could get away with it, but once they've made an agreement, they won't break it." *I hope,* he thought, to himself.

The truth was, the Xirkaali were a puzzle he had yet to solve. Even the indefatigable Eran had come up with little from her searches. Nothing solid, at least. As ridiculous as it sounded, Merytan's library simply wasn't big enough. Eran believed that the answers they sought might be elsewhere. In Ej, perhaps – or the great libraries of Elvenholme.

Valan saw no reason he couldn't take Eran with him when he returned to Elvenholme. She was proving herself useful as a research assistant if nothing else. And with Merytan's backing, he'd be able to get her access to what remained of the official records of the old elven empire. There might be something in there that could help them.

And they did need help. He feared that the Xirkaali weren't going anywhere anytime soon. The elves would need every bit of information and every ally they could get to simply hold the line; an overwhelming force would be required to fully pry their lost territories from the grip of the invaders. Some would argue against it, of course. Some might even claim that the problem was for the southern kindred to deal with alone. But others would see what Valan saw: the Xirkaali were a threat to all of the kindred, everywhere.

He paused before the internal gate. Alesha stopped as well. "I need the assistance of one of the battlemages," he said. "Can you spare one?"

"Why?"

"I'm going to the docks. I need to contact the Neriticans. If they attack the Xirkaali, all of my hard work could be undone."

Alesha grunted. "I hadn't thought of that."

"Lucky for you I did," Valan said, discreetly omitting that Aeron's part in the decision. From Alesha's expression, he suspected his ploy was in vain. "Yes, and Ser Aeron thought it might be a good idea as well."

Alesha chuckled. "I can spare one. Qyalthris is at the hostelry just inside the gates, seeing to the injured there. She can help us."

"Us?"

She smiled tightly. "Someone ought to be there in a military capacity, don't you think? And I'm the only officer of sufficient rank left, other than Ser Aeron."

"On the whole, that's the way I prefer it," Valan said, without thinking. He winced as he realized what he'd said. Solibos, for all his idiocy, still had supporters in the city. He didn't think Alesha was one of them, but there was no reason to risk annoying her.

Thankfully, she laughed. A harsh laugh, true. But he relaxed somewhat. "I honestly didn't think Ser Aeron had it in him," she said.

Valan smiled sourly. "Nor did I. Perhaps we elves are rubbing off on him." He'd considered telling Merytan that Solibos was still alive, but decided against it. Why burden her with the knowledge that he was a captive? More to the point, why risk the chance she might want to get him back? In all likelihood, Solibos would be dead soon enough. He was bound to irritate the Xirkaali, and from what Valan had seen, they weren't the sort to put up with an annoyance for very long. The thought filled him with a certain warmth. If he'd done one useful thing here, it was that.

"What are you smiling about?" Alesha asked, suspiciously.

"Nothing. I'm simply pleased it's over." Valan indicated the gate. "Shall we?"

The Red Star hostelry had suffered significant damage to its roof from rockets, but was otherwise intact. Valan thought Hrinmeer would be pleased about that, or at least would have one less thing to complain about. The halflings had set it up as a hospital; the courtyard was full of wounded, all being treated by halfling saucerors and a few elven mages, those who could be spared from other duties.

Alesha led Valan through the lines of injured soldiers, towards a lean-to erected to protect the worst of the wounded from the sun. A halfling sauceror and an elf mage crouched over a grievously wounded halfling warrior. As Valan watched, the elf placed a hand on the ugly, red slash on the halfling's chest and murmured something. A moment later, motes of light danced across the wound, and the flesh began to slowly knit itself together. Valan cleared his throat. The sauceror looked up and held a thick finger to her lips.

Alesha crouched, so that she could meet her gaze eye-to-eye. "Maggie, we need Qyalthris. Can you spare her?"

The sauceror, Maggie, patted the mage, Qyalthris, on the arm. "Go on, love. I'll make do, and it sounds like they need you for something important. But hurry back, eh?" Qyalthris nodded and rose stiffly. She was younger than Valan had expected; barely old enough to be an apprentice. Her robes were speckled with soot and blood and other things he didn't care to think about. But when Alesha explained what they needed, she gave them a wan smile.

"Easy enough to do. From what I've heard, the riverguard have been swarming around the docks since yesterday, harassing the Xirkaali barges. The Xirkaali retreated upriver, but the riverguard are still there. You don't even need a spell to contact them."

Valan rubbed his hands together. "Excellent. Still, no doubt a spell will be more efficient in locating an officer or a chieftain or whatever they call their leaders." He smiled. "Besides, it's always best to be impressive when contacting potential allies."

Qyalthris in tow, they made their way out to the docklands. Everywhere Valan looked, the city was torn between celebration and worry. The few citizens left were doing what they could to clean up the damage done by the Xirkaali rockets, but he feared it would take more than a few days to erase the effects on the city.

The docklands were no different; worse, in fact. Jetties had been burnt to the water-line, or else made into temporary emplacements. They groaned beneath the weight of wooden bulwarks and overturned wagons. Halflings patrolled the shoreline, keeping an eye on the shattered line of burnt-out barges still floating some distance from the docks.

The halfling mercenary captain, Trosbert, was waiting for them when they arrived. He gave a lazy salute as he caught sight of them. "Ser Aeron sent a runner to let us know you'd be coming," he said as he led them onto the largest of the remaining jetties. "The riverguard have been quiet since the Xirkaali tucked tail and fled for solid ground. But my people say they're still close by. Whether they're keeping an eye on us or the Xirkaali, I can't say."

Valan nodded. "Either way, we'll get their attention soon enough. Qyalthris, if you would…?" He gestured to the river. The mage nodded and whispered softly, conjuring a small ball of light into her palm. She blew gently on it, and it whisked away, darting across the surface of the water like a glow-bug.

After a few minutes of silence, Valan asked, "And how long does it take?"

The mage shrugged. "As long as it takes."

Valan was about to reply when he felt a tremor run through the docklands. The surface of the river began to heave, and the halflings on guard shouted in alarm. Trosbert muttered a curse and reached for his sword, as did Alesha. Qyalthris gestured sharply. "It's nothing to be concerned about. Something is coming."

"That sounds quite alarming, actually," Valan began. Before he could get much further, however, a swirl of froth built in the waters before him. For a moment, he thought a whirlpool was forming. Then the surface of the river split, and a familiar figure appeared.

Axel rose from the foamy waters atop a shimmering bubble. "Valan Cormys. I told you that I would be returning. And so I am." The mage sounded tired; looked it, as well. His clothing was ragged and torn, his cloak in tatters. But he stood tall.

Valan laughed in relief. "Axel! I hoped that this sudden rescue was your work."

"Mine, and more than mine," Axel said. As he stepped lightly onto the dock, the bubble evaporated, depositing several halflings and a towering placoderm beside him. Valan stepped forward quickly to greet the newcomers. He recognized Captain Bimson among the halflings and felt a prickle of relief. That was one burden they could take off of Aeron's shoulders, at least.

The halflings on the docks rushed forward with a great shout to greet Bimson and her companions, despite Trosbert's shouted orders. Valan stepped aside, to avoid being trampled, and found himself looking up at the placoderm. The Neritican was larger than any Valan had ever met face-to-face, and smelled of the sea's depths. He had a heavy trident in one claw, and the head of a Xirkaali warrior in the other. "You are to be speaking for the elves?"

"I – yes. Yes, I do," Valan said, trying to ignore the blood pooling at his feet. The head appeared to have been wrenched from its adjoining neck in a display of brute force impossible for any elf to replicate. "I am Valan Cormys. Ambassador to the court of Lady Merytan of Callenspire."

The placoderm nodded in satisfaction. "I am being Tidewarden Nemon." He offered Valan the head. "This is being a token of our esteem." Valan gingerly took the gory trophy and looked around surreptitiously for a place to deposit it.

"I – ah. Yes. Thank you. Much appreciated."

Nemon bared his teeth in what Valan hoped was a smile. "I am here to be discussing an alliance between our peoples. I offer the aid of Medu'Syth in the destroying of our mutual foes. This is being agreeable, yes?"

Valan smiled. "Oh yes. Yes indeed."

CHAPTER FIFTY-TWO
Aeron

Three days after the Neriticans had arrived, the Xirkaali departed, as they'd agreed. Despite Valan's assurances, Aeron hadn't been sure they would. But the diplomat had been right; the Xirkaali didn't lie. They'd agreed to leave, and so they had.

Understandably, the city was jubilant. The mood in the council chamber, less so. Aeron, exhaustion weighing him down, sat at the table, trying to pay attention to Valan's words. "We've done it," Valan said, with some relief.

"Ser Aeron did it, you mean," Alesha said, sharply. The elf had become one of his biggest supporters since the battle in the forecourt. All it had taken was saving her life. Aeron pushed the thought aside and tried to concentrate on what the others were saying.

Valan nodded and waved this aside. "Yes, yes, of course. Regardless, this is a time for celebration. To old friends and new alliances!" He held up his cup, as if in toast. No one joined him. He shrugged and knocked it back regardless.

"They are retreating – but they'll be back," Aeron said. He looked at Nemon, who stood a short distance from the table, arms crossed over his chest. The placoderm nodded.

"The little one is being right. The Xirkaali will be back, in greater numbers. And we will not be here to be saving you when they are coming." Nemon bowed to Lady Merytan. "Though we are being allies, we are having our own battles to be fighting."

"You have done more than enough, Tidewarden Nemon," Merytan said, softly. She looked as tired as Aeron felt. But relieved as well. As if a weight had been lifted from her shoulders. Valan and the others looked the same. But Aeron felt no relief, and no lifting of the weight. Callenspire was just the beginning. "That you came at all, after the years of discord and mistrust between our peoples, was more than any of us expected."

"At the very least, I hope you'll consider killing a few Xirkaali on your march to the sea," Valan said as he poured himself another drink. "Not too many, you understand. But a few might encourage them to move faster." Nemon chortled.

"That much, I am thinking, we can be doing." He looked at Aeron. "We will be hunting them as we are going and spilling their blood where our paths are crossing. While they occupy our coasts, we will be making war on them. That, I can be promising you."

Aeron nodded. "And we will help you, if we can. I'm told you're conducting raids along the coast, yes? Well, those raids might be easier with a few trained bands to help."

Nemon peered at him. "Perhaps," he said, speculatively. "Your folk are more effective fighters than I expected. The ones we brought endured much, and without complaint."

Aeron felt a swell of pride at Nemon's words. He'd been as surprised as anyone to see Hannah and the other *Thunderchild* survivors, and hear their tales of adventure in the jungle. "As the elves have found, we make for decent allies. But we'll leave it for now. I need to stretch my legs, and you need to discuss matters amongst yourselves."

Nemon grunted, and Lady Merytan smiled sadly. "Yes, we have much to discuss. The future is murky, and we must find our way through as best we can." She looked at Nemon. "Hopefully together."

"As the Great Current wills," Nemon rumbled.

Aeron took his leave then, and left them to talk about the future. He made his way down to the streets below, where celebrations were in full swing. No one noticed him; the elves had other things on their minds. He was grateful for it.

The siege had been short, but the city had endured much. The scars of the Xirkaali munitions would remain for some time, he thought. Maybe the elves would use magic to repair them. The thought saddened him somewhat. Erasing such markers was a sure way to forget what had happened. Then, maybe that was what the elves wanted.

Eventually he made his way back to the Red Star, where his people were celebrating. The sound of music and laughter rose from the courtyard, and Aeron made his way around back and into the space he'd taken for his own. Plans, maps, and messages lay where he'd left them. He looked down at them, wondering what came next.

A cough alerted him to the presence of someone at the door. He turned to see Hannah. "Captain Bimson. Shouldn't you be out celebrating?"

"My apologies, Ser Aeron. I saw you duck in here." She indicated the windowsill, and Aeron gestured for her to sit. She did so and said, "You tried to warn me."

Aeron paused. "I did."

"I – I wish I'd listened," she said, softly. She looked out the window, into the courtyard, where the survivors danced and sang and ate. Aeron recognized the look on her face. He'd seen it often enough in the mirror. The guilt – the bewilderment – *why did I survive, when others didn't?* – a question with no satisfactory answer. "I was… thinking. About a friend. Kortys."

"The elf. I only met him briefly. He seemed a solid sort."

She nodded. "He's dead. I didn't think he could die. He always seemed… invincible to me, when I was a girl." She swallowed. "I wish I'd been there. I might have done… I don't know. Something."

"You can't think like that. Torturing yourself with what-ifs and could-have-beens is a sure way to go mad," Aeron said, sitting down beside Hannah. "For myself, I'm glad you weren't there, because you might well have died like Kortys. Might be selfish of me, but I'm glad you're alive. Anas will be relieved as well, I know." He looked up, shading his eyes against the sun. "*Windwalker* should be back with supplies in a few days. If you want to return to Gerinhaf…"

Hanah shook her head. "No, Ser Aeron, I don't." She looked away, and, after a moment, said, "I think I'll stick it out for the duration. I owe that much to Cogman, and Kortys, and all the others we lost."

Aeron nodded. He felt the same way himself. His doubts were still there, still lurking at the back of his mind, but something had changed. The Xirkaali weren't invincible. They could be beaten. Maybe not by him, but someone would. He was about to say as much when Hannah shot to her feet. A Neritican entered the hostelry; not a placoderm or a riverguard, but some other type that Aeron didn't recognize.

"You must be this Tricklebrook fellow I've heard so much about," he said, rising from his seat.

The gillkin studied Aeron for long moments, and then said, "And you are being Aeron Cadwallader. It is being a pleasure to be meeting you." He held out his hand, and Aeron took it. Before either of them could say anything more, Valan burst into the hostelry.

"There you are! I've been looking all over for you."

"What? Why?"

"There's a Xirkaali on the other side of the bridge!"

Aeron stiffened. "Just one?"

Valan nodded. "The one in charge. She's apparently waiting for you."

"Me?"

Valan shrugged. "That's what she said. What should we do?"

"Meet her," Axel said, softly.

Aeron looked at him, seeking answers in the mage's dark eyes. Axel nodded slightly, and Aeron straightened his shoulders. "I suppose I'm meeting her."

He had his aralez saddled and rode out to the bridge. A temporary wooden replacement had been laid across the gap, uniting the two sides once more. Wyn trotted across and stopped on the far side, where the Xirkaali waited, atop her own steed. The leonine monstrosity growled at their approach, but she soothed it and slid from the saddle. Aeron brought Wyn to a halt and did the same.

They faced one another in silence for several moments. Then, Aeron cleared his throat and said, "Your army left without you."

Shulgin shrugged. "It will take little time to catch them, slow as Parga moves." She slapped her steed's scaly flank, eliciting a grunt from the big beast. Wyn woofed nervously, and the creature growled. Shulgin soothed it with a clout on the side of the head. "Besides, I felt I owed you one last chance to surrender."

Aeron chuckled and patted Wyn. "No, thank you."

Shulgin nodded and looked past him, at the city. "You fought well. But we have taken your measure. When we return, we will take Callenspire."

Aeron hesitated, and then nodded. "I expect so. But you'll have to earn it."

Shulgin bared her teeth; a smile, he thought. "The dance of steel is never easy."

"Is that what you call it, then? A dance?" Aeron asked, without thinking.

Shulgin nodded. "Yes. What do you call it?"

"A waste," Aeron said, softly. Shulgin tilted her head. Aeron sighed. "Sometimes – most times – I regret taking up the sword. I was so eager to be a soldier, a general, that I did not understand the implication of what it meant. Of the decisions I would have to make. If it is a dance, it is not one to enjoy."

It was Shulgin's turn to hesitate. He wondered if she understood, or if his words were incomprehensible to her. The Xirkaali were a warrior people; it was as natural as breathing to them. Finally, she said, "What would you have said, if we had not been interrupted?"

Aeron looked away. "I don't know," he replied, after a moment.

Shulgin nodded. She was silent for a time. Then, "The pumpkin was delicious."

Aeron chuckled. "I'm glad."

Shulgin pulled a cloth bundle from beneath her cloak. "I had this made for you. A gift, as I promised. A badly-judged one, perhaps." She took the bundle and offered it to him. Aeron carefully unwrapped it, and stepped back. In his hands was a Xirkaali blade – but fashioned for a halfling to wield. He lifted it and found it lighter than he expected. It was well-balanced, and intricately wrought.

"It's beautiful," he said, truthfully.

Shulgin grunted in satisfaction. "Steel is sacred to us. Only a hemicyon may wield steel, in the empire – or those we permit to do so." She peered at him. "Know this, Aeron Cadwallader: should you survive all that is to come, and your people take their proper place as citizens of the empire, you will be allowed to carry that blade. Because you are worthy of the steel, of this I am certain." She knocked her knuckles against her cuirass, for emphasis.

Aeron set the sword down. "If that day comes, I will do so," he said, diplomatically. "But I will fight your empire for every foot of ground until that day."

Shulgin gave a bark of laughter. "I would expect nothing less!" She looked down at him, her gaze speculative. "Enjoy your victory, Ser Aeron. For when we next meet, I shall be ready for your tricks."

"Perhaps I shall have some new ones to show you," Aeron said.

Shulgin snorted. "I look forward to it." She gazed at him for a few moments more, as if memorizing his face. Then she turned and stalked away. Aeron watched her go and then turned his attention back to her gift. He stared at the sword, admiring it. It truly was a beautiful thing, if deadly. He ran his thumb along the edge and winced as blood welled. He sucked on his thumb a moment and then laid the flat of the sword across his shoulder. He watched the Xirkaali begin their withdrawal; not a retreat. Never that. A strategic withdrawal, to deal with a larger threat.

As he turned, he saw Valan and Axel hurrying toward him. "She wanted to give me a gift," he said, indicating the sword. Valan frowned.

"A funny sort of gift," he said.

"They are being a funny sort of people," Axel said. He watched the Xirkaali depart with an inscrutable expression. "But determined. They will returning, I am fearing."

"She said as much," Aeron said. He extended the sword and peered down its length. "And next time, we won't have the Neriticans to rescue us." He looked back at the city. "I think we need to evacuate. And quickly."

Valan blinked. "Abandon the city? After what we just went through?"

"Yes," Aeron said. "Victory here was never about holding the city. It was about buying time for Ej – and Elvenholme – to prepare for what's coming." He swept the sword out. "This has all been a feint, Valan. Just to ensure that the elves survive a few days more. But we can't hold Callenspire against another siege."

Valan made to protest, but Axel cut him off. "He is being correct. What is needed to be doing has been done. The course of the future is set. The war is being started, but it will not be the rout I am seeing in my dreams. That means we are having a chance, however slim, to survive the coming storm."

Valan grimaced, then sighed and looked away. "So, what now?"

Aeron weighed the sword in his hand. "We fall back to Ej and make ready. Vieshlar is lost, or will be, soon enough. But we'll make them pay a heavy toll for every inch of ground they take. They'll know they've been in a fight, if nothing else."

"You say 'we,'" Valan said. "You intend to stand with us?"

Aeron looked at him. "We honor our debts," he said, simply. "You gave the Ej-folk a home, and so we'll defend yours – whatever comes." He looked up, at the bright sky overhead and the sun, and loosed a slow breath. "But that's for tomorrow."

Valan grinned. "True. For today, I'm suddenly in the mood to celebrate."

"Celebrate what, exactly? I wouldn't call this a victory, as such," Aeron said.

"Another day of life," Axel said. "New friends, and future success."

"I'll drink to that," Valan said, with a laugh. "In fact, first round is on me, eh? Let me treat you both to the hospitality of Callenspire – while it still exists, at least."

"You two go ahead," Aeron said. "I want to wait here for awhile."

"I will be waiting as well," Axel said. Valan shrugged.

"Suit yourselves. I think I've earned a drink or six." He left them with a backward wave. Aeron watched him go, and then glanced at Axel.

"Am I right in guessing that your plan becomes a bit fuzzy, after this?"

Axel nodded. "Yes. There is much that I am not knowing. It might be that my part in these matters is being concluded."

"And mine?"

"Perhaps yours is being done as well." Axel paused. "I am not thinking so, however. There are being battles to be fought, cities to be defended – enemies to be defeated. I am thinking your services are being needed for some time, Aeron Cadwallader."

Aeron sighed sadly. “That’s what I was afraid of.”

EPILOGUE

Hejun

Hejun looked down at the dead placoderm with something like regret. He had led the latest foray against her defenses; a skilled warrior. But not skilled enough. They had caught him unawares on the docks, with a lucky rocket strike; crippled him, insomuch as such a creature could be crippled. He had revealed nothing under questioning, however, and had refused to serve the empire, as was to be expected from such an implacable enemy. As with the former lord of Ruhaindo, that had left her only one option.

She cleaned her blade with a rag and considered whether the body should be burnt with the others. The smell of smoke lingered on the air, and the cries of the wounded mingled with those of the hungry gulls that flocked to the feast below.

The bay and the mouth of the estuary were awash with wreckage and the dead. Bodies floated on the tide and were carried ashore by the current, where they became food for crabs and birds or other things. A cloud of gulls circled the bay, their cries drifting down like rain. The smoldering mass of the dead kraken lay across the docklands of Evanvale, filling the air over the bay with the stink of its passing. There were still Neriticans in the bay, she knew, concealed deep beneath the waters, waiting for the command to advance once more. They had been driven back for the moment, but tomorrow would be a different matter.

For now, the only thing to be done was to count the dead.

“Bring me something to eat. Executions make me hungry,” she growled to the human soldiers on guard nearby. She indicated the body. “And have this removed. Return it to the sea, with all due honor.” They hurried to obey, and she returned to her bench, with its table of maps and ledgers now in disarray. Over the last week, reports of Neriticans moving inland had doubled. It was clear to her now that they had waited for the Xirkaali to commit themselves to the invasion before attacking. The reasons why they might have done so escaped her, however. As ruses went, it seemed somewhat lacking. Then, who knew what went on in the minds of such creatures.

She stared at the maps, trying to see into the heart of the enemy. But as ever, the motivations of the water-breathers remained opaque. It was as if there were another game being played, somewhere above her, and her own battles merely byproducts of that unknown struggle. Advance and retreat, like waves crashing against the shore. She picked up another missive, then set it aside unread.

A week. They had lost a week. The invasion had not quite stalled, but it had been slowed. For every gain, there was an equivalent loss. A trade; this for that.

“Staring at them won’t make them go away,” Obair said from behind her. She turned to see him coming up onto the wall, carrying a bowl of something orange.

"Is that pumpkin?" she asked, eagerly, detecting a familiar scent.

"Shire pumpkins," Shulgin answered, as she followed after Obair. "Fresh from Callenspire." Hejun rose from her bench and Shulgin bowed.

"The city…?" Hejun began, but she saw the answer in Shulgin's eyes. "You failed," she said, flatly. Shulgin hesitated, then nodded.

"The city stands," she said. Her tone was almost, but not quite, apologetic.

She might have gone on, had Obair not cleared his throat and said, "Admiral Khulan is also here."

"You see how he announces me, cousin?" Khulan barked, as she shoved past Shulgin. "As if I, the great Kaiju-killer, am a mere afterthought in the heavy considerations of Obair. The insult of it, the effrontery, the – is that pumpkin?" She plucked a piece from the bowl and chewed it to stringy ribbons with grumbles of delight. "Delicious."

Hejun took a piece for herself. "Shire…?" she murmured, eyeing it. Shulgin nodded.

"One of the kingdoms of the halfkin, somewhere to the north. Apparently, they are quite fond of it as well." She paused. "I was… given them as a gift. By Aeron Cadwallader."

"A halfkin, I presume?" Hejun said. The pumpkin was quite good.

"Yes. The elves put him in charge of the defenses at Callenspire."

Hejun blinked. "Really? Why?"

"Because he is rather skilled at it, as it turns out," Obair said. Khulan snorted.

"Yes, yes, very good. Would you like to hear my report now, cousin? Given that I've come all this way?" She filched another piece of pumpkin and sat down on the bench. "We've had some successes, though the Neriticans have been laying traps for us up and down the coast," she said, tapping several points along the coastline between Evanvale and Grishamvu. "They've buried wooden spikes in the shallows to pierce our hulls, and onto the beaches to slow our disembarkation and make us easy prey for their attacks."

Hejun nodded. "But the landings continue?"

"For the moment. Several of my subordinates have reported that they've also hidden lengths of net, seeded with shards of sea glass and bits of rusted metal, everywhere. They pull the nets taut and catch our soldiers as they come ashore, injuring or even killing them." Khulan made a fist for emphasis.

Hejun rubbed her muzzle tiredly. "How clever of them."

"Yes. And they're making use of our own fortifications, using them against us."

"Inconsiderate," Hejun muttered. Khulan nodded.

"Very. But, as you noted, clever."

"But not clever enough, I trust."

Khulan rubbed her snout with a knuckle. "No. We can outfight anything, on land or at sea. But every fight costs us a little more blood, a little more time. I've had to lift the blockade of Grishamvu in order to reinforce Iron Beach and the other remaining camps." She looked out over the bay. "How goes it here?"

"You see the wreckage, I assume," Hejun said, bitterly. She selected another piece of pumpkin from the tray and chewed it angrily. "They've retreated for the moment, but I've had to call back the raiding parties to reinforce Evanvale."

"All of them?"

Hejun grunted. "No. Blackthorn will fall within a few days, or so Han assures me. I've sent Gorcha to reinforce him, which she will enjoy I expect."

Khulan glanced at Shulgin. "And Callenspire?"

"Callenspire stands," Shulgin said. "For the moment, at least."

"So you failed?"

Shulgin growled softly, but said, "I thought my forces could be put to better use here."

Khulan snorted. "Did you now?"

"The Neriticans marched inland, to reinforce the city," Shulgin said. Khulan paused, clearly startled. Shulgin went on. "I could have taken the city, but not without paying a heavy toll. And I might not have been able to hold it."

"A strategic withdrawal, then," Khulan said. Shulgin nodded and looked at Hejun.

"When I learned of the Neriticans, I thought it would be wise to preserve what forces I had, in case of disaster." Then, in a challenging tone, "Would you have done differently?"

Hejun hesitated. Finally, she sighed. "No, daughter. I would not. You… did well."

"She is learning," Obair said. All three of them looked at him, and he looked away, his expression one of innocent reflection. Hejun chuckled ruefully.

"Yes. I think it is safe to say that we are all learning new lessons here." She looked pointedly at Khulan. "Even you, Khulan."

"I am learning I do not like Neriticans. Then, I have known that for some time." She held a piece of pumpkin. "I do like this pumpkin. We should definitely take this… Shire for our own. And some halfkin to farm it for us."

"I brought more than pumpkin back," Shulgin said. Hejun looked at her.

"Oh?"

"A prisoner."

Hejun glanced at Khulan. "What sort of prisoner?"

"An elf."

Khulan sniffed. "We have elves."

"A noble."

Hejun picked a string of pumpkin from her teeth. "We have nobles."

"This one is… different." Shulgin gestured, and two spearwardens marched an elf up onto the wall. Hejun realized that they'd been waiting below for Shulgin's signal. "Allow me to introduce Lord Solibos of Callenspire."

The elf wore neither armor nor finery, but something in his face told Hejun he had been born to both. He hesitated, and then knelt before her. The elf was bedraggled; humbled. The journey from Callenspire had not been kind to him,

Hejun thought. Then, Shulgin was not the sort to be considerate of a captive's feelings. Hejun leaned toward him. "Tell me, Lord Solibos… are you ready to serve the Xirkaali Empire?"

Solibos met her gaze squarely. *Not so humble as all that then,* she thought, wryly. There was a fire in him still; a hungry heat. What did he desire? Power – no. Power was a cold need. Heat derived from anger; humiliation. Spite.

"I… am," he said, hoarsely. Shulgin nudged him with her foot. "Matriarch," Solibos added, with a venomous glance at his captor. Shulgin didn't appear to notice, but Hejun did.

She waved her daughter back and stood. She gestured for Solibos to do the same. The elf licked his lips and rose.

"You will serve us, and in return, you will be given high honors and made a citizen of the empire with all the rights and considerations due to you," she said, formally. Solibos bowed his head.

"Yes, Matriarch."

"Good." She paused. "How would you like to serve us, Lord Solibos?"

He looked up. "Callenspire," he said, and she heard the bitterness in his voice.

Ah. There it is, she thought. She understood now why Shulgin had brought him all the way back here. Despite her initial assumptions, it had become clear that the elves were as hierarchical as her own people, if in somewhat subtle fashion. They followed strong leaders, though that strength was less in the sword arm than in force of personality. Solibos was strong – or would be, with the might of the Xirkaali Empire at his back.

"In time," she said. "Until then, there is much to be done, and your aid would be greatly appreciated. We Xirkaali are not fond of politicking or games of influence. We… lack the necessary mindset. But you elves are skilled in these matters."

Solibos straightened. "What do you wish of me, Matriarch?"

Hejun gestured back into the city. "Ruhaindo. We hold the city, but not the heart of its people. You will win it for us – and all that comes with it. You will teach your people what you have learned, so that they might follow your example."

Solibos arranged his face into an expression of polite acquiescence. "I will do my utmost to serve," he said, and Hejun noted the careful phrasing but said nothing. She gestured in dismissal, and Shulgin had her spearwardens remove him.

"Well, finally," Khulan said, when he was gone. "Took one of them long enough to take the bait. I was beginning to fear that the only cure for their obstinance was extinction."

"Do you trust him?" Obair asked, in a mild tone.

Hejun and Shulgin snorted at the same time. "Do not be ridiculous, old man," Shulgin said. "He is a snake, that one. I offered to return him to the elves, you know – they declined. I expect that they had good reason."

"But he will be useful, as a figurehead if nothing else. The rightful ruler of a city in enemy hands is a potent weapon, for the right wielder." Hejun tugged thoughtfully on her ear. "Eventually, he may well turn in our hand. But until then, we shall make good use of him." She looked at Shulgin. "What of this halfkin general you met?"

"The one who gave you this delicious pumpkin," Khulan clarified.

Shulgin was silent for a moment. "Clever. Practical. If he lives, we would be well served to entice him to our cause. The halfkin are… industrious. They employ a form of alchemy similar to our own, and there is much we might learn from each other."

Khulan laughed. "Is this my cousin's pup who is speaking? Surely you cannot have changed so much in so little time."

Shulgin twitched irritably. "I know only what I have seen."

Hejun waved Khulan to silence. "Shulgin is right. If we are to conquer, as we must, it would be better to do so without unnecessary slaughter. Why kill the calf, when it will eventually provide milk?"

"Because it is delicious," Khulan said. "And we are not talking about calves, cousin."

Hejun laughed. "No, we are not." She picked up one of the maps and gesticulated with it. "But we do not have the resources to fight for every scrap of jungle. So why fight at all? The elves have left us no choice – the Neriticans cannot be bargained with – but these halfkin? Perhaps we should send an envoy to them, in their mountain fastness, and see if they possess as much common sense as Shulgin believes." She paused and plucked the last piece of pumpkin from the tray. She eyed it before popping it in her mouth. "At the very least, we'll get more of this delicious pumpkin."

"And Callenspire?" Shulgin asked.

Hejun looked out over the bay. "Callenspire will fall, if not today then tomorrow. Or a month from now – a year, even. And all of Vieshlar with it. It is as inevitable as the tide." She turned to look at the others.

"Let us hope we all live to see it."

About the Author

A professional author since 2007, Josh has over thirty novels to his name, as well as numerous short stories, novellas, and audio scripts. Born and raised in South Carolina, he now resides in Sheffield with his wife and daughter, as well as a highly excitable dog and something he hopes is a cat. A complete list of his work can be found at https://joshuamreynolds.co.uk/.

See more Tales of Pannithor

Look for more books from Winged Hussar Publishing, LLC – E-books, paperbacks and Limited-Edition hardcovers. The best in history, science fiction and fantasy at:
https://www.WHPSupplyroom.com
Instagram: WingedHussarPublishing
Facebook: Winged Hussar Publishing LLC
For information and upcoming publications